EVERY LAST DROP

A NOVEL

SARAH ROBINSON

D1166995

To Brittany Maynard, you will not be forgotten.

To Betty Sullivan and Laurian Eckle, two of the strongest mothers I know.

PROLOGUE

A FIELD of water betrays the spirit that is in the air. It is continually receiving new life and motion from above. It is intermediate between land and sky.
  - Walden by Henry David Thoreau

WHEN I WAS about nine or ten, my father caught me reading an erotic novel. Once he got over the fear that his daughter might be a pervert—spoiler alert: I'm not...I think —he sat me down and told me every story is not meant for every audience. I assured him I'd never read anything like that again, and, out of respect for my promise, waited a full five minutes before I went right back to reading the rest. I'm practically a saint.

The thing was, it had nothing to do with the sweaty scenes where things fit together that I was wholly confused about at my age, but the fact that these had been my mother's books. I'd found them in a box of her things long after she'd died, and every page I read, I read with her. My heart broke and was mended right alongside the characters, and I cried over the same tear-stained pages my mother had. I laughed at romantic quips and imagined her beside me, sharing the joke.

Books captured my soul, and completely changed the way I saw the world. The shared experience of knowing those who read these words were aching with me, giggling with me, loving with me was captivating. Being able to write like that, to bring people together, soon eclipsed my childhood dreams of being an actress, a truck driver, or the bearded lady at the circus. Yes, there was once a time I'd wanted to be the bearded lady.

As I grew into an adult, and that beard never did grow in (small miracles), my goals evolved. I started adding to the things I wanted out of life, but writing a book was always there. Now I'm twenty-eight years old, and with all the wisdom and knowledge from my extensive time on this planet—*note the heavy sarcasm*—I've come up with three goals for my life.

To write a book. *Here we go.*

To become a mother. *Soon.*

To marry the love of my life. *Check.*

When I started writing this journal, I hadn't really intended it to become *the* book, but you know what they say—we make plans and God laughs. I had already married an amazing man years earlier and was working toward the second goal on my list. I meant for these pages to tell the story of my journey into motherhood, and the ensuing ups and downs. It was going to be about new life and lost life, about how I raised my little sister after our mother died, and how I'd known even then, that motherhood was my greatest aspiration.

I had never planned to show this to anyone outside of my family, but still, it would be written. I would have written a book. And I was so damn excited to tell the story I'd been writing my whole life, finally on paper this time.

Was.

Because I thought I knew the story already. I thought I knew how it would end. I had no clue this story *was* meant for everyone, and every audience. If I had known, maybe I would've started writing it sooner. Maybe I'd have changed the ending.

The problem is, I won't live long enough to do that.

And when you read this book, you're going to want me to. At least, I hope you will. I hope you'll wish for a miracle, for the words on the page to transform into an epic tale of *almost, so close, our prayers were answered, Hallelujah!* But after that moment of hope, you'll need to remind yourself a miracle isn't coming.

This story isn't a cautionary tale. It's just life, and life ends.

I wish I could write a happily-ever-after like my mother's novels, where the greatest of romances can conquer death. But that isn't going to happen, and I'm really sorry it won't. I wish I would live long enough to write you those stories, but I am dying.

And my story dies with me.

CHAPTER ONE

Monday, March 24, 2014

"BABE?"

"Mmm."

"Tessa, wake up."

"Mmm, I'm awake. See?" I raised an arm in the air for a brief moment before dropping it down on the soft blankets covering me. I'm sure it was quite convincing, despite my sealed-shut eyes.

"I've got an anniversary gift for you." His voice was teasing, tempting.

I decided I could open my eyes for a present.

"What is it?" I pushed up on my elbows to find my husband, Kyle, sitting on the edge of the bed, freshly showered and fully dressed. I yawned and wiped the sand from my eyes. His brown hair was darker when wet, his green eyes excitedly staring me down. I'd never understand how he had this much energy in the morning when I could easily roll over and go back to sleep.

"Here, open it." Kyle handed me a rectangular object, clumsily covered in red wrapping paper. It looked as if he'd smothered the gift in glue, then tossed it into a pile of gift wrap, hoping something would stick. Honestly, I wasn't even sure there was a gift inside or if it was just a wad of paper—knowing Kyle and his pranks, it could be either.

I grinned, sitting up fully and crossing my legs under the blanket. Placing the present in my lap, I not so delicately ripped it open.

Kyle leaned forward and kissed my forehead. "Happy anniversary, babe."

I tore off the last of the wrapping and looked down at a beautiful black leather-bound journal. Immediately lifting it to my nose, I took a big whiff of the pages. *Mmm—paper.* Nothing smells better than freshly printed paper, whether it's books or pages ready to be filled with words. I weighed the gift in my hand and ran two fingers over the soft surface. Writing by hand is one of life's great treasures and I was already overflowing with things I wanted to share between its binding.

I looked at him, my brows raised and a hesitant smile pulling at my lips. "Is this for my book?"

He nodded, pride shining in the hidden spaces behind his eyes that only I knew existed. "Yep, you've been talking about it for years, and I know how you hate computers."

"Computers are one click away from ending humanity," I quipped, still barely believing how lucky I was to have a husband so supportive of my dream to become a writer. He knew me—my soul, my very being. I pushed away from the mirror in my heart that made me stare at how inadequate I was compared to him.

Kyle laughed. "You sound like your dad."

"I've been called worse," I said with a forced chuckle,

then lifted up the journal. "Is this your hint for me to start writing my book?"

"I thought with today being the doctor's appointment, you could start keeping a record of the entire fertility treatment process, the pregnancy, and everything that goes along with it. When our kid is older, he can read about how hard we worked to bring him into the world."

"Or her," I reminded him.

Kyle tossed me a wicked grin. "As long as the baby's healthy, that's all that matters."

I shook my head, grinning as my defenses lowered inch by inch. I knew he wanted a son. Most men want a son. I couldn't blame him for that, but I also knew he'd love a daughter, too. He was going to be an amazing father, and there was nothing in the world I wanted more than to be able to give this dream to him—and to me.

Whether or not I'd be a great mom was another question. Kyle didn't know I thought about that but I did. All the time. I wanted to be a mother more than anything, but that didn't mean the concept wasn't terrifying to me. I have to set an alarm on my phone to remember to feed the dog. I'm not sure the same concept works for children.

"Where's Beast?" I looked around the meticulous bedroom—mostly Kyle's doing, not mine. My style is organized chaos, while his is more organized...actually organized.

"Where do you think?" Kyle laughed and lifted the blankets, letting a rush of cold air surround my bare legs while at the same time revealing our fluffy white dog, fast asleep. He was a Bichon mix, weighing in at eleven pounds of pure defiance.

"Of course." I pulled the sleepy pup into my arms and cuddled him.

He stretched his paws and yawned with the confidence of knowing he was the real owner of this house. Beast began waking in earnest in my arms and wagged his tail excitedly, looking between Kyle and me.

"Do you think we'll forget about Beast when we have Baby Falls?" I asked, using our last name as our future baby's nickname.

Kyle laughed just as the dog stood in my lap and pawed at my arm. "I doubt Beast would ever let us."

"Stop, Beast. Ow!" I reached to push him off, but he jumped up and tried to scratch at my head instead. I ducked my face into my hands and wiggled away from the demented dog I loved so much. His attack on my head was soon foiled when a lump in the blankets distracted him and he had no choice but to attack it.

"Why does he always scratch your head? It's the weirdest thing." Kyle stared at us in amusement.

I shrugged, unsure.

"You should yell at him when he does it."

"I can't yell at Beast!" I say in a mock-baby-voice as I scoop my dog's face in my hands and kissed his wet nose. He licked my mouth at the same moment and we accidentally traded salty tongue kisses. "Gross."

Kyle ruffled the curly white fur on Beast's back. "You spoil him too much."

"Nonsense, Beast needs all the love." It was a phrase Kyle and I had been saying to each other since we met, and now Beast had all our love, too.

"I'm the one who's gone half the time. *I* need all the love." He raised one brow, his tone suggestive.

"Too bad you're already dressed and showered," I teased, cuddling Beast tighter against my chest.

The pup squirmed in my arms, trying to escape, finally

making me give up and let him go. The tiny white ball of fur bounded across the bed and onto the floor where he found a chew toy and tossed it in the air with his mouth, chasing after it.

Our house was mostly spotless and organized in every way except for one thing—Beast. His toys littered the floors, and he had a terrible habit of carrying bits and pieces of his food in his mouth and hiding it in random nooks and crannies.

Aside from his mess, the rest of the bedroom was clean lines, soft earth tones, and billowy fabrics. I craved comfort and nature, trying to bring the feeling of Mother Earth into our home. The curtains were thick, keeping out the light. The carpet was plush and brown, matching with the other fabrics in the room, which were either starch white or soft beige. There was an occasional pop of color, like the red throw blanket on the end of our bed, but mostly I loved the muted feel. It felt like me—calm, a little sullen, with a dash of attitude whenever it decided.

"I'll make us some breakfast, and then we should get going to the doctor." Kyle stood from the bed and handed me a steaming cup of coffee I hadn't noticed on my nightstand.

I immediately scooped the mug from his hand and took a few gulps, regretting it only slightly as the hot liquid burned my tongue. The discomfort didn't stop me though, my love for coffee in the mornings undeterred. "Thanks, babe."

"Oh, I picked up some extra ibuprofen for you. It's in your nightstand if you still have a headache," he called over his shoulder as he headed for the hall.

And I forgot to buy you an anniversary present. Wife of the year. I must have been an amazing folk hero in another life to deserve him. It had been two years since we married, and he still treated me like a queen. My friends had all warned that once married, he'd slowly stop doing all the things he'd first done to woo me. Maybe that would still happen one day, but there was no sign of it yet and I certainly wasn't holding up my end of the bargain.

I was really great in bed though. So, there's always that.

I stretched and clambered out of our comfy king-sized bed, pulling my clothes off, my mind drifting to thoughts of a possible past life. I wasn't particularly religious, though I had been raised Catholic. I stopped attending Mass in college and never felt the need to resume. It always felt more a duty to check off for the week than anything else.

I pulled on dark jeans and a loose-fitting cable knit sweater. It was still cold outside, but mostly due to the Chicago wind. Walking into the master bathroom, I stuffed my light brown hair into a loose bun at the base of my neck and brushed a few swipes of blush onto my cheeks. I dabbed brown mascara onto my already long lashes, topped with a subtle gold shadow I'd been told made my blue eyes stand out.

Kyle once told me my eyes remind him of ponds. Dark blue and slightly murky, as if something were hiding beneath the surface. I grinned devilishly at the thought. I liked feeling a bit mysterious—how when swimming you worry something might nip at your toes but you don't know what. It doesn't scare you from the silky water's embrace, but it's enough to keep you moving, hoping it won't catch up.

Putting the makeup away, I surveyed the bathroom for any mess but found none. Kyle must have already taken care of it. All his training from a decade in the U.S. Marines made him the resident clean freak. *Great, so I couldn't even do that for him.*

I really needed to get him an anniversary gift.

I stepped around Beast to pick up my phone and scanned through my text messages, while at the same time brushing my teeth. There were a few from my boss, but nothing urgent. I'd been an assistant at a law firm for the past few years, despite my lifelong goal to be a writer. We needed the paycheck, and I enjoyed the work for the most part.

Okay, that was a lie. Honestly, I don't even know why I said it.

I'm *trying* to enjoy it. I go to work every day and tell myself *this will be the day you'll fall in love with your job.* Then that turns in to tomorrow, and then the next day, and a year goes by and I still hate my damn job. Don't get me wrong—it's a great job and I know I'm lucky, but that doesn't mean I'm happy.

I guess that's kind of the common theme here.

Finished with brushing my teeth, I pumped some lotion onto my palms, hoping to calm the blisters that had become a part of me at this point. Kyle and I had a ridiculously expensive membership to a climbing gym downtown which we loved, but it really did a number on my hands and feet.

"Tessa, we've got to go!" Kyle called from the steps.

I grabbed my new journal. Beast led me out of the bedroom and down the hall, pausing at the open door to my left. He disappeared into the room, making me peek in after him. The little pup stood in front of the crib, surveying the room, then headed past me and down the hall.

I lagged behind and studied the nursery we'd set up months ago when I'd been pregnant. We lost the baby not long after. The pale purple walls were as gender neutral as we could agree on, with heavy drapes keeping the room dark for months.

It was still waiting to be filled. We all were.

I sighed, heading to the end of the hall and down the stairs. Kyle called for me again. Upon finding Beast, I led him into the kitchen and poured food in his bowl then secured a baby gate in the doorway to keep him quarantined on the tile floors with his toys.

"Be good, Beast. We'll be home soon."

He was already busy spilling the contents of his bowl onto the floor, oblivious to our departure.

My usual melancholy took a back seat and excitement swarmed my belly like butterflies on fast forward. Today was the day we'd been waiting for. Things were looking up, and for the first time in over a year, we had hope.

Because today, Baby Falls, is the first day of fertility treatments.

• ღ • ღ • ღ •

"HOW OFTEN ARE YOU HAVING SEX?" Dr. Dana Hill stared at me over thick, black glasses with a level of seriousness I envied. How did she ask such personal questions day in, day out, and not burst out laughing? Or blush with embarrassment?

"Uh, often." Kyle fumbled on his words, crimson spreading across his cheeks.

"What's *often*? Two to three times a week? More? Less?"

I decided to answer for the both of us. "About four times a week, sometimes more."

I put my hand on Kyle's to calm his nerves. I never minded talking about our sex life. It's hard to stay quiet about it when you're married to the physical embodiment of God's gift to women. To this day, I cannot understand why someone with his impossibly good looks was interested in a mousy brunette like me.

Kyle is certainly not as open as I am though, and if the color of his cheeks was any indication, he was more than a little uncomfortable at the doctor's line of questioning. I tried to stifle a grin at the irony since Kyle had been raised one flower blossom shy of being a full-blown hippy. His lackadaisical parents, Elias and Dixie Falls, were children of the sixties and nothing short of a stereotype, but somehow, they had the opposite effect on most of their three children. Kyle and his sister Kat were conservative to the point of polo shirts as a religion. Their brother Kurt was somewhere in between, not fitting into any mold, but certainly nothing like his parents.

"Four times a week," Dr. Hill repeated, scrawling notes on a clipboard. "How long have you been trying to become pregnant?"

"About a year and half since we first decided to start trying. Kyle is in the U.S. Marines, so he was gone on his third tour into the beginning of last year. He was deployed a lot the first few years we were together, actually. Since he came home last year, he's been stationed close by, so we've been able to ...uh, practice...regularly."

"I see, and you stopped using condoms or other types of birth control?"

"Oh, were we supposed to?" I replied with a straight face.

"Tessa," Kyle said in warning while his face tried to remain serious, but then he snorted a laugh. "Yes, Dr. Hill, she went off birth control a year and a half ago, and we haven't used condoms since we were married."

Based on the frown on Dr. Hill's face, she didn't appreciate my joke. "And, Mrs. Falls, you've had steady periods every month? No chance of conception?"

Struck with sudden sadness, I dropped my eyes to my hands, fiddling with the strap on my purse.

Kyle placed his arm over the back of my chair. "We conceived a year ago, but lost the baby at nine weeks."

It was still hard for me to voice the words. A few friends had assured me miscarriages were surprisingly common, and nine weeks was barely anything—a follow up medical procedure rarely necessary since the body naturally cleans up after itself. They told me I couldn't feel the baby yet, so it wouldn't make much of a difference.

But it *had* made a difference. I might not have yet felt a kick, but I felt the presence of a life that wasn't mine, and yet...was. I'd fallen in love, and hugged my waist, telling my little son or daughter how much I already loved them.

And just as sure as I'd felt the flicker of life inside me, I had felt it leave.

There was no agonizing pain, no terrifyingly massive blood loss. It was nothing like the movies had led me to believe. Instead, it was quiet and somber. It was slow and deliberate. My body was supporting life one minute, then clearing it away the next.

The tiny heart had stopped beating, and it was as simple, and complicated, as that.

"Ages?" Dr. Hill was firing out questions. I might have missed a few since I had tuned out, but Kyle seemed to be keeping up for the both of us.

I took a deep breath, slowly exhaling and imagining my negative thoughts and memories leaving with it. That's what my therapist had taught me to do after the miscarriage. It was a process, but I was working my way toward being happy again and today wasn't the day to think about loss or heartaches. We were taking our first steps toward making our family, creating a second Baby Falls—though we'd never forget our first. Life's all about choices.

Today, I was choosing to be happy.

I needed to be happy.

"I'm thirty years old," Kyle told her.

I glanced sideways at him, a teasing grin on my face. "And I'm twenty-eight."

I needed to joke about something, anything, and ever since Kyle had turned thirty in January, I'd enjoyed kidding him about his 'old' age. I told him once I turned twenty-nine in September, I'd stay that age for the rest of my life. His response to that was to go through our entire kitchen to find every birthday candle we owned, counting out twenty-nine and throwing the rest away.

I squeezed his hand tighter at the memory, a dopey smile pulling at my lips. It's no wonder I wanted to start a family with this goofball.

"Do either of you have any health issues I should know about?"

"Not that I know of," Kyle answered.

He still looked so nervous, and I wanted to tell him it would be okay, but I guess this was what we were here to find out.

I shook my head. "Me neither."

"What about these headaches you marked on your intake form, Mrs. Falls?" Dr. Hill stared at me again, as if accusing me of lying. She needed to relax...like, a lot. I wondered if she could write prescriptions for herself. If so, she should.

I shrugged. "Well, it asked me if I ever had any headaches, and I said yes."

"How often? Are they severe?"

"Uh, a couple times a week. More often and more painful lately than they were at first. I think it's the stress of this process. We've been trying for a baby for a while, you know?"

Dr. Hill fixed on me for a moment, squinting, as if deep in thought, before returning to her paperwork. "I want to run some tests. Mr. Falls, I'll need a sperm sample from you first. The nurse out in the hallway will give you everything you need and show you to a private room. Mrs. Falls, I'll need you to come with me to the fourth floor so I can run some scans after we do a blood test to check that you're not pregnant now."

"Scans for what?" I pictured being stuck in a giant donut-looking machine accidentally malfunctioning and trapping me forever.

"A full body scan will tell us if there is anything we need to worry about, cysts, malformations. At your age, pregnancy shouldn't take a year, and in light of your miscarriage, we need to know what's going on, so we're going head-to-toe."

I immediately suspected she wanted to bill my insurance for expensive tests. "What does fertility have to do with my toes?"

Dr. Hill rolled her eyes—a *doctor* rolled her eyes at me. That was a first. I kind of liked her a little now. "With no recent medical records to refer to—since your last physical was in college—I must rule out all possible problems before we proceed."

I made a face behind her back, and Kyle stifled a laugh. So sue me. I didn't like going to doctors. My father didn't either, and he never made me go unless I was sick. I wouldn't have gone in college if it hadn't been required. In my opinion, it makes absolutely zero sense to go to the doctor when healthy, just to risk picking up a nasty virus in the waiting room and ending up worse than when I walked in.

I gave Kyle an envious look. "So, you get to look at booby magazines, and I get a full body scan. I bet this is how the feminist movement started."

Kyle laughed, circling an arm around my waist. "It's going to be okay, Tessa."

I shot him the squinty glare I'd learned recently from watching Dr. Hill. "For you, maybe." He was a little too eager about all this, if you ask me.

"I'll think of you the whole time, babe. I promise."

"Well, obviously," I replied, wiggling my brows suggestively.

"Mrs. Falls, are you ready?" Dr. Hill was suddenly in my face, and I realized without the desk between us, this woman had a serious lack of social etiquette. Also, she'd definitely eaten tuna for lunch.

"Can't wait," I told her, pretty certain she wouldn't pick up on my sarcasm.

As I followed Dr. Hill down the hall, I heard Kyle behind me asking the nurse for the Wi-Fi password so he could use the internet on his phone instead of magazines.

Bastard.

CHAPTER TWO

WEDNESDAY, *March 26, 2014*

"I'M NOT sure I can take another day off work this week. The U.S. Marines don't exactly give you free rein on sick days, babe." Kyle frowned, stirring a jar of tomato sauce into the spaghetti on the stove.

"Yeah, but you work at the recruitment center now. Plus, Dr. Hill says she needs us to come in person for our results." I stuck a finger into the pot and slurped the sauce off my fingertip before he could bat my hand away. Beast barked at our feet, as if to tell me to share.

"Why can't she do it over the phone?"

"I don't know. Maybe she feels bad telling you over the phone your swimmers aren't working," I said, teasing, though every part of me hoped it had nothing to do with bad news.

"My swimmers are fine. Maybe your batter missed the ball."

I grimaced, sticking my tongue out while walking to the

cabinets and pulling out our dinner plates. "My batter? That sounds horrifying. Where on earth did you learn that metaphor?"

He grinned proudly. "I just made it up."

"That figures. I officially ban any baseball talk in regards to my uterus."

"You can't do that!" He actually sounded upset. *Men are so weird.*

I cocked my head to the side, my brows raised. "So, you wouldn't mind me writing in my book to Baby Falls that Daddy says you're taking so long to get here because Daddy can't throw strikes?"

"Maybe he will become a famous baseball player and see this as the beginning of his fated journey to athletic stardom." Kyle waved his hand dramatically through the air while Beast followed his movements with sharp eyes, waiting for one of us to drop a tasty morsel of canine-poison tomato sauce.

"Fated journey? You've been talking to your mom again, haven't you?"

"They're up in Alaska, looking for a yeti or something."

I snorted a laugh. "There are no yetis in Alaska. Yetis live in the Himalayans. Amateurs."

"That's Dixie and Elias for you," Kyle said, shrugging.

I paused, tapping an index finger to my pursed lips.

He furrowed his brow. "What?"

"I'm trying to decide if I'm more weirded out by you calling your parents their first names, or that they are off searching for mythical creatures on the wrong continent."

He came up behind me, wrapping his arms around my waist and kissing my neck softly. "And the verdict is?"

"I'm strangely okay with both."

"And I'm strangely okay with you." His breath sent

shivers across my skin. "Speaking of strange trips, have you checked your email today?"

My eyes popped open. "Oh my God—today's the day!"

Kyle held up his phone, grinning. "I got the permit. I got picked in the lottery. Did you?"

"I haven't checked!" I shrieked at the top of my lungs, digging around in my pockets frantically for my phone.

"Don't be upset if you didn't," he cautioned. "The chances of us both being picked for the Half Dome are slim to none."

The Half Dome Day Hike at Yosemite National Park was a climber and hiker's dream trail, and we'd been trying to get picked to go forever. You could only get permits in March via lottery and we'd both missed out and not been chosen the last two years.

I finally managed to find my phone and pull open my email, scrolling through a ton of junk mail until I finally found the right one. "I got it! I got it!"

Waving my phone in his face, I jumped up and down then threw my arms around his neck in a giant bear hug. "We're going to Yosemite!"

"I can't believe we both got in!" Kyle said, hugging me back. "This trip is going to be amazing."

"This is our year, babe. We're going to kill it." And I was really beginning to believe that.

Kyle laughed. "You're a strange one, Tessa."

"What's so strange about me?" I said, teasing and unsure if I actually wanted an answer. We're talking jumbo-sized can of worms here.

"What's so strange about Tessa Falls? Hmm, do we have all night?" He kissed me again, chuckling against my skin.

"Nope, we're on the clock. Beast demands an answer in one sentence or less."

"Beast does?"

I nodded, motioning down to the dog, who had wormed his way between our legs.

"Hmmm...the strangest thing about Tessa Barnes is she chose to become Tessa Falls," he said.

I tried to hold the corners of my lips still, his coaxing voice making me turn to face him. Wrapping my arms around his neck, I found his mouth with mine and thanked him for the moment of sincerity. I was more comfortable in constant witty banter than I was with raw feelings, but his words were exactly what I needed to hear. It was exactly what I needed to feel—wanted.

"Schedule the doctor's appointment for Friday afternoon, and I'll see if Gunny will let me leave early." Kyle brushed his lips across mine. "It shouldn't be a problem though."

"Yes, sir, Staff Sergeant." I pressed my hips forward, my tone suggestive.

He groaned, always loving when I call him by his rank, and inhaled deeply, his nose still pressed against my shoulder. The sensation caused my skin to prickle with a chill before heating up and traveling south.

"You know what I think?" His voice was now deeper and husky.

I moaned lightly in response, urging him to finish his thought.

"I think we should go upstairs and practice before dinner."

"Practice what?" I asked.

"Making Baby Falls."

• ∞ • ∞ • ∞ •

WEDNESDAY, March 24, 2010

"I GOT SOMETHING FOR YOU." Kyle grinned at me excitedly.

The man had no poker face. I'd known he had a surprise up his sleeve ever since he first picked me up for our date. It was cute. He was cute. The last three months of dating him were cute.

Cute, cute, *cute.*

And I'm not a cute person—never have been and never wanted to be. Yet somehow, I was dolling up to see him and gushing to my friends about everything he did. I'd even tucked the receipt from tonight's movie rental into my purse as a memento.

That's the levels of depravity we're talking about here.

Someone, send help.

"What is it?" I wedged into the couch farther, pulling my feet underneath me.

He hopped up and walked to his jacket, slung over a chair in the corner, and retrieved something from the pocket. We'd already eaten at one of my favorite restaurants in downtown Chicago then rented a movie to watch at my place. I was a big fan of movies on the couch—same show, but you could take your shoes off...among other things.

He handed me a medium-sized brown box. "Open it and find out."

I grabbed it and ripped the top to find a red heart inside. Smiling, I glanced up at him, wondering if this meant what I thought it meant.

"Are you giving me your heart?" My voice sounded a lot

more hopeful than I intended. I bit my lip, hoping I hadn't sounded as desperate for his answer as I really was.

Instead, his fingers found my chin and tilted my face to him. "I love you, Tessa. I'm in love with you and have been for weeks." His wide smile seemed to go on for days as he reached into the box and pulled out the heart. I hadn't realized it at first, but it was the kind of heart-shaped box that was filled with chocolates. "But you should open the heart."

Lifting the lid quickly, I immediately burst out laughing. "Kyle!"

The heart was filled with small airplane bottles of booze —all of my favorite brands. Hershey's kisses acted like buffers between the bottles and each little chocolate had a paper ribbon that said "I love you." If I had had any doubt that he was my perfect man, it was certainly wiped clean now.

"I couldn't think of anything that would better describe our love than booze and kisses," he said, a mischievous grin on his face.

I pulled out a tiny Jack Daniels and shook my head, chuckling. "I accept your booze—and chocolate-filled proclamation of love, but I have one caveat."

I felt like throwing my arms around his neck and kissing him to kingdom come. Or until one of us does—preferably me first. But I had conditions first.

He looked so surprised I thought his eyebrows would touch his hairline. "You have a caveat to me loving you?"

"Yes, I'll let you love me with one condition—"

He snorted. "Oh, now you'll let me?"

"I'm not done," I said in warning, my index finger pointed between us.

He held his hands up in defense, pausing for me to continue.

"As I was saying, I'll let you love me on one condition—I

get all the love. Every last drop of love in your heart is for me, nothing held back ever."

"Every last drop," he repeated, clearly amused.

I pushed my chin up. "Those are my terms."

Kyle scooted closer on the couch and pulled me to him, settling me on his lap as my arms circled his neck. I took the opportunity to sniff his collar, blushing slightly at my indulgence. I'm pretty sure his scent is half the reason I started dating him. Something about it was intoxicating, compelling, and perfectly mine.

"Tessa Barnes, I hereby guarantee you have all my love." He covered my lips with his, stealing the very breath from my lungs.

I tasted his sincerity and wanted more, took more, and gave more. After several heated moments, I pulled away and looked at him with mock seriousness. "Can I get that in writing and notarized?"

He laughed, shaking his head and reaching over me to grab two mini bottles of booze. "I'm going to need a drink if you're going to add more conditions to this." He handed me one. "Drink up, woman."

"Yes, please," I said, taking it from him and unscrewing the top. "Although, you know, you're still getting laid tonight whether I'm drunk or not."

He grabbed the DVD remote and started the movie. "Oh, I know."

His cocky attitude and sly smile suddenly irked me and I huffed. "I take it back. Maybe I'm not in the mood."

He chuckled, putting the remote down as the opening credits rolled onto the screen. "Whatever you say, babe."

"Hey, Kyle?" A rush of nerves hit my stomach as I considered what I was about to say.

"Yeah?"

Heat rose to my cheeks and I averted my gaze. "I'm in love with you, too."

He grinned. "I know that, too."

A smile twitched at the corner of my lips as I burrowed into his side. Okay, so cute isn't too bad.

I think I'll keep him.

CHAPTER THREE

FRIDAY, March 28, 2014

"DID YOU TAKE SOME IBUPROFEN?" Kyle pulled the car into the hospital parking lot, casting worried glances my direction.

"Yeah, this morning." I pushed my sunglasses against my face, hoping the pressure and darkness would ease my headache. "But it didn't help much."

"Maybe you should get checked out by a doctor, Tessa. There has to be something they can do to get rid of them. They've been getting worse."

"No more doctors right now. I'll be fine." I shrugged it off and climbed out of the car. After tucking away my journal, I hung my purse over my shoulder and tilted my chin down, allowing my hair to cascade past my cheeks and block out the sun.

Kyle locked the car and wrapped his arm around my shoulder as we walked through the glass doors and into the lobby. The hospital was huge—a campus of buildings adjoining or separated with only a small walkway. Dr. Hill's office was on the west side and by the time we'd walked all the way there from the parking garage, I was exhausted.

When was the last time I'd made it to the gym? I made a mental note to get my ass back there immediately because clearly I was getting out of shape.

Kyle kissed my temple, as he always did, and I swear that alone made the pain in my head subside and exhaustion in my body dissipate. Sometimes I wondered if love had magic powers. Like if you love someone hard enough, you could do anything. You could manipulate time and space, or live outside the boundaries of reality. Maybe love wasn't enough to change the world, but it could change one person's world, and Kyle had changed mine.

When I was six years old, my mother passed away from breast cancer. I don't remember much from before her illness, but my father always told me she'd loved me and would always be with me. Some days, I think I can feel her —a hand on my shoulder wanting me to know I'm not alone. Only loving hard with everything you have can do that, and when I go one day many, many years from now, I hope to do the same for the people I leave behind.

"Hi, we have an appointment," Kyle stated to the receptionist when we entered Dr. Hill's waiting room.

"Name?"

"Kyle and Tessa Falls."

The receptionist cast a furtive glance in my direction and cleared her throat. Her face quickly went neutral and she shuffled a few papers around before coming out from behind the desk and motioning for us to follow. "Come with me, Mr. and Mrs. Falls. I'll get you guys set up in Dr. Hill's office and she will join you in a minute."

Something felt off, as if she knew something I didn't, and I wasn't a fan.

"Kyle, I don't know about this," I whispered. When I glanced up at him, I saw he had the same suspicious look on his face.

He wrapped his fingers around mine and brought my hand to his lips, kissing my knuckles softly. "Don't worry, beautiful. I've got you."

His smile warmed me, and I relaxed as we were guided to the office.

"Can I get either of you something to drink?" the receptionist asked while opening the office door.

We both shook our heads.

"Okay. Dr. Hill and her colleague will be here in a moment."

"Her colleague?" Kyle asked what I was thinking, but the receptionist had already left.

I took a seat, keeping my hand wrapped in his. Something didn't feel right.

"Tessa, Kyle, how wonderful to see you again." A too-cheery version of Dr. Hill walked in and greeted us with soft handshakes, the kind where the second hand covered our joined hands. It felt too friendly for the grumpy doctor I'd come to know from our last visit.

"Dr. Hill." Kyle stuck with a curt greeting.

"Let me introduce you to Dr. Spencer Page." Dr. Hill moved aside, revealing an older man in a white coat who reminded me of Santa Claus. If it wasn't March, I would've thought he was here to hand out candy canes or give me a gift. Despite my current unease, I instinctively trusted this man.

"Mr. and Mrs. Falls, it's lovely to meet you both." He

shook our hands—a softer handshake than Dr. Hill, almost limp—then perched on the edge of Dr. Hill's desk.

Dr. Hill walked around to sit behind her desk "This is difficult to say, so I'm just going to dive right in." Still oddly cheery for whatever grim news she was about to deliver.

I said a silent prayer—which was newsworthy on its own—that my teasing hadn't jinxed my husband's swimmers. I turned to look at Kyle, pledging then and there that I was going to love him even if he couldn't give me children. We could adopt or foster or whatever. I'd love our children whether we conceived them ourselves or not. This wasn't the end of the word.

We'd face whatever the doctor was about to tell us.

"Tessa, I found something worrisome on your scans, so I asked Dr. Page to consult."

"What?" Kyle and I asked at the same time. He squeezed my hand harder.

"Dr. Page?" Dr. Hill said, deferring to him, her cheery appearance dissolving into nervousness that increased mine tenfold.

Dr. Page cleared his throat. "Mrs. Falls—"

"Tessa, please," I corrected him, mostly trying to delay whatever he was about to say.

"Very well, Tessa." He unfolded a file in his hands that I hadn't noticed before. "Dr. Hill consulted me about your scans because I'm a neurosurgeon, specializing in oncology. I examined your scans thoroughly." He paused, taking a deep breath that seemed to be stealing my own. "The results reveal what appears to be a tumor in your brain."

My mouth fell. "A tumor? *In my brain?*"

I honestly couldn't understand what he was telling me. I'm not sure he was even speaking English. It was only late

March, but I was suddenly looking around the room for signs of an April Fool's joke.

"We will need to do a biopsy to confirm the exact nature of the mass. There's a lot we don't know yet," Dr. Page continued.

I looked past him to Dr. Hill, who dodged my gaze and fiddled with a pen on her desk. The air in my chest was stagnant, but if I could have, I would have screamed for her to drop the damn pen and look at me. Tell me to my face what was happening. Instead, she sent in some Santa-looka-like to deliver the worst gift possible.

There had to be a mistake.

"Biopsy? As in *cut* into her brain?" Kyle finally spoke.

When I saw his eyes were wide with fear, I began to feel it, too.

"Technically, yes, but biopsies are small, and we try to be as non-invasive as possible. If during the procedure it looks like I can remove the entire mass, I will. But in all like-lihood, it will just be a small piece."

"Non-invasive, *but in my brain*," I repeated, not sure if he understood he made no sense.

Clearly, the man had no idea what he was talking about. I was twenty-eight years old. I was short, athletic, and petite, barely weighing more than Kyle's massively muscular legs combined. He had to be looking at the wrong scans—this kind of thing didn't happen to people like me.

I'd done everything I was supposed to do.

I eat organic. We shop at the farmer's market and source local products. We rarely eat sweets or drink pop, except for special occasions. The worst thing I've ever done is drink alcohol, but these days it's mostly red wine, which is good for my heart, or so I've chosen to believe. I run at least five mornings a week with Kyle by my side, and I drink the recommended eight cups of water a day. I even use an app on my phone to keep track of it, where every glass I drink waters an imaginary little plant. I have a freaking forest by now.

I am doing everything right.

"When can we do it?" Kyle's voice was firm, his jaw set in a hard line as if he was biting down. The corners of his lips pointed south, and the soft stubble from his beard somehow had gone from a sexy disheveled look to tired and worn.

"Ideally, today. This should be done as soon as possible," Dr. Page said.

"You want to cut into my brain today? *Today?!*" I reiterated, completely aware of how shrill my voice sounded. "Wait a minute, you said you specialize in oncology. Does this mean I have cancer? Is the tumor cancerous?"

"That's what the biopsy will tell us," he said, but there was a flash of sorrow on his face that made me think he already had an awful guess.

I sat back in my chair, now clutching Kyle's hand with both of mine.

Dr. Page continued talking, explaining how the biopsy worked, and the procedure's intricate details, but I could only watch his lips move. His beard bounced and jiggled with each word, the room silent around him.

He knew. I could see it in his eyes and the way he shook his head. He *knew* it was cancer. But he was wrong. *This is wrong. I am not sick.*

I do not have cancer.

I do not have a tumor.

I just want to have a baby. We're only here to talk about babies.

"If it is cancer, what then?" Kyle's words cut through my silence.

"It's hard to project that before the biopsy. Every tumor is different. However, it doesn't look very large yet, meaning with treatment, the outcome could potentially be optimistic. We'd need to do the biopsy long before we could make that call though."

Optimistic about cancer—the irony.

"I'm going to give you guys a few minutes to talk in private," Dr. Page said.

"And, uh, fertility treatments?" Kyle rubbed his hand on the base of his neck.

Dr. Hill looked up at Kyle's question. "We're going to wait until this is resolved before we continue."

I wanted to punch her in her scrunched up, stupid face.

She wanted to wait until *this* was resolved. My tumor, some sort of pending transaction. I snorted, an awkward inward chuckle at the thought. Like I'd accidentally overdrafted my bank account and was cut off until I was back in the black. My denial skittered me to the edges of hysteria, and to be honest, I wasn't convinced they knew the first thing about fiscal responsibility.

"Oh." Kyle's voice dripped with sadness.

"I'll wait for you in the hallway to take you for prep and blood work," Dr. Page told me, before summoning Dr. Hill to follow him, which she reluctantly did.

"I'm so sorry about this, Tessa." Dr. Hill put a hand on my shoulder as she walked past me.

I wanted to shrink from her touch, but I thought it too dramatic. None of this was her fault—I knew that—but it didn't make me any less angry and ready to find someone to blame. *Tag, Dr. Hill is it.*

The door clicked closed behind them. There was a

lump forming in my throat, making it difficult to talk, but it didn't matter. What was there to say? I had a tumor in my brain. Or this was the cruelest early April Fool's joke ever, and I'd be murdering everyone soon.

I bit down on the inside of my cheek in an attempt to keep from screaming.

Leaning over the desk, I grabbed the pen Dr. Hill had been fiddling with. In one quick motion, I snapped it in half. Staring at the two ends dripping with ink, I dropped them on her desk, watching black liquid pool into a puddle on her large desk calendar.

When the puddle grew larger—which didn't take long as there was a surprising amount of black ink in such a small pen—I reached into my purse and pulled out my journal. In less than a week, I'd managed to add four entries and had been feeling pretty confident about the start of my book.

I pressed the book open to an empty page and laid it over the puddle of ink, paper side down, and let it soak through the blank pages. After a few moments, I picked it up and closed it, allowing the wet pages to stick together. I didn't know how to write about today. So instead, today's entry would be black. Sticky. Dark.

Exactly what I was feeling inside.

I wanted to run. I wanted to scream and cry. I wanted to tell the doctors they were wrong—they were making a huge mistake. I wanted their medical licenses hanging on my wall of people who had once wronged me. If I had a wall like that.

I should definitely get a wall like that.

Kyle didn't move, staring at the chaotic, widening puddle of ink. It was probably less than a minute, but it seemed hours passed before he exhaled loudly and rotated his chair to face mine.

I did the same, our knees bumping against each other.

He grabbed both my hands, sandwiching them between his and rubbed them together, as if to warm me.

"I guess your swimmers are fine," I said, breaking the silence.

He chuckled lightly. "Not necessarily. We never got to that."

"True." I angled my head toward the pen. "Did you want to break something, too?"

"I think I already have." He pressed my hands to his chest over his heart, his face twisting in pain.

I leaned into him, dropping my forehead in the shallow dip between his neck and shoulder. I exhaled slowly, feeling his heart pumping fast beneath my palm. I tried to restrain myself, but a rebellious tear slid down my cheek and dropped to his forearm.

"I have cancer in my brain," I whispered, tasting the concept on my tongue to see if I could say it aloud.

"You don't know that," he corrected, but I heard the hesitation in his tone.

He leaned back to look at me and wiped my escalating tears with the pads of his thumb, his cheeks as stained as mine.

I sniffed. "But what if I do?"

"Then we'll follow whatever the doctor tells us...and beat it."

"What if I don't beat it?" I was surprised to hear the thought from my own mouth. I was generally a very positive person despite my sarcasm, or the creeping sadness that had been overtaking me since the miscarriage. But I'd committed pen homicide, inked up a doctor's desk, and was assuming the worst possible scenario. Quite the roll for a perpetual optimist, but, I figure when someone tells me potential life-ending news, I'm allowed a moment of doubt and fear. Probably a little insanity, too.

I planned to treat myself to every bitter spoonful.

"You're unstoppable, Tessa. You know that, I know that, and the world knows that. There's never been anything to keep you down." His jaw set firm, he looked more confident than I did, and I wanted to believe him. "I love you, Tessa. We'll get through this." He ignored my joking as he wiped at my wet cheeks again. He knew me too well and wasn't letting me mask my nerves.

"I love you, too, Kyle." I bit the inside of my cheek again, tasting blood this time. I liked it. Something about the metallic flavor reminded me I was still here. I wasn't dead yet.

I'm still here.

"Do you want me to call your dad or sister? Have them come meet us here?" he asked, his cheeks pulled down in a frown that seemed to be taking up permanent residence.

"No, but you probably should anyway. They'd kill me before this tumor does if they found out I hid this from them. Oh, and find someone to feed Beast."

Kyle's eyes flashed anger, but not at me. "This isn't going to kill you, Tessa. I won't let it. It's just one step on our way to becoming parents. We need to fix this, then we'll have our baby. One step at a time."

He stared at me hard, and I could see he was willing himself not to cry, but tears were falling anyway and had been since we started talking. Tiny, beautiful tears cascading down his chiseled, rough features. The dichotomy was breathtaking on him, and I couldn't think of the last time I'd seen him cry.

"You think we'll still have a baby?"

Kyle nodded firmly, turning to rub his cheek against his

shoulder to wipe his tears. "I know we will. We almost did once, and we will again."

Nothing inside me believed him, but I didn't tell him that. My head ached again, but the throbbing in my heart overshadowed it. The idea of leaving behind the man I loved, never having a family—Kyle never being a father—the thought was unbearable.

My body trembled and tears pooled on my lower lashes.

Kyle pulled me into his arms, and I curled into his chest.

My voice dropped to a whisper. "Kyle, I'm afraid."

I was afraid I would never be a mother. I was afraid it was cancer.

And I was afraid it would kill me.

"I'm here, babe," he spoke softly into my hair, his arms wrapped around me.

I wanted him to squeeze me tighter, so I pressed farther into him. He obliged, holding me together to keep me from falling apart.

"I need all the love. Every last drop," I said, repeating our cherished phrase. I wanted our love to be strong enough for this moment, and strong enough to fix this. Love can do anything and I only had one request.

"You've got my everything, Tessa."

CHAPTER FOUR

FRIDAY, *March 28, 2014*

"NO LUNCH? I didn't have time to eat breakfast this morning." I scrunched up my face as I sat on the edge of an examining table, trying my best to keep the thin paper gown from exposing my lady bits to everyone in the room. Which, by the way, was a lot of freaking people. The room was stuffed with nurses, orderlies, and other people in official-looking uniforms I didn't know.

This was so weird.

There was no other way to describe it except weird. This morning I was going about my life as usual, and a few hours later I'm about to have my skull opened up. To say I was adjusting to this news would be a total lie.

I was *not* okay.

I don't want my head cut open. I don't want to be in a damn paper gown in a room full of strangers. I don't want to have cancer.

Please, God, don't let me have cancer, I prayed silently,

something I'd been doing more and more of. I wondered if that would have made the difference, if maybe God would have spared me all of this if I'd prayed more and gone to church every Sunday. Sure, I ate organic and ran a half marathon last year, but maybe those things didn't matter at all.

"It's better to have an empty stomach when going under anesthesia. If all goes well, you'll be having dinner in a few hours," Dr. Page assured me, interrupting my thoughts.

"If? Don't you mean when?" Kyle practically growled from where he stood next to me.

"Of course, Mr. Falls. Your wife will be fine. It's only a small procedure to see what's going on inside." The doctor pointed at my head, and I briefly considered biting off his finger.

Kyle glowered at him, squinty-eyed with his arms crossing his chest. His shoulders were back and his feet far enough apart to put him in the intimidating stance I knew he'd learned in the U.S. Marines. He was angled away from me, but still managed to remain close. Everything about him screamed *protector,* and to be honest, it was kind of hot.

Normally I'd be laughing at the strangeness of being in a thin, paper gown with a nurse attaching all sorts of things to me, or cracking a joke about whether or not the shiny clamp on my index finger could reveal to the room how I wanted to jump my husband. But laughter seemed so far away and I couldn't fathom finding it.

"Mrs. Falls, I'm Delores and I'll be prepping the surgical area for you." A younger woman with the prettiest smile approached, pushing a tray on wheels. It had shears, a razor, and liquids I didn't understand.

"What do you mean by *surgical area?*"

"I'll need to shave a small area of your hair away so the

doctor can do his job." Her smile was so welcoming, I almost missed what she'd said. "This is the hardest part for most of our female patients."

I ran a hand through my hair, letting my long, wavy brown locks drift through my fingers. It was one of my favorite features, the only cooperative thing about my looks. It fell naturally just the way I wanted with very little effort.

My hand dropped to my lap and Kyle wrapped his hand around mine. "Okay."

Delores picked up the shears and sectioned off a square to one side of my head. She twisted the hair around her finger a few times, then snipped off the strand at once. I cringed at the sound, closing my eyes so I wouldn't see my hair in her hand.

There were a few more snips and then a buzzing sound as an electric razor rattled against my skull and brought it down to stubble. I stayed still with my eyes glued shut, pretending I was elsewhere. I jolted slightly at the cold sensation as she spread a cool gel over the spot and ran a razor blade across it a few times.

"There you go. You're ready." Delores smiled and began packing her things.

I willed myself to say thank you or something polite. But I wasn't grateful; I was only trying not to cry.

She handed me a small mirror, and I swallowed as I tilted my head to the side to see my new bald patch.

There it was—the physical reminder that I was not normal. I was not healthy. There was something wrong and it couldn't—or wouldn't—be hidden. The shaved spot stuck out like a dead fly in a champagne glass, taunting the rest of my thick hair. This was the problem with hair; it didn't matter if the rest might make a shampoo model jealous, just like it doesn't matter how delicious that metaphorical champagne was. There's still a dead fly in it.

"Don't tell me where I can and can't go in this God forsaken building!" A gruff male voice yelled from the hallway outside my room. "You think you're keeping me out of an exam room? I've stormed whole villages!"

Kyle and I looked at each and smiled as my father burst through the doors.

"Tessa!" He sounded relieved and terrified at the same time, bounding over to me and then wrapping me in a bear hug. He was the only man I knew with a larger and more intimidating stature than my hulk of a husband. I shared my father's brown hair and blue eyes, but the similarities ended there. For everything I was tiny, he was large. His nose was large, his eyes were large, his ears were large—his entire body, large. The man was a walking giant and could look really intimidating if he wanted to. Thankfully, I knew he was nothing but a big softie underneath it all.

"Daddy, I'm so glad you're here." I nuzzled my nose into his shirt and hugged him tightly. I'd known he'd come as soon as he heard, living as he did only a few minutes outside Chicago in our hometown of Northfield.

I'd been a daddy's girl since the day I was born, and would be until the day I died. Didn't matter what mistakes he made, I loved him no matter what. He'd been the sole caretaker for my younger sister Elly and me after my mother died when Elly was only three years old. He'd struggled—we all did—but his love and commitment to us had never wavered.

"It's okay, sunshine. I'm not going anywhere. I'll be here through the whole thing." He squeezed me tighter, and I needed it so much I almost cried out at the relief of feeling safe in my father's arms. He'd called me *sunshine* ever since

I was a baby after a popular song lyric, his *sunshine on a cloudy day*.

"The doctor said I might have cancer," I told him, blurting it out.

"Bull-fucking-shit. Doctors are always assuming the worst, a bunch of quacks," he huffed, spouting another of his many conspiracy theories. "Don't believe a word they say."

"Dad, I saw the scans."

"My doctor's been trying to show me scans of my lungs for years, trying to get me to quit smoking. They're getting paid by the pharmaceutical companies to try and make me buy those quitting patches."

"Dad," I said, chastising him with my tone. He'd been smoking my entire life and no amount of begging had convinced him to quit. That was the thing about Master Sergeant Glenn Barnes—once he'd made up his mind that he was right about something, there was no one that could convince him otherwise. Being in two wars had given him the chance to see so much corruption and devastation that he trusted no one and nothing at this point, looking for scandals around every corner now.

"Master Sergeant Barnes," Kyle said, breaking up our discussion and greeting my father with a military style salute before devolving into a hearty handshake and hug. My father was former U.S. Marines, so to say he was proud of my choice in a spouse would be an understatement.

"Kyle." My father's voice was sad. "Are you taking care of our girl here?"

"I'm trying, sir."

"Good man. Where's the doctor?" At my father's mention, I looked around and realized we were down to an orderly and a nurse, but no Dr. Page.

"I'm not sure." I shrugged. "Did you tell Elly what's happening?"

"Yes, and she'll be on the first plane out tonight from JFK. She'll be here at least a week to make sure you're okay."

"She's able to take that much time off classes?" I asked.

Elly was six years younger than me and in her last year of college at New York University. She was studying physical therapy, and I couldn't be prouder of her. We'd been inseparable growing up, and as strong as I was trying to be, I really needed my best friend.

"It's actually her spring break, so it doesn't interfere with anything but her beach plans," Dad explained.

Kyle stroked a stray piece of hair behind my ear. I could feel him lingering above my newly shaved spot.

Dr. Page walked in, and everything about him was all business—you could practically see the mental checklist behind his eyes. His dark blue scrubs were topped with a red cap over his white hair, masks draped around his neck.

I wondered if this was how Santa looked on Christmas Eve, his sleigh packed and six billion houses to visit in one night. Dr. Page looked ready for six billion houses, or at least one tumor.

"Mrs. Falls, how are you feeling? Any questions about today's procedure?"

I had a hundred questions but none he could answer. Why was this happening to me? Would I ever be a mother? Was I going to die? Around Christmas time, did people ask him for gifts? I felt like Dr. Page could probably only answer the last one, but I refrained, shaking my head no.

"Dr. Page, I presume?" My father stuck out his hand.

Dr. Page shook it. "I am."

"I'm Greg Barnes, Tessa's father." Their handshake took

a little too long, and looked a little too tight, some sort of silent battle of wills happening between them I didn't understand.

Finally, Dr. Page let go and stepped back. "Thanks for being here, Mr. Barnes."

Dad grunted. "Wouldn't be anywhere else."

"Everything should go fine—no reason to worry. To reiterate, we're only doing a biopsy today." Dr. Page turned to me. "I'm going to open up your skull, take a small sample of the tumor for testing. If I see the tumor is in a favorable position where it can be removed, I will do so, but from the scans, I must tell you that is unlikely."

I nodded again, my voice trapped beneath my fear.

"Can you hop on this bed, Tessa? The orderlies will wheel you to the operating room where they will then transfer you onto the table while I prep. Mr. Falls, this nurse will lead you to the waiting area." The doctor motioned toward us and pointed staff in our direction.

Kyle grabbed my hand and squeezed, helping me down from the table and onto the bed. "Can't I walk with her to the operating room?"

"I'm sorry. Standard procedure, Mr. Falls."

"I'll walk next to the bed until we get there, then," Kyle compromised, not asking permission. He pulled the starched hospital blankets across my legs. I wanted him to curl in bed with me, hold me through the entire operation. If it wouldn't break every infection control policy possible, I'm sure he would have.

"Mr. Falls, there's really no need, she'll be fine." A nurse tried to draw him away, but I clamped a hand around his forearm.

He didn't budge. "Are you kidding me? My wife is about to have her head cut open, there's definitely a need."

"We'll both walk her down, then I'll make sure Kyle gets to the waiting room and stays put," my father intervened, two hands on his son-in-law's shoulders.

I exhaled slowly, pushing everything out of my lungs and focusing on calming my pulse. This was happening, there was nothing I could do to stop it. I inhaled slowly, filling my chest and lungs entirely before letting them collapse again.

"I'll be right here when you are done, babe," Kyle told me, my hand in his while he walked beside the bed.

The orderlies pushing me were fast, and their urgency frightened me. I clutched his hand tighter. "Kyle, in case I don't make it out of there—"

"You will, Tessa. I won't let us be apart again."

So much of our marriage, and even dating, had been long distance because of his deployments overseas. This last year together had been everything we'd hoped for, and he was right—I never wanted to be apart again.

Still, I needed to say it. I needed him to know. "But just in case, I want you to know how much I love you. You're everything to me, Kyle. My entire life. I wouldn't have it any other way."

He lifted my hand to his lips and kissed it.

"All the love, Tessa."

I smiled, closing my eyes and hoping for everything. For one thing.

For a miracle.

CHAPTER FIVE

FRIDAY, *March 28, 2014*

"THAT'S BUSH LEAGUE. I was promised dinner." I frowned at Delores as she took my blood pressure.

"Dinner was hours ago, hun. We can get you a light snack or something, but nothing heavy. After being under anesthesia, you'd risk an upset stomach."

I touched the bandage around my head, cringing at the twinge of pain. I was being rude, particularly since Delores had been so kind to me. But when someone's fingers have been on the wrong side of your skull, you tend to feel a little bitchy.

Kyle rose from his chair beside my bed. "Babe, how about I run out and get you something?"

"If I'm craving pickles, will you judge me?"

His brow furrowed. "You want pickles?"

"Yes. Preferably fried." I'd never had them before, but they sounded perfect. Don't ask me why—I haven't a clue.

Delores raised an eyebrow. "Not fried. Your stomach will have lots to say about anything fried. Regular pickles might be fine. Weird, but fine."

Kyle nodded, tossed me a bewildered grin, and headed out the door.

I watched him go, my head angled to admire his perfect...stature. Okay, I was ogling his ass, but it's not my fault. He was yummy and powerful, and I could use some power right now.

Lying in a hospital bed with needles in my arm was unnerving. This place was depressing, despite the nearby poster of a cat hanging from a tree branch encouraging me to *hang in there*.

My father was at O'Hare picking up my sister. I was missing him already, plus, I was dying to see Elly.

Poor choice of words.

"Mrs. Falls?" Dr. Page's deep Santa-style voice boomed as he pushed aside the privacy curtain between the glass door and me.

"What's up, doc?" My best Bugs Bunny impression won me a small twitch at the corner of his lips. It was almost a smile; I'd take it. I needed all the optimism and pep I could manage to fake right now. The usual creeping sadness was threatening to make its way back in and it was taking every coping skill my therapist had taught me to keep it at bay. Deep breathing, mindfulness, meditation—I was pulling out all the stops to stay positive, but, damn, life was pretty shitty at the moment.

"How are you feeling?" he asked.

"I'm okay, a little headache." The worst part was over and that thought was carrying me through. Plus, the pain medications. Those were fantastic.

He glanced down at the papers in his hands and when

he looked back at me, my optimism quickly tanked. Sullen and somber—this wasn't good news. "As you're aware, I was hoping to remove the entire tumor. That wasn't possible as I discovered the tumor has spread feelers to other parts of your brain. I'm most worried about its proximity to your optic nerve."

My heart thumped behind my ribcage, and I felt a wave of nausea pass through me.

"It gets worse, doesn't it?" My expression begged him to tell me I'm wrong.

"The results aren't what we'd hoped for," he said.

I chewed on the corner of my thumb, trying to keep the nausea down. "My husband's getting dinner. Should we wait?"

"That's up to you. Whatever you'd be more comfortable with." Dr. Page thumbed the papers again.

My stomach twisted in knots; wishing I'd picked a better time to be hungry. I couldn't wait for Kyle. I had to know now. "Just tell me."

"We rushed the results of your biopsy. It's a Grade 2 Diffuse Astrocytoma." Dr. Page hugged the clipboard to his chest, his sad eyes fixed on me. "It is malignant, and we must act fast to keep the cancer from progressing."

Silence fell between us, only the beeping of the machines interrupting every few seconds.

"Well," I started, blinking rapidly. I felt like a pierced balloon, deflating, scrambling to find my words. I only had one. "Fuck."

"My thoughts exactly," Dr. Page echoed.

Every fear from earlier was bombarding my thoughts, my heart, my stomach. I wished I had waited for Kyle. I wished I'd waited for my dad or Elly.

The first time I'd ever heard the word *cancer* was when

my mother was diagnosed with it. Then my little sister was born, becoming my whole world. I'd heard the word thrown around a few times after that, but I had been so focused on my sister and being a kid, it hadn't seemed a big deal. No one had ever told me to worry about it, or see it as something serious, especially since my mother went into remission soon after treatment.

When her breast cancer came back three years later, she wasn't as lucky.

I was old enough the second time to understand how scary the word was. My teachers whispered it to each other, pity in their eyes when they looked at me. The doctors had always sent us from the room before speaking with my parents.

But my dad never said it. No one said it. *Cancer.* My mother had cancer.

Now I have cancer.

And the word seemed even scarier this time than it ever did before. Amazing how powerful just a word can be. I wanted to run from it—ninja jump out the hospital window like a skilled stunt woman from the movies so it couldn't catch up with me. My father always used to tell me that I needed to stop running from things. "Face things head on, Tessa," he'd say. That's not really what my life was about up until now. I'd married the first man who'd seriously paid attention to me—thank God he happened to be the perfect man for me anyway—and I'd taken the first job to offer me a contract. I'd graduated college from the first school to offer me admission and moved in to the first house the realtor had shown us.

I wasn't picky. I wasn't difficult. I was go-with-the-flow. But...was that really a thing? Or was I just avoiding life and making any decisions at all? Now here I was facing the potential end, and it would be nothing but choices from here on out.

Ironic.

"So, um, what now?" I faltered my words, still unsure, hugging my knees to my chest, the thin hospital blanket covering me. I could feel tears threatening to leak, but I took a deep breath and pushed them down.

It barely worked, but I was waiting for Kyle. I couldn't break down alone. I couldn't.

. "I have a treatment plan outlined. I think we should get started right away if you're open to it."

"Kyle's going to be back any minute," I reminded him.

"I'll bring him up to speed," the doctor assured me. "Monday morning, you'll start radiation. Five times a week for six weeks. After that, we'll repeat the scans to look for changes. The goal is to shrink the tumor and its feelers. If those diminish, I can remove the full tumor during surgery. The goal is for you to be cancer free in a few months."

I watched him. His beard bobbing with each word. Radiation. Surgery. *Cancer.* Words I feared would become too normal a part of my vocabulary.

"So, two months of radiation and another surgery," I repeated.

He nodded. "Yes."

I sat up taller, straightening my knees as I thought this though. I needed to keep it together, because I couldn't spend the next few months miserable and pessimistic. It wasn't who I am. I'm *not* that person. I needed to look for the silver lining as much as I needed air to breathe.

And the lining was that it was only two months. Nothing can be so terrible if it's only for two months. This entire ordeal would be an ugly bump in the road behind us soon enough.

"Babe?" Kyle walked in with a small brown bag and approached the bed. "Doc? Did you get the results?"

My eyes swung from Kyle's hopeful face over to Dr. Page, and I gave a small nod of approval. Dr. Page repeated everything in greater detail, and I watched my husband's face go from hopeful to devastated to determined, and everything in between.

Finally, Dr. Page left and we were alone.

"What's two months?" I plastered on a smile, hoping he'd see a confidence in me I didn't feel in myself. "It's nothing. You've been deployed longer and we made it through."

Long eyes met mine, a depth in them I wasn't strong enough to explore. "Two months," he said, his voice soft and meek—something I'd never heard from him before.

I reached my arm to him, beckoning him closer, and he obliged my request. Crawling into the bed beside me, only the blankets separated us as he pulled me to his chest. I lifted my arms to his neck, careful to maneuver my IVs around us. My lips moved to his, and I spoke everything in my heart through our kiss.

I told him two months was so short, we'd barely notice. I told him two months was nothing compared to the rest of our lives, to our family, to Baby Falls. And I told him these two months sounded like the scariest thing I'd ever imagined.

When we parted, Kyle leaned toward the side table where he had set down the bag of food he'd brought in with him earlier. Beside it was my journal, which he must have brought with him because I hadn't seen it before then. I smiled slowly, wrapping myself in good feelings at how well my husband knew me.

He picked up the journal and laid it on my lap. "Let's write it down."

I shook my head. "We're not doing fertility treatments anymore, Kyle. We may never have a baby. What's the point?"

"The point is you've always wanted to write a book. Now you're going to have a few weeks off work, and knowing you, you'll be bored. Take this time to write. It's okay if it isn't about parenthood."

I considered what he said as I leafed through the pages. The big reveals of today made writing a book seem an impossible goal. I turned to a clump of pages stuck together with dried ink and pulled them apart slowly—the smeared ink blot from Dr. Hill's pen.

I stared at the black words that weren't words at all, and it was probably the truest thing I'd ever written.

"I can't. I can't write about this," I said.

"Why?" Kyle pushed a stray hair from my eyes, pausing when he came to the bandages.

"I wanted to write a happy story for our child. Something he or she could learn from, love with, something to smile about. Nothing about this is positive."

"Being positive has nothing to do with rainbows and unicorns, Tessa. It's about putting your best self out there each and every day. You're the most real and honest person I know; you can't help yourself. Our future child isn't the only one who could learn a thing or two from you or your book," Kyle replied.

My head against the pillow, I looked into his deep green eyes. He was right. I'd had this beautiful journal less than a week. A giant black ink blot couldn't be its last entry. I owed my dream more than that.

I owed *myself* more than that.

I think Kyle could see the agreement in my eyes because he handed me a pen from his pocket. Smiling, I took it and tucked myself closer into his side as I flipped open the journal to the next empty page.

CHAPTER SIX

SATURDAY, *March 29, 2014*

"BEAST!" The white fluff-ball of fury charged straight for me the moment I walked in our front door the following morning. A baby gate dangled from its hinges in the kitchen doorway behind him. His little body slammed into my outstretched arms when I bent down to greet him. There was so much force behind his run, I nearly fell backward into Kyle.

Kyle laughed, walking around my embarrassing display of cooing and cuddling. "He obviously missed you."

I snuggled my cheek into his warm, soft fur as I cradled him in my arms. He wiggled nonstop, panting in excitement as he twisted his body to attack my face with kisses. Suddenly, he stiffened, stretching to get a closer look at the bandage on my head. He sniffed lightly, the tiniest whimper emanating from him.

I cuddled him tighter and wondered how much he understood, or had understood, all this time.

"I'll never understand why you didn't get a real dog," my dad said gruffly, following Kyle inside after he had driven us both home from the hospital.

"Beast is a real dog!" I buried more kisses in his fur. "Just the mini, fluffy version of one."

Dad grunted at that sentiment. If it wasn't at least sixty pounds and a Labrador, then it wasn't a dog. He wasn't much of an animal person anyway and never let us have a dog when I was a kid. Instead, he allowed us turtles. Don't ask me why a ten-pound dog wasn't an acceptable pet, but a ten-pound snapping turtle given to me for my tenth birthday was. The damn thing ended up growing so large we had to give it to a local university with a safe turtle lab—because there is such a thing, apparently. When a U.S. Marine raises two little girls by himself, the results get strange.

"Tessa!" I looked up from booping noses with Beast to see my baby sister walk through the entryway.

The gorgeous blue-eyed blonde looked nothing like me with her perfectly toned everything and long legs surpassing my height by several inches. Physically, we were complete opposites, but our personalities were one and the same. I'd like to think I'm the funniest, though. She got the height gene, give me humor at least.

"Elly!" I held out my arms for her and she rushed right in. We clung to each other, gently rocking back and forth. It was as if we were two magnets who'd been kept apart for so long, and when we found our other halves again, we held on for dear life. "I'm so glad you're here. I missed you so much."

"Right back at ya, big sis." She pulled back, holding me at arm's length to look me over. Her fingers lingered on the side of my head, a frown pulling at her lips.

"It doesn't hurt," I said, trying to assure her. I did not enjoy the look of pity in people's eyes, and I especially didn't want to see it in hers.

Elly moved past my comment with another quick hug. "I have our whole day planned, Tessy."

I smiled; it had been a while since anyone had called me Tessy. In fact, I think Elly is the only one who ever had.

"Lay it on me." I followed Beast into the kitchen and poured myself a glass of water.

Elly trailed behind and began rattling off her list. "I've got all nine seasons of *One Tree Hill* on DVD geared up and ready to go. The living room has been converted into a dine-in movie theatre extraordinaire! We're going to binge watch Chad Michael Murray, eat popcorn, and talk throughout the whole thing so we have to rewind every thirty seconds."

"Oh my God, I *love* that show!" I clapped excitedly but quickly realized I resembled a twelve-year-old girl. I awkwardly dropped my hands and cleared my throat, acting nonchalant. "Yeah, sounds fun."

"Dork," Elly said, snorting and grabbing her own glass of water.

When we'd both finished, she herded me toward the living room. I did a double take when I walked in, stopping in my tracks. Hadn't I only been gone a day? My living room had large velvet curtains hanging across the windows, darkening the entire room. The couches faced a different direction than before and had a large movie screen projector set up on a table behind them, ready to project Chad Michael Murray in all his glory on the wall. She'd even thought to line the coffee table with magazines, books, candies, a bowl of popcorn, and a random assortment of other goodies.

I balked, still taking it in. "Am I in the wrong house?"

"You're not in a house anymore." Elly grinned, taking a seat and patting the cushion beside her. "You're in the Barnes Movie Theatre."

"Don't you mean Falls?"

"Hey, you might be a Falls now, but we will always be Barnes sisters," she informed me with a pointed finger.

I smiled, taking the seat next to her.

Kyle entered the room a moment later and had a similar heart-stopping reaction to mine. "What fresh hell happened in here?"

"We're having a movie day," my sister said simply, hanging over the back of the couch as she fiddled with the projector.

"Not a movie day, a *One Tree Hill* day," I clarified.

"Have fun, but don't ask me to clean this up. That's on you, Elly," he said, exiting the room the way he came.

She stuck out her tongue at his retreating back. They loved each other but bickered like siblings. It warmed my heart to see how they'd taken to each other, even when they were at each other's throats.

"Where did you get this stuff?" I inquired, shifting my weight to lean my head against her shoulder on the couch as the first show began.

"Well, I planned to go to an AV rental store in South Side that promised to have them cheap, but when I got there, I found this guy selling the projector from the trunk of his car for a steal. I had to snatch it up."

I lifted my head and stared at her, trying to assess her seriousness.

She looked confused at my horrified glare. She was either the bravest woman alive or the dumbest. "What?"

"Elly! Seriously? Was Dad at least with you?"

Her brow furrowed. "No. Why?"

I'm going to go with the dumbest.

"Don't go to down there alone again. And for goodness sake, don't buy stuff from the trunks of strangers." I wondered how my little sister was still breathing. She might have gotten the height gene, but apparently, I got both humor and common sense.

She frowned, pouting slightly. "But it was a steal."

"Yeah, I'm sure that's *exactly* what it was." I burst out laughing, imagining her traipsing around the south side of Chicago asking sketchy drivers for a look in their trunks.

Despite our best effort to get through all nine seasons—almost two hundred episodes—we only managed to watch three episodes before we became too antsy and had to move around. I loved a television binge day as much as anyone, but I'm naturally an active person. Plus, staring at a screen was doing nothing for my headache.

We settled on leashing Beast and taking him for a walk. The doctor had cautioned me against anything more than light exercise right now, which I felt was already punishment enough, but they'd also put all fertility talk on hold indefinitely. Children were off the table, and I was put back on birth control for now.

Way to kick me in the ovaries when I'm already down.

They'd asked me if I wanted to be prescribed an antidepressant, too. Like the news of my cancer and loss of motherhood were automatic depression triggers and I was going to drown in their wake. I'd said no, but...I'm still considering my options.

Getting out of the house and taking a walk was a good temporary antidote. Kyle had gone to work—I'm assuming to talk to them about his schedule for the next six weeks—and my dad was busy cooking dinner.

"You know what today reminded me of?" I said to Elly, watching Beast nose-deep in a neighbor's rose bush, debating whether to rip it to shreds like he'd done to all our flowers.

Elly shooed him away and we kept moving. "What?"

"That day we skipped school and stayed home to watch movies when we were kids." I grinned, remembering how it had been easy to fool my dad since he worked such long hours. I was the adult in the house most of my childhood, so the responsibility of taking care of Elly often fell on me.

"*You* skipped school. I was merely a pawn in your delinquent ways," Elly said with exaggerated effect, waving to a neighbor who'd called hello from her porch.

"If that's what you need to tell yourself," I teased her, waving as well.

Beast focused his attention to two preteen boys on skateboards barreling toward us. He began barking as if someone had put a megaphone in front of his face. I glanced around the quiet townhomes, hoping he hadn't disturbed anyone. We stepped on to the grass to let the skateboarders pass by, pulling a non-compliant Beast with us, before heading back in the direction of the house.

Quiet descended while we walked, stopping every few feet for Beast to sniff or pee on something.

"Are you scared?" Elly asked.

I didn't meet her eyes, but, instead, watched Beast, now straining on his leash in hopes of catching a sparrow hopping across the sidewalk.

"A little bit. Mainly because I don't know what to expect, but it'll be over soon." I waved my hand as if to dismiss the very idea of fear, though the truth was much different. Ever since I'd heard my diagnosis, it felt like fear was seeping through my pores—pungent and corrosive. Yet,

I was masking the scent, keeping it from my family. I wasn't sure they could handle my fear on top of their own.

"It's okay to tell me, you know." Elly lifted her chin. "I'm not a kid anymore."

"You'll always be my kid sister, baby girl." I wrapped an arm around her shoulders—which wasn't easy with the height difference—and gave her a quick squeeze.

"Yeah, but you don't need to protect me or take care of me anymore, Tessy. Let me help you."

"You're here, and that's help enough," I assured her, sidestepping Beast when he unceremoniously stopped in the middle of the sidewalk to sniff a crack.

"I'm going with you to every appointment this week." Elly took a heavier step than normal, making a loud stomp against the concrete as if in demand.

Beast jumped in surprise and growled at her feet, then went back to sniffing a mystery smudge on the concrete beneath him.

"I'd like that," I told her. "Kyle and Dad both have work during the day. Crap, that reminds me, I should call my boss and tell him what's happening."

"Are you going to quit?"

"Not if he doesn't make me. Maybe he will let me take a medical leave instead, or work shorter hours. I'm not sure what the protocol is for this." I pondered the idea as we returned to the house with Beast in tow.

I couldn't help but feel overwhelmed at how much one little tumor was going to disrupt my life.

CHAPTER SEVEN

MONDAY, March 31, 2014

"YOU CAN CHANGE in the bathroom over there. Here's a gown," the radiation therapy technologist said, a smile on her lips that barely reached her tired eyes.

"It won't work in my regular clothes?" I asked, already certain she would say no but giving it a shot anyway.

She looked at my jeans and sweatshirt, frowning. "Not those, sorry. If you wear leggings and a T-shirt next time, something like that would work fine. Just no metal or thick fabrics."

I changed and balled my clothes on a shelf in the bathroom, hoping it was okay to leave them there. Kyle and Elly were in the waiting room, and my dad was home with Beast. I didn't want him to come to the hospital if it wasn't necessary. I knew how hard it was for him after what he went through with Mom.

"Perfect. Are you ready?" the technologist asked when I emerged from the bathroom.

"I think so."

She motioned for me to follow her, and we went down a short, inner hallway that led to a set of double doors. Inside, a giant machine dwarfed most of the room, making it look smaller than it probably was. The walls had a dark, industrial look and signs indicated they were lined with concrete and lead—thick and impenetrable to contain the radiation.

I followed her inside, my steps slowing, and my eyes widening at the gray monstrosity waiting for me.

"Lie down here for me, Mrs. Falls." The technologist moved to a thin table in front of the radiation machine and tapped on its surface.

It looked cold as ice and my skin immediately puckered at the thought of touching it. Gingerly, I sat on the cool surface, a shiver going through me. "Can we turn on the heat in here?"

"Unfortunately, the machine must be a certain temperature. I'll get you a blanket once you lie down."

She left the room into what looked like an even smaller room. I watched her through a tiny, tinted square window centered on the wall while she grabbed a blanket and reemerged.

Pulling my feet up onto the table, I tried to find a comfortable way to lie down. My legs were bent by a wedge under my knees and my head was sandwiched between two boards that kept me from turning my head to the side. I stared up at what looked like a giant, metal circle pointing down at me—the tallest part of the machine.

The technologist draped the blanket across my legs and torso, warming me. I tucked my arms under it, grateful for the added heat. She positioned the table I was on closer to the machine, pulling several panels out from the sides so they were pointed at me as well.

It was overwhelming my entire field of vision, like this was my entire world now. And in a way, it was.

"How long do I have to be in here?" I lifted my head past the confining boards, watching her move panels and fiddle with the machine.

"The treatment itself is only two to three minutes," she assured me.

I lowered my head to the table. "I guess that's not too bad."

"I need to put a holder over your head to keep you still, ensuring the radiation is focused on the correct location," the technician explained, her face appearing over mine. She held a white object with bolts on the edges.

"A what?" The panic in my voice was obvious. "What is that?"

She gave me a small, sympathetic smile. "It's a type of hard mesh. I'll place it over your head, and then I will secure it to the table. I know it's frightening the first time—it is for everyone. However, it's imperative your head be completely still. This will ensure that happens."

"What if I promise not to move?" I swallowed hard, but she positioned it above my face anyway. I was already held in place with the boards by the side of my head, further restraints seemed cruel.

"It's not as scary as it looks, I promise. Plus, it's only two minutes. You can do this," she tried to encourage me, lowering it closer to my face, the plastic pressing down and pushing my skull to the table.

The material covered every inch of my head and neck, pinning me down and crisscrossing over my eyes, nose, and mouth with only the tiniest opening for me to breathe. I could barely see at all and my breathing was made shallow as my jaw was forced closed and my nose squished.

I was doing my best to handle it, trying to breathe slowly and concentrate on anywhere but here.

Then I heard the bolts locking into place next to my head and I panicked.

High pitch shrieks emanated from deep inside me, completely out of my control. I flailed my arms and tried to get off the table, but from the neck up, I was paralyzed.

"Mrs. Falls! Calm down!" The technologist sounded as panicked as me, immediately unfastening the holder.

I couldn't stop screaming.

I jumped from the table the instant my head was free. Standing crouched in the middle of the room, my chest heaved, eyes wild as I cried, covering my face in my hands. "I can't do this!"

"I know it's frightening, Mrs. Falls, but it will be over quickly. I have to put it on you. I have no choice—it's for your own safety," she tried to explain.

"I can't. I can't." I was sobbing now, my face surely bright red with embarrassment.

She was only doing her job, I knew this, but what I hadn't known was what to expect from the doctor's vague warning that I might feel claustrophobic. To be completely pinned down and paralyzed was another matter entirely.

"What if I get your husband? Maybe let him talk to you for a few minutes?" she asked, leading me back to the table and encouraging me to sit.

I sat, as far from the machine as I could, and only because my legs were shaking so hard I feared I'd collapse if I stood a minute longer. "Yes, please. Can he be in here with me?"

"Definitely." She smiled, but, again, it didn't reach her eyes. "When the actual treatment starts, he'll need to stand in the other room with me for his own safety, though."

I nodded, relieved, as she left to find Kyle. My cheeks heated, wondering if he would be ashamed of my reaction. He thought I was strong. The treatment hadn't even started and I was crying.

I'm *not* strong.

It's only day one. I have six more weeks of treatment and so far, I couldn't handle the first thirty seconds. My chin dropped in shame, and I squeezed my eyes shut, breathing slowly. *It's just a mask.* And a little claustrophobia. And two to three minutes. Then I'd be done...until tomorrow. And then the next day. And then after that, we'd be having a baby. That's what we were here for. That's why we were doing this.

We were going to have a baby.

"Tessa?"

My head snapped up at his voice, and my shoulders slumped in relief as he came toward me. I reached my arms out to him, hopping off the table only to stumble forward, forgetting how shaky I still felt.

"Babe, are you okay?" He grabbed me before my knees buckled completely and wrapped me in his arms, smoothing the hair off my face.

"I don't think I can do this, Kyle." I was sobbing again, this time into his shirt.

"The technologist told me you don't like wearing the mask?"

"It's not *just* a mask, Kyle. It's bolted to the table, covering my entire face and neck. I panicked. I shouldn't have, but I panicked." I hid my face against his chest.

"Show me," he instructed, leading me to the table.

I pointed to the white mask sitting abandoned on top. He picked it up, turning it over. It looked tiny in his large hands, less intimidating. Kyle shifted to the technologist, motioning for her attention.

"Ma'am, can you strap me up in this thing? Like you were doing for my wife?" he asked, maneuvering around me to sit on the table.

"What? That's not really..." she trailed off, confusion overtaking her expression.

"It's fine. It'll just take a second, right?" He gave her a reassuring smile, handing the mask to her. "I just want to try it."

I stepped back and watched as he swung his feet up and lay down.

"Okay, but only as a quick demo. Breathe normally and try not to move," she instructed, bringing the mask against his face and neck.

It stretched to accommodate his larger head, and his nose was more squished than mine had been. His chest rose and fell faster as the technologist fastened the bolts into place around head and neck.

She stepped away and let me move in beside him.

Kyle breathed out. "Fuck, this is awful."

At least, that's what it sounded like he said. His voice was muffled and strained, a mash of sounds and syllables. His head was imprisoned between the table and the mask, every bit as unmoving as I'd been moments before. I glanced down at his hands, white knuckled and clutching the table's edge.

Slipping my fingers around his, I frowned, unsure of what to say. My big, strong marine was strapped down like a lab rat, helpless and hobbled and it was all for me. He wasn't sick. He didn't have to do this. He didn't have to be a part of any of this...but he was.

If he could do this for me, I could do it for me.

The technologist stepped back to the table and began unfastening everything, slowly freeing him from the confines of the mesh prison. He bolted upright and rubbed his hands across his face and hair, pushing hard and massaging his skin firmly.

I pulled his hand to mine and kissed his palm before pressing it to my cheek. "I can't believe you just did that. You're crazy."

"Yeah, well, so is whoever invented that shit." Kyle shook his head then leaned in to kiss me, cradling my face in his palm. "If I stay here with you, do you think you can do this?"

I nodded, summoning every ounce of courage inside me, and we traded places.

Kyle leaned over and kissed me after I'd lain down on the table. Once the technologist stepped in, I could still just see him in my peripheral vision until she brought the mask down over my face. I closed my eyes, breathing as slowly and deeply as I could manage.

"Babe, I'll be with the technologist while the machine is on, but I can still see you. I'm still here," he told me as the tech ushered him with soft words into the other room.

I tried to nod okay, but my head was immobile. I tried to talk, but the air was gone from my lungs. Fear replaced every sense, and I fought hard to keep it from overwhelming me.

Instead, I raised my hands, giving him shaky thumbs up. Random beeping scattered around the room and I knew the treatment had started, though little else indicated the massive levels of radiation shooting into my brain.

They had said it wouldn't hurt, but I had expected to feel *something*. There was no heat, no pressure, no pulsing... nothing except a few random beeps.

I'd done some research on my treatment and knew it wasn't devoid of side effects though. One day soon, maybe even today, I could experience symptoms as minor as a dry mouth to as serious as seizures. In about two weeks, I'd start to lose my hair, and, if lucky, I might avoid the scalp burns radiation often caused to the skin.

I exhaled slowly through the hard plastic against my face and tried to remain calm. A tear escaped the corner of my eye, trailing down my cheek to the table below. I concentrated on its movement, feeling it cross my skin as the time slowly ticked by.

"All done!" the technologist cheerily announced with the sound of a door swinging open roughly two minutes later.

I held my breath, waiting for her to remove the mask, waiting to be free.

"You did great, babe."

His fingers wrapped around mine and I clutched his hand like a much-needed lifeline. I still couldn't respond—any attempt to speak was only garbled sounds.

"Hold still, I'll have you out of there in just a second." The technologist's face appeared above me as she unfastened the straps by my right ear. I wasn't sure why she had said to stay still. Obviously, I wasn't going anywhere.

The moment I was free, I slid off the table, not wanting to be there a second longer than necessary.

"That's it, we're all done?" I asked, massaging my neck with my hands, stretching it from side to side.

"Yes, ma'am. The first time is always frightening, but I promise it'll get easier each go." The technologist gave me a warm smile then began repositioning the panels on the machine.

"Why don't you get changed and we'll head home?" Kyle suggested.

I nodded my agreement, heading for the bathroom to retrieve my clothes.

"See you tomorrow!" the technologist cheerily called as we left.

I hated her for it.

All I wanted was to crawl into bed and never get up again. I hated being reminded this wasn't a one-time thing. I hated knowing I'd be doing this nearly every day for six weeks. Then I frowned, because the truth was, I didn't hate her or this hospital.

I hated having cancer.

CHAPTER EIGHT

WEDNESDAY, *April 23, 2014*

"WHAT ABOUT SOME WATER? Will that help?" Kyle asked me.

I turned my head warily to look up at him. He stood in the bathroom doorway wringing his hands, a tightness in his face.

"I wouldn't keep that down either." I groaned, tilting back over the toilet as I vomited again.

I'd spent much of the last three weeks, and all of today, worshipping the porcelain throne and sacrificing my stomach contents to it. Today was by far the worst my nausea had been, and as the evening ticked by, there were still no signs of relief.

"I'm going to call the doctor and see if you can take more anti-nausea meds."

"I can't take it more than twice a day," I reminded him.

"But you threw it up. They have to have something for

you." His tone was so forlorn, so hopeless. "This is the worst I've seen you yet."

I wanted to say it would be okay, that they'd warned us about side effects, but I felt as helpless as he looked.

The first week hadn't been so bad. I still had energy and managed to go to work every day after my morning treatments. Elly had still been on spring break, so she had accompanied me to each appointment, and most of the time my dad did, too. Kyle had to work so he was there only for the first treatment, but when he came home, he waited on my every need.

Elly had had to return to New York for school before the second week, but she called daily to check on me. She'd come again once the semester ended in May and spend the summer with me, which I looked forward to. In a way, I was glad she had left when she did, sparing her from seeing me at my worst. Each week the side effects of radiation worsened, hitting me harder, and I spent most days either vomiting or curled in bed with headaches.

My boss gave me short-term disability leave until my treatments would end and I recover from the final surgery. I had wanted to keep working, but it had quickly become unmanageable with my symptoms. Dr. Page had warned that radiation on the head often came with severe symptoms, but I still hadn't expected it to become my entire day in, day out.

It hadn't just consumed my life, either, but my family's, too. It was in the third week that I saw Kyle crying. I'd rarely seen him cry before, but there he was standing over the sink staring out at our tiny patch of a back yard with tears streaming down his face. He didn't know I had walked in or was watching him, and he didn't know I knew I'd caused those tears.

Some days I wondered if I could send my family away, so they wouldn't have to watch me get sicker and sicker. I saw the memories of my mother's illness in my father's eyes. When he looked at me, I saw her and I hated every reminder, but cherished every moment I got to spend with her in his mind. I knew this was tougher on him than I'd ever understand.

I didn't want to put any of them through this, but Kyle kept reminding me it was only for a few more weeks. He clung to the timeline as if it were the only thing grounding him, as if he could get through this only if he knew there was an end in sight. We were all counting down the days until the treatments ended in May, collectively holding our breaths.

"Dr. Page says we need to come in right away." Kyle reappeared in the doorway two minutes later, mid-heave as I curled over the toilet bowl, stomach bile all I had left.

He rushed forward and pulled the hair off my shoulders, keeping it from falling into the line of fire. I continued to vomit for a few more seconds, my shoulders shaking and my stomach clenching.

When the worst was over, Kyle offered me a wash cloth with his free hand, and I wiped my mouth clean as I sat back on my heels.

"Oh," Kyle said, sounding shocked as he released my hair and stared at his hands.

I followed his gaze to see a thick clump of my long, brown hair dangling from his fingers.

He began to stammer apologetically. "Tessa, I'm so sorry. I didn't mean to."

"It's fine. That's not the first time." I waved it off, pulling up to my feet and grabbing my toothbrush.

I didn't want to look him in the eyes. If I did, I'd most

certainly cry. I'd been losing hair for a week, but it had been light at first. Just small wisps here and there, then a little more each day. My hair was thinning and there was still a bald patch on one side, but it didn't look too ghastly yet.

Yet.

The last two days had changed this hope. It was falling out in chunks now, and I'd tried to hide it from Kyle with a hair band or a strategic ponytail, but it was quickly becoming futile.

His stricken expression stared at me in the mirror while I brushed my teeth, so I closed my eyes.

"Um, Dr. Page says we should get you on an IV of liquids and some anti-nausea medicine, so you can't throw up the medications," Kyle quietly explained before exiting the bathroom.

I could hear him rummaging around in our bedroom drawers as I finished brushing my teeth, probably packing a bag for me.

"I think that was the last of it. I'll be fine," I assured him as I walked out of the bathroom, holding the wall for support. The room was spinning around me, but I refused to admit this to him.

"The hell you are." He frowned at me, zipping closed a duffel bag on the bed. "You need fluids to replenish everything you lost today, and you look dazed."

"Just a little lightheaded. It's really not a big deal. I probably just need to sleep."

"No, we're going to the hospital. The meds you're on, plus the radiation? It's no joke, Tessa. We need to make sure your body has the help it needs." He swung the duffel bag over one of his shoulders and wrapped his other arm around my waist.

"Fine." I leaned into him, inhaling his natural musk that had always comforted me.

Until this second.

Suddenly, a felt a burning in the back of my throat as my stomach churned and threatened to return to my mouth. I dashed back to the bathroom and prayed to God I'd make it in time. I heaved over the toilet with an intensity that made me feel like all my insides were about to abandon ship.

Calming down, I wiped my mouth with tissue paper after the worst of it had passed and sat back on my heels. Tears stung my eyes, not out of sadness, but because the force of my sickness overwhelmed me. I tried to tuck a piece of hair behind my ear, but too many strands fell away, tangling in my fingers instead.

"Babe?" Kyle was hovering again.

"Can I have some water?" I croaked out, sounding aptly exhausted.

He turned to leave, but I reached for him. I needed something to hold. Everything was moving. I was moving.

I was falling.

Black.

"Tessa!"

· ♋ · ♋ · ♋ ·

FRIDAY, April 25, 2014

"WE CAN KEEP her here the rest of the day for observation, but honestly, she'd do better at home with her nausea under control now and fluids back up. I'd like to arrange for a nurse to come by your house daily for at least the next week to check on her and administer an IV." An older male voice hovered somewhere above me, but I kept my eyes closed and my breathing slow as if I were still sleeping.

"So, she would be hooked up to all this stuff at home?" This voice definitely belonged to Kyle.

"Yes, she needs to stay fully hydrated to have the best chance to fight the cancer. She needs to be at her best."

"She *is* fighting it. She fights it every day, doc. You haven't seen her like I have, but she is fighting like hell." Kyle sounded mad, making me feel bad for the other man.

Sometimes I liked to make Kyle angry on purpose, my insides clenching deliciously at the reminder of how his jaw tightened and his eyes flamed, all while he never for a moment lost control. But I did...and I loved it. All the times we'd spent wrapped around each other, him pressed deeply inside me. I never once considered it might be the last, never once thought maybe our days were numbered. That *my* days were numbered.

"Mr. Falls, that's not what I'm saying. Her symptoms are normal. I want her to have the best resources to help her body fight this," the doctor assured my husband. "We will get control over this."

I've never felt much control over my life, and often find myself grasping at straws and pretending that it helped. Pretending that a broken pen and stained desk top made up for a doctor's cold demeanor. Pretended that hiding an anchovy in the lining of my middle school bully's backpack made up for how she and her mean girls squad turned up their noses at me. Pretended clear, plastic wrap over the gym teacher's toilet seat in his private bathroom would make up for when he teased me for starting my period halfway through volleyball practice. It was miniscule and petty, but I'd felt better.

Silently, stoically, and a little psychotically, I'd taken back control.

Now the only thing ever actually in my control—my own body—had been stolen from me. Everyone thought they had the answers, feeling confident *we got this*...we can beat cancer. With each treatment and onslaught of symptoms afterward, I was finding that harder and harder to believe.

"Fine, let's set up the nurse visits. I'll check with our insurance." Kyle sounded resigned.

Money. Another thing no one warned me about. Some of my shots cost several thousand dollars. *Seriously*. A vial of liquid bent on making me vomit for hours costed nearly five thousand dollars. Kyle's insurance through the military is excellent, but even so, it's barely enough and our savings account is dwindling fast.

"Once she is awake and the nurses have done the morning vitals, she can be discharged. She'll need to be on bed rest at home. Nothing exerting."

"Thank you, Dr. Page." The bed sagged by my feet and a strong hand rubbed my calf for a few quiet moments. "He's gone, Tessa. You can quit pretending now."

I kept my eyes closed, but a small smile crept over my face. "How'd you know?"

"You weren't snoring."

I opened my eyes and shot him an angry glare. "I do *not* snore!"

"Whatever you say, babe."

He was laughing so I pulled up into a seated position and crossed my arms over my chest. "I don't!"

It was the first time I'd stopped and looked at him since he'd brought me to the hospital. I had spent most of yesterday sleeping and hooked up to anti-nausea meds which had made me drowsy. He'd missed work two days in a row to stay by my side, which was no small feat for him.

His normally bright green eyes were dull and drooping. His hair was disheveled, his shoulders slumped, and his clothes were wrinkled; the same outfit he'd worn when we had arrived here. Thinking back on it, I realized he'd never left my side.

"Ready to go home?" I asked, wanting him to get some rest as much as I wanted to be out of here.

"Of course, but are you? They can't rush you out of here if you're not ready."

"I feel much better. Plus, they're sending a nurse to visit me." I paused, biting my bottom lip and looking down at fidgeting hands.

"What's wrong?" he asked.

"I don't know, it's just a nurse...coming to our house. It's so..." I paused, unsure how to finish the sentence. Honestly, I didn't know what to think or why it bothered me. It felt strange. My independence was a point of pride, something I cherished. A daily visit from a nurse felt...senile.

"Tessa, don't over think this. She'll only come by to administer injections and check your vitals, pretty basic. It doesn't mean anything more than that," Kyle assured me.

I nodded, knowing he was right, but still disbelieving. It *wasn't* basic. It was another reminder, now daily, of my illness and how I couldn't take care of myself. How I wasn't the independent person I had been before cancer had crept into my brain.

How I wasn't in control anymore.

CHAPTER NINE

SATURDAY, *April 26, 2014*

"DELORES?" I looked up from the kitchen table where I sat gingerly nibbling the edge of a piece of plain toast, as my dad escorted the familiar woman into the room. Delores was sporting hot pink scrubs adorned with kittens, a jarring sight at first, but I was instantly obsessed with how proudly she wore it. Her strut had a confidence I'd long since been missing in my own. "What are you doing here?"

"New job, hun. When I saw your name on the roster, I was like 'Oh, I know that girl!' Figured it's a good first assignment for me since I just saw ya'." Delores spoke as if she had known me for years, though we'd only met a few times. Still, I had bonded with her more than with any other hospital staff member over my stays.

"So, you're not at the hospital anymore?"

"I am. Doing both, got a teenager who's eatin' me outta house and home. But let me tell you, I'm lovin' this job better already. Boss lets me pick my own scrubs, not those boring hospital blues. A girl needs a little color every once in a while!" She bopped up and down with every word, placing her bag on the kitchen table as she spoke.

I was surprised she had a kid, let alone a teenager. She looked too youthful to have lived so much. I watched her extract from her bag sterilizing pads, gauze, needles, and vials.

"How's the nausea today? Did you have a treatment yesterday?" she asked.

I nodded. "Yeah, before I was discharged. It wasn't too bad yesterday, but I threw up once this morning."

"You eaten anything yet?"

I glanced down at the nearly intact piece of toast in front of me, only a tiny bite taken from it. "Not much."

"Honey, I know it seems twisted, but the more nausea you feelin', the more you need to be eatin'," Delores said, filling a syringe with clear liquid from a vial.

I wondered if she could pronounce the letter g, even though I liked her dialect without it. It was comfortable and familiar, instantly filling me with trust and assurance. "That does seem twisted," I agreed.

She shrugged. "Well, it's the truth, hun. You need food and energy to fight that tumor in ya head." She put down the needle and opened an alcohol swab packet.

I pulled up my shirtsleeve so she could administer the anti-nausea medication, but she shook her head.

"Gotta get ya to bend over for this one, hun." She stood in front of me, shot in one hand, swab in the other.

My eyes widened. "What?"

"The shot goes in your tush, hun. Needs the deep muscle."

"My tush isn't very muscle-y," I stammered, stalling.

Delores smiled innocently like a shot in the ass while

bent over my kitchen table wasn't a big deal. "You ready?" she asked, undeterred.

"Um...I guess. Will it hurt?" I stood and turned my back to her. Pushing down the band of my favorite yoga pants that had never seen the inside of a yoga studio, I bared my cheek.

"A tiny pinch. You'll be fine."

The cold, wet alcohol swab swept a small circle over my ass, causing me to shiver. Seconds later, I felt the pinch and inhaled sharply at the pain. The cold liquid injected into me, invading my body.

"Oh wow, wrong moment to come get some breakfast."

I turned my head to see my dad standing in the doorway, looking ten shades of red past uncomfortable. I wanted to laugh or tell him it was fine, but nothing really felt fine about today. My mind was blank and overloaded all at once.

"Ain't nothing you hadn't seen changing her diapers," Delores reminded him.

My dad quickly turned on his heels and shuffled out. "Yeah, uh, Tessa, I'll be in the living room if you need me," he called over his shoulder.

Delores chuckled. A moment later, the needle pulled away. "There, see? Not so bad."

Gauze swabbed the injection site and I breathed out, relieved the sharp pain had been replaced with the soft cotton. Finally, Delores returned to her supplies and I pulled my pants back to my waist.

I stood awkwardly, wanting to sit, but unable since my ass was stinging. I ran my hand through my hair, taking care to avoid where the biopsy had been done.

Delores clucked her tongue softly. "Oh, hun."

Her voice sounded so sad that I looked at her in alarm.

"What?" I croaked out, surprising myself at the raspy scratch in my response.

Her gaze was on my hand, and I followed it to see my fingers tangled with clumps of light brown hair.

"This been happening for a while?" she asked.

If anyone else had asked me this, I would have lied out of embarrassment. I'd have been irritated they even asked in the first place, and probably had a snippy reply ready for them, but not with Delores. Her words came from a place of maternal love, radiating care and kindness that couldn't be mistaken for anything else. She wasn't teasing or prodding, only caring.

I nodded in affirmation, afraid if I spoke again, I might cry.

The truth is, I feel silly for still being so vainly attached to my hair. I've known that I would lose it eventually, and I also know that when treatments are over it will grow back. That's just the nature of radiation, and after all, it's just *hair*. Even still, every lost tendril was a stab to my heart. As if my femininity, what made me a woman, was being taken from me.

As if, I was losing myself. Maybe silly, but...maybe not.

"Hun, how about you let me take care of that today?" Delores asked, her voice softer than before—if that's even possible.

I returned to the kitchen chair, positioning my offended ass cheek off the seat's edge to avoid direct contact. "What do you mean?"

Delores shrugged, calmness to her movements that in return, calmed me, too. "I cut my boy's hair all the time. It'd only take a few minutes to shave it off and then you don't have to be shedding pieces of yourself all over Chicago."

I swallowed hard, picturing a bald head. "I don't know..."

"Hun, it's coming off no matter what. You know that, right?" Delores was blunt, but somehow her words still came off as kind. It was an impressive feat, and it ignited a small flame in me. She suddenly became my teammate, and her support filled me ever so slightly with a strength I'd been missing.

I bit my lip, studying her gentle expression as I considered her proposal. Finally, I nodded.

She clapped her hands triumphantly. "All right, let's do this. It's time you got the first say about something." She headed toward the doorway. "Fuck cancer."

I laughed at her sudden energetic outburst, my flame growing hotter. "*Fuck* cancer."

"Hey, anyone got an electric razor?" Delores called out, sticking her head into the hallway. "We 'bout to kick some cancer ass in here!"

My dad quickly brought everything she needed, his eyes on the ceiling the entire time, probably worried he'd see my naked cheeks again. This only made me laugh harder—especially when he clipped the doorjamb with his shoulder on his way out and cussed up a storm.

"Men, I swear," Delores muttered, rolling her eyes at his retreating figure.

I waited as she put everything together, running my fingers through my hair again and again. It was still soft against my skin but had thinned dramatically. I hadn't noticed how much until now, and my flame flickered, dampened ever so slightly.

As silly as it may or may not be, I'd miss this feeling. I'd miss my hair.

"Here we go; I have everything ready." Delores fluffed

the ends of my hair and smiled. "You're gonna look great. You look like ya' got a smooth head under that hair."

"I...what?" *Was that a compliment?* "Is that good?"

"Oh yeah, you want a smooth head, means your mom did somethin' right." Delores tied a towel around my neck and plugged in the electric razor. "See, me? I didn't know all that when I had my boy. Was just a teenager, no one told me I gotta make sure he had a smooth head."

"What would you do if he had had a lumpy head?" I laughed even as I heard her turn on the razor. I was nervous and terrified, and a mix of other unpleasant emotions, yet Delores's voice and storytelling distracted me.

She stood facing me, parting my few remaining hairs into smaller sections with the razor. "*If?* Girl, that boy's head is like a mine field of speed bumps. Momma said I should have smoothed his head when he was a baby, rub it until it had no more lumps. Babies heads are like Jell-O, make 'em into whatever shape you want."

"You shaped a baby's head?" *She had to be lying.*

"Girl, you listening?" She put one hand on her hip. "I was *supposed* to, but I didn't know, so I didn't do it. Shoulda though, 'cause that boy is a walking mountain range."

I laughed, enjoying the banter. "What happens if you shape it wrong?"

"I dunno, you end up with an ugly ass cone-head baby? Or maybe that little football head baby on that cartoon. Don't do that, though—nobody wants to play sports with a baby's head."

Tears invaded my eyes for a new reason, my flame brighter than ever before. My insides were light and warm, and I wanted to throw my arms around Delores to thank her for bringing laughter to this ugly moment. Hell, I was laughing so hard she had to stop shaving so she wouldn't nick my skin.

Delores joined in alongside me. When our laughter finally subsided, she was ready to get back on task. "You good, hun?"

Seamlessly, the intensity of my laughter turned serious and stoic. I wondered if she had done this on purpose. It was as if she knew laughing and crying were almost the same, and she hadn't wanted to see my tears. A lump formed in my throat as I nodded, satiated from the strength she'd given me, but fully aware of the seriousness of this moment. "Go ahead."

Delores eyed me as if she knew I was lying, as if she knew I wasn't ready. No woman was.

I thought of Kyle as she turned the razor back on. He'd suggested I shave off my hair a few times. He saw me crying one day when I found too much hair on my pillow, so his solution had been simple: chop it off. If it wasn't on my head, I couldn't be sad when I saw it fall out. It hadn't occurred to him I'd be sad every time I looked in the mirror or ran a hand over my smooth head.

Yet here I was, taking both his and Delores' advice because simply put, this problem needed solving. My emotions would just need to get with the program because they were both right—this wasn't something I could avoid.

A large lock of hair dropped past my face and I gasped, stiffening as she continued to shave my head. Keeping my head still, I glanced at the floor, or at least as far down as I could see without tilting my head.

I was surprised by the lack of hair beneath me. I knew Delores was at least halfway done because I felt the coolness on my bare skin, but I'd pictured a massive mountain of discarded hair at my feet and that just didn't exist. There hadn't been much left to shave off.

"All right, I'm almost done," Delores said. "After this spot, I'll even everything out."

"Is there anything left?" I asked, hopeful I'd grown a thick mane impenetrable to her razor, to radiation, to cancer.

"Oh yeah, I left a big Mohawk down the middle," Delores said.

I squawked, my eyes wide. "What?"

"Relax, I'm teasing! It's just a lil' peach fuzz all over. When we were kids, my sister had a lil' mustache, and Momma said we weren't allowed to tease her about it, so my other sister and I started calling her Peach Fuzz." Delores laughed at the memory. "Told her it was just a cute nickname, but really, we were poking fun at her mustache without Momma knowing."

I laughed, remembering more than a few occasions when I'd teased Elly growing up. The razor was now off, and in its place, she held a pair of scissors and was closely examining my head, I'm assuming to catch any stray hairs the razor had missed. Finally, certain she had cut them all, she stepped back and smiled.

"I used to bleach my upper lip every month before all this. Haven't needed to lately, because it's gone. Haven't needed to shave my legs, either," I mused, not having thought of it before.

I raised my hand to my eyebrows, soft and feathery, lighter than before. I wonder how long until I lose those, too.

"I wanna call that a silver lining to cancer, but—" Delores paused for a moment, tapping her finger against her jaw as if in thought.

"It's still cancer," I finished for her.

"Yeah." Delores removed the towel from around my neck, wiping at a few stray hairs, and put her things down on the kitchen table. She picked up a handheld mirror and gave it to me.

I lifted it to my eyes and stared at my reflection.

Sliding a hand over the fuzzy surface of my head, I studied my new look. My scalp was white—very white. Pale with tiny brown dots of hair barely poking through the surface. Some areas had no brown at all, just completely bald. Then there was the still-healing scar where the biopsy had been.

My appearance reminded me of Frankenstein. I felt hideous. No hair. Gross scar.

Hideous.

I put the mirror down on the kitchen table and chewed the edge of my lip. Delores patted my shoulder then returned to putting her things away. I avoided eye contact with her, not wanting her to think I was upset with her. She'd actually been the best part of this, distracting me with funny stories during the worst moments, but I was suddenly worn and tired.

Finally, Delores finished packing her bag and winked at me. "At least you got a smooth head."

I burst out laughing, and Delores quickly joined in.

At least I had a smooth head.

"I'll be back tomorrow for your next shot. You have yourself a good Saturday; try and do something fun," Delores instructed as she headed to the door.

I followed her out slowly, feeling self-conscious of my new hairdo—if you can call it that.

"Tessa?" My dad's voice sounded behind me in the hallway after I closed the front door behind Delores.

I turned to him, noting the pull of his brows and frown on his lips.

"Wow." he said, after a long exhale. "How do you feel?"

I shrugged. "Okay, I guess. Kind of tired."

He nodded toward my head. "I remember your mom when she did that. You look so much like her right now; it's like I'm looking at her."

"Oh." I touched my head gingerly, cringing. "Is it bad? Do I look okay?"

"Sunshine, you look beautiful. You always have and you always will," he assured me, taking several steps forward to hug me tightly. "Just like your mom."

I leaned into him, allowing the comfort to envelope me.

"Tessa?" Kyle's voice broke our embrace.

I turned to see he'd arrived home from work and was standing in the doorway. Part of me wanted to cover my head, but my body froze under his scrutiny. "Hey," I said, nerves shaking my voice.

"You're beautiful," Kyle said, greeting me with a kiss. "I love it."

My muscles released, and I deflated into a smile, knowing the man I was so attracted to still though I was beautiful. He was my fairytale; he always would be.

My dad cleared his throat. "How about you kids go take Beast for a walk? You could use the time to talk."

The moment my dad spoke, Beast rounded the corner barking. He knew those words well—they were his favorites.

"Oh, so that'll wake you up?" My dad rolled his eyes as he exited the room. "Damn lazy excuse for a dog's been sleeping in the sunny spot in the living room all day."

Kyle smiled and pulled his jacket back on. "I'd love to go on a walk with you."

I nibbled the corner of my lip at the idea of going

outside with my new hairstyle. I opted for stalling. "Can I change first? I'm still wearing my yoga pants."

"Sure, I'll leash up Beast."

I took the stairs slowly, not hurrying. I didn't know why going on a walk felt weird. It shouldn't. Kyle and I spent much of our free time walking, or hiking, or anything outdoors, but everything was different now that I looked like...a cancer patient.

Disrobing as I entered my bedroom, I scoured my drawers and settled on a dark pair of jeans under a flowery blouse. I tugged on a pair of boots that came partway up my shins, then finished with a brown, leather jacket I loved. Standing in front of my mirror, I surveyed my body.

Everything from the neck down was normal...me. From the neck up, not so much.

Frowning, I headed into the bathroom and brushed on a slight blush to my cheeks and some mascara on my thinning eyelashes. Stepping back, I realized the mascara was sparse because my lashes were so few. I swiped on some eyeliner as a fix, adding a little to my eyebrows to thicken them, too.

My bald head still stuck out like...a bald head.

Glancing down at my hands, I realized that all of my blisters had mostly healed. It'd been at least a month and a half since I'd been at the climbing gym. I didn't have the strength I once had, and the idea of pulling myself up a rock wall seemed unfathomable right now.

Kyle called from downstairs, "Tessa? You ready?"

"One second!"

I rifled through some old shelves in my closet, hoping to find a scarf or bandana. I had few hair bands, as my thick hair often broke them, and I normally opted to wear it down.

"Sunshine?" My dad's voice brought me to attention,

standing in the doorway behind me with a large wooden box in his hands.

"What's up, Dad?"

He motioned for me to follow him, and we returned to the bedroom. "I thought maybe you might want these," he said gruffly, shoving the box toward me without looking into my eyes. That was pretty normal for him. He wasn't one for emotion or sentiment and eye contact was all vulnerability —something he wanted no part of. "It's nothing, really."

Curious, I took the box from him and opened it. Inside were small triangles of thin, silky fabrics folded over a velvet lining with such care, that it practically dripped luxury.

"Are these Mom's?" I asked, even though I recognized the scarves immediately.

"Yeah, I thought you might like them. Especially now that, uh..." he trailed off uncomfortably.

Tears stung at my eyes from his kind gesture.

"You kept these?" I examined each one, reveling in the feel of the soft silk. "I thought her stuff was donated."

He shrugged. "Most of it was, but I kept some of my favorites. It's silly, I know." A flash of nostalgia washed over his face. "Your mother spent so many years collecting those. Then when she got sick, she used them to cover her head. I don't know, I thought maybe—"

I threw myself against his large, brick chest, wrapping my arms around his shoulders, and squeezing my eyes closed.

He tensed for a moment, then relaxed and circled his arms around me as well.

"Thank you, Daddy. This is...it's perfect."

He squeezed me tighter and kissed the top of my head. "I love you, sunshine."

He released me and left the room, leaving me alone

with my new gift. I wiped an escaped tear from my cheek as I lifted a soft pink scarf from the box. It had been one of my mother's favorites, and I remembered it well.

I'd never known what happened to these scarves after her death. She had worn them all the time, talking about them to anyone who would listen. They were Hermès, a symbol of wealth and prosperity in her eyes. She'd spent most of her childhood in poverty, and I think it made her feel like she always had to prove her worth, and in some strange way, these did that for her. Little pieces of fabric gave her the confidence she hadn't been able to give herself.

I hadn't liked them for the bragging rights, but for the soft way they had complimented her pink cheeks, or for how they felt against my shoulder when she would lean close. The way they smelled like her when I would hide in her closet and drape them over my hair, pretending I was all grown up like the woman I loved.

I lifted one to my nose and inhaled, smiling when triggered memories flickered behind my eyes.

"Tessa, come here!" Her high-pitched voice carried into my bedroom where I was playing with my dolls.

"I'll be right back," I told my dolls as I skipped out of the room and down the stairs, finding my mother standing in the kitchen with her hands nearly elbow deep in a bowl of who-knows-what.

"Oh, good. Tessa, help me." She was so beautiful when she turned and smiled at me that I had to pause for a moment to admire her sparkling white teeth, dazzling blue eyes, and tiny button nose that fit her face perfectly. Her skin glowed and her belly protruded slightly from under her white shirt where the existence of my future sibling was beginning to show. Her head was covered in a soft pink silk scarf, and completely bald underneath.

"What do I do?" I asked.

"My hands are dirty mixing this meatloaf; can you turn on the radio over there? We need some music in this house!" She nodded to a large boom box on the far counter.

I pulled a small wooden stool over in front of it, ambling up to reach it and pressing the power button. Music instantly filled the room, and I paused to listen to the upbeat tune.

"Do you know this song, honey?" my mother asked as I climbed off the stool and pulled it across the kitchen next to her.

I hopped up and grabbed her pants for balance, holding steady as I peeked over the counter. "No?"

"Ob-La-Di, Ob-La-Da," she told me as she started singing along and swaying her body side to side.

I leaned unsteadily backward with her movement, deciding to grab the counter and climb up there instead. "That's not a word, Mommy!" I insisted as I hoisted my bottom onto the counter and turned to face her, watching her make meatloaf as she sang.

"Sure, it is," she said.

"What's it mean then?"

"It means Tessa is the best little girl in the whole wide world." She winked at me as she finished with the meatloaf and shaped it into a pan before pushing that into the oven.

"Nuh uh, you can't trick me." I giggled, putting my hand over my mouth to hide my smile as my mother washed off her hands.

"Don't cover your beautiful face, darling. I just can't go a minute without seeing my little girl's smile." Mommy kissed my cheek as she pulled my arm down with her still-wet hand before lifting me into her arms, her big belly bump between us.

I wrapped my legs around her back as best as I could, facing her, and proudly letting her see my smile.

"Dance with me, Tessa," she told me, swaying with me in her arms as my one arm wrapped around her shoulder for support and the other was held tightly in hers. She bounced and moved around the kitchen with me singing loudly and I joined in when I could. I quickly got the chorus down, but hummed along to the rest.

Giggling, I leaned my head against her shoulder, feeling the ends of her soft silk against my cheek. I closed my eyes and tucked in tighter to her chest as she continued to sway along to the beat.

Looking at my reflection in the mirror, I lifted the soft pink scarf and wrapped it around my head the way my mother had worn it. She had had cancer twice, once when she was pregnant with Elly which went into remission after Elly's birth, and then again, a few years later, which finally cost her life. I bit my lip at the memory.

If my mother could dance and sing with cancer, I could go outside with no hair.

Nodding at my reflection, as if to give myself permission, I took a deep breath and left to join Kyle.

CHAPTER TEN

SATURDAY, *April 26, 2014*

"DAMN IT, BEAST!" Kyle spun around attempting to untwine the leash our dog had wound around his legs.

I giggled, watching them as we stood at the entrance of Grant Park where the pup's excitement at so many people had gotten the better of him. "This is why I should be holding the leash. I never get tangled up."

"Or we could just get a dog that acts like a normal freaking dog," he replied.

"I think that option's long gone."

Kyle shook his head in annoyance, despite his wide smile, finally freeing himself to resume our walk. I ducked my head, trying to get used to the cool breeze against my bare skin, sneaking beneath the thin scarf.

It surprised me how few people stared at me. I had thought leaving the house hairless would be a giant bill-board with a red arrow pointed at me, but that was not turning out to be the case. In fact, they ignored me now as always. Attention stuck on their phones, few eyes even made it to my scarf. Occasionally, someone would do a double take as if to reassure themselves that their eyes weren't playing tricks on them. The moment they realized they were in fact looking at a bald woman, they moved on with little more than a slight blush or quickly averted gaze.

"Look, there's a concert playing." Kyle pointed toward the far side of the park where a transient crowd had gathered to watch the show.

"Let's go!" I headed that direction, pulling him along. I was always eager to hear new music.

When we reached the crowd, we found three young band-mates with a sign identifying their group as *Mama-Dear*. A fresh-faced blonde with a girl-next-door look was singing from a small stage. Her voice echoed despite no microphone. The two men behind her also sang—one played a guitar, the other a mandolin. They harmonized perfectly. The man with the mandolin watched her with adoration and I couldn't stop from smiling at young love.

"Dance with me?" Kyle asked, extending a hand.

"No one is dancing," I replied but still took his hand. We watched the trio sing an unfamiliar song. With the mix of country and pop, I guessed they'd written the lyrics themselves, and I liked it.

Soft and passionate, they sang about betting on love and taking chances, that it was worth it in the end. I felt the notes slide over me, closing my eyes. The words were reminiscent of my current ordeal—I was betting on my life, betting on surviving the next few weeks, betting on remission.

I was betting on me, on us, on growing old together.

Kyle whispered in my ear, "Since when do we need others permission to dance?"

I popped open my eyes as Kyle pulled me by my free hand against his chest. Beast's leash draped across our intertwined fingers, and Kyle circled my back with his other arm. I moved my hips with his, swaying to the song.

"Such a romantic," I said, teasing.

"Only when I have the right inspiration."

"What's inspiring you now?"

"My beautiful wife," he answered, not missing a beat.

"Not so beautiful anymore." My cheeks grew warm thinking of the thin scarf hiding my head.

His gaze dropped to my lips, then returned to meet my eyes. A seriousness stole away his smile and I knew unequivocally that everything he was about to say was honest and from his soul. "You couldn't be more wrong," he countered. "You're gorgeous—with or without hair."

"Kyle." I sighed, moving stiffly in his arms, uncomfortable with how real things had just become. He was being nice and I knew he'd always think I was beautiful, but I also knew what I really looked like.

He shook his head then tilted my chin up to look at him, his fingers brushing against my skin. "Nothing changes how much I love you, or how beautiful you will always be to me, and to everyone else. Not even cancer."

I let him have a small smile, but doubt still filled me.

He narrowed his eyes, searching mine. "You don't believe me."

The words sounded almost accusatory, like I'd hurt him, and I blinked quickly in surprise. "No, I, uh..."

Kyle handed me Beast's leash and walked off, causing the dog to strain at the end, trying to catch up with him. I frowned, wondering what he was doing as he weaved through the crowd toward the band. He approached the female singer, who had just finished a song and was asking for recommendations. They exchanged whispers. She glanced at me, smiling, then nodded.

Kyle strutted back to me, pride seeping from his big grin.

"This next song is dedicated to Tessa from her husband, Kyle. He says she is the most beautiful woman in the world. I have to agree," the lead singer announced as she pointed out Kyle and me to the crowd.

Heat bloomed across my cheeks as I blushed deeply, taking Kyle's hand for another dance. The crowd clapped and cheered, and not a single face looked horrified by a girl without hair in a bright pink scarf. I saw only affection and acceptance, and I couldn't stop smiling.

The band played another song, the lyrics about love and soulmates. It was perfect. It was us. We swayed against each other, Kyle humming near my ear, his cheek against mine.

"You're so sweet," I murmured a few minutes later, feeling deliciously loved. Everything about this moment was simple but passionate. Muted, but loud in love.

"I love you, Tessa."

"You didn't have to do all this to tell me you loved me," I reminded him, giggling and falling back on humor to ease my discomfort at being complimented. "Aren't public displays of affection supposed to be embarrassing?"

Kyle shrugged. "Love out loud, or don't love at all. Wearing your heart on your sleeve is just letting the world know you found that something special everyone wants."

I leaned against his chest again, dancing slowly as Beast bounced at our feet. "I can't believe you still like me without hair." I sighed, smiling.

"Like doesn't even come close," he said with a small chuckle. "You're fucking gorgeous, babe, and I *love* it. I'd be more than happy to prove it to you as soon as we get home."

I laughed at his innuendo, feeling as sexy and loved as he'd always made me feel. Pulling back slightly, I examined his expression. He was telling the truth— and possibly imagining me naked. "I wish I wasn't putting you through this. You're so amazing, and this is so...I just wish I wasn't doing this to you." I hated the pain my cancer was causing him. Even with our vows of *in sickness and in health*, I knew neither of ever expected the first part to come so soon. "I honestly feel like I'm such a shit wife. Like I have been for a long time."

The honesty poured out of me faster than I realized, and I wanted to take it back as soon as I said it. It was too real, too true, and I didn't want him to know I felt that way.

Kyle's face twisted as if I'd just fed him a whole handful of lemons. "What? Are you serious?"

Well, it was too late to back out of it now. I nodded slowly. "It's not like I'm waiting at home for you every night with a warm dinner or even remember our anniversary unless you remind me."

"Okay, so you're not the type of woman to remember dates on a calendar or slave away at new recipes every week. That doesn't make you a good wife or not." Kyle was adamant in his tone, his hands gripping my upper arms as he made sure our eye contact never broke. "But you text me silly GIFs of lady and the tramp slurping spaghetti when I'm having a long day, and you answer my mother's phone calls even when I avoid her, and you let me put my cold ass feet on yours to warm them up even though you hate it."

"I...Well, yeah, but—"

"You yelled at the dry-cleaning lady when she burned a hole in my favorite shirt and wrote them the most scathing Yelp review I've ever seen. You're willing to defend me at the drop of a hat over something as minor as a shirt, Tessa," he reiterated. "And remember that time the waitress at Tiki Tacos asked me for my number? You licked my face at the bar right in front of her and declared 'Mine!'"

"You yelled at me for that!" Tessa reminded him.

"But I've never laughed so hard or loved someone so much," he countered. "You make every day fun. You make every moment of my life worth living to the next. You're my reason for going, and *that* makes you the most amazing wife a man could ask for."

I swallowed the lump forming in my throat at his sweet words. "Even with everything I'm putting you through now?"

"Tessa, *you* are not putting me through anything. Don't push me away. Not now. Not when we need each other the most." He stared me right in the eye, demanding I hear what he was saying.

I nodded, biting my lips. I was pulling back, and he knew it. He wanted to take this journey with me, he wanted to be by my side, and I wanted to let him. "I won't. I promise."

Kyle untangled Beast's leash from around our legs once more, then taking my hands, he spun me around into another dance. I laid my head against his chest, listening to his heartbeat in tune with the music, flowing from their instruments to his very core and into mine.

"What if something happens?" I said barely above a whisper, unable to keep my fears completely at bay.

He released my hand, wrapping both arms around me instead. "Nothing will happen."

"I have cancer, Kyle."

He looked down at me, the serious expression back. "Which means the worst has already happened. *And we're still here.* We're still fighting, and we're going to win."

"How can you be so confident?" I asked.

He shrugged. "How could I not be?"

I rolled my eyes, but couldn't keep the smile from creeping onto my face. "I'm serious, Kyle."

"So am I, beautiful," he said, wiggling his brows suggestively before kissing me.

When we parted, I laughed, taking Beast's leash and walking back toward the path. "You're a goofball."

He caught up to me a second later. "You married that goofball."

I smiled. "Until the end."

"Nope." Kyle shook his head. "There's no end to us, Tessa. There's only forever." He wrapped an arm around my shoulders and laid a kiss on my scarf.

I smiled. I wanted it. Every word.

Only forever.

CHAPTER ELEVEN

Thursday, May 15, 2014

"THIS WAS YOUR LAST TREATMENT, are you excited?" the technologist asked, lifting the hated mesh holder off my head.

"I don't know about excited, but I'm definitely ready to be done with this thing." I pointed at the mesh holder as she put it aside.

"I can imagine." She helped me off the table. "The surgery is tomorrow, right?"

"Yeah," I confirmed, not wasting any time heading for the door. She had turned out to be a sweet lady, but I was done with this room. This place. All of it.

"You'll do great!" she called after me.

I pushed through the heavy doors, giving her a thank-you wave over my shoulder. It took all my effort to open the door, so the more reserved wave would have to do.

Six weeks of radiation and I looked every minute of it. I slinked down the hallway toward the waiting room where either Kyle or my dad had sat every day, shuttling me back and forth. Today it was my dad, since Kyle was working so he could take tomorrow off for my surgery.

I reached the end of the hallway, holding the rail the entire way and glancing up at the round mirror in the corner the staff used to see around corners to avoid collisions of beds and patients.

The moment I saw my reflection, I realized my mistake. It was like staring at a ghost.

The obligatory sweats hung loosely from my hips, no metal allowed. My face was a washed-out, pale oval, cheekbones pushing against my skin. Nothing defined me from the off-white wall behind me.

There were no eyebrows to echo my mood, no lashes to bat and hide behind, no pink signs of life in my cheeks. My already small frame was even smaller now—my skin nearly translucent. Tiny blue veins marked my body, one of the few reminders I was still alive.

Because I *was* still alive. Or something like that.

Standing straighter in defiance, I released the handrail and readjusted the bright green scarf over my entirely smooth head. Even the fuzz was gone, replaced with scattered red blisters on my scalp instead. Taking deliberate and slow steps, I made it to the waiting room without assistance. Radiation had made my body weak, but *I* wasn't.

Cancer doesn't get to win.

"Sunshine? You ready?" My dad hopped up from his seat and dropped a magazine on the table nearby.

"Yep, I'm done." Truer words had never been spoken. I took his offered arm and leaned against him. "*So* done."

"Let's go home, then." He kissed the back of my hand affectionately. "Want to stop and get something to eat on the way? You didn't have breakfast."

I shook my head and settled my free hand on my stomach that had begun somersaulting at the mere mention of food.

His brows furrowed. "Tessa, you need to keep eating."

"I'm not hungry."

He grunted. "Delores will be here in the afternoon. We should ask her for more anti-nausea meds."

Poor Delores. I don't know how she wasn't sick of me yet. She came each afternoon, administering my medications and setting aside my pills for bedtime and the following morning. She listened to my whining about aches and pains and anything else. I was grateful for her, partially because my daily medications were overwhelmingly. There was no way I'd make heads or tails of it without her. But, I also appreciated who she was, and the support I felt just by her presence.

"I guess the meds will help," I replied, too tired to say more.

"What about some toast?" he tried again as we entered the elevator to the parking garage.

"Dad." I put my hand over my mouth, willing my stomach contents to stay where they belonged.

"Sorry." He raised his hand in resignation, despite his usual persistence. It wasn't that I wasn't hungry, or even that nausea was the worst part of it. Food just wasn't fun anymore. Before I became sick, I'd always loved to eat and had the curves to show for it despite my regular exercise routine. I had always described my body type as *works out but definitely enjoys cheese. Often.*

Everything's different now that my body is barely my own. My curves have long since melted away, the first thing to go with the weight loss from my treatment. My taste buds are now almost nonexistent and I can't smell a thing, which makes eating like forcing rubber down my throat. Add to these wonderful symptoms nausea from the meds, and it's no wonder food had lost all appeal for me.

"New topic, then," my dad said. "Your sister will be here on Saturday. She finishes her last final tomorrow."

I exhaled with a smile, relief flooding me at the thought of my sister being back by my side again. "I can't wait to see her. Though I don't want to mess with her final tomorrow by having her worrying about me in surgery."

"I think she'll worry either way."

"Tell her not to," I added, knowing it was useless. "She needs to focus on her test, not me."

My dad laughed, a deep belly laugh that shook even the arm I was holding on to. "Elly's never been one to listen to her dear old dad, Tessa."

This was true. Of the two of us, she'd always been the rebellious, stubborn one. I envied her, having never had the chance to be a kid, to be irresponsible and just live for myself. I never wished for something different because I do truly love my life, but sometimes I wondered what it would have been like to be a regular kid. To have a mom who hadn't died, a father who wasn't often deployed, and a little sister who didn't need me to be the parent we were both missing. I didn't regret it, and I wasn't bitter, but sometimes I wondered.

My dad started the car and drove out of the parking garage. "What time do we need to be here tomorrow for surgery?" he asked.

"Seven o'clock in the morning."

He grunted again—the majority of his vocabulary was made up of different grunts, but this grunt was his doctors-are-stupid-and-seven-in-the-morning-is-crazy grunt. "Those damn doctors are up with the roosters. Probably trying to make it look like they actually do shit."

I laughed, more to myself than to him. "I mean...they *are* going to cut into my head." *That was some definite shit.*

Honestly, I didn't mind the early hour. In fact, I wished it was today. Or right now. I wanted this done. Finished. Over. The end. Six weeks of my life had been on hold, waiting for this, waiting for the tumor to come out. Then, I could finally move on.

I would be able to say I'd beaten cancer. There was no other acceptable outcome. I was not my mother. I would not die alone in a hospital bed with no one to hear my final words.

That wasn't me. That wasn't my ending. I am a survivor.

I *will* beat cancer.

• ღ • ღ • ღ •

FRIDAY, May 16, 2014

"WHAT AM I SUPPOSED TO WEAR?" I was almost bouncing with excitement, standing in my closet surveying the options, Beast rolling around on the carpet at my feet.

Kyle leaned against the doorframe, watching me pack a bag. He was rubbing the sleep out of his eyes since it was only five in the morning, but I was too eager to sleep. "I don't think it matters, Tessa. They're going to make you change into a hospital gown."

"Not for now. I mean after the surgery. I have to walk

out of the hospital in something kickass. Something that says *I kicked cancer's ass.*"

"I could have a shirt printed up saying that." His lazy grin warmed my heart.

"I think I'd prefer a billboard. Right over Millennium Park. *TESSA KICKED CANCER'S ASS.*" I made a congratulatory gesture with my hands imagining the sight.

Beast rolled over, perching on my feet and cementing me to the spot.

"I'll get right on that." He laughed, leaving momentarily before reappearing with a small package. "Speaking of getting shirts printed, I got you something."

"A present? Ooh, give it here!" I lifted my feet—dislodging the dog—and walked to Kyle, taking the gift from him. Moving to the bed, I sat on the edge with it in my lap.

Kyle shifted his weight from one leg to the other. "It's just a little something for today. For beginnings."

Pride beamed through his smile, and my heart leapt in response. Pulling the wrapping off, a small piece of fabric unfolded in my lap. The material was starched white cotton and when I flattened it against my thighs, I realized it was a baby onesie. The front had a big red heart and then black letters spelling out *I love my Mommy.*

"Kyle! This is adorable!" I held it up against my chest, hugging it to me. "You know I'm not pregnant though, right?"

"Obviously," he said with a small chuckle, sitting on the edge of the bed next to me. "But after today, we can go back to hoping for a little person to wear that onesie. These last six weeks...well, it's fucking sucked for all of us, but especially you. This is something to look forward to—you, me, your family. This is what we're holding on to. This is what's going to get us through."

"Oh, Kyle," I whispered, staring at the heartfelt gift in my hands. "I'm so lucky to have you. Thank you."

"I'm the lucky one, babe. All the love." He pulled me against his side and kissed my cheek. Standing, he headed for the doorway and glanced back at me. "Ready to go in twenty?"

"I'll be right down," I said, watching him leave.

Looking down at the onesie in my hands, I let a few quiet tears glide down my face. They weren't sad tears, or overwhelmed tears, or even tears of pain. These were tears of hope, of excitement, of optimism. The best kind.

I smiled and folded the onesie into a tight bundle, tucking it into my bag for the hospital. I wanted it with me. I didn't want to forget what the last six weeks had been for. It wasn't just my life, it was our entire family, our entire future.

I returned to packing what I'd need for a few days into the leather weekend bag Kyle had bought me for my last birthday. I'd meant to finish packing last night, but I'd been sick most of yesterday and barely able to leave the bathroom.

My phone pinged and I pulled it out of my pocket, smiling when I saw my sister's name on the screen. There was also a well-wishing text from my boss. Both messages wished me luck today, along with many prayers. I needed every bit of it.

I thanked them and returned the phone to my pocket.

Wrapping a purple silk scarf around my head, I surveyed my appearance in the mirror. Even though I'd be taking it off in a few minutes, I needed the scarf. Partly to keep my head warm, but mostly, I'd gotten used to it being a part of who I am right now. I didn't feel naked or on display when I wore them. Instead, I felt glamorous and connected to my mother in a way I hadn't before.

Contrary to my glamorous scarf, I opted to keep on my pajamas for the morning commute. They weren't really pajamas anyway, rather, Kyle's shirt and ill-fitting lounge pants.

Everything I wore was ill-fitting these days. Pants hung off my hipbones, which protruded too far from my waist. My skin stretched and hung in a sad manner, as if it were clinging to my bones.

Sighing, I surveyed Beast, whose snout was nose deep in his crotch, one back leg over his head. Snorting noises came from his self-manipulations, and I gagged slightly. Thank God, he's cute.

"Give it here. I'll carry that." My dad motioned toward the bag in my hands as I walked out of my bedroom.

Gratefully, I handed it over, not wanting to waste the limited energy I had on carrying luggage. "Thanks, Dad." I followed him down the stairs, Beast on our tail as we reached the bottom.

"Do you want something to eat or drink?" Kyle asked, standing by the open front door, car keys in his hand. My dad walked past him with my bag, heading for the car.

I shook my head. "I can't. Nothing heavy in my stomach before surgery."

"Oh, right. Well, I'll make sure to have something yummy waiting when you're done, babe," Kyle assured me.

"To celebrate," I added. Because, damn it, we *would* be celebrating. Today was for celebrating. Well, in a few hours.

"Definitely." Kyle looked relieved, and I felt it, too. We were ready for today. We were ready for it to be over. He helped me shrug on a jacket as my dad walked back in, my bag no longer in his hands. "Glenn, can you lock Beast up in the kitchen while I get Tessa into the car?"

"Sure, but it won't make a damn bit of difference. He always slams through the gate before we get home anyway," my dad muttered, stalking off toward the kitchen with Beast under one arm.

I buttoned my jacket, laughing at my dad's remarks. Warmth enveloped me and I pushed my hands in the jacket pockets. Though almost summer, my new paper-thin skin made me perpetually cold. A pair of loafers finished my less-than-subpar look as I stepped out onto the front porch. "Okay. I'm ready."

So damn ready.

The drive to the hospital was quiet. Not awkward or uncomfortable, just quiet. We knew today would be tough, but it was blue skies after that. Sure, I'd have checkups and different therapies to return me to my old self again, but the worst would be behind us. A calmness comes with knowing the worst thing you'll ever go through is behind you, and at only twenty-eight years old.

After registering with the admittance staff, we were ushered into a small hospital room where a nurse told us to wait for the doctor. She gave me a gown and showed me to a private bathroom where I could change. Once barely-adorned in my paper coverings, I sat on the edge of the exam table and fidgeted, waiting.

"Tessa, sit still. You're making me seasick," my dad grumbled from his chair a few feet away.

I grinned. "Can't help it. I feel like I've had eight cups of coffee."

"You haven't had anything," Kyle said with a snort, leaning against the far wall.

I shrugged. Didn't matter.

"Good morning, Tessa," Dr. Page greeted us, walking into the room. "And family."

We all sat up straighter, giving him our full attention.

Kyle grabbed my hand and squeezed it between both of his. "Morning, doctor."

"Yes, sorry to make everyone come in so early. We usually do surgeries as soon as possible so the day can be spent monitoring the patient, but, uh," he paused and licked his lips, flipping through a clipboard chart in his hands.

I narrowed my eyes. He wasn't reading the charts, just turning pages. My dad glanced in my direction, and I saw a similar worry in the crinkle of his eyes.

"What's going on, doc?" Kyle seemed to sense it, too.

"Tessa, I'd like to discuss a change in your prognosis. Would you like to do that privately?" He gestured to my husband and father, offering them a polite smile.

I shook my head emphatically. "No, they can stay. I want them to stay."

Please just take me to surgery. Cut me open, yank out the tumor, and let me put this day so far behind me, it can never catch up.

"Very well. We examined your scans from earlier this week, hoping to see a decrease in tumor size and spread. Six weeks of radiation should have done this—significantly. The tumor should've been more manageable so we could remove it today."

"Should've?" I interrupted. Panic fluttered through my abdomen. I swallowed heavily. *Was that sorrow in his eyes? No. God, no. Please, don't say it.*

"We won't be doing the surgery today, Tessa. I'm so sorry. The tumor did not diminish." Dr. Page inhaled deeply before continuing. "In fact, it grew and spread. At this point, we'd classify it as a Grade 4 glioblastoma, and inoperable."

Wide-eyed, I clutched Kyle's hand. A strangled sound came from my dad's direction, but he didn't look at me. I glanced sideways at my husband. He was barely breathing, paler than the white hospital walls.

My stomach somersaulted. My heart pounded against my ribcage.

I don't understand. Today was the last day. It's over. The nightmare is over.

"What are you saying?" I asked, my teeth clenched and each word coming out choppy. Separated. Confused. *I don't understand.*

"Tessa, the treatment protocol you went through was aggressive—the most aggressive we have for this type of tumor. Unfortunately, it was not successful. Surgery at its current mass would be fatal, and further treatment would most likely be ineffective. In my medical opinion, our best option is to treat the symptoms, address the pain, and make you as comfortable as possible."

"As comfortable as possible until what?" *Don't say it.*

Dr. Page stood a little straighter, maybe steeling himself. "This tumor is terminal, Tessa."

A strangled, shrill sound shot out of me. My chest ached, and I pushed my palm against it. My lungs tried to fill but weren't cooperating. I swallowed air greedily until I could form words again. In. Out. In. Out. Breathing. Alive. *I'm alive.*

"I'm dying?" I breathed out, shuddering each syllable.

"I'm so sorry," Dr. Page confirmed with a nod of his head.

I shook mine in response. "No."

"Tessa," Kyle began to speak, but I put my hand up to silence him.

"*No.* I am not dying. I am twenty-eight, Dr. Page. I'm twenty-eight-freaking-years old. There has to be something you can do. There has to."

"Sunshine." My dad placed his hand on my shoulder, but I brushed him off, keeping my eyes on the doctor.

"How long?" I demanded, anger flooding me.

Dr. Page didn't falter. "Six months would be my estimate. At most."

Kyle gasped loudly, as if just hearing the news for the first time.

My dad's head dropped, his chin to his chest.

Tears stung my eyes and a lump formed in my throat, but I shook my head. I shook it away and told myself this was wrong. *This was completely wrong.*

"There has to be something you can do. There has to be something that will fix this!" My volume raised with every second. I pushed up off the table warily, my energy zapped from my body.

"I'm happy to recommend doctors for a second opinion. In fact, I'd encourage that," Dr. Page said, jotting something down on the clipboard in his hands.

"I want a second opinion. I want third and fourth opinions. I want anyone's opinion, but this one." I gritted my teeth, glaring at him as if this were his fault. "I cannot die, Dr. Page. Not yet. I'm not ready to die."

"I'll arrange for it immediately." He pushed his glasses up his nose, and then he was gone. One last glance of sadness and he'd left us to cope with the news. It was barely dawn and he'd walked in and ruined my entire day—my entire life.

It sounds harsh, but I don't give a crap. Life is harsh. Cancer is harsh. *I get to be harsh right now.*

"I want to go home." My voice was barely above a whisper, but fury dripped from each word.

"I'll pull the car up front," my dad said, rushing for the door as if eager to leave.

Kyle picked my bag up off the floor and placed it on the exam table next to me. "Do you need help getting dressed?"

The room was small and empty except for the two of us, but his stooped shoulders and giant build seemed to take up half of it. Every time his chest rose with a breath, the oxygen seemed to drain from the room.

Everything was closing in on me. There wasn't enough space.

I *needed* space.

Clutching the table's edge, I swallowed hard. "I want to be alone."

"I'll wait in the hall. Take your time." Kyle touched my cheek with the back of his fingers, but I refused to look into his eyes. I refused to let him see me cry. One second of his gaze would break me.

He left me alone in the tiny, collapsing room and it didn't get any bigger in his absence. It somehow seemed smaller.

I unpinned my gown from behind my neck and back, letting it fall in a puddle at my feet. My chin to my chest, I scanned down the length of my body. My breasts were smaller than before, sagging against jutting ribs. My stomach trembled slightly, curving inward. My hips seemed they were only there to hold up pants. My legs were thin, but not in good way. They barely showed any muscle, the skin tight over my bones. My thighs were bruised from frequent shots. My hands and arms punctured from numerous IVs, replaced recently by the PICC line jutting out near my elbow and taped down against my arm for better access to shrinking veins.

Stepping over to the floor length mirror, I lifted my hands to touch the scar from my biopsy. It had healed weeks ago, but no hair grew there. The skin around it was red, peeling, swollen. I had rubbed a burn balm on it daily that Delores had brought me, but radiation burns heal poorly when the cause was inside eating its way out. I pressed my hands to my skull—hard, squeezing, unrelenting, as if choking the tumor from my brain.

A few centimeters beneath my fingertips was a mass that would end my life.

It was right there below my fingertips, yet untouchable.

I ran my hands down my neck, my sides, and then wrapped them around my waist in a small hug. Breathing deeply, I told myself to hold it together. People were waiting for me, depending on me, needing me. I couldn't fall apart.

Turning from the mirror, I moved back to the table and zippered open my bag. I pulled my clothes out in one big bundle, and a small white cloth fell to the floor.

It was the onesie Kyle had given me this morning.

The pressure behind my eyes became too much. It had to have its turn. I *had to* feel this. I had to lose this, lose everything. It was all being taken from me and I had no choice but to watch it slip away...watch everything slip away.

The first tear slid down my cheek, falling upon my naked chest and traveling the length of my body. The rest were seconds behind. I clutched the onesie to my stomach and twisted my hands in the fabric.

I would never be a mother.

There was no more *after* and no more *one day*. There was no more. Period.

For the first time since my diagnosis, I realized what it all meant. With barely six months left, my dreams were not going to come true. Cancer wasn't just killing me—it was killing everything I would have been.

Would have been. I was already talking about myself in the past tense.

Heaving sobs racked me. I hugged the onesie to my stomach tighter, my womb barren and empty beneath. My body tilted forward, my knees bending. I folded into myself in a desperate attempt to keep from falling apart completely.

Seconds. Minutes. Hours passed. I didn't know. I didn't care.

My tears slowly dried, but more were coming. I could feel the pain regenerating within me, waiting until my body could physically grieve more. It was mourning whether I wanted to or not.

I was dying. Six months, at best.

Lifting the onesie to my face, I rested it against my cheek. I prayed for the child who would never wear it. I prayed for the mother who would never hold that child. I prayed for the father who wouldn't have either of them. I prayed for the family we'd never be.

And when the prayers were over, I tore the fabric in half and tossed its pieces in a nearby trashcan.

I turned away, and pulled on my pants. Tightening the drawstring, I secured it around my small waist. My shirt slid over my top half easily, my mother's scarf on my head. I wet a cloth in the sink, wiping the tear stains from my cheeks, dabbing my puffy eyes.

Finally, I slid on my jacket, but I didn't feel any less cold. I'd been cold for months.

I'd thought it was the weight loss, or maybe the radiation had made me less able to self-regulate heat. But now, I wasn't so sure. Maybe the chill had been my fate, the cold my tumor, the bleakness my future.

Death had been embracing me for months, and only today could I see it.

I was dying. Six months, at best.

CHAPTER TWELVE

SATURDAY, *May 17, 2014*

A COOL, wet object pressed against my cheek, and I swatted it away with a hand that had tucked under a pillow. Unrelenting, it returned and pushed into my cheek accompanied by a small whimpering. Blinking open my eyes, I stared into Beast's beady pupils.

A slobbering lick was next, Beast's tongue slapping against my cheek loudly, causing me to grimace and push him away. When I rolled onto my back, Beast took it as an invitation to climb aboard, mounting my chest, and renewing his slimy assault on my face.

"Beast, my God, give me a second to wake up," I groaned, squeezing him tighter to me which both appeased his need for closeness and kept his stinky tongue off my face.

"Morning, babe. How are you feeling?" I turned my head to see Kyle lying next to me, propped up on one elbow as he stretched out on his side. The way he was leaning looked like he'd been awake for a while, still and pensive, not a single sign of sleep on his face. Part of me wondered if he'd slept at all last night.

"I'm fine, just tired." I probably wouldn't have been able to sleep either, but the ravaged condition of my body made staving off sleep impossible. Even with the bit I did manage, it had been restless.

"Your sister should be here soon. I heard your father leave earlier to go pick her up at the airport."

"Not necessarily. Dad's super anal about airports. He always gets there a minimum of three hours early, even if he is just picking one of us up." I snorted a giggle, barely audible.

"Oh." Kyle sounded confused, but even more tired. There was an emptiness in his words, an exhaustion behind his eyes that seemed to go a lot deeper than missing sleep. "Well, at least you'll see your sister at some point today."

I stroked Beast's soft fur, his head on my chest, his breathing slow and calming. I'd spent yesterday in bed after getting home from the hospital, not wanting to talk, not wanting to do anything, or be with anyone. Hiding seemed preferable to the hellhole my life had become.

I wasted the day on a Netflix binge until my laptop overheated and the inevitable buffering sign disrupted one too many episodes of *One Tree Hill* to be tolerable. Kyle convinced me to eat some soup for dinner, but I barely kept that down. After, I let sleep consume me, and it did for most of the night.

"Do you want to talk?" Kyle asked, sounding as unsure, his eyebrows pinched and his lips pursed.

I know I should try to make this easier for him, but damn it, it wasn't easy for me. I feel so angry, and I should.

I'm allowed this anger—I've earned every bit of it. "There's nothing to talk about."

"Tessa, come on. I know this is tough for you—it certainly is for me—so, I can't begin to imagine what's going on in your head. But that's why I'm asking, because I want to know. I don't want you going through this alone, not when I'm right here to help you, to hold you, to carry as much of this for you as I can."

"That's the problem, Kyle. You can't help. The tumor isn't in your head, it's in mine. You can't do anything. I can't do anything. It just...it just is."

He bit his lip and was silent a moment before shaking his head.

"Yes and no," he said. "Yes, I don't have a tumor, but, no, there is definitely something I can do. I can help. I want to. I want to be here for you for all of it. If I could trade places with you, I would. But I can't. So, please let me do something. Anything, Tessa. I *need* to do something."

"Kyle," I protested, but he nudged Beast off my chest and pulled me against him, lifting the blankets so I could curl in next to his naked body.

I molded my body to his, seeking the safety of his embrace.

"Let me be there for you, Tessa," he repeated. "I will do anything."

I bit the inside of my cheek to keep from crying. I did enough of that yesterday to last me years—as if I even have years left. Shallow breaths, I swallowed the emotion.

"I don't know what I need." I sniffed, dropping my forehead into the dip between his neck and shoulder. "There's no manual for this. There are no instructions. I don't know what I'm doing, and I have no idea what I need."

"That's okay. We're going back to Dr. Page on Monday

to find out what to do. We'll get pain meds and set up hospi —um, set up the care you need." His voice faded, stumbling over his last words.

A thick lump formed in my throat at the word he couldn't say. I swallowed hard, breathing deep in an attempt to keep my distance. Keep that word far away. Keep reality away. *Hospice. I'm twenty-eight years old.*

This is what dying people do, I reminded myself. *I'm dying.*

"Babe, it's okay." He rubbed my neck, sliding his hand from my hairline down to my shoulder.

"No part of this is okay, Kyle. I have so much left to do, to live...or had. I *had* so much left to do."

"You're right," he agreed.

I felt something wet hit my cheek and wiped it away, angry at myself for crying. I'd been walking waterworks since yesterday, and it freaked me the hell out. That's not who I am. I am tough. I can handle anything. Growing up with a father working all the time and a dying mother, there hadn't been time for breakdowns and tantrums.

A sniffling sound tore me from my self-deprecating thoughts. I lifted my head from Kyle's chest to see the origin of the escaped moisture. Tears pooled in his eyes, sliding down his nose sideways onto the bed where my cheek had been moments earlier.

If my heart wasn't already broken into a thousand pieces, it would've shattered then. Maneuvering my body higher on the bed, I wrapped my arms around his neck and pulled his head to my chest. He clung to me, his arms around my torso like a vice while I leaned back on the pillow.

His tears poured freely, trembling, sobbing. I rocked him with the give and take of our soft bed, consoled him with soft murmurs of how it'll be okay. It didn't matter that neither of us believed it. Neither of us knew what was going to happen, but the one thing we were sure of is nothing would be okay. Not again.

Never again.

· ♋ · ♋ · ♋ ·

SATURDAY, May 17, 2014

AFTER SEVERAL HOURS of pillow talk and encouragement, Kyle and I rose from our bed by mid-afternoon. Slowly moving around the kitchen, I pulled out granola and yogurt for breakfast. Kyle had taken Beast for a walk and the house was quiet for the first time in a while.

Standing at the kitchen counter, I used a mortar and pestle to crush the granola into a fine dust before sprinkling it in my yogurt. I used to love the crunch of granola under my teeth in a spoonful of parfait, but six weeks of unsuccessful treatment stole that luxury from me as well. Small, yet vicious radiation blisters ran down the inside of my throat. Anything I swallowed scraped past them like a blade shredding my esophagus. Even something as soft as yogurt, or a glass of water, made it burn and ache with fury. Smashing the granola into crumbs was the only solution to get food down while minimizing the pain.

"Tessa?" someone called from the front hallway.

"In the kitchen." I finished preparing my food and brought it to the kitchen table.

"Sweetie, I *so* wasn't expecting you to show up on my roster today. They must have discharged you fast after your surgery." Delores waltzed around the corner in her usual perky manner. Today, she was sporting bright green scrubs decorated with fast food restaurant logos. It was hilariously unique, and completely Delores.

"Yeah, well...here I am." I spooned yogurt into my mouth, hoping that would get me out of further questions.

Delores dropped her bag onto the kitchen table and scrutinized me. I looked away, feeling naked. Her sigh was audible. She'd figured it out.

"There was no surgery," she stated, waiting for me to confirm.

I nodded, the lump in my throat silencing me. I was beginning to get used to the restraint, the tears, the pain. I wondered if this was what my next six months would look like.

"How long, Tessa?" she asked, her voice soft. She sat beside me, took my hand, cradled it in both of hers.

"Six months," I croaked. Turning back to my meal, I forced the yogurt down my throat. I was so anxious in that moment, I barely concentrated on the clawing scrapes of the food passing my blisters and sinking into my stomach.

Delores didn't respond; she squeezed my hand tighter, her calloused hands rubbing mine. It was sweet. It was kind. It was comforting, as if she knew I didn't have the words—because I didn't. So, I let her hold me, even the smallest part of me. For several minutes, I ate yogurt and she held my hand.

"Hi, Delores." My dad walked into the kitchen carrying a large suitcase and garment bag draped over his shoulder. He placed them on the floor near the hallway, tired eyes lifting to find me.

Delores nodded curtly. "Afternoon, Mr. Barnes."

I tried a small smile on for size, but when he moved and revealed who was behind him, my smile fell. Elly stood there in an oversized sweater nearly engulfing her lanky frame, her hair piled high on her head, carelessly messy. Her disheveled appearance wasn't what made me pause—it was her face.

Elly's skin was blotchy, bright blue eyes puffy and rimmed red. Shoulders hunched, and her lips were frowning so fiercely, they seemed to point at the ground. Her lashes were sparkling with teardrops and her eyes downcast, avoiding mine.

"Elly?" I pushed to my feet, releasing Delores as I walked over to my sister.

Her shoulders bounced and she shook her head rapidly, but said nothing.

"Elly, please talk to me." My pulse quickened in my ears. I knew she knew. My dad had to have told her on the way here. I hadn't seen her since the first week of treatments, but she wouldn't even look at me now.

"Dad told me." She lifted her chin slowly, her eyes bleary, teaming with unshed tears.

"Oh." I dropped my hands to my side, unsure what to say. No one had told me the best way to tell people my prognosis, especially people I loved. I'd spent my entire life protecting Elly from pain, and now I was the one delivering one of the greatest hurts she'd probably ever experience.

The very thought sickened me.

"Tessa, this can't happen." She suddenly launched forward, throwing her arms around me and sobbing into my shoulder. I stumbled back for a moment, finding my balance, which was a feat in my weakened state. Hugging her, I caressed her back, her body heaving up and down with the strength of her cries.

"Elly, it's okay," I coaxed, lowering my voice.

"It's not! It's so fucked up! First Mom, now you..." she trailed off. I felt a dampness in my shoulder as she continued to cry.

"You're right." I rocked her gently, hoping to calm her. "It's not fair. I know, baby girl."

My dad stood behind Elly, rubbing his neck uncomfortably. He seemed as lost as I felt for the right thing to do or say.

"I'm sorry, Tessa," he said to me. "I wanted to tell her before we got here, so you wouldn't be overwhelmed. But, uh..."

"It's fine, Dad," I assured him.

The guilt stayed on his face. Despair in his eyes, he wrapped his arms around both of us, sandwiched Elly in the middle. She continued to cry with as much strength as before, no ending in sight. Little paws jumped up on my leg, scratching at my knees for attention, but I ignored Beast. Kyle joined us, throwing his arms around the entire group.

We stood in a giant bear hug, four people clambering for life not to rip us apart, not to let me go. Yet the only thing I wanted to do *was* let go. I wanted out. I wanted away from this moment—it was too much.

Aside from those few minutes alone in my hospital room, I'd spent the last day helping others feel better. I had assured my family I only wanted to sleep yesterday, that everything was okay. My dad and Kyle checked on me countless times, and I calmed their fears each time. This morning when we awoke, Kyle had needed comforting, and now so did my sister. The only person who had received the news without needing solace had been Delores.

I needed solace, and I was the only one going without.

My eyes found Delores—desperate, pleading. She cracked a wry grin, gesturing to me that she understood my request. Reaching over the table, she knocked a hand against my empty bowl and sent it crashing to the ground.

It clattered against the tile loudly, and everyone broke apart, releasing me. I closed my eyes in a silent prayer, thanking the good Lord for bringing this woman into my life.

"Oh! That's my bad," Delores said, bending down to scoop up the intact bowl. "It's all good. It didn't break. Clumsy fingers."

"Are you okay?" Kyle asked, before helping her clean up the mess.

My dad muttered something under his breath like *how could a nurse be clumsy*, but then he ushered Elly out of the kitchen and began helping her carry her bags upstairs.

"Time to take Tessa's vitals anyway," Delores said to Kyle. "Sorry to break up that love huddle. That was getting me right here." She tapped her heart. "Right in the ticker."

Kyle gave her a funny look then kissed me on the cheek before he left the room next.

"You okay?" Delores turned her attention to me.

"Yeah." It was an automatic response. "Thanks for saving me back there."

"No problem." She shrugged. "Kinda disappointed the bowl didn't break though. That would have been hella dramatic."

I smiled slowly, though there wasn't much behind it. We sat at the table and I rolled my sleeve for her to take my blood pressure. The tight line of her jaw flexed for a moment while she focused on the task, a stethoscope on the inside of my elbow, the other end tucked into her ears.

She counted. I waited. The cuff tightened. My heart throbbed.

Delores's eyes glistened, giving away her real feelings. I knew she was as upset over the news. She was my nurse, but she'd become my friend—she cared about me, and I cared just as much about her.

"I'm not really okay," I answer her question again. "But I'm trying to be. I want to be."

She smiled. "That's all you need to do, Tessa."

CHAPTER THIRTEEN

MONDAY, May 19, 2014

DOCTOR'S OFFICES are not made for this many people. All four of us were crowded into one tiny exam room with a table in the center, making it at capacity. No one could walk in without slamming the door into my dad's back, but since he was sandwiched between Kyle and Elly, he wasn't going anywhere either. Propped up on the table, I was the centerpiece.

At least, I was fully clothed this time.

The new doctor didn't need to examine me physically. He had looked over my blood work, scans, and all the other goodies I'd brought with me from the last few months. I was fully aware I wasn't going to like what this doctor would tell me, or the next. That's why I have three different doctors scheduled this week to check, triple check, quadruple check.

I had pushed off my appointment with Dr. Page until Friday, wanting to get every other opinion before sitting down and talking about what I want for the end of my life. Because this couldn't be the end of my life. *It just couldn't.*

"Mrs. Falls?" A voice entered the room with an *oomph* as the door smacked my dad between the shoulder blades. He pitched forward. "Oops, you okay, sir?"

A young nurse stuck her head in farther and slid through the opening, needling her way in. My dad assured her he was fine, squeezing himself behind the table and out of the path of the door. A middle-aged man in a doctor's coat entered next, doing the same shuffle through limbs and medical equipment to get to me.

"Are you Mrs. Falls?" he asked.

"Yes, and you're Dr. Burton?"

He nodded. "Mrs. Falls, I've gone over your scans and blood work, and I'm afraid I can't offer you more than what Dr. Page has already said."

I blinked, not expecting him to dash my hopes so quickly like that. "There's nothing? Nothing you can do?" I asked, feeling a sense of déjà vu.

"We could possibly continue treatment to prolong your life expectancy, but there is no cure. That could give you a few more weeks, maybe even a month or two." The doctor was curt, but there was no malice to it. He spoke slowly, letting me absorb his words, but he didn't sugar coat anything.

"What kind of treatments?" Kyle interrupted, squeezing my hand.

"Chemo, radiation, possibly a combination of both. There are experimental drugs we could try, but your tumor is aggressive. It's unlikely they would work if they didn't work already." He paused, frowning. "And there are the side effects to consider."

"But it would give me more time? These treatments?" I reiterated, ignoring his warning.

"Potentially, but there are no guarantees. Your last six weeks of radiation should have drastically reduced the size of the tumor. Instead, yours grew substantially." He flipped through some pages on the clipboard he was holding, as if to confirm what he was saying. When he found what he was looking for, he nodded and looked back at me. "Treatment could prolong your life if the tumor does what we want it to do."

"But my tumor doesn't have a history of doing that," I finished his sentence.

"Yes," he said, confirming what I didn't want to hear. "You'd also be experiencing all the side effects of radiation again."

"She can at least try," Elly spoke up from behind a nurse. "Right, Tessa?"

"She definitely can," he confirmed, turning to look at me. "I'd love to help you do exactly that if those are your wishes, Tessa."

"Let's do that then," Elly volunteered for me, and I felt a sinking in my gut at the idea.

Dr. Burton kept his focus on me. "I'd like to fully discuss the process with you before you decide. Your records indicate you suffered with a lot of symptoms from the radiation in the last six weeks. You had to be hospitalized in the middle of it, correct?"

I shuddered at the reminder. "It wasn't an easy time."

His frown deepened. "A new round of treatments would be worse. There'd be extreme nausea, boils lining your throat and mouth, possibly your esophagus. Your scalp would suffer first-degree burns, skin peeling, blistering. There would be headaches, temporary blindness, vertigo, itchiness, weakness, and a lengthy list of other symptoms. I know you've already experienced a good bit of these, but it wouldn't get better—it'd get worse. That being said, it might be worth it, Mrs. Falls. It might give you more time."

I watched Dr. Burton's shoulders slump as he spoke, and I could tell he had little faith in any other outcome. The way his eyes widened every time he looked at my chart, it was clear he agreed with Dr. Page.

I'd been given a death sentence.

"Is that something you want to do, Mrs. Falls?" the doctor asked.

My family looked at me expectantly, hope in their half-hearted smiles and pained expressions. The truth was I didn't want to give up. I'm not a quitter. I never have been. Part of me wanted to try if only to say I did, to ease the strain on the faces around the room. They were rooting for me, maybe even more than I was rooting for myself.

But they hadn't lived in my body for the last six weeks. They watched and they comforted, but they didn't feel it. They didn't know the torment of a disease leaving you a shell of your former self, literally. This *had* been me trying—six weeks of excruciating trying.

And it had failed.

As I looked at their faces, a quiet, despondent voice in the back of my head said *never again*. Not even for a few more weeks.

Never again.

I pushed those thoughts aside. I couldn't think like that. I couldn't let cancer win. There were still three doctors left to see this week who might have an answer the others hadn't. A miracle drug, a clinical trial, a fairy godmother, anything other than the torment of the last six weeks again.

"I have to think about it," I said finally, despite the pit in my stomach telling me I already knew the answer.

"We've gotta be optimistic, right, babe? What's there to think about?" Kyle asked me.

I looked into his green eyes, wide and pleading. "Right, gotta stay positive..." I agreed, my voice trailing off.

Everyone was looking at me. I mean, there were literally five sets of eyes glued to me, waiting for me to say I'd do it. To say I'd try.

I couldn't say no.

I couldn't say I never wanted to do a single treatment again, even if it meant leaving them sooner. I couldn't say I didn't want to keep going, only to be in so much pain again. Love was pain, and they were in pain loving me. *Maybe I owe it to them. Maybe this is what love is.*

"Sheila will get you several informational packets about it, and you can decide in your own time." Dr. Burton motioned to the nurse behind him.

I exhaled, appreciating the reprieve from having to give an answer right then and there.

"Sounds like a plan, doctor." Kyle grinned, the first time I'd seen him smile in a few days. Maybe since before Friday's bombshell.

Dr. Burton nodded at Kyle, then looked back at me. "Mrs. Falls, if you do decide on continuing treatment, it will need to start within the next week. The sooner, the more effective."

My body tensed at the rushed timeline. "If I started now, would that mean I'd be going through treatment until... the end? I'd be sick the entire time?"

I knew I had little time left, both doctors had confirmed it more than once, but I didn't feel it. I didn't *feel* like I could die tomorrow, despite what I looked like.

"We'd definitely do our best to limit your symptoms, but we'd try to continue treatment as long as possible. With some luck, that would give you more time."

A non-answer if I'd ever heard one.

Kyle nodded excitedly and my sister looked relieved. Even after seeing the hell I'd been through the last six weeks, they looked like the doctor had handed them a miracle. I wasn't sure we were all hearing the same thing, because nothing he'd said was making me feel optimistic.

"I'll think about it," I repeated, mentally pushing the knot in my stomach down as far as possible.

"It's more time, Tessa. Doesn't that sound better?" Kyle said, pushing again.

I tightened my jaw in frustration.

"Yeah, this will give us more time," Elly added, stepping closer to me.

"It will give *you guys* more time, sure," I snapped.

Instantly, I wanted to pull the words back into my mouth. The wounded look on my baby sister's face hurt worse than any tumor ever could.

My dad squeezed my shoulder lightly. "Tessa."

"I'm sorry. I don't know if I want more time. Do you remember the last six weeks? Because I do. Hell, I remember every torturous second of it." I shuddered. "If this is all I get, do I want to spend my final days like that?"

I closed my eyes at the truths I couldn't hold back. My head hanging, I didn't look at any of them. I couldn't see the pain I'd caused on their faces. My heart heavy and pounding in my chest, I realized exactly what I'd said. *My final days.*

I'd never said it before. Not aloud.

I'm dying.

"This is actually a very common response," the doctor

said, speaking to my family first then turning to me. "It's completely understandable to want to spend your final days feeling as normal as possible, Tessa."

There were those words again.

"We can arrange for hospice care and manage your symptoms with palliative care to make everything as pain-free as possible," he continued.

My brows furrowed. "What pain? I mean, if I'm not doing further treatments, what will happen to me?"

Everyone looked at Dr. Burton.

"As the tumor grows, your headaches will worsen. You'll likely have seizures, increasing in intensity." Dr. Burton looked straight at me as he spoke, never faltering. "Eventually, you will lose your eyesight. You will suffer numbing, and then paralysis, throughout your limbs first, then your whole body. As that happens, you will lose independent functioning. Your internal organs will start to shut down. After that, it will happen fairly quickly."

"I'll die," I finished his thought for him.

He nodded.

I swallowed hard. "I'll be trapped in my own body, and then I'll die."

"I'm very sorry, Mrs. Falls," Dr. Burton said, his shoulders dropping slightly.

Kyle's hand tightened around mine. I wished the doctor would just say *yes, you're going to die trapped in your body, like a human coffin*. But as I stared at him and saw the sadness on his face, I realized maybe an apology was all he could say. No one was entirely comfortable around death, not even doctors.

"Does that have to happen? I mean, that's just..." Elly's tiny voice trailed off.

I glanced at her. White as a ghost.

"Unfortunately, that is the progression with this type of brain tumor." Dr. Burton frowned. "There isn't any way to avoid it without taking things into your own hands."

I jolted, as if something had bitten me. "Suicide? I'm not going to kill myself."

"Of course not, Mrs. Falls," Dr. Burton replied, his expression regretful. "I'm sorry, I didn't mean to imply anything. It's not even considered suicide, despite the moniker 'physician assisted suicide,' so I can assure you there is no judgment. I shouldn't have even mentioned it."

"I'm not going to kill myself," I repeated with a little less ferocity this time.

"We want Tessa with us as long as possible," Kyle added.

No matter what was implied in Kyle's words, but I bit my tongue. The *what* mattered to me. It mattered a lot, and I wasn't sure Kyle would ever be okay with that.

My dad's face was shadowed in doubt when I turned to look at him. It mimicked what I felt, and a wave of relief poured over me that maybe I wasn't alone. Maybe he understood.

"We'll get you the paperwork. Look it over. Do some research. Take your time deciding," Dr. Burton said, reaching out to shake my hand. He and Sheila then left us alone in the examining room.

"How about I get the paperwork and you guys head to the car?" my dad asked, eyeing me with worry.

"I'll go with you, Dad," Elly said.

I shot her a small smile.

My family got it. I didn't know how, but they did. They got that I needed a few minutes of quiet. I needed to process this in my own way, and they probably needed to process it away from me, too. They needed to cry and be angry and hate what was happening, but they wouldn't do it in front of me. They would try to protect me from it, and I needed them to.

Alone in the exam room with Kyle, I stood and looked around. Walking to the counter next to the sink, I picked up a jar of tongue depressors and opened the trash can with my foot. Turning over the container, I emptied the unused sticks into the garbage.

"Tessa?" Kyle frowned as I closed the lid and put the empty jar back on the counter. "What are you doing?"

"Throwing away tongue depressors." I held up my hands like it should be obvious.

He laughed. "I can see that, dork, but why?"

"Oh." I looked at the trashcan and shrugged. "Because they're depressing."

Kyle laughed again and wrapped an arm around my shoulders, leading me toward the door. "At least, it wasn't a pen this time."

"There's always next time," I told him, waiting for the brokenness inside me to hit its peak, for the news of *there's nothing we can do* to shatter me entirely, but it wasn't. I wasn't breaking. I *was* hurting. My heart was swollen with how much it ached. But I wasn't shattered.

Somehow, I wasn't breaking.

· ෆ · ෆ · ෆ ·

THURSDAY, May 22, 2014

· · ·

MY EYES ACHED from hours of staring at my computer screen. I squeezed them closed and rubbed my knuckles into the sockets, attempting to see straight. Giving up, I closed my laptop and laid across the bed. Beast hopped up and curled into my side, falling asleep while I stroked his fur and stared at the ceiling.

Doctor #3, #4, and #5 all had said the same thing as Dr. Page and Dr. Burton. The tumor was inoperable. I'm only twenty-eight, but it doesn't matter. The treatments, the tests, the prayers—none of it mattered.

Cancer *will* win. It will kill me. Six months, at best.

Every doctor described slightly varying treatments that could prolong my life. Full brain radiation, chemo, experimental medications. They each told me I had options.

But I didn't really.

I'd spent days researching each one. I'd read every informational packet they'd given me, every research article, every journal. Kyle had had to work this week, and so I'd spent my days home alone with Elly. We watched movies, went on walks with Beast, and gossiped about the old days. Nothing deeper than that—she couldn't handle it. I couldn't handle it. I knew they were waiting for me to decide, to tell them I what option I'd chosen. To tell them I was going to fight, I was going to beat an unbeatable cancer.

I wasn't doing any of that. So, I said nothing.

I made excuses. I pretended to need a nap, when I was actually on my laptop, the faint hope left that something would tell me what the right choice was. I bit my lip and released it, counting the dots on the ceiling tiles above me. I was coming to the same conclusions as the doctors.

I had options, yes, but every result would be the same. I had a Grade 4 Glioblastoma. It was going to kill me. Treatment might give me an extra month or two, maybe more, but nothing would add another year, another lifetime. Everything would be a bandage on a gaping wound, hiding it, but fixing nothing. Each attempt at holding off the inevitable would make me sicker and sicker, miserable and paralyzed until the day I took my last breath.

It would be everything I'd experienced the first six weeks multiplied by thousands. I wouldn't have a chance to do anything on my hypothetical bucket list. I wouldn't even be able to get out of bed. The side effects would start almost immediately, and they'd never go away.

A few months ago, I'd been excitedly celebrating winning a permit to hike in the Half Dome at Yosemite Park, now I was excited to climb a set of stairs without seeing stars. That dream was long dead—even though I begged Kyle to go on it without me. Spoiler alert: he'd refused. Shocker.

My hand stroked Beast while I imagined this fight to the death. I pictured Kyle holding my hand as I lay withered in bed, and Delores wiping the vomit from my chin. Elly's horrified expression as I became unrecognizable. My father's pain while he watched yet another loved one succumb to cancer.

I didn't want this for them.

I didn't want this for me.

I thought of the other option, of doing nothing. I'd still have symptoms—blindness, seizures, paralysis—but I'd have time. I'd have a few extra months to spend with the people I loved. I'd have time to write the book I'd been procrastinating on the last few weeks when my symptoms had prevented me from doing anything but surviving. I would be myself...longer. Even if that wasn't very long at all.

The options seemed ironic. One gave me more time on the planet, but less time as me. The other gave me more time as me, but less time on the planet. And yet, both offered a false claim of time—the one thing I wanted most. Time was intangible, a guess the doctors used to try to measure life, death, and everything in between. They wanted to make sense of something senseless, and I understood that desire, but it was still only a guess. We were all just guessing.

I dropped my hand to the bed beside me. Tightening my muscles, I laid still. Closing my eyes, I took slow, deep breaths and pretended this was it. I was paralyzed and blind. The cancer had come for me, and I was just waiting for death to be next.

The seconds ticked away. I waited, frozen.

Time is nothing without spirit, without the ability to enjoy it. A punishment for some, and a blessing for others. A reflection of the soul, not hands on a clock. I swallowed slowly, wondering if time was really what I wanted, or if I just wanted to enjoy the time I had left.

Opening my eyes, I knew I didn't want blindness. Fluttering my fingers, I didn't want paralysis. I didn't want cancer to have the final say of how I spent my last moments. I didn't want poison poured into my body in hope of a few more miserable months.

Cancer didn't get to be in charge. Maybe this was why I didn't feel entirely broken. Maybe this was why I felt a sliver of inexplicable power in the face of it all.

I didn't want more time. I wanted a choice.

And I knew the choice I wanted to make.

CHAPTER FOURTEEN

FRIDAY, May 23, 2014

"HOW ARE YOU DOING TODAY, TESSA?" Dr. Page asked, entering the exam room with an oversized clipboard and a nurse on his heels.

I stared at him. "I've had better days. You know, like before I found out I was dying."

Today's motto is fuck it and fuck you. And I'm not even sorry.

"Oh, of course." Dr. Page cleared his throat. "Well, hopefully we can reach some decisions today that'll help ease you through this transition."

My brows pushed together, wondering if he moonlights as Charon, ferrying people across the River Styx. Anything short of that side job, he won't be able to ease me through this 'transition.' Death was staring at me from the opposite shore, and there was only one seat open on my ferry ride.

"Tessa, have you made a decision?" Kyle prompted me.

He was standing between my dad and Elly, waiting for

me to say I was going to fight this to the end. I'd go down swinging, battling unseen forces. I'd never let it win; I'd never surrender.

That's what they wanted me to say.

That was what they'd been waiting for me to say for days. It was also why I'd dodged every one of their questions since I made my decision. The truth was I still wasn't certain how I wanted to die. My only certainty was, despite their hopes for a miracle, I *was* dying, and I didn't want to give up what little time I had left fighting for more.

I kept my focus on Dr. Page, a desperate plea in my eyes. He followed my gaze to my family and nodded, understanding. "Would you folks mind giving Tessa and me a moment alone, please?"

"What? Why?" Kyle stammered, nerves dashing across his face.

"Just routine." Dr. Page held open the door and everyone but the nurse shuffled out.

"Call us when you need us, Tessa," my dad said.

I smiled reassuringly at my dad as he pulled Kyle along with him.

I knew Kyle was nervous, and his way to quell those fears was through trying to gather as much information as possible. To be there for every moment. To control what was happening to us. I wanted to grab his hand and tell him death couldn't be controlled, and that was okay. That I was angry about everything, and that was okay, too.

But I said nothing, nodding instead. "Just a couple minutes, guys."

Elly blew me a kiss, following the men out.

The nurse closed the door behind them as Dr. Page sat on a rotating stool and looked at me. "So, we're not doing treatment?" he asked.

I shook my head.

"Let's talk about palliative care, then."

That simple. Relief rushed through me, my shoulders sagging as the air in my lungs pushed out in one loud exhale. There was no argument, no second guessing, no explanation. This was my choice. These were my options.

He gave me a half-hearted smile—mostly pity—and pulled a pamphlet out of the file folder he was holding. I took it from him, leafing through slowly. Muted blues. Clear statistics. Soothing, somber phrases. It read so quiet, resigned. Peaceful.

"I'm going to prescribe some pain medications and anti-seizure medications. At this stage, both will be on an as-needed basis. We'll reevaluate dosage as things progress."

I nodded again.

"Have you thought about hospice care?"

Not happening. "I don't want to die in a hospital," I replied, adamant.

"Hospice isn't usually in a hospital, rather a separate care facility. They strive to feel just like home," he assured me.

I wasn't buying it. "I'd rather be in my own bed, at home, with my dog and my family." There was no chance in hell I was changing my mind on this.

"Understandable. We can arrange for that. In the meantime, you'll have visiting nurses checking your vitals and helping you with your medication. It's more expensive, but hopefully your insurance will cover it." Dr. Page jotted a note on the file.

Biting my lips, I rolled them between my teeth. I released them, took a deep breath, and asked what I was afraid to know. "How long will it take without treatment? What will it be like?"

Dr. Page lifted his head, focusing on me again. His expression was careful, poised, and it dampened my anxieties for a moment. "Over the next few months, you'll develop worsening headaches. You'll fatigue more easily. You may experience seizures within a couple months. Your vision will slowly regress—black spots, blurriness, possible blindness. Once that happens, it won't be long. Eventually, you'll start to lose sensation—numbness—in parts of your body, then your entire body. You'll be paralyzed which will cause your organs to shut down. It won't be long after that— maybe hours."

Dropping my head to my hands, I tried to focus on breathing. In. Out. Filling my lungs. Exhaling out. *Breathe, Tessa.* Lifting my head, I searched the room for something to focus on—something to ground me. A skeleton hung in the corner from a metal pole. I counted each bone, head to toe. It's missing a finger. I pictured it with skin. I pictured it alive.

I pictured it as me. *Was it really that simple?*

Bones. Skin. Here. Gone. In. Out. *What was the point of any of it?*

"What if I don't want to go through any of that? If I don't want to be a prisoner to my own body?" I was sounded desperate, but I didn't care. "Isn't there something I can do?"

Dr. Page shook his head. "I wish I had a better answer for you."

"It's my *life*, doc," I told him. "I need *something*. I can't die like that. It's so..." I shudder, my entire body trembling as I pictured what he'd described. "There has to be a better way, Dr. Page. *Please.*"

He paused and glanced at the nurse standing beside him. Her eyes were brimming with tears. She was trying to be less obvious, nose down leafing through papers in my file. Dr. Page, the Santa-lookalike seemed conflicted, unsure of what to say next. Or better yet, knowing what he wanted to say, but unsure if he should.

"What?" I pushed, wanting to hear it.

Inhaling, Dr. Page explained, "In cases such as these, it's not unheard of to look into death with dignity. It's a very personal decision, one none of us can, or should, make for you. It would also involve a lot of logistics to make happen, which might not be how you want to spend your time left."

I frowned, unsure where I'd heard the phrase before. "Death with dignity?"

"It is sometimes referred to as physician-assisted suicide. It is only available for terminally ill patients who have no chance at recovery. It is only legal in two states, neither of which are Illinois."

"*Suicide?* Are you going to 'Dr. Kevorkian' me? Just kill me here and now?" I balked, baffled as to why two doctors had now mentioned suicide.

Suicide was wrong. It was selfish. I'd been told that all my life. A girl from my very-Catholic high school had killed herself during my freshman year, taken a whole bottle of pills and couldn't be revived. Not once had I heard a single word of sympathy for her. No one discussed how much pain she must have been in to do such a thing, or why she'd made such a drastic choice. No, sympathy was reserved for the innocent people she left behind. She'd hurt them with her sinful actions, and we'd grieved for them—not her. Blame was tossed around as easily as the latest high school rumor, everyone shaking their heads in disapproval at her grave.

I might not be the best Catholic in the world—or even consider myself Catholic at all anymore—but that ideology had been ingrained in me my entire life. The Church's stance on suicide was clear—suicide was an unforgivable mortal sin. It wasn't an option.

So, why did it keep coming up?

"It sounds more gruesome than it is." Dr. Page tilted his head to the side slightly, easing back in his chair. "It is legal in Vermont and Oregon, though it looks like other states, and maybe even federal laws, will consider it soon. Of course, none of that is guaranteed forever. All it takes is one new president to change everything. I hear in 2016 we may even have our first female president. For now, anyone who chooses to go this route needs to move to one of those two states and establish residency. Once they do so, they make an oral request for the medication to a doctor. It's two medications, mostly a very high dosage of barbiturates. The first puts you to sleep, and the second stops your heart."

I blinked, trying to imagine taking pills and knowing in minutes my life would be over.

Dr. Page continued. "Once an oral request is made, the doctor waits fifteen days, then you make a second oral *and* written request in the presence of no less than two witnesses who have no vested interest in the matter. You will need to be psychologically assessed, determined if you're capable, informed, and voluntarily making the decision. If—and that is a *big* if—you pass each of those steps appropriately, you will be prescribed the medication to use at the time of your choosing. Even then, less than half the patients who receive their prescriptions end up actually taking it. Like I said, a very personal choice."

I shook my head, trying to wipe the idea from my mind. I don't even know why I was listening to this—it was *not* an option. "My family would freak. I can't. I can't even consider it."

But I *was* considering it. The very idea...I could be in control. I could choose when cancer stole my life. I could choose. It was the first hint of power I'd felt in months, the first time I'd realized I could have a voice...not only in my life, but also in my death.

It was intoxicating.

"That is perfectly fine. It is completely your choice to make—not mine, not your family's. In fact, that's the only thing I'd encourage you to consider. Don't decide the rest of your life based on what other people will say. Base the decision on what *you* want—it's your life and it's your death. No one else can experience this with you. You will be alone in the end, and you need to be alone in this decision."

His words hit me like a stack of bricks dropped on my head. I bit my tongue and swallowed my nerves, the thought echoing in my head.

You'll be alone in the end.

My mother. She died while my father was at work, and we were with the sitter. Only a nurse or doctor by her side, and even that's just a guess. It was after the September 11th tragedy, and despite my father's protests, national security mattered more than having a dying wife in the hospital. We weren't prepared. No one had expected it so soon. No one had expected a young mother to leave behind two children and a loving husband either.

Everything about death is unexpected...unless it's not.

"I'm doing palliative care. I could never—" I paused and exhaled slowly. "I need to think about everything."

"Of course. I have your prescriptions here. This one is for seizures, which hopefully we won't encounter for a while." He held up one script, then another. "This one is for nausea, which should decrease as the radiation leaves your body. You'll notice you're feeling better soon. You'll gain some weight, feel stronger, even possible hair regrowth. The radiation makes you *feel* sick, so as your body heals, it will become easier. This last one is for pain."

"If it's going to get easier, why do I need these?" I tucked the scripts into my purse anyway.

"The symptom relief will be temporary. As the cancer grows, new symptoms will arise and your health will decline. For now, the nurse will come once a day to check your vitals, but we will eventually need to increase the visits as things progress."

Progress. Ironic. I'd always thought of progress as a good thing.

"Do you have any questions?" he asked.

The nurse in the corner glanced up at me, her eyes red.

"Why?"

It was all I could think to ask.

I'm twenty-eight. I'd done everything *right*. I'd lived a life I'm proud of, but not nearly enough of it. I wanted more. So, my only question...*why?*

"I wish I knew the answer, Tessa. I wish we could predict and prevent diseases before they ever occurred. Maybe science will figure it out one day, but now?" Dr. Page shook his head with a heavy sigh. "We simply don't know. It's unfair. It's tragic. I wish I could do more—I wish I could change this for you. All I can do is suggest talking to your minister, if you're religious. It might help you make sense of everything."

The nurse sniffed and rubbed her cheek against her shoulder.

"I'm going to eat an ice cream sundae with every topping tonight. None of that how-many-points-to-not-be-fat fake ice cream. I'm eating full fat, caramel and hot fudge ribbons with every candy topping," I told them, slowly at first, then hastening as I thought about all the things I wanted to do.

Everything I'd said no to, to be healthy, to add years to the end of my life, to love my body. All the gluten-free shit I'd sworn to friends tasted as good as warm rolls right from the oven, slathered in butter. I'd wanted to feel good, look good, *be good* in a body that had always been meant to betray me.

Fuck. That. Shit.

"And fried Oreos," I added. "I'm going to finally try a fried Oreo."

Dr. Page smiled and the nurse let out a loud burst of laughter.

"Sounds like a great idea, Tessa," he said.

"You both need to have one, too." I pointed at Dr. Page, then at the nurse. "Promise me. Promise me you'll both eat fried Oreos."

"I've never tried them," the nurse admitted.

"Me neither." Dr. Page grinned. "But I promise."

The nurse nodded. "I promise, too."

"Good. Don't wait. I never should have waited," I told them, talking about much more than a fried treat.

CHAPTER FIFTEEN

FRIDAY, May 23, 2014

"HEY, BABY. WHAT ARE YOU DOING?" Kyle found me in our bedroom while I was changing from loose jeans into even looser sweatpants.

Beast was on the bed, but when he saw Kyle, he stretched and trotted from the room.

"I'm going to take a quick nap." I yawned, pulling on a T-shirt. "It's been a long morning."

"Tell me about it." He came up behind me and kissed my neck. He yanked his shirt over his head, then tossed it into the hamper. "I'll take one with you."

He kicked off his shoes and sat on the edge of the bed, watching me. I busied myself pumping lotion into my hand from a bottle on the dresser. Rubbing it in, I tried to ignore how close my bones were to the surface. At least my skin was soft now—the roughness of once being a climber was long gone from my hands. I actually felt feminine for the first time in a long time; ironic since my body had lost most of its curves.

Clearing his throat, I heard him take a deep breath as if he was about to say something. He paused, cleared his throat again. I kept my eyes on my hands until he finally said what was on his mind.

"What did you end up telling the doctor?" he asked, his voice smaller than I'd ever heard it before.

I'd known the question was coming. It's why I'd avoided eye contact and was re-lotioning my hands for the third time.

"Tessa?" he asked again.

I rubbed the final bits of lotion in, exhaling slowly before climbing under the covers. "I got a few prescriptions —pain killers, anti-seizure, nausea. Delores is visiting every day, and when things get worse, there will be around-the-clock care to help me at home."

"Hospice." The word rolled off his tongue as if he were tasting it, testing the flavor. His grimace told me he didn't like it.

"Hospice, but at home," I replied, pulling the covers down enough to watch him climb into bed beside me. "I want to die here, Kyle. With you and my family by my side. Not in a cold, hospital room. I want to go peacefully, comfortably."

He was quiet a minute, turning his body to stare up at the ceiling. "You're not going to fight?" His words pierced through me, his anger seething beneath. It wasn't directed at me, but it gutted me anyway. "You're not going to do anything, Tessa?"

"There's nothing I can do." A whisper this time. "Kyle, I'm dying."

His head shook against the pillowcase. "There's always

something we can do. There are treatment options, Tessa. Radiation, chemo, experimental drugs." His voice heavy with sorrow, his hands rubbing his forehead, tears welling in his eyes. "There's a chance, Tessa."

Frustration pushed at me, bristling my insides, making it harder to control my tone. "A chance for what? A few more months of pain and suffering, of not being able to enjoy our time left together? Is that what you want for me?"

"If it means being with me longer, then yes!" he shouted.

His sudden burst of volume made me jolt against the sheets. Pushing up onto my elbows, I stare at him, mouth open. "You don't mean that."

He climbed out of bed in a flurry of blankets, groaning as he began pacing the room. "Tessa—I—I..."

My heart thumped in my chest, watching emotions play across his face as heavily as guilt sunk in my stomach. I was doing this to him. I could fix everything—take away his pain. I just had to fight for something I didn't want to fight for to do it.

Finally, Kyle paused in front of me. Burdened eyes turned to me, and he took my hand in his. "I don't want you in pain. I just want you *here*. I want you 'til we're old. I want the forever we always talked about."

"Kyle," I said, sniffling and searching his deep green eyes. "I don't have forever. Not anymore. I have here, now. We only have this moment."

He pulled me to him and hugged me against his chest. "My love for you is greater than a moment, Tessa."

"That's all we have," I whispered, loving every inch of this man. "That's all we get, Kyle."

"This is so fucking unfair," he whispered in reply, burying his face in my shoulder.

"Come on." I pulled him farther onto the bed, and we crawled under the covers together.

His arms wrapped my stomach, my back to his chest. At my smaller weight, his arms circled entirely around me and then some. I'd never been particularly heavy, but I'd also never known a thigh gap I hadn't rectified with carbs. I liked that about myself. I flaunted the few curves I had, and I looked damn good in a bikini. Now I was no different from a hanger, as if I only existed to hold up the clothes on my back.

Despite this, I felt like my old self in my husband's arms. The same warmth, the same tightness. Powerful, wanted. I felt desired as a woman when his length reacted to my proximity, pushing against my lower back. This was our normal, our simple.

Cancer had no say.

Our souls married into one, ceasing to exist separately: healthy vs. sick, living vs. dying, man vs. woman. He kissed and caressed me in the most delicate ways. Despite my exhausted body, I wanted him and he wanted me. It was *normal*, and we needed this.

Gentle hands, slowly removing my clothes one piece at a time. I was a porcelain doll beneath his fingertips, and he cared for me with everything he had. It'd been a while since we'd been together, and, despite my frail and bald body, our muscles remembered each other as if they'd never been apart.

His lips stole mine as I shattered against him, consumed by him. I felt him in my core, telling me he loved me with every thrust. When he pulled my hips tighter against his, I felt the outpouring of his affections inside me and I cried.

I cried because this had once been us hoping for a baby.

We'd thought we had forever. We'd thought we'd have a family.

We'd spend the rest of our lives wrapped around each other, teasing each other's bodies, bringing each other to the brink of ecstasy, hold each other as we fell over the edge.

Now he had a forever that would last long after I was gone. Six months, at best.

"Tessa?" Kyle fell against the mattress, pulling our naked bodies together, draping the sheet over us. "Why are you crying?"

I sniffed, pushing away a tear with the pad of my thumb. "I don't know how to sum it up in words. I've missed you. I've missed us just being us. I'm going to miss *us*."

He wiped the tears from my cheeks with his lips. "Don't talk like you're already gone, baby."

"Haven't I?" My heart throbbed against my rib cage, reminding me of all I'd lose. "It feels like it."

"No, you haven't gone anywhere. We still have time. We still have time to be together, to be us. To do all the things we've always wanted to do. Maybe it's good you don't want to do the treatments—we'll be *us* longer."

Kyle spoke slowly, clearly coming around to the idea. He wanted more time. I did, too, but time wasn't everything —even when it meant so much.

"There's not enough time for every single thing," I reminded him.

"Why not? I'll take a leave off work." Kyle ran his fingers down my jaw line. "We'll write a list of everything you've ever wanted to do."

"We can't have a child."

Kyle didn't respond, but I watched his throat bob as he swallowed. He squeezed me a little tighter.

"I'm so sorry, Kyle," I continued, attempting to stifle the threat of tears anew.

"Don't be," he replied. "This isn't your fault."

"I know, but it's still ruining everything. We talked about kids for so long. We were trying, then I lost the pregnancy, and now I'm—"

Kyle put a finger to my lips. "Tessa, stop. We'll drive ourselves crazy thinking that way. It's not in the cards for everyone to be parents. That's just life. We tried. That's what matters."

I blinked back tears. "Can we pretend for a moment?"

"Pretend what?" he asked, tracing the tips of his fingers down the side of my face and neck until he reached my collarbone.

"That we're going to be parents," I whispered, curling closer to him. "That we have forever."

"Are we having a boy or a girl?" he asked. No hesitation. I loved him so much in this moment. He settled onto his back, both of us staring at the ceiling, the blanket pulled to our chins, and our hands linked between us.

"A girl," I answered.

"Do I get a say in naming her?" I could hear the smile in his voice.

The corners of my lips lifted. "Depends, what would you name her?"

"Mildred? We could nickname her Milly."

I laughed. "You don't get a say in naming her."

He squeezed my hand, a low, throaty chuckle.

"What about Elise?" I offered.

"I like Elise," Kyle said. "Elly would, too. Wasn't she named after your mom?"

"Yeah, Elizabeth. I think Elise would be an homage to

her, but still unique." I knew my mother would have approved. "Still her own."

"Elise will have your light brown hair, but my green eyes," he added.

"Definitely your eyes," I agreed. "She is tall like you, too."

Kyle smiled. "And she has your button nose."

"And your meticulousness and organization," I said, teasing.

"Nah." Kyle chuckled. "I think she's artsy and creative, like you. Everything in its place, but all of those places a little off from the rest of the world. She's got your wit. She's known for her ability to make everyone around her laugh."

I grinned. "Just snarky enough to not be called rude, but too snarky to be considered sweet. But she'll be loved."

"She'll be loved." Kyle's voice was quieter now. "She'll be loved more than any one person could ever be, and it's because you'll be her mother."

I didn't say anything. Instead, I squeezed my hand tighter in his, my teeth clenched. My chest throbbed at the thought of her tiny face and little baby fingers and toes. I pictured her in my arms, warm and soft. She called me *Mama*. Kyle had his arms around us both, and he was so obviously head over heels in love with her. He was entirely at her beck and call, and she knew it—she knew she was loved.

Because she was. She is. She would have been so loved.

Without my permission, her image faded away to nothing, my lap cold and empty. She wasn't there. She never was.

We never were.

Kyle angled to his side to face me, draping an arm across

my waist. He nuzzled his nose against my neck, whispering. "You're loved, Tessa."

"All the love?" I repeated our phrase to him, not looking at him.

"Forever and ever."

As he kissed across my collarbone, I realized for the first time how wrong our statement was now, and how much I didn't want that for him. I pushed the painful thought away and wrapped my arms around his neck.

"Forever and ever," I agreed.

"So, have that with me, Tessa. Fight this with me," he whispered, his jaw clenched tightly. "Fight the cancer. Don't give up."

Was he serious? "Kyle—"

"Think of Elise. Think of the three of us together. Think of what we could be." He sounded desperate now, his voice pleading. "Think of me, Tessa. Don't leave *me*."

My heart shattered into a million little pieces. "There's nothing left to fight, Kyle. I'm dying. One way or another... I'm dying."

He let go of me and rolled on to his side, facing away from me. He was quiet for several seconds, a heavy blanket of despair dropping over us. "I don't know if I'll forgive you for doing this, Tessa. I expected you to fight. I expected more."

And my heart broke for him, and for me.

• ɷ • ɷ • ɷ •

SATURDAY, May 24, 2014

. . .

"SO THAT'S IT, THEN." Elly looked at her hands folded in her lap, ignoring the bowl of cereal in front of her, surely soggy by now.

I sighed, wishing for something I could do to ease the tension. "This is going to happen no matter what I do—or don't do."

She nodded, as she had the entire time I explained my decision. "I know. I get it."

I reached out and squeezed her upper arm. "It'll be okay, Elly."

"Of course it won't be okay, Tessa." Her eyes widened. *"You're dying.* Nothing is okay about this."

I bit my lip, saying nothing.

"None of this is okay," she repeated slower this time, standing from the kitchen table. Her cereal sat abandoned as she rushed away. I knew she was trying to hide her tears from me, but I wished she hadn't.

My dad walked in, glancing at Elly's retreating figure then turning to me. "Everything okay?"

I grimaced at the word choice. "Not really."

He scratched his scruffy beard before pulling coffee grounds and a filter from the cupboard to make a fresh pot. "Kyle told me about hospice."

I pinched my brow. "Are you angry, too?"

"Not about hospice," he told me, grabbing a fresh mug. "I'm angry any of this is happening in the first place, but I'd never be angry you're making the right decision for you, sunshine. After everything with your mother, I don't blame you one bit."

"What do you mean?" I pushed off the chair and refilled

my glass of orange juice for another round of medications waiting for me on the table.

"Your mother kept trying treatment after treatment until the very end. That was the right choice for her, because if there was any chance she could stay longer to be with you girls, she'd have taken it." His sad eyes filled with the briefest of hope, then fell to a grimace. "But it came at a cost."

He held the mug in his hands, steam from the coffee billowing into his face, but he wasn't paying attention. "She was in so much pain. The entire last eight months were in a bed, hooked to machines and tubes, unable to care for herself. She lived longer than they predicted, but the way she lived... I wouldn't wish it on my worst enemy. She put on a brave face. I don't think I ever knew the true extent of her pain. Eventually, she was just waiting. She was ready to go, but God let her lay there in pain for so long. I kept begging Him to take her sooner, but she just lay there."

A few memories, bits and pieces, resurfaced as I swallowed my medication. Her face, her eyes shining as she looked at me. The way her fingers curled around my hair, pushing it behind my ear. How soft her lips felt against my cheek when she kissed me goodnight every night even when she couldn't get out of bed. "She was never not smiling. She made everything seem fine—safe."

My dad smiled, his far away gaze back on me now. "She didn't want you girls to be hurt. Everything she did was for her girls. I wish I'd been there more."

"You had to work, Dad."

"When my wife was dying? I could have left the service, or demanded more time off. I could have made her my priority, made you girls my priority. I could have done more." His voice quivered as he spoke through gritted teeth.

Over twenty years ago, yet the guilt was still so prominent in his features that it seemed barely no time had passed at all. "Maybe I was gone on purpose, too afraid to watch her go. I did many tours in my career, but I was too much of a coward to hold my wife's hand when she died."

I shuddered at the thought of the last few days, the idea that I could actually be ready to die, then have to wait, and wait, and wait for a higher power to choose my last breath. My family anguishing by my bedside, counting every rise of my chest. It seemed medieval in its cruelty.

My mother had gone through that, and I couldn't imagine her suffering. I thought of the stories I'd heard of her final days and the little pieces I remembered—her barely-there body wasting away as she wished for death to come and it just...didn't. Only pain and agony for days and days. Until it finally did.

Why did she have to wait like that? Why did she have to suffer?

I definitely didn't want to die. I wasn't ready today. But I know I'd have to be ready, whether I liked it or not, a lot sooner than I'd ever imagined. Pain, seizures, blindness, paralysis. I'd want to die, and yet, I'd have no choice. Not on how soon I'd die, or how long I'd be hovering on the edge of death waiting to tip over.

Ironic, really.

Dr. Burton and Dr. Page's words snuck through my mind, and I wondered if it would be so bad to choose. If it would be so bad to pick the day I'd die, the way I'd die. To take back control of my life, and my death.

"Dad," I began, but he waved me off.

"Tessa, take these next few weeks, or months, or however long, to do something worth doing. Something you've always wanted. I spent too much time avoiding the uncomfortable, the far reaches. Be daring. Be bold. You've nothing left to lose."

My heart swelled at the sincerity of his tone, the depth of his words. "Live in the moment and make a bucket list," I replied, trying to lighten the mood.

"I never liked that term," Dad said, sitting down next to me at the kitchen table. "It's too much pressure."

"Well, whatever it's called, I know what I'd put on it," I told him after swallowing the last of my pills. "First, I'd learn how to make the perfect pancake. Mine are always blob-shaped."

Dad laughed.

"And I'm going to smoke pot," I continued, my dad laughing harder now. "I want to travel to another country, too. Not far, because I'm unsure how sick I'll be. Just one last stamp on my passport—maybe Niagara Falls."

"Niagara is beautiful," Dad agreed. "So, weed and waterfalls. What else?"

"I don't know... hmmm. I'd definitely want to spend every day possible with you, Elly, Kyle—and, of course, Beast." I stared at the sleeping dog under the table, smiling. "I want to finish writing my book. And...and I want to celebrate my twenty-ninth birthday."

"Your birthday is four months away," my dad replied, his voice quiet.

"Yeah, it is." Because I wasn't sure I'd make it either.

CHAPTER SIXTEEN

TUESDAY, *June 17, 2014*

"DELORES?" I glanced at the kind nurse as she pulled a clip from the tip of my finger after measuring my pulse, which had only strengthened in the last month. "Can I tell you something and you won't repeat it to my family?"

"Well, I've never been known for my ability to keep a secret, hun, but I can try."

I shrugged. I was going to tell them eventually; I just wasn't sure how. "I went to see Dr. Page again yesterday."

"Yeah?" Her eyes widened eagerly. "Prognosis changed?"

"Nope. Still dying. Still pissed about it."

Delores exhaled loudly, disappointment flooding her face. "Jeez, hun. You're blunt, I'll give you that."

"Sorry." I grinned, then took a deep breath. "I asked Dr. Page how to...there are pills I can take at the end to..." I paused, unsure of how to finish the sentence.

"End your life?" Delores finished.

Nodding, I watched her face for a reaction, but there was none.

She continued jotting down my vitals in her notebook. "I get it. Before I became a nurse, maybe I wouldn't have. But now? Seeing what I've seen, seeing how the end can be...I get it."

I exhaled so loudly I surprised myself. I hadn't realized I'd been holding my breath.

Delores continued. "In every terminal patient I've had, there comes a day when they're ready. Done everything they wanted, said their goodbyes, and accepted it, but sometimes the body and mind disagree. They're ready to die, but the body is still holding on. That's the worst—watching them suffer and they don't know how long it'll be for."

"That's what I'm most afraid of. If I have to go through this, if it *has* to happen, if I have to die..." A lump formed in my throat at the thought, but I pushed past it. "Then I'd like to have the final choice. The when, the where, the how."

One brow raised, Delores smiled. "Fuck that cancer."

"Exactly. Fuck it." I grinned, leaning back in my chair. "I've spent my entire life doing what others wanted, going with the flow, taking care of other people's needs."

"Nothing wrong with that," Delores added, gesturing to her uniform. "Plenty of people that way."

I loved her for her running commentary on what was most likely a monologue. I was sort of talking at her, rather than to her. Trying to see how it sounded aloud. Speaking for the sole purpose of seeing how the words felt out in the universe.

Sour, dramatic, haunting, and all the other adjectives I'd predicted fell flat. It wasn't horrible; it wasn't even painful. *It was relieving.* I'd spent three hours in Dr. Page's office yesterday discussing it, leaving Kyle oblivious in the waiting room. There was no doubt he could sense a difference when I exited. Thankfully, he didn't push. He just bundled me into the car and drove us home where we spent the rest of the evening binge-watching television shows I'd never had time for before.

We'd barely spoken over the last few weeks. He'd still not come around on the fact that I wasn't fighting the cancer, but he was trying. I could see that he was trying. We'd still cuddle and make love, but the intimacy was strained. The conversation was muted.

I was getting stronger as the radiation left my body, and my hair was growing back. It was slow, and sometimes barely noticeable, but it was a process. The first few weeks, I'd only wanted low-key. I'd wanted to curl up on the couch, go on short walks, and eat delicious food.

Thankfully, my appetite was returning. My throat was healing and the nausea subsiding, so I began to eat more. I wanted to try everything—new restaurants, new cuisines, new flavors—and we did. We went to a new restaurant every day, or Kyle grabbed carry-out which we ate in bed. They'd cut his work hours almost in half for the last month, and, soon, he'd go on leave completely until ...

Until.

Elly had to finish the summer semester, but she'd be back soon. My dad visited every day, usually around lunch, to dote on me. He would have happily stayed all day, but respected the importance of my time alone with my husband. I knew he loved Kyle like a son, and didn't want him to miss time with me like he'd missed with my mother.

"I don't want to be the person who takes care of everyone else anymore," I told her. "I want to take charge of what time I have left. I want to be a little selfish, focus on what's best for me. Period."

Delores nodded like she understood. "Then do it, girl. Do what you need to do. Nobody gonna blame you for doin' you."

"I'm not sure." I thought of how Kyle and Elly had reacted to the news that I wouldn't pursue further treatments. I couldn't imagine they'd find favor with my latest decision either.

Have I decided?

"Well, what'd Dr. Page say?" Delores asked.

"He said I'd have to move to Vermont or Oregon, where it's legal. Said he didn't think I'd want to spend what time I have left packing, unpacking, establishing residency, etc."

Delores frowned. "He's got a point. Moving is a special sort of hell. My boy and me moved into a new apartment when I got this new job, and damn, I thought that was the answer to all my problems. It's big and super nice—all renovated and stuff—but wouldn't you know it, the moment my kid dropped a ball on the ground, it went and rolled into the corner."

I furrowed my brow. "Huh?"

"The whole floor is tilted! I'm living in a crooked apartment! But hey, I got stainless steel appliances and a marble countertop that makes my sister jealous, so you win some, you lose some." Delores shrugged.

I tilted my head back, laughing as I imagined Delores walking around an apartment with a crooked floor. "You're kidding!"

"I wish." Delores waved her arms emphatically. "I won a robot vacuum on the radio last month. Piece of crap can't climb up out of the corner. That corner clean as hell though."

I laughed even harder, almost choking on the intensity of it. "Your calf muscles will get a workout every time you walk to the bedroom," I said, teasing between pants of laughter.

Delores pointed one slim index finger at me. "You kid, but you'll see. I'm gonna have me calf muscles like Serena Williams." She pointed down and flexed her leg, popping out the muscle. "Like *bam!*"

I laughed until I couldn't anymore. She giggled along with me, putting away her equipment and finishing her notes. The conversation lulled as our laughter died down, leaving room for reflection. My thoughts returned to the idea of moving. It did sound awful...but more awful than the alternative?

"It should be legal everywhere, you know?" I finally said, frustration mounting. "I shouldn't have to move. My life is here."

"You right," Delores agreed.

I chewed on the side of my thumbnail. "I guess in the big picture, it wouldn't be all that hard to move. We'd need to rent a place and go to the DMV. We don't have to let go of this place, since Kyle will need to live here after."

"Don't you like Chicago?" Delores asked. "It could be hard to be away from home."

"I've been here my entire life," I replied, considering for the first time how little I'd ventured in my life. "I love it, but I think I'd also love to live somewhere new, even if only a few months. Vermont sounds so beautiful..."

"Ooh, and you're a writer, too. Creative types is all they allow up there, I hear." Delores pointed to the journal in front of me on the table, open to scrawled pages.

I'd written so much in the last few months that it actually seemed I might cross this particular goal off my list. I didn't know what the purpose was exactly, or what I'd wanted people to know, to walk along this journey with me.

I just wanted them to remember me—to know I'd mattered once.

"New England *is* the perfect place for a writer," I agreed with Delores.

She finished filling a syringe and then connected it to the PICC line on my arm. I watched her plunge down on the top, the pain-relieving liquid pressing into my veins seamlessly. As much as I hated how the permanent IV device looked on my arm, I loved not being pierced every day.

Delores dropped the syringe into a red box for biohazardous materials. "So, you really going to do this?"

"I think so," I admitted, though no one else even knew.

She smiled and patted my shoulder. "I'll miss you, girl."

I placed my hand on hers. "Thank you, Delores."

"Oh, I haven't done anything, hun." She shrugged, a sweet smile on her lips.

"Yes, you have," I assured her.

She was the one person who let me take care of myself, instead of taking care of her. I could talk to her about what was happening without having to console her. I loved my family, but I walked on eggshells around them. I tailored my words to make it easier on them, knowing this would be one of the worst things they'll ever go through and it was my fault.

Delores, on the other hand, saw this all the time. She cared, probably more than any nurse I've ever met, but she didn't need to be cared *for*. She was stronger than most and maybe she had to be with this type of job. People needed to know there are others in this world who innately give, and never feel the need to take. That kindness exists even in the most difficult of places, and the most difficult of circumstances.

Delores was, and always would be, one of those people —her and her Serena Williams calves.

•ဢ•ဢ•ဢ•

WEDNESDAY, June 18, 2014

"I'M LOOKING FOR FATHER JACK?" My voice was slightly hesitant as I spoke to the middle-aged woman seated at the front desk of the church office.

"He's doing confessions in the chapel right now. You're welcome to wait here, or go to confession," she informed me.

Thanking her, I quickly retraced my steps out of the office and around to the front of the large cathedral where my family usually came on major holidays. Despite our lack of attendance, everyone still tried to attend a few times a year. I guess it was because of laziness that we hadn't kept up with going, because I enjoyed church when I did.

The main chapel was large and shaped like a cross with the altar at the farthest point from the main doors. Confessionals were to the right, behind large columns almost hiding them from view. Being mid-afternoon and mid-week, the auditorium was nearly empty.

One woman was kneeling in the front row, her hands together in prayer. A few church officials bustled around the altar, leaning over a large book. A few more attendees were scattered in pews, either with heads bowed or staring at the large crucifix over the front podium. Whispered chants and praises filtered through the air, the mood heavy and serious.

Nervously, I wondered what I was doing there—looking to the church for permission for something I'd mostly decided already. I certainly had never claimed to be a good Catholic, and I tended to find strict rules oppressive. I never understood what waits for us on the other side, but now that I'm a few months away from it, I felt like I had to find out. I needed to know what's next...if there's anything at all.

And it kind of seemed like the thing to do—go to church on Christmas, Easter, and when you're dying. Like every other mediocre Catholic.

Movement to the right startled me, a tall woman with red-rimmed eyes exiting the confessional. Taking this as my opportunity, I quickly replaced her in the booth.

"Forgive me, Father, for I have sinned. It's been...um, well, I guess it's been years since my last confession," I admitted. The last time I'd gone was once in college, and I wished I felt guiltier about that.

I don't know why I hadn't been back because I remembered it had been a moving experience. I'd talked about my regrets partially hooking up with half the lacrosse team and earning the nickname Teasing Tessa for the first half of my freshman year of college. I'd gone a little wild with the freedom of being at university, and I didn't like a lot of the choices that I'd made with alcohol or boys. Thankfully, that chapter of my life didn't last very long and I quickly found solace in running and hiking, building solid friendships through that instead of partying.

"Years?" I heard the priest's voice through the decorative grated panel between us. I was kneeling in front of it and could see his shadow, but nothing more. "That's quite some time. What brings you in today, dear child?"

"I have a few questions. I, um..." I paused, unsure of how to blurt out my diagnosis.

"Anything you say here is between you and God. Feel free to speak freely."

I nodded, feeling a little less nervous. God already had the run-down of my situation. "To be honest, I didn't come to confess. I'm hoping you can tell me what will happen to me when I die. How do I know I'm...right with God?"

He paused for a moment then cleared his throat. "Are you dying, dear child?"

I stared down at my clasped hands clutched furiously. "Yes. I have terminal cancer."

He sighed, long and forlorn. "This is truly difficult. I am so sorry you are going through such a tragedy. I'll certainly be praying for you."

"Thank you, Father."

"To answer your question, at the moment of death, our souls separate from our physical bodies. There will be no more pain or suffering, only Christ our Lord. According to teachings, all souls will be judged for eternal life in Heaven or the damnation of Hell. Those of us who aren't saints, meaning the majority of us—including me—will find ourselves somewhere in between."

"What's that mean—*in between?*" I asked. It sounded terrifying.

"A temporary punishment for souls to purge the sins limiting our ability to fully envision and enjoy God in Heaven. It is truly a blessing, since it means you *will* be going to Heaven. We just need to clean up a bit first. When you asked if there is a way to know if you are right with God, I think that is your answer. Before death, after death, all we are ever doing is trying to get right with God. We will always fall short, and He knows this."

I sat back on my heels for a minute, pondering his words. It didn't sound as frightening as I'd envisioned. More of a next step than a last. "What's it like?"

"I couldn't say, dear child. I could only guess as well as you. I do know the Lord tells us not to be afraid," Father Jack replied. "Does death frighten you?"

"No, not particularly. Everything leading up to it, though. That scares me," I said honestly. "Pain, paralysis, seizures...why? I'm already dying, isn't that enough?"

"God allows hardships in our lives for a reason, but it's not always easy to know what those reasons are."

Tears pricked my eyes. I looked at the ceiling of the confessional, hoping to blink them away. *This isn't fair. It's too much...too soon.*

"I get a sense there is more on your mind," Father Jack continued.

I peered through the decorative slats between us, squinting to see his face, but it was dark and shadowy. Deciding not to hold back, I cleared my throat. "Is it true anyone who..." I tried to find the words somewhere in my jumbled-up brain. My cheeks flamed hot, a nervous churning in the pit of my stomach.

"Go on, dear child," he prodded.

"Is it true anyone who, um, ends their own life..." I closed my eyes. "Is it true they automatically go to hell?"

There was an audible sadness in his exhale. I'd heard it before, an image of my dad's pained face flashing before me, reminding me of how many people would be affected by this.

When he finally spoke, I was surprised not to detect judgment in his voice, only kindness and empathy. "Are you considering suicide?"

"Not suicide. Not today, but..." I babbled, trailing off.

"But once your symptoms progress and the end is near?" he finished for me.

I nodded, then remembered he couldn't see me. "Yes. If I go to Vermont, doctors can give me a medication to help me. Then, in a few months..." I trailed off again.

A silence passed, unnerving me. I waited as calmly as I could, my knees on the kneeling board and my hands clasped together.

A softly mumbled *amen* broke the quiet. Father Jack continued. "Are you baptized?"

"I am." As an infant, according to my dad, though I couldn't remember it.

He made a low humming sound before he spoke. "Well, the Catholic Church's position remains steadfast. The killing of any human being, whether at your own hands, or someone else's—and no matter the reason—is a mortal sin."

"I'd go to hell," I surmised. Mortal sins don't just weaken, but sever entirely one's link to God, condemning their soul to hell for eternity.

Father Jack didn't say anything for a moment, and I wondered if he was trying to find a nice way to tell me I was a doomed hellion.

"Maybe, but I am not sure that is always the case."

I frowned. "But you just said—"

"Officially, the Church has a clear stance," he cut me off. "It is a mortal sin, and I urge you to consider every option carefully. There are *always* other options."

I sighed, feeling both confused, and already a sinner.

"However," Father Jack continued, leaning toward the divider between us and lowering his voice. "Personally, I am of a slightly different mind. I believe God knows our hearts and minds before—and during—a decision such as that and *that* is what we are judged on. God does not blindly condemn us. He looks at our hearts, our motivations." He paused again.

I could practically hear him considering his words carefully, and I leaned forward, desperate to hear what he had to say.

"There is always time to repent, even after death," he finally said. "But more importantly, God loves us, and He does not want us to suffer."

The lump in my throat swelled. I closed my eyes, saying a silent prayer. Asking a million questions and begging for one answer—why? Why me, and why at only twenty-eight years old? Why couldn't I have my happily-ever-after with Kyle and our future family?

Why, God...why?

Sniffing back tears, I tried to get out my final question, cracked and broken. "If He doesn't want suffering, why is He letting me suffer now?"

Father Jack sighed again. I could feel his anguish mixing with my own. "I wish I knew, dear child. I wish I knew. All I do know is whatever you decide, He loves you. That will not change."

He loves me. That will not change.

I thanked Father Jack and left the confessional booth with a stack of reading materials and verses from him. Returning to my car, I sat in the driver's seat and put the key in the ignition. I went to turn it but couldn't bring myself to actually make the move. Instead, I just sat there, staring at the steering wheel and letting tears cascade down my cheeks.

Opening the piece of folded paper Father Jack had given me, I turned to the first verse in the Bible that he had scrawled out that he wanted me to read. I opened the Bible app on my phone that was mostly there for decorative purposes—I admittedly didn't read it nearly enough—and looked it up.

For I am sure that neither death nor life, nor angels nor rulers, nor things present nor things to come, nor powers, nor height nor depth, nor anything else in all creation, will be able to separate us from the love of God in Christ Jesus our Lord. [Romans 8:38-39]

Something clicked in my heart and the tears poured even harder than before. He loves me. That will not change. The Bible tells me so. It's written right there in black and white.

He loves me. That will not change.

I knew without a doubt what I wanted to do now.

I was just so damn terrified to do it.

CHAPTER SEVENTEEN

WEDNESDAY, June 18, 2014

BEAST WAS the only one in the house when I returned home from my "confession" with Father Jack. He greeted me at the door, tail wagging, and rolled onto his back, presenting me with his belly to scratch. Too exhausted to bend, I rubbed him with my foot for a minute before heading into the kitchen.

My stomach growled slightly, but my throat felt sore from crying so much earlier. After I'd left church, I'd sobbed in my car for what felt like hours. There was sadness, there was frustration, but the majority of my tears were relief.

I had made my decision.

I would die, and there's nothing I could do about the end result, but how I got there *was* in my control. The idea of being a slave to my own body, unable to move or breathe on my own, was terrifying. Losing the ability to see my loved ones, gripping seizures...I could choose differently.

I could choose when I would die, and who would be

there. I didn't have to go out alone like my mother, her husband at work and her children with the sitter. I could squeeze their hands and say goodbye, and, for me, that's the right decision.

Dreading this choice, I'd thought it would feel like giving up, but it didn't. It felt like taking charge. It didn't *feel* like a sin. It felt powerful, calming, and even healing.

"Hungry, sunshine?"

I startled, turning toward the kitchen entrance to see my dad with a white paper bag, smiling at me. "Hey, Dad. I didn't hear you come in."

"Lost in thought, huh? Come on, sit down. I got us some broccoli and cheddar soup from the deli on the corner."

"Sounds perfect." He dished out two servings into glass bowls and placed them both on the table, then joined me. The aroma made my stomach growl eagerly. "Thank you, Dad."

He waved his hand like it was no big deal. "Don't worry about it. So, what'd you do today?"

I swallowed my first bite, relishing the creamy taste. "I went to church."

He paused, a spoonful of soup midway to his mouth. "Church?"

I smiled, understanding his surprise. "Yep, church. I came to a decision. I've been thinking about it for a few weeks, but I know for sure now. It's what I want to do."

"You know I'll support you in anything, sunshine," he assured me, placing his hand on my forearm before returning to his soup.

Taking a deep breath, I steadied and looked him in the eyes. "I want to move to Vermont."

"What?" His brows lifted almost to his hairline as his

spoon paused mid-air again. "Tessa, why on earth would you want to move *now*? And Vermont?"

"Vermont is the closest state to us with the Death with Dignity act. A doctor will prescribe me medication to help me..." I paused, still unsure of how to phrase it. "I want medication to help me die."

Dad's spoon fell to the table with a clatter, droplets of creamy soup splattering against the table top. "*What the fuck?*"

I dropped my hands to my lap, fidgeting and looking down at my soup, steam still billowing. His response unarmed me, my nerve gone.

My dad stood and walked over to the counter, grabbing paper towels and returning to wipe up his mess. "Sorry, Tessy. Caught me a little off guard with that, but I'm digesting it. I'm...I'm digesting it." He sat down after the table was cleaned, and rested his chin on his hands. "So, you have to move to Vermont for this? Nothing closer?"

I shook my head. "It's not allowed everywhere—only in three states."

"That seems odd. Politics for you, huh? Always trying to tell us what to do with our own bodies." He returned to eating his soup with a shrug. "Bunch of criminals, if you ask me."

"You're not mad?" I asked, surprised by the quick shift from shock to lunch.

"I'm far too old to be taking politics personally anymore, sunshine."

"Not that. I meant, my decision. About the medication...about dying."

His hand squeezed my forearm again. "Tessy, a few months ago, all I wanted was for you to have the family of your dreams. A month ago, all I wanted was for that tumor to shrink. But today? All I want is for you to live the rest of your days without pain and with as much happiness as possible. When life says you can't have your dreams, you don't give up, you just pick a different dream."

My chest swelled with pride at being his daughter. Kind blue eyes smiled back at me. There was pain in his expression—an overwhelming amount of pain—but something else was there, too, and so much stronger. He loved me enough to let me make the right decision for me.

"Thank you, Daddy," I said, my voice small and childlike.

"Nothing to thank, baby girl." He fidgeted with a napkin for a moment. "Can I ask you one question, though?"

"Of course."

"If you do move and get the medication..." he glanced at the floor as he trailed off, then he took a deep breath and raised his eyes, not quite meeting mine. "If you do this, when is it going to happen?"

"I don't know," I told him, honestly. "Not soon. I'll wait as long as I can. A few months, maybe?"

He nodded thoughtfully, still not meeting my gaze. "I don't like this, but I'll support anything you want, sunshine."

I sniffed back tears and stared down at my soup. "Thanks, Dad."

"Like I said, nothing to thank. Plus, I'm not the one you need to convince. Kyle's not going to like this, and don't get me started on your sister."

Kyle walked into the kitchen and dropped a few grocery bags on the counter, catching the tail end of my dad's rant. "What am I not going to like?"

Standing, my dad picked up his bowl. "I'm going to go eat out on the porch."

I frowned. Elly would definitely hate it, mainly because she hated the idea of me dying. To her, this would be me stealing more time from her. She'd struggle to understand I don't want her last memories to be of me unconscious in a hospital bed. But Kyle? I had no idea how he'd react. We'd already barely been talking because of my decision to stop treatment. Now I wanted to end my life.

Honestly, I might be ending my marriage.

"Okay, I'm getting nervous now." Kyle frowned and looked between me at the table and my dad's retreating figure. "What's going on, Tessa?"

I told him everything.

He sat staring at me intently as I explained everything; the move, the medication, the priest, the doctor, every last ounce of thought I'd put into making this decision. I laid it all out for him and begged him to understand.

Kyle's green eyes stared back at me, incredulously. He shook his head slowly, as if he couldn't believe what he had heard. Then in an abrupt move, he stood up from the table and slapped his palm against its surface.

I jumped in reaction. It wasn't frightening, but it was loud.

"Not a chance," he said firmly between gritted teeth. "This isn't a game, Tessa. This is your life. No, it's *our* life. You can't just make such a rash decision like this when it affects so many other people."

"It's not rash—" I began.

He shook his head again, cutting me off. "Tessa, you can't be serious."

"I've spent the last month thinking about it, Kyle. I've prayed about it, talked to multiple doctors, and researched the hell out of it." I kept my eyes locked on his. "I've decided."

Guilt swarmed in my gut and I felt like the world's biggest bitch. Doubt crept through me and I swallowed hard, trying to remind myself why I'd made this decision in the first place. It was *for* them. So they wouldn't see me suffer. So they wouldn't stand by my side for hours, days, weeks, months watching me waste away into nothing. I didn't want that for them as much as I didn't want that for me.

Kyle stepped away from me, turning to face the counter. His palms on the granite, his chin against his chest, his shoulders trembling as a sob left his throat. "You can't kill yourself, Tessa." His face hidden, his voice strangled. "You can't."

"I'm already dying." My voice dropped to a whisper. I wrapped my arms around my own waist in a much-needed hug. "It's already happening."

He shook his head and turned for the door.

"Where are you going?" I asked, wanting to reach for him but frozen in place.

He paused in the doorway and ran the palms of his hands across his face and over the top of his head.

"We need to talk, Kyle." I stood to follow him, my limbs feeling weak. The fight already leaving me.

His hand on the doorknob, he looked back at me, but his eyes never actually met mine. "I can't even look at you right now, Tessa."

With that, he left.

CHAPTER EIGHTEEN

*W*EDNESDAY, *June 18, 2014*

"I GET IT, Tessa. You want to take control of what's happening." Elly sighed into the other end of the phone, sniffling intermittently. "But have you tried *everything*?"

She emphasized the last word so strongly, I felt her desperation through the phone.

"You heard the doctors, Elly." I looked at my feet where Beast had curled on the end of the bed, covering my toes. Kyle's spot was empty. I wasn't sure I'd be able to fall asleep without him there. "There's no miracle coming."

"Don't say that. You don't know," Elly immediately interjected. She was so young—bad things don't happen to good people, and death can be defeated. "There could be new breakthroughs in oncology, and if you took those pills, you'd miss it."

"Elly," I started, the most confident tone I could muster. "I'm okay with what's happening." That wasn't entirely true. "Or at least, I will be. I'm trying to be. Death comes for everybody at some point."

"You're twenty-eight," she reminded me. "You're supposed to have another sixty years. I'm supposed to have another sixty years with my sister."

"I know, baby girl," I said, sighing. "I wanted that, too. At least this way I have time to enjoy the end, say my good-byes? That's certainly better than being hit by a bus and it all being over in an instant."

She groaned. "If those are my only two options, that's pretty shitty."

I chuckled, pulling my sweater tighter around me.

"Let's talk about something else. This is just... it's too early," Elly said. "Is Kyle home yet?"

I looked toward my bedroom door, as if he'd burst through. Fiddling with the edge of the blankets, I swallowed the lump in my throat and shook my head. "Not yet. He's not answering his phone either. I have no idea where he is, or when he's coming home."

"I'm sure he's on his way. He probably needed a walk to clear his head."

"An eight-hour walk? I'm sure." Sarcasm dripped from my lips. I was angry. I was really fucking angry he'd made this all about him when I was the one going through the worst of it. Hell, he'd made the last few weeks about him with his stony silence. I wanted to be understanding because I knew this was hard for everyone, but I was angry. And, damn it, I had a right to be.

"You okay?" Elly asked after a moment of silence passed between us.

"I'm a little ticked off, honestly. I'm not trying to be selfish, but I needed his support, or at least his under-standing, or willingness, to talk it through with me," I confessed. "For him to up and disappear for hours without telling me where he's going, or if he's coming back... it's mean."

"I don't think he's trying to be mean..." Elly started. I recognized the tone she gets when she's about to launch into a lecture, which I always found funny coming from my little sister. "There's no manual on how to behave when you get news like this. He married you expecting more than half a century together, and he barely got a few years. Then you tell us you want to die even earlier than you would have. I'd be angry if I were him. Hell, I *am* angry and I'm not him. This isn't fair. None of it is."

I let a beat of silence pass before I answered. I know she's right, because I felt the same way they did. I wanted half a century with my husband, a lifetime with my sister. I wanted all of that, but I didn't have a choice. And in the midst of it all, they got to point their frustrations at me, when I've nowhere to point mine. Cancer was the enemy, and, yet, I seemed to be the only one to remember. "You're right, Elly. I'm sure he'll be home soon."

"Definitely. Don't wait up for him though, it's already pretty late. You need sleep."

"I won't. Not sure I could, even if I wanted to. My energy level is not what it used to be."

There was a heavy pause from her. "I was going to say feel better, but..."

"You can still say it," I assured her. "Just because I'm *not* getting better doesn't mean I don't want to feel it."

"Okay. Feel better, Tessa."

"Thanks, baby girl."

We said our good nights and then hung up the phone. Reaching down, I lifted Beast and brought him to my chest. Pressing my face into his soft fur, I cuddled him. He squirmed and fought me, pulling away and burrowing his way under the blankets.

Sighing, I turned off the bedside lamp. Grabbing my pillbox and glass off the nightstand, I dumped tonight's medication into my hand and swallowed them with a gulp of water. I'd become a pro at it now. Months ago, I'd barely taken multivitamins because swallowing seemed impossible. I panicked and gagged up the soggy pills every time. Now, I took a handful at once without a second thought.

Tucking myself into the blankets and hugging my pillow, I closed my eyes and willed sleep to come. Every part of me was exhausted, craving the relief sleep could provide. But my body resisted. I lay there for minutes, or hours—I couldn't be sure after a while. My mind circled everything from the past few months, how much my life had changed, how much it still would.

Until my diagnosis, I'd never talked much about death. My mother had died, but it wasn't a topic we brought up often as a family. It hurt my dad too much to mention her, so Elly and I avoided the topic. Soon it was like she'd never existed. The few memories I have of her are fuzzy and warm, but so far away, as if I have to wade through my mind to find them.

I wonder if that will happen to me.

If in ten years, I'll be a faded memory in Kyle's mind. Just a woman he once kissed, once loved, once married. If I'll be the sister Elly once trusted, once adored, once looked up to. The reality was they would live longer without me than they ever did with me.

Fear gripped me—not at the thought of dying, but of being forgotten.

Maybe that's why I wanted to write this book. Maybe

it's why I wanted to leave something behind to remind people I was here, I mattered...once.

A creaking sound from behind startled me as a sliver of light fell across my arm. "Are you still awake?" Kyle's voice was husky and low; the way it always was when he'd been drinking.

"Yeah," I whispered, not turning to look at him.

I didn't know what I was feeling—angry, hurt, embarrassed. It just felt safer not to make eye contact. I felt exposed and vulnerable, and that's not usually who I was, or who I wanted to be, even in the little time I had left.

The bed shifted behind me and a breeze hit my shoulders as the cover lifted enough for him to crawl under. The smell of whiskey tickled my nose when he pressed his body against my back, his arm around my waist. A wave of nausea rolled through me, but I pushed it down. My sense of smell had become so sensitive during treatment that anything strong left me feeling sick.

Kyle didn't say anything at first, and for a moment, I wondered if he'd fallen asleep. Finally, he sighed deeply, his breath hitting the top of my fuzzy scalp. "I'm sorry, Tessa."

"Never be sorry for what you feel," I replied, not really meaning it.

"Well, I *am* sorry for how I reacted, and for the things I said. For how I've been acting the last few weeks. I was cruel, and no matter how I feel, there's no excuse for that." His words were ever so slightly slurred, but the anguish in his tone was unmistakable.

I let his words hang in the air for a moment, savoring them, rolling them over in my hands as I debated what to do with them. They were heavy and sharp, pointed on my skin and burning in their sincerity. His sincerity was transparent and I ached to let go of the anger I'd been harboring against him.

Finally, I pushed back on the bed, pressing farther into his chest. "I forgive you."

And, truthfully, I did. It was just a decision I made as simple as that. His words had hurt, but I understood he was in pain, and hearing the sorrow in his voice melted my anger. With so little time left, forgiveness was easier to find.

"I hate this, Tessa," he whispered against my neck, sending shivers across my skin. "I hate that I'm going to lose you."

I ignored the heaviness pressing down on my chest and wrapped my hand around his. Bringing it to my lips, I kissed his knuckles, then pressed the back of his hand to my cheek. "I hate it, too."

"Tell me again. Tell me what it is you want to do. I want to understand."

A weak smile played on my lips. "Are you sure?"

"As sure as anyone can be when their wife dying." His words weren't bitter, only sad—so sad they fell from his lips, weighted with agony.

"I want to choose when the end is, Kyle. Before things get too bad, before I go blind, before I'm paralyzed. I want to pick the date and time and go peacefully, while I still feel like myself."

"How will you know when?"

I shrugged. "Right now, I haven't a clue. But I think when the time is right, I will."

He clutched me a little tighter. "What do we need to do?"

"I'd like to move to one of the states it's legal in, like Vermont. Then find a doctor and go through the process of getting the medication. We'd still keep this house, since you'd probably return after I'm gone. I think I'd enjoy living in a new place for a bit. I grew up in Chicago. I've never branched out."

"We've always talked about it," he confirmed, drawing circles with his thumb on my palm.

"It would be nice to have one last new experience," I whispered.

His body tensed behind me. "We should probably move soon then, maybe this week? Better to get a head start and get the medication since we don't know when you'll need it."

I nodded. "Yes."

A few minutes of silence passed before Kyle spoke again. "I'm going to miss you, Tessa."

I rolled over to face him. His arms circled me, holding me close. I placed my hands on his chest, my legs wrapped around his, and I looked at him for the first time tonight thanks to the moonlight streaming through the window behind me.

His eyes were shallow with dark circles underneath, his lips turned down in a frown that seemed permanent. His clean-shaven jaw from this morning was now prickly, and his hair was mussed in every direction.

"I'm not going anywhere, Kyle. Not really." I put my palm flat on his chest over his heart. "I'll always be *here* with you, loving you. You'll have all my love for the rest of my life and beyond."

He kissed my forehead. "I wish the rest of your life matched the rest of mine."

I frowned. "Me, too."

"This changes nothing, Tessa. I promised you all my love, and you'll have it. Forever."

I searched his eyes, wondering if that was what I

wanted. If I really wanted this man to hold on to me so tight, he'd never have room for anyone else. I wasn't sure it was, but it didn't feel right to talk about it tonight. Today had been hard for both of us. He needed time to adjust to what was happening as much as I did.

I pressed forward and placed my lips to his, gently at first, then with fervor. He pulled me closer, propping himself up on an elbow and leaning over me. I lifted my arms to wrap around his neck and clung to him as if it were possible to never let go. Our tongues met, and he tasted like whiskey, but I didn't mind it this time.

I needed him. I needed to know every part of him and I were connected, that we understood what was happening, what we were losing. That we owned each other in a way no one else ever could.

His fingers hooked my pants and underwear, sliding them down my legs. I gripped the bottom hem of my shirt and pulled it over my head, then grabbed his and did the same. He kicked off his pants and boxers, climbing on top of me and pressing his warm skin to mine. Random aches and pains shot through me, but I pushed their power away, demanding to have this one normal moment.

He held the bulk of his weight on his hands. I was still too frail to handle much, but we kissed, and we kissed hard. We kissed as if it might be our last, because neither of us really knew if it was. His hands slid across my breasts, his touch sending lightning through my veins, and it warmed me to know I could still feel like that. I could still feel something other than constant pain.

I was dying, but every part of me came to life beneath him.

His hands moved farther south and he touched me in that way he knew I loved, because this was us, and we knew each other inside and out. He manipulated my body until I was panting and arching against him, begging for him. Obliging my request, he centered his hips over mine and pressed inside slowly, carefully. I moaned at the welcome intrusion and gripped his shoulders.

He showered soft kisses from my forehead, down to my cheek, my jaw, my neck, before finding my lips again. "Tessa, look at me," he urged.

I realized my eyes were closed. When I opened them, I saw his eyes glistening. "What's wrong?"

He shook his head, still pressed inside me. "I don't know how to be okay with not having *this* forever—having you."

My fingers caressed both sides of his face. "Some love is strong enough to live a lifetime in only a few years."

"I wanted forever anyway," he replied.

"Me, too." I held his face in my hands and kissed him deeply, pressing my hips against his to urge him to continue. I told him I loved him with everything I had, and he gave me all he was. It was slow and sensual, sad and sweet. It was every feeling we had been holding, saving, waiting, wanting.

It was a joyful embrace and a tender goodbye.

CHAPTER NINETEEN

Sunday, June 22, 2014

"MAYBE I SHOULD HAVE HAD a goodbye party or something. It feels weird—just up and leaving, and never coming back," I told Kyle while placing clothes in a large suitcase on our bed.

Kyle shrugged. "Let's have one then. We can delay the trip a few more days so you can say your goodbyes."

I frowned. "Is it bad if I say no? I don't feel ready for goodbye yet, you know?"

"Tessa, you can do whatever you want. This is your time."

I consider his words. "I just don't feel like I'm... *gone* yet. I still feel like me."

"So, we'll wait." He smiled, a slight uneasiness under his expression. "There's no rush."

That wasn't true. Everything felt rushed to me. There's a timer on everything I do now, and not enough time to do it all.

I didn't want to say goodbye yet, but once I moved, it *would* be too late. All my family and friends were here, not in Vermont. Luckily, the people more important to me—Kyle, my dad, and Elly—were coming with me. Beast, too, of course.

My dad walked into the bedroom holding an envelope up. "Tessa, I printed your confirmation info, but you'll need to get your boarding passes at the airport."

"Thanks, Dad." I took it and tucked it into my purse. Returning to packing, I opened my nightstand and transferred my medications and vitamins to my suitcase. No small feat since there were so many.

"Are you and Elly going to be ready soon, sir?" Kyle asked my dad.

"Yep, boxes are already good to go. I'm picking up the rental van tomorrow morning, packing it, then driving to Vermont. I'll pick up Elly along the way. By the time we get there, hopefully you kids will have picked a place."

"The real estate agent is taking us this afternoon to a few furnished homes. We'll stay at a hotel for a day or two until everything is finalized," Kyle confirmed.

"Hotel confirmation is in that envelope, too." My dad pointed at my purse. "Oh, and Beast's papers, too."

I put a hand over my heart. "Thank you so much for everything, Dad. You've been my rock through this."

"I agree, thank you," Kyle echoed.

My dad waved his hand dismissively, heading out of the room. "Don't mention it, kids. I'm ready to take you to the airport once you're packed, so let me know. We need to get a move on. Your flight is in six hours. At this rate, we're going to be late."

I rolled my eyes and traded a knowing look with Kyle, who was trying to hide his smile under his hand.

"Did you hear that, Beast?" The dog jumped on the bed next to my suitcase. "You're going on a trip!"

"I packed his things and enough dog food for a couple days," Kyle said, ruffling Beast's fur. "We can buy more when we get there."

I took Beast's face in my hands, giving him a kiss on the bridge of his nose. I was nearly packed since we were only bringing a few days of clothes and personal items. My dad and Elly would drive the rest up.

"Did you talk to your boss?" Kyle asked.

"Yeah, he was very sympathetic. He said he had a temp working there while I was on disability, so he'll probably hire her on to fill my role."

"That's good. I know you were worried about leaving him stranded."

"I liked my job." I sighed. "It wasn't too taxing, but I enjoyed it. I felt important there. I made a difference, in my own way."

"Tessa, you're important no matter where you work, or what you do, or what happens in the next few months."

"Five months," I added, still unsure how time could feel as if it were racing full speed and stuck on pause all at once. The doctors couldn't give an exact estimate, but I was clinging to their guesses anyway.

"It could be longer. We don't know," Kyle reminded me. "No doctor can predict that with real accuracy."

"Did you get my birth certificate out of the safe?" I switched topics. "We should probably bring any important papers with us. I need to go to the DMV to get a Vermont identification card."

"Yeah, I've got it, but I think you'll have to wait a couple more days for a lease to establish residency."

"You're probably right; I'm just anxious."

"We have time, Tessa." Kyle zipped up his suitcase then turned to me with a frown. "I mean, sort of."

I nodded, because he was right—time was the one thing we didn't have.

· ღ · ღ · ღ ·

SUNDAY, *June 22, 2014*

"THAT'S THE LAST BAG," Kyle informed us as we stood around his car ready to go to the airport.

"I'm going to walk Beast around the block quickly since he'll be cooped in the carrier for a few hours." My dad gripped the dog's leash and headed down the driveway.

Turning toward the house, I headed for the front door. "I want to double check that I didn't forget anything."

I heard Kyle reply, but couldn't make out what he'd said since I was already stepping inside. I closed the door behind me and stood still, surveying the now-bare coat and shoe rack to my right, then the large mirror on my left. My reflection still startled me on occasion, even though my hair was growing, a thicker film of fuzz covered my scalp. I still wore my mother's scarves. I'd regained a few pounds, but not many. My color was returning. Sweaters looked large on my frame, and makeup still couldn't help my hollow appearance.

All the times I'd stood in front of this same mirror, prepping to go out on the town, or on dates with Kyle, felt so long ago now.

Inhaling slowly, I walked farther into the house, coming to a stop in the kitchen this time. I ran my hands across the top of the kitchen table, every meal with friends and family replaying in my memories. The kitchen was stark and cold with Beast's bowls and toys missing from the floor. Swallowing my nostalgia, I continued to the living room, just as comfortable and homey as it had always been. A few pictures were gone from the shelves. We had packed them to bring with us, wanting to keep those memories close, but the loss didn't make this room look any less lived-in.

Big plush couches and colorful throw pillows welcomed me and so I sat, and stared out the window as I'd done a thousand times before. The small back yard hedged against a busy road on the top of a small hill. Chicago unfolded before me and it was busy and gray, but beautiful all the same. This had always been one of my favorite places to sit and write because of this view.

"Tessa?" Kyle entered the living room behind me. "Are you okay?"

"I'm just saying goodbye to the house." This wasn't okay. None of this was okay.

"Oh." He cleared his throat. "Do you want me here or should I wait outside?"

"I think I want to be alone for a minute."

I stood when he left. There was nothing in this room for me anymore except the view. I pulled my cell phone from my pocket and snapped a picture of it, so I wouldn't forget.

As soon as the thought crossed my mind, I realized its absurdity. I scanned through the large album of photos I'd taken over the last few years in my phone. The images burst through the screen, reveling in the most photogenic moments of my life. They were the instances of beauty, the times I found love, and the joy I wanted to bring with me into the future.

I hadn't known I wouldn't have one.

My chin dropped to my chest, and I exhaled it all, leaving only the throbbing pain of goodbye traveling through my veins. I left the living room for the stairs in the hallway. I normally took them two at a time before the cancer had weakened me, forced to move slower with small, careful steps. Right now, though, it's a choice. I inched up the steps with purpose—demanding to be in this moment. To feel the familiar give of the creaking wood beneath my toes when it dipped slightly. I might never feel it again and I'd walked past it more times than I could count without giving it a second thought. It was crazy to miss a broken stair, but I knew I would.

The top of the stairs came faster than I'd wanted and the room on my left made me pause. Staring at the door-knob, I wondered if I could even go in there.

I'm not ready.

I walked past it to the door at the end of the hall and entered my bedroom. The large bed beckoned me and I crawled onto it, cherishing the softness as I rolled onto my back and stared at the ceiling. There was an odd paint swipe in the white that was slightly darker than the rest of the ceiling and I wasn't sure why I'd never seen it before now.

Turning my head to the right, I saw our small window that faced the street. I could hear Beast barking out front and my dad's voice. It never was very well insulated, but I hadn't minded. I wasn't bothered by other people's noise—I often found it comforting. A reminder that there was life in the world and I wasn't alone, even when Kyle was deployed.

To the left, the bathroom and closet doors were open,

the shelves bare and the products that normally littered the counter gone. It looked like it had the first day we moved in, before we'd filled it with love and loss.

Closing my eyes, I concentrated on the bed beneath me. I remembered every tangle of bodies from the very first time Kyle and I made love to the last. I found comfort in knowing Kyle will be the only man I've ever given my body to in that way. I'd dated before I met him, but never went very far physically. I wasn't religious or a prude, I just only had enough room in my heart to give it away once.

A lump formed in my throat when I realized that wouldn't be true for Kyle. I hadn't been his first, and I wouldn't be his last. I wanted him to find another great love, someone who'd give him everything I had, and more. I wanted him to have a family, even though I wouldn't be a part of it. My fingers brushed the tears from my cheek. My chest ached and swelled as I lay the hopes I'd had for my future with Kyle down beside me. I pulled myself up from the bed and left those dreams behind.

Closing the bedroom door behind me, I made my way to the top of the stairs. The long forgotten door beckoned me again and this time my hands found the knob. I stepped into the room and turned, closing the door but keeping my nose inches from it. Staring at the white wooden panels, I pressed one hand against the grain and filled my lungs.

I could feel everything I'd lost behind me. I wasn't sure I could turn and look at it. But I did, slowly.

I hadn't been in here since before my diagnosis, since before I'd known we'd never fill the crib against the wall. We'd never coax our child to sleep in the rocking chair, and we'd never laugh and play with the bin of stuffed toys to the side. Thick, inescapable drapes kept the room as dark as possible, but I could still see everything I'd meticulously designed and put together in preparation.

I'd been almost three months pregnant when I'd painted the pale purple walls for the child I hadn't known was already dying inside me. It had all been still so new, and yet I loved our child with every possible part of me. Kyle had been deployed and wouldn't be home until right before the birth. I was strong enough to handle pregnancy on my own. I was sure of it.

I was also in this room when I'd felt a sharp pain in my abdomen, when fear clutched my heart and never let go, when I knew, suddenly, I was empty. It wasn't an agonizing pain, just enough to make me pause. I didn't know the exact moment, but I knew I felt life inside me, and then I didn't.

She was just gone.

I reached forward and ran my fingers along the top of the crib's railing, spotting something inside I'd forgotten. I retrieved the worn teddy bear and held it to my chest. Dipping my head, my cheek rested on the soft surface.

My mother gave me this teddy bear before she died. I'd watched her sewing it and filling it with stuffing. She'd told me what was happening, and how she wouldn't be around to see me grow up. She'd said she loved me so much that she couldn't take it all with her, so instead she was going to leave her love inside the bear. She'd sewn in a small red, fabric heart hidden in the stuffing, and told me to give it to my child one day so she could love them too.

I'd promised I would.

Tears cascade down my cheeks, soaking into the bear as I leaned against the crib and slid to the floor. Sobbing, I buried my face in the bear on my knees. My cries shook my body with such strength I wasn't sure I wouldn't just die right now.

I cried for the child who would never feel his or her grandmother's love, and for the promise I could never keep. For the child I had loved, but hadn't protected. For the man I loved who had been as broken by the loss as I had been. And I cried for me.

I cried for everything I'd never be, never see, and never feel.

The door creaked open and a path of light fell on me. Kyle closed the door behind him and came to sit beside me. He lifted my frail body into his lap, peppering soft kisses against my streaked cheeks. I curled into his chest, the teddy bear squeezed between us, and twisted my fingers into his shirt. His arms trembled around me, his chest moving unevenly beneath my face, and I knew he was crying, too.

We sat against the crib of our dead daughter and we cried for her—for the grandmother who'd never hold her grandchild, the child who'd never be held by her mother, and the mother who only had a few months left.

CHAPTER TWENTY

SUNDAY, *June 22, 2014*

WHEN THE PLANE honed in on Burlington, Vermont, I knew I'd made the right decision. From above, the city was picturesque with mountains on one side and Lake Champlain on the other. Brick facades on many of the buildings gave it the classic New England look that excited the writer in me, an innate sense of belonging to the stoic structures.

For the first time, I felt a resounding peace with the move. No matter how or when I would die, I'd get to experience living in a new place that already felt familiar. It was as if I'd checked something off my bucket list that I hadn't even known was on it. When we deplaned, the crew welcomed us to Burlington with wide smiles, eagerly pointing out baggage claim and the rental car counter.

Even Kyle seemed brighter in the hospitable small city. "You should probably text your dad. Let him know we got here safe," Kyle said, catching my eye over the roof of our rental car.

Beast and I climbed into the passenger's side, then I pulled my phone out of my pocket. "Yeah. He was worried, but he'll be here in two days."

"Fathers worry. No changing that." Kyle started the car, retrieved his phone, and plugged the real estate office's address into his GPS. All set, he interlocked his fingers with mine, resting our hands on my leg while he drove.

I suddenly thought of his parents, wondering what they knew. "Have you talked to Elias or Dixie lately?"

"I sent them a message through their camping guide, so hopefully it gets there. I sent a few emails, too, in case they ever get near Internet."

I frowned. "They don't use email much."

I'd never had much interaction with them, but neither had Kyle. They were free spirits who believed children were peers, without need of handholding or guidance. Kyle had had to teach himself early how to survive in the world. It sounded okay in theory, but it also meant they weren't close. There were no hard feelings between them...just emptiness.

"I'll keep trying. It would be nice to see them again before..." his words trailed off.

I'd like to see them before I died, too, but I understood how hard it must be for him to say it. "How many houses are we seeing today?" I asked, changing subjects. "Should we grab some lunch first?"

Kyle's brows furrowed as he glanced sideways at me. "You're still hungry? We ate on the plane."

I shrugged my shoulders, knowing this was news to both of us. "That was a few hours ago. My stomach is growling."

I'd spent most of the last few months vomiting and refusing food. I was still dealing with some side effects from radiation, but they were decreasing every day and I was slowly—albeit, *very* slowly—beginning to feel like my old self.

"If my wife wants food, we're getting food," Kyle said. He squeezed my hand, then kissed my knuckles. I could almost see the tension easing from his face at the news.

An hour and a half later, we left a quaint little café with full stomachs. We'd tried a few restaurants, but most closed at insanely early hours. This was definitely a unique town, every place quaint and small, yet warm and friendly. Plus, every restaurant had been completely fine with Beast joining us, which was truly the highlight for me.

The real estate office was no exception. It was tucked into a brick office complex near the water with gold plating on the doors that screamed of importance. Gorgeous art of landscapes decorated the inner waiting room and a curvy blonde in a dark pantsuit greeted us.

"Hello, I'm Carly Wellings. How can I help you?"

Kyle reached out a hand. "Hi Carly, we spoke the other day about looking at furnished listings?" He then gestured to Beast and I. "This is my wife, Tessa. I'm Kyle, and our dog here is Beast."

I shook her hand next, noting the strength in her grip. It was rare to meet a woman with a strong handshake, and I immediately knew I'd like her.

Carly's face lit up with recognition. "Yes, of course! I've got three lined up for today. Just need to put a sign on the door in case anyone stops by, but I'm ready to go."

She bustled casually about the office grabbing her purse and phone, and taping the sign on the front door. Everything about her—and this town—had a mellow feel. No one was in a rush, and everyone was just...relaxed. Growing up in a busy metropolis had never afforded me that luxury, and I was savoring every second of it now.

We left our car in her parking lot and piled into hers, reaching our first destination only a few minutes later. It was a white manufactured home below our price range, and looked every bit of it. I only had to walk a few feet in to know I wouldn't live there. It felt used and worn, held together by sheer will. There was nothing homey about it, and now that I'd tasted this town, I couldn't settle for less.

Beast pulled at his leash to leave, echoing my sentiments. Carly apologized and drove us to the next location— a blue ranch-style home with a gorgeous brown roof. I was hesitant to say no, because it really was nice, but so much larger than we needed. It wasn't until I saw the view from the living room—directly into our neighbor's kitchen a few feet away—that both Kyle and I quickly decided against it.

Our last destination for the day was a green-shingled bungalow with a bright red front door that immediately made me smile. I'd had a thing for red doors ever since I'd helped my mother put on her makeup when I was a toddler. One of her compact mirrors had a bright red door on the back. It whispered expensive and lavish—but not showy— just silently decadent. The perfect description for who she was.

I'd spent years looking for a mirror like it and had finally found the spa that made them a few years ago. I'd purchased a dozen, and the clerk had looked at me strangely, but I didn't care. I wanted to have one in my purse, my car, my room...everywhere I'd be where I'd want to remember her.

"Kyle, I love it." I grabbed his hand when we climbed the front steps, Beast a few strides ahead.

He laughed, wrapping an arm around my shoulders. "You haven't seen the inside yet."

I wasn't concerned. "I can feel it. This is the place."

When we stepped inside, everything was wood, stone, and brick combined seamlessly in a way that felt as if the house had grown onto this piece of land all by itself. The owners hadn't skimped on the amenities, however, because every appliance was top-of-the-line.

"Every room is nicely furnished, but there's plenty of free space for you to add your personal mementos while you're here," Carly explained, walking us through each room. "The best part is you're backed onto Lake Champlain. You have your own dock and motorboat down on the end there."

I followed her pointed finger to outside the kitchen window where an expansive body of water greeted me. A dark wooden dock jutted off the grass with a white rowboat bobbing at the end. It was as beautiful as one of the photos from Carly's office, but I could smell the water and hear the splashing against the dock. There was an instant tranquility to the scene and the house that told me my initial impression was spot on.

Carly opened a door off the kitchen, and Beast immediately rocketed out into the back yard, running laps around the grass, only pausing to dig holes and toss dirt around.

"Beast!" Kyle scolded the dog, clapping his hands. "Stop it!"

Beast lifted his face, revealing a dirt beard all over his fluffy white face. Then he returned right back to digging.

"Christ," Kyle grumbled. "Damn dog."

"Can we afford this?" I asked Kyle, still mesmerized. With the recent medical bills, I'd lost track of our finances. I used to be the one in charge of our bills, but ever since my diagnosis, Kyle had taken over.

Carly's eyes lit up and she lifted a hand to catch our attention. "Rent is actually $50 a month under your max."

"Works for me." Kyle gave me a questioning look, and I nodded my head. I wanted this home. "When can we move in?"

"It's move-in ready." Carly pulled a file from her bag, flipping it open. "You'll need to sign some paperwork and get the homeowner's approval, but I should have a final answer for you within two days."

"Beast already moved in." I watched him circle the yard again, laughing at his prancing.

"He loves it!" Carly agreed then turned away from the yard to face us. "What lease term were you thinking of? The average is a year, but we could ask the landlord for something else, too."

Kyle's gaze fell to the floor, shoving his hands in his pockets. "Um, I'm not sure."

"Well, how long do you plan to stay in the area?" she asked.

"Less than a year," he replied, glancing sideways at me. "Maybe a few months?"

I pushed my shoulders back, lifting my chin. "What he's trying not to say is we're only going to be here until I die."

Carly froze, her eyes sliding from Kyle to me, and then back.

"I have cancer," I continued. "The doctors give me another few months. Maybe five."

She blinked a few times, clearing her throat loudly. I could see her mind working, though I wasn't sure what she must be thinking. No agent would want someone dying in their listing, but it was going to happen no matter which house we chose—plus I wanted the homeowner to know. I needed them to be okay with it, for my own peace of mind.

Carly finally managed to speak, "I'm so sorry. That is awful."

Well, this is awkward. "Do you think they could do a six-month lease with the option for a few more if something changes with my health?" I asked, changing the subject.

"I'm sure we could work something out," Carly replied. "The owner of this house moved south to be with his kids after his wife died of cancer—here, I believe. So, I think he'd be more than understanding about it."

"Really?" Kyle's face twisted with puzzlement. "That's an odd coincidence."

It was, but it also wasn't—cancer certainly wasn't uncommon. I wasn't sure if I was creeped out or if I liked the symmetry.

"It is. Kinda like it was your destiny to be here to... well, you know," Carly murmured, an innocent smile on her face that made me want to smack her a little. Just a little, though.

I refused to believe it was my destiny to die before I turned thirty, but I tried to appreciate her attempt at reaching out.

She clasped her hands together. "Okay then! Let's get the paperwork started."

A yawn overtook me, the chill rolling down my spine. "Sounds perfect. I'm ready for a nap after traveling all day."

"You guys just came up from Chicago, right?" She tilted her to the side, tapping a finger to her lips as if she wasn't entirely sure of what she wanted to say next. "I've got to ask...why do you want to move *now*? With everything going on with your health?"

I felt my cheeks heat, a blush creeping up at the question. Odd, since I wasn't embarrassed by my decision. Clearing my throat, I decided for the truth. "Illinois hasn't legalized death with dignity like Vermont has."

Her eyes widened. Kyle looked everywhere but at me.

"Oh, I didn't..." She rubbed her hands together, fidgeting. "Wow, that's, um... It's just not often we hear about that. It's brave. I supported the legislation when it passed last year."

Her rambling was so uncomfortable even Beast started whining and put his head down.

I waved a hand in an attempt to change the topic yet again. "I appreciate it. I really wish all states legalized it."

"Mmhm. Sure." She nodded her head a bit too vigorously. "I'm probably going to need to mention this to the landlord, of course. Some people are particular, you know? Uh, let's head back to the office and finish the paperwork. Good? Great. Fantastic. That's...um...yes, let's go." Carly bee-lined for the front door.

Chuckling, I turned to Kyle. "Was it something I said?"

He wasn't laughing. "I didn't consider what it would be like telling other people."

"I hadn't either," I admitted, realizing I needed to think of a better explanation for next time. "Do you think we won't get this place now?"

Kyle shrugged, holding the front door open for me. We lowered our voices as we stepped out onto the porch, but Carly was already sitting in the driver's seat ready to go. "I'm not sure," he said. "I never knew much about this until the last few days."

I hoped it wouldn't affect our application. "Fingers crossed."

I was as new to the entire concept as he was, and although I'd gotten a jump start on research, I'd seen him reading every journal article possible over the last few days. I hadn't considered how others might have an issue with it outside of my family—at least, not to the point where we might be denied a rental home.

Maybe that was naïve.

I gathered Beast and piled back into the car. Two hours later, every line was signed, initialed, and ready to go. She had our phone numbers and would give us a call in the morning to confirm whether we could have the keys or not. If all went well, we'd spend the next few days moving into the new place, getting my dad and sister set up here, requesting a new license from the DMV, and meeting with a doctor.

An entire new chapter of our lives was starting and neither of us knew what to expect. We were trying to prepare ourselves for it, to be ready for whatever may come, but we weren't even close.

CHAPTER TWENTY-ONE

MONDAY, June 23, 2014

"I'VE CALLED and set up a doctor appointment for tomorrow with Dr. Protos," Kyle said from where he sat at the desk in our hotel room.

"That's fine." I peeked out for only a moment before burying my head under the pillows again. My skull was cracking open, tearing in half and taking my sanity with it. I'd taken the medications prescribed specifically for headaches, but they hadn't had time to kick in yet, so pillow compresses and darkness were the next best thing. "I'm not sure I'm getting out of bed. I did too much yesterday—the flight, touring the houses—it was too much."

I could hear Kyle push his chair away from the desk, then felt the bed sag as he sat on the edge a moment later. "You don't have to; I'll take care of everything. Just sleep."

"Can you check in with my dad? I think he's driving to New York today and spending the night with Elly, then coming here tomorrow."

"Already talked to him while you were sleeping; he's doing fine," Kyle replied, rubbing my leg over the blankets. "He spent half the call grumbling about crazy drivers and the lack of government funding going into improving highways or something."

I chuckled, then winced at the following pain. "Sounds like Dad."

Kyle's phone rang and I groaned, holding the pillow tighter over my head.

"Hello?" He paused, and I could hear the sound of someone on the other end of the line. "That's wonderful news. I'll be by shortly to get the keys!"

"Was that the real estate agent?" I peered out from under the pillow to see him pocketing his cell phone. "Did we get it?"

He nodded, his mouth in a wider grin than I'd seen him sport in weeks. "Yep. We got the bungalow."

I lifted one brow. "Man, you were really worried we wouldn't, huh?"

He looked down at his hands for a moment, then returned to the edge of the bed and plopped down beside me. "It's not about you or me. I've been reading more about the Death with Dignity Act. The opposition is...vocal. It's only been allowed here for the last year, and, since then, only two people have actually gone through with it—none who moved here to do so."

"It's a small state, Kyle. There were more people who were prescribed the medication, but didn't end up taking it," I countered, leaning my head on his shoulder and curling into his side. "It's never anyone's first choice. It's our last."

Beast jumped on to the bed and wedged himself between us, twisting on to his back and closing his eyes.

Kyle sighed and squeezed an arm tighter around me. "Are you sure about this, Tessa? Are you sure you want to do this?"

I stared at the pastel photo of a flower on the hotel wall across from the bed. "Right now? Yes, I'm sure this is what I want to do. In a few months when things are deteriorating? I'm not sure."

Kyle's brow furrowed. "Why go through this if you're not sure then?"

An ache in my chest throbbed harder as I thought about the best way to explain myself. "I want the option. Sure, I know I might change my mind later, but if I were to wait until then to get the medication, it might be too late. I could be too sick to go through the entire approval process." I ran my hands down the length of my torso, straightening the slouchy tee I was wearing. "Despite the headaches, I've actually been feeling better lately. My hair is growing again; my appetite is returning. I look a little less like I'm dying, but we both know in a few months—probably sooner—it won't look that way." I gestured up and down my body. "I won't look like *me*."

Kyle laid his hand on top of mine, interlocking our fingers. "We don't know anything for sure, Tessa. Miracles happen all the time."

"Maybe, but maybe my miracle already happened. Maybe a six-month warning to say goodbye *is* exactly that." I ran my free hand through Beast's soft fur, swallowing the lump already forming in my throat. "Maybe meeting you and spending my last few years completely in love is the biggest miracle I could have ever asked for."

"Tessa—" he started.

I couldn't let him stop me. "I'm serious, Kyle. I think I've lived a pretty miraculous life already. I'd obviously love it if suddenly my cancer disappeared, but I have to be realistic. That's not going to happen."

He placed a warm, lingering kiss against my forehead and I closed my eyes. "You be realistic; I'm going to be hopeful. Then we'll have all bases covered."

Laughter fell from my lips as I turned my body into his for the briefest of moments. "That sounds perfect."

Another sweet kiss and short embrace, then he slid off the bed and pulled the covers over Beast and me. "Get some rest, Tessa. I'm going to meet the agent and get our keys. We can move in tonight."

"Okay. Text my dad the address."

He nodded and leaned down to kiss me again. I yawned and stretched, then curled into the blankets and promptly fell asleep.

• ღ • ღ • ღ •

TUESDAY, June 24, 2014

"TESSA!" My sister's voice traveled across the yard to where I stood on the dock with Beast, watching boats bob on the lake.

I turned and began walking toward her, arms open wide. "Elly!"

Beast beat me to her, running full speed and slamming himself into her legs. She laughed and leaned down to give him a quick cuddle before greeting me with a big hug. It'd been a while since I'd seen her, despite our daily texts and phone calls. She had been busy taking online courses over the summer before her final year of college, and had managed to get ahead enough credits to be able to take off the fall semester and still graduate in May.

Pride didn't even begin to describe how I felt about her big brain and amazing work ethic. It was impressive as hell, honestly. I'd never had that kind of drive or ambition, which was fine with me since I loved my life. But for my baby sister? Oh, I wanted her to have it all.

She hugged me stiffly, her arms barely bending. "Oh, am I hurting you?"

"A hug won't break me." I squeezed her tighter until she finally gave in and embraced me like normal. "I've missed you so much, girl. How's school?"

Her face lit up. "This time next year, I'll be a college graduate."

"You're doing amazing." I held her at arm's length, pride pumping through my veins. "I can't wait to see you walking across that stage."

She paused, her brows furrowing and her smile strained.

"Oh, right." I suddenly understood what she was thinking. There's no chance I'd be there to see her get her diploma. "Almost forgot for a second."

She swallowed hard, looking down. "Tessa..."

"It's okay," I interrupted. "It honestly is. I've accepted what's happening, even if I forget sometimes. I'm not going to spend the time I have left lamenting over what I can't change. You shouldn't either." I'd left my anger behind in Chicago and I had zero plans to let it follow me here.

Elly didn't look convinced. "You're right. Um, well, Dad's starting to unload the van. There isn't much on there."

"We didn't need a lot," I replied. "Just personal touches and clothes. Have you seen your room yet?"

"No, I'm excited!" Finally, the first genuine smile I'd seen on her since she'd arrived. "The bungalow is so cute, and this view...holy shit." Elly gazed toward the water and inhaled loudly. "It's amazing. I feel relaxed just looking at it. Like the perfect vacation spot...um, except—"

"Let's just enjoy the view, not the reason for why we're looking at it." Despite our morbid purpose, she needed to loosen up. I liked forgetting sometimes. I didn't want to be reminded every second of how few I had left. "I'll show you your room before I leave. I've got a doctor's appointment in a few."

"Can I go?"

I shrugged, never minding the company. "Sure, but it might be boring."

"I don't mind." Elly linked her arm with mine as we headed to the house with Beast on our heels. "I don't care what we're doing, Tessy. I just want to spend every minute together. It already doesn't feel like enough."

"Because it's not." My heart ached at the thought, but I tried to push the pain away. "Not even close."

An hour later, Elly, Kyle, and I were ushered back into an exam room at the doctor's office. We'd left my dad at home to rest since driving all day had worn him out.

"Dr. Protos will be right in," a nurse informed us. Elly and Kyle sat in folding chairs against one wall while I climbed onto the padded exam table. "Did you bring the scans from your previous doctor?"

Kyle handed her a copy of my medical records. The envelope wasn't as thick as I'd expected. Just a thin packet of films. It didn't really do justice to the magnitude of the tumor's presence in me.

She took the scans and left us to entertain ourselves with outdated magazines for almost thirty minutes. Finally, a middle-aged doctor entered the room adorned in a long white coat and stethoscope.

"Hi, folks. How are we doing today?" He was cheery and friendly, but I was honestly so irritated by the long wait that I automatically hated him. Okay, so maybe I hadn't left *all* my anger in Chicago. He extended a hand, which I shook—but I didn't like it. "So, Mrs. Falls, these scans. Are they the most recent?"

I nodded my head. "There are two sets, actually. The first was a month ago, and the second was last week."

He flicked a switch on a white panel on the wall, which lit up. Placing my scans against the bright surface, he stood and stared at them for a moment. "Have you had these results read to you yet?"

"Not yet," Kyle spoke up. "We got them right before we moved and didn't have a chance yet."

"I see." The doctor glanced over at my husband, then back at the scans. Finally, he switched off the light. "Well, there is a significant difference between the two scans."

The sudden tenseness in his voice made me squirm.

"What's that mean?" Elly asked.

Dr. Protos shoved his hands into his pockets and turned to face me. "The tumor is growing faster than your doctor originally predicted. It's remarkable, accelerating at this speed."

My stomach began doing somersaults. I hadn't antici-pated more bad news after *you're dying*. That seemed like the worst case, but *you're dying quicker* is so much worse. "But I feel fine. My headaches are here and there, but that's about it."

"That's completely normal," Dr. Protos confirmed with

a small nod. "You're healing from the radiation, which can make symptoms decline. The cancer, however...it's progressing quickly. At this rate of growth, more severe symptoms—vision loss, seizures—will begin to develop in the next eight weeks."

"*Two* months?" I asked, nearly choking on my words as they tumbled from my lips. "I was told five. *Five months.*"

The doctor switched back on the light behind my scans and began pointing out to me the difference between the two, leaving no doubt. Two months until my symptoms worsened. Four months until I died...at best.

"Shit." Kyle exhaled loudly. "That's much sooner than we thought."

A month might not be very long, but when there's one less before death... it felt as if a lifetime had just been stolen from me.

Dr. Protos continued, "I'll prescribe anti-seizure and pain medications to make you as comfortable as possible. Do you have hospice care in place? My staff can make some calls for you, help get you into one of the best facilities in the state."

I nodded as if I was listening instead of trying to summon the courage to ask for what I really wanted. "I also need a prescription for secobarbital or pentobarbital."

His mouth fell open slightly and he looked wide-eyed between Kyle, Elly, and me. I sat taller and pushed back my shoulders, unwavering. Kyle did the same, but Elly dipped her chin, her hands clenched together so tightly, they were turning white.

Dr. Protos pulled his hands from his pockets and crossed his arms over his chest. "This is why you moved to Vermont? The death with dignity legislation? It is legal as of last year, but it's still extremely rare. I believe it's only occurred twice since—and certainly not at this practice."

"I'm aware. I've done my research. I've made my decision, and I'm more than ready to go through the steps necessary," I assure him. "What do I need to do?"

"I apologize, Mrs. Falls, but you'll have to seek that type of aid from someone else." He was already backing toward the door, like he was about to make a break for it. "I won't be a participant to assisted suicide. I'm a God-fearing man, Mrs. Falls."

"You're a doctor...in a state where it's legal," I sputtered, blinking hard in confusion. I could feel the heat of embarrassment already rushing up my cheeks. "I'm terminal, you said so yourself. I meet all the criteria."

He nodded, but it already felt condescending. "I did say that, but we don't get the right to hasten death along. When it's our time, it's our time."

Kyle stood from his chair so fast, it almost flipped over behind him. "Says who?"

"God." Dr. Protos simply shrugged, not even remotely fearful of the rage in my husband's eyes. *Mistake.*

"God wants her to suffer?" Kyle was yelling now, stepping closer to the doctor with a menacing expression. "God says she has to wait to die? She has to wait until after her body can no longer handle the pain? *God* says that?"

Elly and I both stood, alarmed at the escalation. She placed a hand on Kyle's shoulder, pulling him backwards slightly. I stepped between him and Dr. Protos, not saying anything, but trying to block their argument from continuing with my body. Not sure what I'd do if they actually started throwing punches, but I hadn't thought that far ahead.

Dr. Protos stood his ground. "Mr. Falls, this isn't up for

debate. I am not legally required to prescribe medication I don't think is in the best interest of the patient—whether it's legal in this state or not. You'll need to look elsewhere, although I truly hope you won't."

With that, he left the room.

"I swear to God, I'm going to kill him." Kyle's jaw was set, his teeth clenched. "That fucking asshole!"

"There are other doctors," I said, barely above a whisper. "It'll be okay."

I didn't even believe myself, but I tried to calm him down anyway.

Honestly, there was no reason why I hadn't expected some resistance. It was foolish to assume every doctor in Vermont would be on board with the state legislation. But, damn...that was embarrassing. The way Dr. Protos had stared at me with disgust...freaking humiliating.

Shaking his head, Kyle growled. "Let's just get the fuck out of here."

Yes, please.

CHAPTER TWENTY-TWO

Tuesday, June 24, 2014

"I CAN'T BELIEVE the nerve of that pompous jackass." Kyle stomped around the bungalow's kitchen after we'd returned home. "He's a *doctor*. He's supposed to help ease suffering—not add to it!"

I didn't respond. He wasn't looking for me to talk sense into him. He wanted to vent and I was more than fine with letting him.

My sister, on the other hand, was clearly itching to speak from where she sat next to me on a stool at the counter. "He could have been more tactful, but I think he's right," Elly finally said.

The hell? I swivel my stool to face her. "What do you mean you think he's right?"

"It's wrong to kill yourself, Tessa. I know I can't change what you're going to do, and I know this might hurt your feelings, but I'd regret it if I never said anything." She popped an orange slice in her mouth and I almost reached out to slap it off her tongue.

Kyle stopped in his tracks. "Are you fucking kidding, El?"

I put my hand up and glared at him. "Kyle! Why don't you take Beast for a walk?"

The dog came bounding into the kitchen seconds later, holding his leash in his mouth. He was upsettingly smart when he wanted to be.

Kyle shot us both an angry look, but grabbed the leash and left with Beast.

I waited until I heard the front door close before I spoke. "Why didn't you tell me you felt this way weeks ago, Elly? You were so supportive on the phone."

Elly stood and walked to the sink, rinsing her hands from the orange. "I am supportive of *you*, but I didn't know what to say. I was so shocked by the announcement in the first place." She leaned against the counter across from me and dried her hands. "I'd never considered the option. Never even knew enough about it to know how I felt. But I've been doing some reading..." She inhaled deeply, finally letting her gaze meet mine. Tears brimmed her bottom lashes, her voice strained. "It just doesn't feel right, Tessa. It's suicide—the easy way out."

"You're right. It *is* the easy way out." I emptied my lungs with a sigh. "But why do I have to take the hard way? Why endure the pain when I can avoid it? What lessons are there in that? The outcome is no different."

"I don't know, but there has to be a reason. God does everything for a reason. He's the only one who chooses when we die." Elly wiped an escaped tear from her cheek. "I've been going back to church and that's what my priest says."

I dropped a hand on top of Elly's. "I went to a priest before I decided, and I feel comfortable with my decision, in part because of my conversation with him."

Elly's brows furrowed, her frown deepening. "You did?"

"I did, and, personally, I agree. God will pick the day and time I die." Her eyes widened when I said that. "I think when I feel the time is right—the gut feeling of knowing *now*—could very well be God. And if He doesn't want me to die when I take those pills, I won't. Something will go wrong, and I'll be kept here." Though that possibility terrified me. "It's happened before. There have been a few people who have taken it, but didn't die, or took an extremely long time to die from it. God *does* decide in the end. but He also provided us with our minds, our free will, our ability to create these medications, make these decisions. God doesn't want me to suffer— if I know anything, I know that."

Elly shook her head. "I don't know, Tessa. It just seems too big a decision. How will you know when you're ready? To never be *here* again? Never see Kyle, or Dad, or me ever again?" Her voice trailed off, a small strangled sound coming from her throat "How do you make *that* choice?"

A tightness formed in my chest at the thought. I'd asked myself that same question more than once. "I don't know, but I'm hoping one day it will just feel right."

She was quiet for a minute, staring out the window over the sink facing the lake. "It doesn't feel right to die when you're only twenty-eight."

"I *am* going to die, Elly." I wondered if she was more upset that it was happening, rather than how.

"Can you *please* stop saying that?" She crossed her arms over her chest, her jaw tight. "Just stop."

"No." I shook my head, my voice sterner now. "At some

point, you're going to have to accept that this is happening no matter what. No matter how."

She shook her head for the millionth time, now staring at a spot on the wall behind me and visibly biting the inside of her cheek. As much as I wanted to take away her grief, I knew from my own struggle in finding radical acceptance in my situation, that this was a path she'd have to walk alone.

"Elly, I'm not asking you to agree with me. Or to change how you feel." I pushed up from the stool and faced her, my palms pressed together as if I was praying. "I'm only asking for you to be here with me, and *for* me. I know that's selfish, but I'd be absolutely crushed if you were so angry, you left."

"I'm not angry, Tessa. I'm..." She sighed, her hands dropping to her sides and her shoulders slumping. "I don't know what I am, but maybe I shouldn't go with you to doctor appointments anymore."

"Fair enough," I agreed, even though nothing had felt fair in a long time.

"I love you, Tessa," she continued. "I just don't like what you're doing."

I swallowed my nerves with a deep inhale. This was the right choice for me, despite the opposition. "I'm not changing my mind, El."

She nodded slowly. "I know."

· ♋ · ♋ · ♋ ·

THURSDAY, July 3, 2014

· · ·

TWO WEEKS and four different doctors later, I was no closer to getting the prescription for pentobarbital than I had been in Chicago. One stated religious reasons, another worried about malpractice suits, another claimed it would violate his oath as a doctor to help and not hurt, and the last said it was just too controversial and new.

For the first time, I was beginning to doubt my decision to move to Vermont, or wonder if I should have tried the West Coast instead. I turned to face my dad who was standing in line behind me at the DMV in Burlington. "Should we be here?"

He glanced up from his cellphone, his bushy brows pushed together. "What?"

"Maybe I should have tried Oregon instead." I shifted my weight from one leg to the other, trying to ignore the ache from standing so long. The problem was the ache wasn't only in my legs, it was my entire body and it wouldn't get much better if I sat down. "What if none of the doctors here say yes?"

"Tessa, it's still new. It takes time for them to get accustomed. But, it wouldn't have been made legal if the support wasn't there, so I'm confident we'll find someone eventually."

It was the *eventually* which frightened me—a luxury I didn't have. I felt tightly wound around a coil, but my dad looked like he hadn't a care in the world. His assured attitude comforted me slightly.

"Next in line!" the clerk behind the counter called out.

I rushed forward and presented my paperwork and identification. She looked it over for a minute, then pointed to another area of the room and handed me a ticket. "Counter B. Wait for your number to be called."

"I hate the DMV. It's all hurry up and wait," my dad grumbled as he trotted alongside me.

"That's one thing I'll never have to trudge through again." I tried for a lighthearted chuckle. Truthfully, though, if I had to stand in a thousand DMV lines to live longer, I would.

"I can't hear you talk that way, Tessa." He looked down, shoving his phone in his pocket. "I just can't."

"Sorry." I appreciated him coming with me today. Elly and I hadn't talked much since our fight, and Kyle was home researching doctors and making calls. "I'll stop."

The next clerk called my number after waiting thirty more minutes, and I scurried to meet her. She took my picture and chatted the entire time about her new engagement. I smiled and congratulated her, but my words were hollow. Honestly, I struggled to find excitement in much of anything lately, which was unusual for me.

I didn't want to spend what time I had left feeling so low, but it was starting to seem like there wasn't another alternative. Everything hurt. My body was either sore or weak, as if I'd just run a marathon, and there was no in between. Occasionally, I'd get twinges of sharper pain shooting through me. The headaches were constant and progressing daily, worse than any migraine I'd ever experienced. I wanted to curl up in bed and sleep for days on end, but I refused to waste my last few days like that.

"About done here, ma'am." The clerk typed quickly on her computer. "Did you want the two-year or four-year? It's a twenty-dollar difference between the two." Her fingers hovered over her computer mouse as she waited for my decision.

"For the expiration date?" I asked.

She nodded and pointed at a chart up on the wall

showing the difference. "Yes, ma'am. How long do you want?"

I wanted four years. Hell, I wanted a lot longer than four years. I wanted every minute I could squeeze out of life. But, I had five months. Four, if Dr. Protos was right.

"I'll take the shorter one," I finally said.

She lifted one brow and cocked her head to the side. "Sure you don't want longer? You gotta renew in person now. It can save you a trip."

I looked over my shoulder at my dad waiting on a nearby bench. "Yeah, I'm sure," I finally said with a sigh. "I won't be here that long."

"Oh, nice. A traveler, I like that." She gave me a conspiratorial wink that made absolutely no sense. "I love to travel. I'll put you down for two years. Go on and sit down 'cause it's going to take a minute 'fore it's ready."

I thanked her and then joined my dad. Carefully, I lowered my body onto the bench and leaned back with a moan of relief. My feet were throbbing, and I desperately needed to close my eyes for a minute. The migraine pulsed inside my skull, and for a minute, I wasn't sure if the pain would make me vomit.

My dad patted my knee and let me rest my head on his shoulder.

"Ma'am?" I jolted, unsure of how long I'd been asleep, or that I'd fallen asleep at all. The clerk stood in front of me, her previous smile turned down into a worried frown. She held out my new driver's license. "Here you go. You're all set, but...you feeling okay?"

"I'm fine, thank you." I took it from her, and my dad helped me to my feet.

She didn't look convinced, but nodded her head anyway. "You folks have a nice day."

My dad took my arm and guided me to the car. Relief overtook me at the feeling of the soft cloth seats, a big step up from the DMV folding chairs. I pulled on my seat belt as my dad put the car in drive, and then studied my license. My eyes flashed to my picture for only a second before I had to focus on something else.

In my mind, I'd thought I was starting to look better, but the picture didn't agree. I was a ghostly color, my skin pulled tight over my cheekbones. They hadn't let me wear my scarf, so my bald head stuck out like a sore thumb. It had a fine layer of hair growing which I thought looked quite thick lately—almost like a purposefully done pixie cut—but that wasn't what I saw in the picture.

My eyes scanned the rest of the card, then I shoved it into my pocket and rolled down the car window, letting the breeze hit my face. "September 30, 2016."

My dad glanced sideways from the driver's seat. "What?"

"That's when my license expires. On my birthday in two years."

He cleared this throat, keeping his eyes on the road. "Oh."

"Yeah." Neither one of us knew what to say, and I wasn't sure why it even bothered me. The clerk had told me it would be two years, but I hadn't thought about the date itself. "I haven't thought about my birthday."

He frowned, his knuckles tightening around the steering wheel. "You said you wanted to celebrate it back when you first found out, remember?"

I nodded slowly, playing memories of past birthdays in my head. Blowing out candles, unwrapping gifts, making resolutions, getting drunk and forgetting them. "Yeah, my twenty-ninth. But, I didn't think about the rest. My thirtieth, thirty-first, fortieth, fiftieth.... all of them. There won't be any more after this September, if I even make it to twenty-nine."

"You're going to celebrate your birthday, Tessa." His voice didn't sound as confident as his words.

"Maybe, but even if I do, I won't make it to Halloween, Thanksgiving, Christmas, or New Year's. There are so many things I've already experienced my *last* of... and I didn't even know it." A lump began to form in my throat, but I tried to push it away. "I didn't dress up in a costume last Halloween. We just stayed home and watched scary movies. Christmas was great, but if I'd known it would be my last, I'd have done more." There was a weight on my chest, like someone was sitting on me, and I realized this was grief. "I'd have tried harder, if I'd known...I'd have done more with my life."

My dad reached over and squeezed my hand. "My Sunshine on a cloudy day, you've already done more with your life than most ever will. You found love; not just any love, but once-in-a-lifetime love. You had a job you loved, a home you worked hard for, a family by your side, and so many people who love you. That's what it's about. It's the little moments that build a well-lived life, and love that builds well-lived people. Those are the memories you'll take with you, and the memories we'll hold on to."

The weight on my chest lightened, even if just a little. He was right. I'd lived a full life, even if it was short. I'd been loved, and I'd loved with everything I had. That's the most I could ask for from this world, and I'd need to be okay with that.

I wanted to be.

CHAPTER TWENTY-THREE

SUNDAY, July 13, 2014

IT HAPPENED EARLIER than I expected—and slower.

My first seizure.

It was like watching the world frame by frame, and then not at all. One minute, I was standing in the kitchen with Kyle while he tried to teach me how to flip a pancake, and the next minute, I was on the ground with everyone screaming.

Everything before that had been normal enough.

I'd woken up a couple of hours ago, unusually cold. Not all at once, but rather in waves. I'd be comfortable one second, then need a sweatshirt the next. My aches were bone deep, and Kyle had hoped to distract me by cooking together. Beast had done his best to interrupt us, walking in and out between my legs, and barking nonstop. It was incredibly obnoxious—even for him.

And then I felt strange. There's no other way to describe it, except that my body felt different than I'd known for the last twenty-eight years. It was strangely calming, yet panic-inducing at the same time. My fingers tingled and my mind felt fuzzy, my stomach flip-flopped and my tongue felt thick. I tried to listen to Kyle talk, but his words came slower, then jumbled, and then he stopped making sense entirely. I wanted to tell him, but I couldn't think of the words. He began moving, inching backwards, then speeding away so fast, I felt dizzy.

I reached for him, wanting him to stay, but my hands found nothing to grasp and everything faded, taking me with it.

"Tessa!" My name. Someone was shouting. It was muted and muffled. *I'm here.*

Then I wasn't.

Nothing.

A tiny sound. Beast barked. He was so far away. *Is he okay?* Then he was closer. Louder. Roaring. *Quiet!* Kyle's voice was deafening in my ear and my dad was there somewhere...somewhere, but my mind couldn't grab hold. Elly was screaming and I tried to tell her to stop, to calm down, but I couldn't hear my own words. *Am I speaking?* One side of my face felt cold and when my eyes opened, I saw tile.

Rows and rows of tile stretched out in front of me. Then Beast shoved his nose into my face, licking me. Kyle pushed him away, dropping to his knees beside me. My sister was behind him, tears strewn across her scrunched-up face. My dad was holding her shoulders, his eyes wide and his face pale.

"Tessa? Can you hear me?"

I stared at Kyle. His voice sounded so funny, like he was speaking through a fan. *Why is he doing that?* When Elly and I were kids, we'd pretend to be robots and press our faces against the fan's cover, talking into the whirling blades inches away. I wondered if Kyle was playing that game. I didn't want to play.

"Tessa, please. Can you hear me?" Kyle asked again, his voice less robotic now. *Is the game over?* "Say something."

I think I nodded, one half of my face still pressed against the cold floor as I lay on my side, but nothing moved. My head ached, as did the rest of me. One side of my body felt numb, tingling beneath me as if it no longer belonged to me. I tried to push against the floor and stand up, but my body didn't respond. *This isn't a game. Something is wrong.* Panic rose in my chest. *Is this it?* The paralysis I'd been dreading...could it happen this fast?

One minute alive, the next, trapped.

"She's in here." I couldn't pin point who was talking now. My sister stepped into my line of sight. Odd. When had she left? "Please help her."

An unfamiliar pair of legs came into view. "Please step back, sir. We need room to work."

Cold hands were touching me. My neck, my wrist. *Did someone just lift my shirt?* My body tilted backward, but not onto the tile. Onto something soft beneath me that suddenly lifted me off the floor and closer to everyone's faces. Faces I didn't recognize.

A bright light shone in one eye, then the other, then back again. "Mrs. Falls, you're on the stretcher now. We're taking you to the hospital. Can you hear me?"

I nodded. *Yes, I can hear you.*

"She's not moving or responding to the light. We need to move quickly."

I tried to tell them they were wrong, that I had responded. They weren't listening.

"I'm coming with her." I recognized Kyle's voice this time, but couldn't see him.

"That's fine. Everyone else will need to drive separately."

We were moving now, passing through the house, floating. The ceiling moved fast, then the porch, then the night sky stretched out above me for only a moment before I was staring at the metal roof of an ambulance. There was a red smear in the right corner. I hoped it wasn't blood.

"Mrs. Falls, if you can hear me, I want you to squeeze my hand." A man was speaking now, and I realized two of his fingers were flat against my palm.

I squeezed his fingers so tight, I was sure I'd snap them right off.

The man gave me a warm smile. "Good. We have movement."

Kyle exhaled in a one loud rush. "She squeezed your hand?"

The man shook his head. "No, but her hand twitched. She was trying." He patted my shoulder. "Good job, Mrs. Falls."

Bastard. I fumed. *Ask me again.*

He did, and the rest of the ride was both incredibly fast and excruciatingly slow. Every time he asked me to move, it became a little easier. I began to respond, then I finally squeezed hard—the proof in the wince on his face.

Ha.

When the doctors took over, I was able to talk in short sentences. Breathless. After an hour of poking and prodding, I could talk and move normally. Half of my body still tingled and felt sluggish, while the rest of me just felt exhausted.

"You gave your family quite the scare there, Mrs. Falls."

I turned my head to see a doctor noting something in my chart next to my bed. He was tall, thin, and balding, and

I liked him right away. He had an easygoing aura about him, light blue, like the sky on a clear day. None of this had frightened him. I wanted that.

"I'm Dr. Morales." He smiled, revealing a brilliantly white set of teeth.

My mouth felt dry, and my tongue heavy, but I cleared my throat. "What happened?"

"You had a seizure—a quite severe one, actually," he said, placing the chart in a slot at the end of my bed. He pushed his hands into the pockets of his white coat. "I'm prescribing a higher dosage of anti-seizure medications. From the look of your charts and speaking to your husband, it sounds like this isn't a surprise?"

I shook my head. "It's not." And somehow, it still was.

"I must admit, I'm surprised to see a tumor that size in someone your age. I am very sorry you're dealing with this." His mouth turned down at the corners in an apologetic frown. "The new medication should, at minimum, lessen the frequency and severity of your seizures. However, it might be time to start looking into finding a hospice facility. It's very likely your symptoms will progress in the coming weeks."

"I'm not going anywhere," I replied adamantly. I would have stomped my foot if I'd been standing. "I'm going to die at home. It's the entire reason I came to Vermont."

"I was curious about that," the doctor said, his gaze shifting to my chart and then back to me. "Your charts are from Chicago, but your residency is here?"

I looked at him carefully, examining his flat nose and bushy eyebrows, before I dropped my gaze to my fidgeting fingers. I was tired of answering questions and being shamed by doctor after doctor. I couldn't do it again. Not now.

"Oh, I see." He suddenly said, his face lighting up with recognition. He inhaled slowly, nodding his head. "You moved here for the new law. Death with dignity."

This time it was my turn to nod, grateful I hadn't had to go through the spiel again.

"Have you already gone through the legal process, received the medication?" he asked.

I shook my head. "I've tried. Every doctor we've gone to has turned me down."

"Really?" His brows shot up. He looked annoyed, though I wasn't sure if it was directed at me. "According to your chart, you're decisively a candidate. But you're having a hard time finding a doctor who wants to be involved?"

"An impossible time," I replied, hoping I wasn't about to start crying.

"I'll tell you what," he started, then paused, exhaling a sigh and crossing his arms over his chest. "I'll help you—if you want, of course."

I sat up on the bed, despite the ache in my back that shot through my limbs at the sudden movement. "You will? Why?"

Dr. Morales shrugged his shoulders, as if he wasn't saying the best thing I'd heard all year. "I believe in the law. Simple as that. There is no reasonable explanation for why someone should go through that type of pain and suffering."

I wanted to throw off the covers and bear hug him. Thank goodness, my weakened state wouldn't allow that.

He continued, "In your case, I'd like to help because if your latest scans are correct, you won't have much time left to legally make this decision."

Um...what? "I don't understand?"

"The law states the patient must be mentally and psychologically capable of making the call. The type of tumor you have will affect your mental faculties, and at the rate it's progressing, that will be soon."

I remembered getting a scan when I first arrived at the hospital today, but it was still a blur. I definitely didn't remember hearing the results, but the alarm in his expression made my stomach turn. "What did the scans say?"

"I don't have the results from today's yet. I examined your previous reports, though. The tumor is progressing rapidly."

"Another reason why I'm having a hard time finding a doctor to help me," I said.

"Give me a minute." Dr. Morales abruptly walked out of the room.

Confused, I waited. A few minutes later, he returned with another doctor who was about half his age. "Mrs. Falls, this is Dr. Paul. I need a witness to hear your first formal request."

They both stared at me. It wasn't unfriendly, rather stoic and serious. I swallowed, clearing my throat when I grasped what he was saying. Glancing between them, my chest rose and fell rapidly, my ears vibrated with a loud buzzing sound I couldn't pinpoint.

Finally, I pushed the words out of my lungs with as much force as I could. "I'd like a prescription for the medication needed to end my life in accordance with the Death with Dignity Act."

My words came out so fast, they ran together. I wasn't even sure if I'd said the right thing, or if there was a transcript I was supposed to follow. It all sounded so stilted and forced.

The doctors looked at each other.

"I'm satisfied," Dr. Paul said. "Send the paperwork. I'll

review the reports and if it meets criteria, I'll sign as a witness." He extended his hand toward me.

I grabbed it and we shook.

"It was lovely meeting you, Mrs. Falls," he said. "You're in good hands with Dr. Morales."

"Thank you." He left and I looked back at my doctor. "So...that's it? You'll prescribe me the medication?"

"That was only the first step." He looked apologetic, but firm. "Next, I'll arrange a session with a psychiatrist who will tell me if you're capable of making this decision. If all goes well, you'll return here in fifteen days to make a second request. If you still feel the same way, that is. Much can change in two weeks."

"I'm not changing my mind," I assured him.

Dr. Morales seemed unfazed. I liked that. I liked that he wasn't invested one way or the other—it was truly *my* choice. "I'll send a psychiatrist recommendation and write the scripts for the anti-seizure medication. Once you have those, you're free to go home. Sound good?"

I nodded. "Yes. Thank you so much."

With a polite smile, he left and I sagged into my pillow, tears springing to my eyes. After a miserable first few weeks in Vermont, things were finally starting to fall into place. I was closer to dying—an inevitability that both relieved and terrified me—but it was finally going to be on my terms.

CHAPTER TWENTY-FOUR

Tuesday, July 15, 2014

"DO you want me to come in with you?" Kyle dropped down onto one side of the overstuffed couch in the psychiatrist's waiting room then let out a loud yawn.

With how many doctors I'd dragged him to in the last few weeks only to be turned away, I didn't blame him for being so tired. The constant disappointment was exhausting, but this weekend's discussion with Dr. Morales felt like progress. It was our first yes, but Kyle saw it as just another *hurry up and wait.*

I shook my head. "No, I think it has to only be me." I lowered myself gingerly next to him on the couch. I was feeling even more achy than usual, and my head throbbed. The last few days had put my body through the ringer.

He flipped open a magazine he'd grabbed from the end table. "Okay. I'll be here if you change your mind."

The inner office's door opened and a middle-aged

woman poked her head out. When she saw us, she smiled and opened the door wider. I pushed myself up to my feet and she stuck her hand out. "Mr. and Mrs. Falls? Hi, I'm Dr. Willow James."

"Nice to meet you." I shook her hand and smiled politely. "I'm Tessa, and this is my husband, Kyle." Kyle stood and shook her hand next.

Dr. James pushed her hair behind her ears, an endearing move that looked almost vulnerable. I liked it, and I liked her. It'd only been a few seconds, but there was a softness to her that immediately made me feel safe. "Lovely to meet you both." She gestured into her office. "Come on in, Tessa."

After I entered her office, she closed the door behind me and waited for me to choose my seat out of the several arm chairs and couches available. I picked one of the smallest armchairs in the corner and then tucked my feet beneath me.

She seated herself in a similar chair across from me, a notepad and pen on her lap. "Dr. Morales gave me some information regarding your circumstances for being here, but I'd like to hear from you. This is your hour. We can talk about anything you'd like."

"I'm not sure where to start..." The scarf on my head felt itchy. I pushed it back slightly, trying to adjust it, then, on a whim, decided to pull it off completely. I wanted her to see it. The scars, the fuzzy patches of hair, the way my skin flaked around the incision. "I have a tumor—glioblastoma—in my brain." I ran a finger over my head to the spot above the cancer. "It's terminal. Meds, radiation...I've tried it all, but instead of shrinking, it grew. I've got until November, maybe. I'm not entirely sure anymore. Every doctor has said something different."

Dr. James exhaled slowly, and her eyes were frowning. I'd never seen someone who could frown with just their eyes, but she was and it was a more real display of emotion than I'd ever seen. A window into her heart that she'd willingly left open and encouraged me to look into. "I'm so sorry, Tessa. It's incredibly unfair someone so young has to deal with this. May I ask, how old are you?"

"I'm twenty-eight. I'll turn twenty-nine on the last day of September, if..." *if I make it that long,* I finished silently.

She seemed to understand my meaning. "Do you want to make it to your twenty-ninth birthday?"

If anyone else had asked me that, I'd be offended. But, there was no judgment in the way she spoke, an understanding that maybe I wouldn't want to live like this and that was just fine. There was no rule that said I had to want to see my next birthday, but even as I realized she was giving me the freedom to say no, I only wanted to say yes. "I want to make it to all of them. Thirty, fifty...one hundred."

She didn't respond, prompting me to continue, forcing me to face the reality of my situation, something I tried to avoid thinking. That didn't work out in my favor often. "I know the rest aren't options, but I do want to make it to twenty-nine. Though, only if I can still be me."

She cocked her head to the side. "What do you mean?"

I pulled on a loose string on the edge of the armchair. "I'd rather die now—able to talk and walk—than die paralyzed in a bed at twenty-nine. That's why I'm here, why I moved to Vermont. To get the medication to end my life when that time comes."

She didn't look surprised, and I guessed Dr. Morales had already told her. "What made you decide this route? Have you researched other options?"

"I've spoken to more doctors in the last few months than

I've spoken to in my entire life," I admitted, a rueful smile pulling at my lips. "There's no uncertainty in my diagnosis, even with other routes available. There's also no question what it'll be like in the end—paralysis, pain, blindness, seizures. I don't want to go through that."

She jotted something down on her notepad. "What about new medicines, clinical trials, experimental studies? Have you looked into those?"

I nodded, my stomach tightening. "There's a clinical trial at a university in North Carolina with a lot of potential, but not in the time frame that'll help me. The research is still in its infancy. Plus, most of the success they've seen were in earlier stages, and my tumor has progressed so quickly, I no longer fit the criteria."

"What if they accepted you into the trial and it could extend your life? Have you tried to apply?"

I was beginning to think my first impressions of her were wrong. "I called and spoke to the lead clinician. He confirmed my tumor was too advanced. On the off-chance I was accepted, the treatment *would* most likely extend my life...but in a hospital bed. There would be hundreds of tests, strict procedures, constant monitoring. I'd never get to go out on my own terms, doing things I've always wanted to, with people I want to be with."

She lifted one brow. "Even for a shot at life?"

My chest tightened, and I tried to exhale my irritation. I needed her to listen to me, not keep repeating the same question. "That would be the best-case scenario for someone without my tumor, my prognosis. I *am* dying, and that study—or any other—won't change that. Hopefully, it'll change things for the next person with a brain tumor."

"Why not you?" Her face was completely blank, not a hint of emotion. Given that I already knew how expressive she could be, I wondered why she was hiding now—or what. "Why wouldn't you try if it means you'd live a long and healthy life?"

My face twisted so hard, I worried it might freeze that way. *Was she kidding? Did she not hear anything I'd said?*

I mentally counted to five, pairing each second with a choice four-letter word I wanted to throw at her. Finally, I replied, "I don't think you understand."

"I do." She didn't miss a beat, and I let my gaze travel past her to her desk, wondering if I'd get a chance to steal and break the glass paperweight she had. I really had to stop soothing my emotions by breaking shit. Maybe tomorrow. "There is a trial that holds the tiniest bit of hope. It could extend or save your life, but you're turning it down. You're not even trying. Why?"

"I am trying!" The words shot out of me in a yell, my fists balled at my side. I was definitely going to break her damn paperweight now. "I am trying to spend my last months *living*... that's the point of all of this. I'd maybe gain more time, but I'd lose the chance to live. *I want to live.*"

Dr. James carefully placed her pen on the notepad and stared at me.

Shit. I shouldn't have yelled. Though, she didn't seem surprised...or even upset. Therapy is a mine field, and my heart had stepped on each one until I detonated.

Christ, this woman was hard to read when she wanted to be. "I'm sorry," I continued. "I don't mean to yell. It's just...I'm not giving up, or suicidal. I don't *want* to die. I *am* dying. There's a difference. I had to accept that fact to be able to find any happiness in my remaining days. I'm going to enjoy the time I have rather than spend it wishing for more."

She placed her notepad on the table next to her then

leaned forward, resting her elbows on her knees. "Tessa, if you're serious about doing this, about ending your life, you need to know what you're giving up. You need to decide it's worth it to you anyway, find calm with that decision in your heart and mind." Her eyes turned emotive again, and this time, I saw pride. She smiled, small and slow. "It sounds like you've done that."

Relief seeped through my body as I realized how certain I was. For the first time, there was zero doubt in my mind about what I wanted. She was completely right—I'd done the work. The only things holding me back were other people's judgements and feelings, but me? I knew what I wanted. This was the right choice. "You did that on purpose, didn't you? Egging me on like that?"

She just smiled and cocked her head to the side.

I leaned back against the couch, my posture relaxing. "I've seen people die slowly...what it does to those left behind. I want to ease the suffering for my family as much as me. I want to be able to decide when it happens...how."

"What if you can't?" she asked, picking up her notepad again and jotting something down.

I frowned. "What do you mean?"

"What if the tumor's growth accelerates and you pass before receiving the medication? Or, what if you're not approved? What then?"

I swallowed at the thought. "There's not much I could do then, is there?"

It was a question, but it also wasn't. I had no idea how things would progress, nor did my doctors. They hadn't expected the treatment not to work. They hadn't expected six months to be too long of a prognosis. I hadn't expected to be facing death before I turned thirty.

"There are people with terminal illnesses who end their lives other ways," Dr. James said, her voice quieter now.

My eyes widened and I shook my head. "No. No way. I mean...yes, I know it's an option, but not for me."

"Why not?"

"I couldn't." It was truly that simple. "Not to my family. To myself. What if my family got in legal trouble for it somehow? What if they blamed themselves? And, in the worst possible case scenario, what if I didn't die from it at all? Or died slowly and in agony? There's way too much risk. That kind of thing happens *all the time*. I literally have nightmares about it. I just can't. I can't. I know what I want to do."

"That's good to hear that you know what you want and you're adamant about your decision." She jotted down a few more notes. "Tell me about your family. Are they having a tough time with this? Surely they want you around as long as possible."

"They do, but the only one opposed to *how* is my sister," I explained. "And she doesn't know what she's asking."

"What do you think she's asking?"

"She's asking for me not to die. Period." I rubbed my right palm up and down my left arm, then switched hands to do the same thing on the opposite side. Soothing. Making it easier to talk about how little time I have left to feel my fingers brushing over my skin. "If she can't have that, then she at least wants more time. It doesn't seem to occur to her what that time will look like. When our mother was dying, Elly was so young. She doesn't remember the pain and torment our mom was in, or what a hardship that was on our father...on me."

Dr. James made a soft humming noise. "What would you do, then? If you didn't get approved?"

I stared back at her. "Are you not approving me?"

She shook her head, sitting up straighter. "I don't know the answer to that yet, and I'm not the final decision point. Either way—approved or not—there are external factors you can't control. All you can control is how you respond to the uncontrollable."

"I don't know what I would do if..." I paused, looking up at the ceiling for an answer. "If I didn't get approved...I'd probably look into alternative medicines or therapies, anything to stop the symptoms, or reduce my pain as much as possible."

"And if that doesn't work?" She was pushing again. Risky, considering the life of her paperweight was still on the line.

The thought of not only dying, but dying a slow and painful death, was terrifying. It overwhelmed me to think of what would happen, how it would feel, how long it could take....

I cleared my throat and fought back the impending panic. "If I have no options, then I have no options. I'll die the same way people have always died, and life will continue on without me."

We sat there quietly, letting the heaviness of the conversation catch up with us. She watched me, not in an uncomfortable way, but because we needed a moment of silence for my life, for my death...for me.

When we finally began talking again, we discussed what the next few months would look like, how I'd deal with it. Every fear poured out of me, letting down every wall I'd built up to protect the people around me from knowing how devastated I truly was. Here and now, I took care of me first. I bled my grief onto her office floor, and then I left it there.

The weight parked on my chest for months was gone. Whether she approved me or not, I had found a resounding assurance inside myself. There were no more doubts, no questions, and that certainty...it was everything.

I left her paperweight intact as a thank you.

CHAPTER TWENTY-FIVE

Thursday, July 17, 2014

"I DON'T UNDERSTAND why we need to discuss it now." Kyle opened the car door for me and offered me his hand. "We already have the legal paperwork done—will, advanced directive, power of attorney. That's more than enough."

I stood with his help then stretched my neck from side to side as we walked up the porch steps and into the house.

"It feels so mechanical," he continued. "I don't like thinking about it."

"I don't either," I reminded him while I pulled off my jacket. "But if I don't tell you what I want now, when will I have another chance?"

He took my jacket from me and hung it in the coat closet. "There's plenty of time."

I nibbled on the edge of my lip. I hoped he was right, but I also knew he wasn't based on the shooting pain radiating from my scalp to my neck. "Either way, I want you to know. Like for my book, my funeral—"

He waved his hands in front of his face, shaking his head. "I'm not talking about your funeral."

"Good, because I don't want one. If you need a small gathering at my burial, fine. But, I'd rather have a celebration *before* I die. With happiness. And dancing. Even if it's just you and me—I want *that* to be my funeral."

"You want to celebrate your death?" He looked incredulous, his brows lifted almost to his hairline. "Have you lost your goddamn mind?"

I rolled my eyes, heading for the couch. *The dramatics on this one.* "Not my death. My *life.*"

He scrunched his brows together and I wondered if I was pushing him too far. This entire topic was hard for him —I knew that. It was hard for me, too.

"I think we should plan a trip." Kyle's spontaneous admission surprised me.

"Yeah?" I perked a little at the idea, despite how zapped my energy levels were lately. "Where do you want to go?"

He joined me on the couch, lifted my legs into his lap, and rubbed my feet. "Better question is where do *you* want to go?"

I tilted my head, melting into the couch cushions thanks to his skilled massage. A groan escaped my lips, my eyes closing. Beast jumped on the couch and curled into the crook of my arm. "I want to go somewhere with water."

Kyle laughed and I opened my eyes to see him pointing out the window at our view. "This isn't enough water for you?"

"Nope." I grinned, pushing up my chin. "I want excitement, energy—not gentle waves on a calm lake."

"You've mentioned Niagara Falls before. We could take a boat under the falls, get completely wet."

I wiggled my brows at him. "That's what she said."

He opened his mouth as if to respond, but then his face seemed to droop, and he shook his head.

"What?" I prompted. "I'm not funny anymore?"

"You're always funny, Tessa." He glanced sideways at me. "But I'm going to miss this. I'm going to miss how you make me laugh."

I swallowed hard, focusing my gaze out the window. My voice was strangled when I finally found it. "Kyle..."

"It's fine, Tessa. We've talked about it enough."

I sat up, pulling my feet from his lap and taking his hand in mine. "No, we haven't. I've talked, and you haven't listened. At the lawyer's office today, I just wanted to say—"

"For the last damn time, I'm *not* getting re-married," Kyle cut me off.

I threw up my arms. "Not tomorrow, obviously. But, you're only thirty. It's completely unrealistic for you to think you're never going to meet someone you'll love in the future. I don't want you to be alone."

His nostrils flared as he tightened his jaw. Fiery eyes turned to me. "That's not up to you now."

I crossed my arms over my chest, never one to back down from an argument. "Kyle, I'm not saying bring a date to my funeral—"

"Jesus Christ, Tessa!" He lifted my feet off his lap, gently placing them on the couch behind him before standing up and walking toward the kitchen.

Beast stood and looked between us, seemingly nervous about choosing sides.

I didn't follow, mostly because my entire body was

drained and a new headache was pounding behind my eyes. Beast settled down, this time lying on my stomach.

My dad walked into the living room a few seconds later. "What's with the shouting?"

"It's nothing." I tried to push away the tears welling on my lower lashes.

"It doesn't look like nothing, sunshine." My dad sat where Kyle had been and gently rubbed my lower leg. "Talk to me."

I kept my gaze focused out the window. "We finalized our wills today, which was fine. We needed that, but it also brought up the conversation of...moving on...without me."

"Ohhhh." He took in a deep breath and released it slowly. "That's a tough topic."

I rubbed the palms of my hands together, pressing them tightly into the other. "I don't want him to be alone and miserable forever, Dad. He should remarry. He should find love after me." I sniffed, running a hand under my nose. "He didn't even want to talk about it—like he would never even consider it."

My dad cleared his throat. "I never remarried after your mom died, sunshine. And I wasn't alone or miserable—I had my two beautiful girls."

It had never even crossed my mind that my father would date or marry again. Not that he couldn't, but I couldn't imagine him wanting to...at least not when we were younger. "I wasn't thinking, Dad. I'm sorry. You had us girls, at least. Kyle is strong, but who will he have?"

My dad squeezed my leg and smiled. "Sunshine, that boy's always going to have your sister and I, whether you're here or not. He's my son. That doesn't change—period."

A slow tear slid down my cheek and I tangled my

fingers into Beast's fur, seeking comfort from his soft side. "Promise?"

"Family doesn't come with an out, kiddo." He stood up, bent down, and kissed my forehead. "I'm sure when he's ready one day, he'll date again. Even then, he'll still have us. We're not going anywhere."

I smiled under the tears that were flowing more freely now. "Thanks, Dad."

He grabbed an empty notepad and pencil, handing it to me. "He may not listen now, but you're leaving a piece of you behind forever in this book. Tell him. Tell everyone, everything."

I take the items, the blank page staring back at me for only a moment or two before I know exactly what my next chapter will be.

This would be the third journal I'd fill, and far from the last. Each one a love story to breathing. To loving. To remembering I'd been here. He'd read it...eventually. I'll be gone so much sooner than he'd like, and one day he might need me to remind him that life is worth living even when you're dying.

And so I keep writing my story.

• ဢ • ဢ • ဢ •

FRIDAY, July 18, 2014

"IT'S NOT THAT HARD, TESSA," Elly said with a laugh as she pushed the spatula into my hand.

I frowned at the pancake she'd just placed in front of me. "If it's so easy, why is yours all lopsided?"

"It's not lopsided. It's...oval?" She shrugged, then tore off a piece and popped it into her mouth. "Plus, it's delicious."

"I can't flip it." I tried to hand the spatula back to her, but she shook her head. Instead, she handed me a bowl of pancake batter.

"You can do it, come on. Just spoon a scoop onto the pan."

"Should I have sprayed it first or something?" I asked, watching the spoonful of batter spread into a large, flat circle.

"I already did. Just wait 'til you see bubbles, then flip." Elly flicked a tiny droplet of batter at me. I jolted in surprise as it landed on my cheek.

"Oh, gaaaaaame on!" I dipped two fingers into the batter and wiggled my brows at her.

She quickly covered her face with an empty plate. "Don't you dare throw it!"

"Fine. I won't." Instead, I dragged my dirty fingers down the length of her arm.

She shrieked and spun away from me. "Gross! That's on my shirt!"

I shrugged, laughing. "But, I didn't throw it."

"You're such a child," she said with a chuckle "It's almost time to flip. Grab your spatula."

I wiped my hand off on a kitchen towel and gripped the spatula. I slid the edge under the bubbling mass, twisted, and slammed the pancake back down on the pan. Splatters of batter danced in several directions, and the entire thing squished to one side.

I made a check mark motion with my hand. "Pancake flipping. Cross that off my list, but I just killed it."

Elly frowned, holding out a plate. "What list?"

"My bucket list." I lifted the finished pancake onto her plate and garnished it with some whip cream.

Elly let out an audible sigh. "Do you have to do that? Talk about *it* all the time? We were having a nice moment. We don't have to dwell on...the rest."

Ha. I wish my body would let me. "I'm not dwelling. I'm making the most of what I have, but I can't ignore any of it even if I wanted to. It's happening, and I'm living with it."

"You're not living with anything," she snapped. "You're *dying*."

I move to the kitchen table, lowering myself into one of the chairs. I'm exhausted from standing the last fifteen minutes—another reminder I can't ignore. "So are you. So is everyone. We're all living until we die. I just happen to have a shorter timeframe than most."

Elly turned off the stove, then headed for the doorway. She paused to look at me. "I don't understand how you're okay with this. How you're totally fine with leaving us." Her eyes glistened with unshed tears. "With leaving *me*."

I started to respond, but she left and I was too tired to follow her. Frowning, I dropped my head back against the chair before letting out a loud groan. I'd been stormed out on more times in the last few days than I could count. No one was talking much. It was awkward and stiff, and I hated it.

I hated that they couldn't see how hard I was trying to hold it together—*for them*.

They needed me to be miserable, demonstrably hurt by my diagnosis, while also slapping on a smile and bucking the fuck up. They needed apologetic Tessa, guilt-ridden for putting them through this, and furious Tessa, wanting revenge on a conspirator I can't see.

I'm none of those. And all of them.

I'm enraged that the life I'd envisioned for myself isn't going to happen. I'm heartbroken Kyle and I will never have the family we dreamed. I'm physically aching at the idea that both my dad and my sister will lose yet another woman they love to cancer. I'm petrified of what it'll be like, what it'll feel like, or how empty it feels to know I'll be here one moment...and gone the next.

I had no answers for them...or for myself. I didn't even know the right questions—the only ruminations circling my consciousness were when? Why?

Why me?

CHAPTER TWENTY-SIX

Friday, August 1, 2014

I DIDN'T LOSE MORE weight, maybe I'd even gained a pound or two. Never imagined I'd be happy about that one day. It didn't mean my odds were any better, but it meant more normalcy, more strength, and more *me*. At least for a little while.

I was sporting a new look these days. A lot less *cancer patient*, and a lot more pale and pixie cut. My spiky, short hair gave me an edgy look that was every bit as badass as I felt when I managed to keep breakfast down.

"Need a coat?" Kyle entered the foyer, watching me slip on my shoes.

"Probably should," I replied, since I'm still always cold, despite the extra pounds. He wrapped the jacket around my shoulders and slid my arms inside. "Thanks."

There was a stiffness to him. The way he was looking down, moving with restraint. He was holding something back, though it was no secret what. He wanted to stop me—

my plans dashing his hopes for a miracle. But, he said nothing.

He opened the front door and ushered me to the car. A few minutes later, we pulled up in front of the hospital and headed up to Dr. Morales office. A nurse pointed us in his direction and we found the doctor seated at his desk, flipping through my file when we walked in.

"Mrs. Falls, great to see you again," he said with a friendly smile. He stood and shook my hand, then Kyle's. We greeted him, then took a seat on the opposite side of his desk. He lifted a file and flipped through a few pages inside. "So, I got the report from Dr. James."

I leaned forward. "What did she say?"

He cut right to the chase. "She believes you know the options available to you, and have come to your decision of your own free will with a full understanding of the ramifications."

I clasped my hands together. "Does that mean I'm approved?"

He shook his head. "No. Dr. James provides a recommendation I will use to make the final determination." Dr. Morales folded his arms on the desk top, focusing his gaze on me in earnest. "Mrs. Falls, in the two weeks since we last spoke or you met with Dr. James, it would be completely natural to have had second thoughts or to change your mind."

"I haven't," I reply quickly, cutting him off. "Not even a little."

Dr. Morales slowly nodded his head, leaning back in his chair. "Let's get started, then. There are quite a few legal steps we'll need to satisfy."

I let out a long exhale, releasing the tension I'd been holding. It was finally happening. After everything I'd done to get here, the relief at knowing it had all been worth it was freeing.

"I'll need a second verbal and written request." Dr. Morales handed me a piece of paper and a pen before standing. "I'm going to ask my colleague to witness. In the meantime, please write down your request."

He left the room, and I immediately began writing.

~~DR. MORALES~~ TO *Whom It May Concern*:
~~It's about goddamn time~~ *I, Tessa Elizabeth Falls, have* ~~fucking cancer~~ *a grade four glioblastoma with a terminal diagnosis. I have chosen to use* ~~dope ass pain killers~~ *palliative care and hospice measures during this time, and want to be prescribed an end-of-life medication. I'm* ~~smart as hell~~ *fully informed and capable of making this decision of my own free will. This is my second request after the* ~~insanely long~~ *fifteen-day waiting period.*
Signed,
Tessa Elizabeth Falls, 8/1/14

"TESSA?" Kyle squeezed my knee as I placed the pen down, finally coming up with a good letter despite no direction and crossing out half of it. "Are you sure about this?"

"I'm sure." I nodded. "I've been working toward this for months."

"I know, but you can change your mind... even after you have the meds. No one would fault you." He laced his fingers through mine. "We could wait?"

"If I wait, I could miss my chance entirely."

Kyle looked so defeated that my heart twisted in my

chest. I brought his hand to my face, laying my cheek against his palm. "Can you do this?"

His eyes found mine, shimmering green as tears welled on his lower lashes. He shook his head. "I'm not leaving." He slid his palm down to my chest, my heart beating beneath his touch. "I want to feel this forever."

My pulse quickened at the low tenor of his words. I was sure he could feel the throbbing ache of my heart against his palm. "Kyle," I started. "I—"

"Dr. Paul, you remember the Falls." Dr. Morales walked in.

Kyle's hand dropped to my lap, where I squeezed it tightly in one of mine. We exchanged greetings and introductions before I handed him the written request.

Dr. Morales took a seat behind his desk while his colleague leaned against the wall, his hands in his white coat pockets. "Everything looks to be in order. Before the verbal request, let's discuss the decision you're making on record—for legal protections." He held up a tape recorder.

I could probably recite the speech he was going to give at this point, but I didn't mind rehashing it. The law was difficult. It needed to be that way, and, truthfully, I appreciated that.

He clicked play on the recorder and set it between us, giving a verbal introduction of who he was and then asking me to state my name and current legal state of residence. Dr. Paul also introduced himself, along with Kyle, before Dr. Morales started his spiel. He reiterated my diagnosis, life expectancy, and confirmed that I understood the limitations to the medical prognosis. We discussed the second, third, and fourth opinions—all of which resulted in the same accounts—as well as Dr. James's evaluation.

He then launched into treatment options, how further

radiation and chemotherapy could possibly extend my life by a few months. I shuddered at the thought of going through those again. The pain had been intolerable, and there was no doubt I couldn't handle a second round. Dr. Paul mentioned clinical trials and experimental medications and procedures I could try. I gave them both a resounding no to each. Feeling certain I understood the choices, Dr. Morales discussed the palliative care I'd be receiving to make my transition into hospice as painless as possible.

Finally, after what felt like hours, he broached the topic of end-of-life medications. "If approved, you'll be taking two medications. Let me make *very* clear, Tessa, that *you* are the only one who handles them."

"Will the nurse be there?" I asked.

He nodded, leaning against his elbows on his desk. "She will, and she'll assist in case of emergencies and to assess time of death. Medication administration is entirely your responsibility. No one can hand them to you, help you take them. Nothing. This has to be entirely decided by you and acted out by you, with no influence from anyone else. Any third-party assistance, no matter how small, can result in legal action—even criminal prosecution."

"Criminal?" Kyle looked as surprised as I felt. "But it's legal."

"The Patient Choice at End of Life statute last year made it legal for the patient to self-administer the medication. Any other involvement isn't protected under that law," he explained. "It's a stretch, but it's safer not to risk it."

"That's fine. I can do it alone." I squeezed Kyle's hand to assure him.

Truthfully, I didn't want anyone to help anyway. My family was already struggling with the very idea of me dying, and I certainly didn't want to add to their pain by involving them further. This was a decision I had to make and be fully responsible for—fully in control of.

Dr. Morales glanced at his colleague who nodded discreetly. "Good. You'll take them simultaneously, but they'll take effect at different times. The first will make you lose consciousness. You'll feel nothing after that point. The second will stop your heart. Your organs will shut down, and you'll be pronounced dead by the nurse soon after."

"How long will that take?" I asked.

"You'll feel the effects of the first medication in a matter of minutes, losing consciousness pretty quickly. There have been rare exceptions of twenty or thirty minutes, but the average is five minutes," he told me.

"And the second pill? The one that stops her heart?" Kyle asked this time, a slight tremble moved through him. I held him hand tighter.

"That is harder to estimate. It varies based on the individual's body, but can be as soon as thirty minutes, to as long as ten hours."

I gasped, my stomach sinking with a sickening thud. *"Ten hours?"*

My main reason for taking the medication was to avoid pain and prolonged death.

Dr. Morales continued, "Correct. However, you'd be unconscious during that time. Your family, on the other hand, would be aware of the situation. It's something you need to consider, if that's a possibility you and your family are ready for."

Kyle's face paled beside me.

"You are able to change your decision at any time. Whether now, or after you receive the medication. If it's after, you'll need to turn the medication over to us to be properly disposed of. Dr. Paul, is there anything I've left out?" he asked the young doctor still leaning against the wall.

"I don't believe so," Dr. Paul confirmed.

Dr. Morales returned his focus to me. "Mrs. Falls, if you're ready, we can hear the second verbal request."

I'd been ready for weeks. "I've thoroughly considered my options, followed the legal steps, and I'd still like to be prescribed the self-administered medications I need to end my life."

Kyle exhaled sharply, turning his head to face away from me.

"Works for me." Dr. Morales looked at his colleague. "Dr. Paul?"

The second doctor stared at me then nodded. "I'm satisfied."

"Mrs. Falls, there are quite a few documents you'll need to sign," Dr. Morales began, pushing my papers into one large file.

I jumped in. "And then I'll get the prescription?"

"I'll send the prescription directly to our hospital pharmacy to fill it. It can be difficult to find pharmacies to fill it, but the hospital will." Dr. Morales put my file in a cabinet drawer, then turned back to me. "However, I can't give it to you today. You'll need to return Wednesday."

"Why can't she have it now?" Kyle asked what I was thinking. These trips were exhausting, both physically and emotionally. I wasn't looking forward to a repeat performance.

"Legally, a forty-eight-hour waiting period after the second verbal request is mandatory before I can write the prescription." He offered me an apologetic smile. "During Wednesday's meeting, you'll have another chance to change your mind, if you so decide. If not, I'll write the prescription and send it to the pharmacy."

Kyle sighed. "Jesus Christ."

I swallowed my irritation—or tried. "Okay, but by the end of Wednesday...I'll have the medication?"

"If you don't change your mind beforehand, yes," he confirmed.

"Damn." Kyle dropped my hand and rubbed the scruff on his jaw. "I didn't know we'd have to wait again."

"We can come back Wednesday." I was annoyed, too, but in the grand scheme of what we'd gone through to get here, I could wait a few more days. Unless a miracle cure for cancer was discovered in the next week, my decision was made.

His brows furrowed. "We're leaving Sunday for a week." Kyle gave me a sheepish smile. "Surprise, we're going on vacation."

My mouth fell open. "A trip?"

"Even better," Dr. Morales said. "More time to consider. We'll schedule for Monday, August eleventh."

Kyle leaned closer to me. "You don't mind waiting longer?"

I shook my head. "Where are we going?"

He winked. "It's a surprise."

CHAPTER TWENTY-SEVEN

FRIDAY, *August 1, 2014*

AN HOUR LATER, Kyle and I climbed into the car, finished with the necessary paperwork. Despite the disappointing news that I needed to come back...again, I was feeling optimistic. The hardest parts of this process were over—*I had been approved.*

"I wish we could have stayed in Chicago." I angled in my seat to face Kyle as he drove us home. "I hadn't expected how much the move would take out of me, or how much I'd miss our home. I grew up there, met you, spent every minute of my life walking those streets." I sighed as a surprising wave of homesickness tore through me. "I would've liked to die at home."

Kyle squeezed my leg. "Tessa." His voice was sad, and though he only said my name, it said everything.

"I know it's silly. It's just... I wish things were different in the world." I let my gaze wander out the window. "I wish I owned my body."

"You do," Kyle tried to assure me. "Your body is yours to do whatever you want with."

"But that's not really true, is it? If we'd stayed in Chicago, the powers that be—whoever that is—wouldn't have let me make this choice."

Kyle was silent. "Would that be such a bad thing?" His voice was restrained, like he wasn't sure he wanted to speak at all.

Guilt rolled through my belly. I'd promised him a lifetime together and then taken it back. I faced the window, saying nothing, and wishing he'd said nothing, too.

• ဃ • ဃ • ဃ •

SUNDAY, August 3, 2014

"I THINK it's time you told me where we're going." I pushed Beast out of my suitcase for the third time. "How will I know if I missed packing something I need?"

Kyle closed the lid of my suitcase. "You're not missing anything."

"Do I need a bathing suit? Or are those days behind me?" I looked in the mirrors paneling the closet door. A chest port was sticking out an inch below my collarbone and my skin was paper thin, burning almost instantly in the sun.

Kyle knit his brows, like he wanted to argue but then decided not to. "No swimming there."

I frowned. "How about a hint?"

"Hmm...there will be water." He zipped my suitcase and lifted it off the bed.

As he wheeled it from the room, I pulled a sweater on and grabbed my purse, smiling at Beast who sat by the door eagerly waiting for me. I was about to follow Kyle when I saw the stack of journals on my nightstand. I grabbed the one on top and shoved it into my purse.

"Tessa, you coming?"

"Yep!" I glanced down at the journal in my purse, then pulled it out and replaced it on the stack. I decided this vacation was going to be for my family and me—no one else. I didn't want the pressure of chronicling every moment for others.

I wanted to live for me. Just for this week.

On that same thought, I removed my cell phone from my purse, too. There's nothing like dying to make you stop living through a screen.

"Come on, Beast, let's go." When I reached the front yard, my dad and Kyle were packing suitcases into the trunk and Elly was placing water bottles in everyone's cup holders, along with little baggies.

"What's this?" I dropped my purse onto the back seat.

"Travel bags!" Elly exclaimed proudly. "It has snacks, tissues, hand sanitizer, and anything else you might need on a road trip."

"Jeez, how long are we driving?" I worried about my stamina for a long car ride.

Elly lifted Beast into the car and took the seat next to me.

"Seven hours to Niagara Falls," my dad answered.

Elly screeched. "Dad!"

"It was a surprise." Kyle sighed loudly then turned to

give me a smile from the driver's seat. "What do you think, babe?"

I clasped my hands together, grinning from ear to ear. "We're going to Niagara Falls?" The smile on my face was all the approval he needed. "Wait, do I have my passport?"

Elly pulled it out of her purse triumphantly and handed it to me.

"What about Beast?" I asked.

"Got his vaccine records." She pulled them out as well. "That's all he needs to cross the border."

I squeezed the dog's fluffy little body to my chest, giving him a kiss on his wriggling head. Smiling, I looked around at the people I loved most in the world, and I knew that it would all be worth it.

Being with them for one last adventure—one last memory—was worth it.

CHAPTER TWENTY-EIGHT

Sunday, August 10, 2014

GOING unplugged for a week had consequences. I hadn't thought it would matter, since I was with the only people I ever needed to call.

I was no longer employed, and not in regular contact with old friends. There was no special reason, I was just happy being with my family and didn't need much more. I had friends in Chicago I'd occasionally grab a coffee with, but no one who I'd cared enough about to mention what was happening, or even warn of my move to Vermont.

Sure, I'd done the obligatory social media post about my diagnosis a few weeks into chemo, but nothing updated since. Everyone was so sure I was going to beat this, and I had no plans to tell them otherwise. I'd posted about my move to Vermont, but never responded to comments. Kyle ended up fielding most of it, becoming everybody's go-to for information, but even he stayed tight-lipped at my request.

I wasn't against social media—in fact, I had probably

used it too much before my diagnosis. I'd been overly concerned with my amount of likes or followers on my posts. But now? There didn't seem to be a point.

I didn't like scrolling through my friend's posts about new pregnancies, engagements, exciting jobs and opportunities. It was a reminder that there wouldn't be anything new for me, and I was okay with that. I really was—or I was trying to be—but I didn't need the reminder constantly shoved in my face.

Lying on my bed while Elly unpacked my suitcase, I powered on my phone for the first time in a week and it wouldn't stop buzzing as new text messages and notifications came piling through. Every message was the same—people reacting in shock to my terminal status. I hadn't posted anything in weeks, so the sudden influx was odd.

Every message was kind and apologetic, but they all wanted something from me. That's the thing no one tells you about death—it's about the living.

All my old classmates, coworkers, acquaintances, they wanted to say goodbye, ask me questions, or offer help. I don't actually need or want any of it. Their requests and offers are for them—to feel important in the final moments of someone's life, to ease their fears that this can't, or won't, happen to them, to make them feel like they made a difference, or did the right thing.

It's not that I don't appreciate the kindness. I do. I'm just *exhausted*. The trip was wonderful, but it took everything I had. My pain was increasing, and my body started aching the moment I woke up. My head was constantly pounding, and sometimes I had to lay still with a pillow over my face in a vain attempt to slow the searing pain behind my eyes.

Holding my phone and reading everyone's messages

was strenuous enough. I dropped my phone onto the bed beside me. "Um...Elly?"

My sister glanced at me from the closet where she was hanging up my sweaters.

"Did you post something online about me?"

"Like what?" Her eyes didn't meet mine, but I knew she saw the *you're-fooling-no one* expression on my face. "I just posted some pictures from the trip."

"Ugh!" I pulled my oversized sweater tighter, hugging myself with the soft fabric. "I specifically said no one else could see those photos."

"I know, but it's a *vacation*." Elly shrugged. "People post vacation photos all the time."

"Not when they look like this!" I gestured my hand up and down my body.

I didn't have to see the photos to know what they revealed. My skin had a slightly gray sheen. I was thinner than anyone should be—ironic, since I'd actually gained weight since treatment ended. I'm not entirely bald anymore, but there was no mistaking my short hair for a fashion choice.

"I picked as flattering pictures as possible for all of us," she tried to assure me.

I rolled my eyes. Flattering was not an attainable state for me anymore.

"But I might have also said this was our last trip together, what your prognosis was, and why we're here...in Vermont." She looked like she was deciding whether she should make a run for the door.

Through clenched teeth, I exhaled and chose my words carefully. "Why would you think that was okay? To post about *my* life to the world?"

She shrugged fast, her hands slapping against her thighs

with a loud clap. "We moved away from everyone we've ever known, to a place we've never been, to...to...to what? And *no one* gets to know?"

Her volume was escalating, her face turning red and splotchy. I couldn't tell if she was anxious or angry and I opened my mouth to respond, but Elly steamrolled ahead. "Our entire life before this is just gone! It's *gone* and you don't even seem to care because you've given up! So, yeah, maybe I told some people. Maybe I thought if more people knew, if we weren't in our own little 'death bubble' up here, then you would have some hope!" Her tone dipped, her volume lower and heavier. "Then maybe you wouldn't kill yourself."

My jaw dropped, but I quickly closed it, grinding my teeth as I averted my gaze out the bedroom window. "Get out."

"Tessa," Elly started.

"Get. Out," I repeated. "Now."

Elly moved for the door, grabbing the frame and looking at me, as if expecting me to change my mind. I continued staring out the window.

When she finally left, I wanted to cry.

I focused on the water—moving and swirling in the bay, nowhere to be but everywhere to go. I envied its freedom, angry at the disregard with which it lived its life. I let rage well up in me, fill me with hot fury as I crawled beneath the blankets and lifted them over my head. Beast joined me, his breath hot against my neck.

I stared at the woven fabric, centimeters away from my face. Wishing it could be over. Wishing I didn't have to decide anything—that my body would do it for me, take the breath from my lungs before I could utter another word. Before I'd have to say goodbye and hurt everyone I loved.

Please, I prayed. And I rarely prayed. But today…
Take me now. End this now. Please.
But I was still there.

· ℘ · ℘ · ℘ ·

"IS SHE AWAKE?" Muted voices drifted across the room, meeting me where I lay curled around a pillow.

"Even if she isn't, she needs to eat. She hasn't eaten since this morning." Kyle. I'd recognize his tenor anywhere.

I squeezed my eyes tighter and raised the covers higher.

"Tessa?" The door opened this time, his voice clearer. "I brought you a sandwich, and some hummus and cucumbers."

My stomach roared awake and I gave up my quest to stay asleep for the rest of my life. Pushing the covers down, I gingerly lifted into a seated position. Aside from quick bathroom trips, I'd spent the rest of the day in this bed and had no plans to leave anytime soon. "I'm awake."

Kyle held the plate up in front of me, joining me in bed.

I took it, eyeing the food with some hesitation. I was hungry, but that didn't mean I would be able to keep my food down. My body was weird like that lately. Both healing and dying at the same time.

"You hungry?" he asked.

I nodded, taking a bite of the sandwich and swallowing slowly. "Thanks for bringing this."

"You're welcome." He still didn't move. "Do you want to come downstairs? I'll make a bigger dinner in an hour or so."

"I'm tired." I also didn't want to be around anyone, but I didn't mention that.

Kyle rubbed a hand from his forehead to the back of his neck. "Elly told me what happened, and I saw the post online. Did you see it?"

"No, and I'm not looking. I've got dozens of unread messages, and I'm not going through any of them. I don't need to explain myself to anyone."

"I'll answer the messages for you, if you want," Kyle volunteered.

Guilt washed over me over how distant I was being to the man who loved me so fiercely. I picked up the half-eaten plate of food and deposited it on the nightstand, then crawled onto his lap.

My head against his chest, I took a deep breath and exhaled slowly. "I'd really like that. I really like you."

He chuckled and kissed my temple. "I like you more."

"I'm sorry I'm so grumpy," I continued, snuggling into him even more.

His arms tightened around me and he kissed my forehead. "You have every right to be grumpy, Tessa. We're all having a hard time adjusting."

A few quiet moments passed before I finally spoke again, almost a whisper. "Are you ever going to be okay with this?"

He rested his cheek against the top of my head. "I'm trying, Tessa."

CHAPTER TWENTY-NINE

MONDAY, August 11, 2014

"READY TO GO, TESSA?" my dad called from the entryway.

I pulled another sweater on top of the one I was already wearing, doing my best to keep the constant chill at bay. "Coming."

When I arrived at the front of the house, Kyle and my dad were already pulling on their shoes. "Where's Elly?"

My dad's face turned sheepish. "She went to town earlier. Said she needed to study for her summer class at the library."

I rolled my eyes, knowing exactly what he meant. Today was my milestone. It was the last day in a long process of jumping through hoops and government red tape to have control over my own life. It was taking back power over my life, my body.

She should be here for that. Instead, she was running.

"I'm sorry, honey," my dad tried to say as we walked to the car.

"It's fine," I lied.

My heart still felt sore when we arrived at the hospital, meekly walking to Dr. Morales' office. Kyle was by my side, but my dad was keeping the car running out front, refusing to pay for parking.

Dr. Morales' receptionist brought us to an exam room where Dr. Morales joined us minutes later. He greeted us with hearty handshakes before taking my vitals. "How are you feeling today, Mrs. Falls?"

I shrugged. "I'm tired. Achy. The headaches are tough."

"To be expected." He flipped through papers in my chart. "You'll need to make sure you're taking care of yourself, not pushing to do more than you can. Taxing your body could be very detrimental right now. Have you had any symptoms, aside from fatigue and headaches?"

"Nope."

He ran me through an eye test, ensuring my vision was not impacted yet, then had me do some breathing exercises, and reminded me about taking my medications regularly. "Did we do any thinking over the week away?" he asked.

"My mind hasn't changed," I replied quickly.

Kyle dropped his chin to his chest, running his fingers through his hair.

Dr. Morales gave a small nod. "I'll put the prescription through now and call down to the pharmacy. It's on the first floor, so you can head on down to get it when we're done here."

I smiled, relief flooding my body. "Thank you."

"The hospice nurse starts tomorrow," he reminded me. "She'll keep me up to date on your vitals, but if you feel anything is wrong or you're having any issues, come in at any time." He glanced up at me, then back down at his prescription pad. "Once you decide on the date you're going to take these medications, I'd like you to call me. We'll talk about it—no pressure—and make sure everything goes exactly how you want it to. Okay?"

He felt like a partner—someone finally on my side, willing to lend support no matter what. No judgment, no emotions, just assistance and assurance. "I'll definitely do that."

"Good. I'll put in the script now." He stood and wrapped his stethoscope around his neck. "I've enjoyed getting to know you, Mrs. Falls. I'm sorry it couldn't be under better circumstances, and I'm sorry I couldn't do more. I'm here if you need me."

"Thank you, Dr. Morales. You've done everything."

A comfortable silence fell between Kyle and me while we made our way to the pharmacy.

"I'm picking up a prescription for Tessa Falls," Kyle spoke to the technician at the pick-up window for me, an arm protectively around my shoulders. "Dr. Morales put it through a few minutes ago."

"Sure. Let me go check." The plump young woman with big eyes batted her lashes at him, blushing slightly.

I smiled at the interaction, proud that the handsome hunk she was eyeing was mine. Moments like this remind me how lucky I'll always be to have loved him, even if so brief.

The technician returned seconds later, her face paler than moments ago. "Um, yes, the prescription came through." She glanced at me, then quickly averted her eyes. "I need to call in my supervisor to fill it. He should be here soon."

"You're not able to fill it?" Kyle asked.

"Uh, I just...well..." She looked so flustered and kept glancing between the script in her hands, to Kyle, then to me. "I could, but I'm Catholic. This script is for..."

"We know what it's for," Kyle replied firmly, his grip on my shoulders tightening. "We just need you to fill it."

"I'm sorry. The policy is my supervisor will fill it if my faith won't allow me to. He's due in a few minutes anyway. You're welcome to sit in the waiting area and he'll call you when ready."

"Are you serious?" Kyle bellowed, his voice echoing off the walls. "This is legal. It's *prescribed*. Call Dr. Morales. Call him right now and he'll tell you."

"Kyle, please." I put a hand on his chest to calm him. "Miss, how long until the supervisor arrives?"

"About an hour."

"An hour! You said he was a few minutes away!" Kyle was not calming down. "This is ridiculous. Call Dr. Morales down here right now."

"Sir, it's not up to—"

"I'll call him then," Kyle interrupted her and stepped away, pulling out his phone.

I shifted my weight from one leg to the next and cleared my throat, standing there alone.

"You don't have to do this, you know," the technician said, barely above a whisper as she leaned over the counter. Her eyes darted between Kyle and I. "It's not natural. This is a *sin*."

My jaw clenched, wondering if it was legal for her to say that to me.

She continued, "It's not up to us to decide when our lives are over. It's up to God."

"God already decided to end my life," I replied.

She looked startled. My words had come out harsher

than even I'd intended, but I wasn't sorry. "Can I pray for your soul then?" She reached her hand out and I recoiled, stepping back so fast I almost collided into Kyle.

"Dr. Morales is coming," he told the technician as he steadied me, his hands on my arms. "You okay, babe?"

I continued to glare at the technician. "I'll be fine as soon as we're home."

Dr. Morales hurried into the waiting room a few minutes later, giving us a quick nod before heading through an *Authorized Personnel Only* door to the pharmacy. I could hear him and the technician having a heated conversation, but couldn't make out their words.

Kyle laced his fingers through mine and kissed my knuckles.

It was one thing to have my family question my decisions, it was another for a total stranger to judge me—to tell me I was *sinning*. How? For not wanting to be in pain? Not wanting to die slowly as my family watched helplessly? Did God really want that for me? For anyone?

I couldn't believe that.

"Mr. and Mrs. Falls." Dr. Morales crossed the waiting room. "I apologize. I didn't realize the supervisor wasn't on duty yet when I sent you down here. I know he'll fill the prescription for you. He and I already spoke about it."

"Can she really refuse to fill it?" I asked. "It's not like we're doing anything illegal."

"You're not. You're definitely not. However, just like you have a right to your choices, so does she. The one thing she *doesn't* have a right to, is to make you feel badly."

I could feel the strain on the corners of my lips from how hard I was frowning, because this felt like another hoop. We were *so* close—then, road block.

Dr. Morales continued. "The law is still so new, and

there are some kinks to work out. It'll be filled within the hour if you don't mind waiting. I can get you some vouchers for the cafeteria while you wait. How about that?"

I shook my head. "I'm not hungry, but thank you."

"Well, again, I'm sorry for the trouble. The lead pharmacist should be here shortly."

"Thank you, Dr. Morales." Kyle's tone was as grim as his expression when we were left alone again, waiting for the clock to wind down. Something I seemed to be doing a lot of lately.

I grabbed a magazine off a nearby side table and began flipping through it as Kyle rotated between sitting and pacing in front of me. My mind flitted to the possibility of ripping it to pieces and littering glossy confetti across the waiting room. A few months ago, I would have done something like that. I've always been a little passive aggressive instead of speaking my mind. This changed me. I'd learned to pick my battles, and to put my foot down for what's really important to me. I was angry with the technician, but she wasn't a battle I wanted to fight. I didn't need to convince her to respect my decision.

But Elly? I *needed* her to understand.

I spared the magazine its shredded fate and flipped through a few more pages. None of the articles kept my attention so I returned it and watched my husband instead.

"This is bullshit, you know," he said when he caught my eye.

I nodded, but didn't say anything.

Kyle sighed loudly. "I can't wait for this to be over."

I looked at him, but he quickly shook his head. "Not you." He gestured between us, then around his head. "*This.* Being in the hospital. Dealing with these ridiculous hurdles. I can't wait for that part to be over."

"Me, too," I said, mostly to comfort him.

Kyle picked up a magazine, scanned through it, then tossed it down. He did the same thing with three more until he gave up and stared at the stucco ceiling.

I stared at everyone, my mind retreating to my little sister. I wished Elly had come with us. I wondered how she'd react to the pharmacist who refused to fill my prescription—if she'd defend me, or side with the technician. The realization that I didn't know if my sister would be there for me, frightened me. I'd never doubted her before, and now when I needed her the most, there was a chasm between us.

Sighing, I pulled out my phone and logged onto Facebook. Since I was stuck here at least an hour, I might as well check my messages from yesterday.

Tessa, we're so sorry you're going through this. Please let us know what we can do to help. Anything you need!

TESSA, my aunt has a homeopathic company that makes all organic balms and remedies. I think you should try some! Don't give up yet!

I'M PRAYING for your speedy recovery, Tessa. It's not over yet. Trust in God, and His faith will get you through.

TESSA, you're so young and a decision like this is forever. You never know what new drugs and cures they'll come up with.

THIS IS SO WRONG. You can't take your own life. That's

suicide! Please reconsider! We're all here for you, but please, don't do this!

THE MESSAGES WENT on and on. Everyone had an opinion. Everyone wanted to say their piece—none of it for me.

Death is the one time your life should be selfish. People I hadn't spoken to in years suddenly contacting me—wanting to know they mattered to me, they care about me. In reality, they had years before I was dying to tell me how much I meant, but life got in the way.

I responded to a few messages, just a quick thank you. The more judgmental messages, I left unanswered. I didn't owe them an explanation. There were only three people whose opinion mattered to me.

My choice was controversial. I knew that. I had to move across the country to make it possible. I knew my family wouldn't love the idea. I didn't expect them to jump for joy or welcome it, but I did expect them to support me.

Maybe that was naive.

I could see the pain in Kyle's eyes. He wasn't on board yet. Elly's certainly not hiding her discomfort with my decision. But it'd been almost two months since I'd told my family and to be honest, that's more than enough time for them to accept this—even if they still disagree.

I had so few months left. Each minute matters.

A sigh escaped me—my millionth in the last few weeks —and I put my phone in my pocket, seriously considering deleting my social media accounts entirely.

"I think this is us." Kyle pointed to an older man with a friendly smile approaching.

"Mr. And Mrs. Falls?" he asked, pulling on the lapels of his white lab coat.

I snapped to attention. "Yes?"

Kyle stood. "That's us."

The pharmacist looked both confident and nervous. "I was filled in on your situation. If you'd like to come over to window three, I can help you."

"Thank you," I said, standing with Kyle's help.

We followed him to the counter, and he went around to the other side.

"We have two medications." The pharmacist held up two orange prescription bottles littered with colorful warning stickers and instructions. I'd never seen so many tabs sticking off a prescription bottle in my life. His voice lowered as he continued, "They should both be taken at the same time, or within a minute or two of each other, but they will work at different paces. The first will cause you to fall asleep, generally within a few minutes. You'll feel nothing beyond that point. The second is capsules you'll break open into water and drink. The taste isn't great, I'll be honest. It will take longer to kick in, but the second one is the one that will stop your heart."

I nodded, absorbing everything like my life would depend on it. *Which it does.* I snorted, mentally laughing at the morbid joke. The pharmacist and Kyle both shot me questioning looks, which made me quickly clear my throat and nod along.

"The instructions are listed on the bottles, as well as this pamphlet I'll put in the bag," the pharmacist continued. He held up a thick stack of papers that could rival a book. "You should make sure your nurse is present when you take these, and don't take them unless you're absolutely ready."

"I understand," I assured him. "Dr. Morales explained the process to us at great length."

"Good." He double-checked the bag. "It's a big decision. I'm sorry today didn't go as smoothly as hoped. My mother passed from lung cancer long before death with dignity acts were considered. Watching her suffer at the end, just waiting...it was horrible. I fully support what you're doing, and I'm sure the decision hasn't been easy."

My mouth parted, surprised at both his personal admission and his candor. I'd almost forgotten what it was like to have someone not walking on eggshells around me. "Thank you," I replied honestly. "I'm sorry about your mother."

"I'm sorry about your cancer," he said.

I liked him even more.

CHAPTER THIRTY

Tuesday, August 12, 2014

MY EYES BLINKED open quickly as a sharp pain slammed down my spine to my toes. I quivered for a moment, trying to handle the onslaught of what felt like millions of needles stabbing me while every muscle in my body locked up.

My breath hitched, and I held it in my lungs as I slowly counted to ten.

Between four and seven, my vision faded to black, but by the time I got to ten, everything had subsided. Only a dull throb in my limbs as my muscles tried to relax.

These sudden aches and seizes were happening more and more.

Groaning, I pushed up to a seated position and slid my legs down the side of the bed. An oversized cardigan was draped over the footrest and I pulled it around my shoulders, my skin shivering from the cold.

"Tessa?" a sleepy voice beside me stirred. "It's early, babe."

I glanced behind me at Kyle. "I know, I can't sleep. I need to stretch my legs."

"Want me to go with you?" Concern etched his sleepy expression.

I shook my head. "I'm just going to make some tea."

"Okay." He yawned as his head hit the pillow. "Love you."

"Love you, too," I replied, feeling something strange behind my words. I felt off...disingenuous.

I got to my feet and made my way to the kitchen, filling the teakettle with water and putting it on the stove. I stood and watched it boil. I'd always heard a watched pot never boils, but I'd never tested the theory. There were so many things in life I'd just taken for granted as *the way it was*, but now? I had so many questions.

The teakettle began whistling after a while. I watched the steam billow from the tip, more aggressive with each passing second. It surged into the kitchen air, screaming at the top of its lungs and I just *let it*. Finally, I pulled it off the burner and poured the hot water into a mug, dunking the tea bag rhythmically. Still too hot to drink, I carried it to the back porch—one of my favorite parts of the house.

A wraparound veranda, it emptied onto the grass with the perfect view of the lake. The water lapped at the edges of the dock, a wall of stone keeping it from merging with our yard. A small rowboat bobbed against the currents, tied to the end of the wooden dock as the morning sun slowly began to rise over the horizon.

I sat in a chaise recliner, stretching my legs in front of me, watching the steam rise from my mug and disappear into the cool, fresh morning air. The aroma filled my nostrils and my stomach growled, though I wasn't hungry. The sun peaked ever so slightly, barely there, on the edge of the lake.

Blowing on my tea, I watched everything around me happening slowly, trying not to blink. Trying not to miss a single second of this moment.

How many mornings had I spent never actually watching the sun rise from start to finish? The myriad of colors was soft and pale, yet bright and vibrant all at once. It was breathtaking and somehow...infuriating. How could something as majestic as a sunrise exist in the same world where cancer kills?

A wet nuzzle pressed against my leg and I looked down to see Beast attempt—and fail—to jump up and join me. Reaching down with one arm, I scooped him onto the chair beside me where he cuddled into the crook of my knee, fast asleep and snoring a minute later.

We stayed like that for a while—him oblivious, and me overanalyzing everything.

I loved my husband, I loved my family, I loved my life. But I didn't feel very *loving*. My cancer would be an easy excuse. No one would expect me to feel chipper with a brain tumor. But my brain wasn't the problem—it was my heart.

I'd spent months uprooting my entire life in pursuit of one thing I thought would fix everything. Now? I was more broken than ever before. It felt as if everything was already over, and I hadn't even died yet.

The sunrise ended shortly, peeking high enough for its colors to dissolve into bright orange. I closed my eyes for a minute, or maybe more, feeling the rhythmic thump of Beast's heartbeat against my leg. I smoothed a hand across his soft fur, focusing on his curls as they whispered against my fingers.

"Tessa?"

My eyes blinked open as my thoughts were interrupted by Kyle. "Yeah?"

"Morning, babe." He leaned over the back of the chair I was sprawled on and kissed my temple. "The nurse is here."

I relished the feeling of his lips against me, soaking in the affection I wanted to want. "Already? She's early."

He glanced at his watch. "You've been out here two hours, babe. Want me to make you some more tea? That must be cold by now."

I sipped the edge of my cup and he was right—it was freezing. I must have dozed off for a bit. Beast jumped to the ground as I pushed to my feet. "Yeah, that would be great. I'm a bit hungry, too."

"What about eggs?" he asked. "I'm going to make some."

A wave of nausea slammed through me and my hand flew to the base of my throat. Shaking my head, I swallowed hard and waited for the feeling to pass. When it finally did, I choked out, "No eggs."

Kyle's face was concerned. "Let's go see the nurse. She'll have meds for the nausea."

He offered me his arm and I slid my hand around his elbow. I was getting weaker every day, definitely thinner now, but not enough to look sickly. I knew it wouldn't be long though.

When we entered the dining room, a tiny brunette was facing away from me, rifling through a medical bag. She began pulling out the items she needed, placing them in an orderly line on the table that she was only slighter taller than herself.

"Hi there," I greeted her.

She turned to me, a slightly crooked smile that added so much personality to her face. I immediately wanted to know her, like her, and trust her. Her bright eyes shone and her hand rested on a swollen, pregnant belly that was so large it seemed she'd tip over. "Hi! You must be Tessa! I'm Malaika—and before you ask, my parents loved unusual names."

We shook hands, and I smiled at her signature North Eastern accent that didn't at all match her African name. A tiny pale woman who'd undoubtedly never seen the sun long enough to tan was the last person I expected to hold such a beautiful Swahili name, but it only made me love her that much more.

"Good to meet you, Malaika. I'm Tessa, and this is my husband, Kyle." I nodded toward her belly. "Congratulations."

She rubbed her hands across her stomach affectionately. "Thanks! I'm due in a little less than three months, but I popped early. This baby is going to be bigger than me."

"You must be so excited," I told her, digging deep to find a way to be happy for her. Babies were always a gift, but...it was a cruel slap of fate to give *me* the pregnant nurse. "Children are such a blessing."

"That's what I hear!" she exclaimed. "This will be my first, so I'm excited. Do you guys have kids?"

"We don't have any kids," Kyle intervened, and I let out a small sigh of relief. "So, what do you need to get started today, Malaika?"

"Nothing, actually," Malaika assured him. "I'll need Tessa to sit down and roll up her sleeve so I can take her vitals. We'll discuss meds and hospice planning after."

Hospice. The word still sent chills down my spine.

I sat down in the chair next to her, lifting one arm out of my cardigan.

Kyle kissed the top of my head. "I'll be in the kitchen if you need me."

"Thanks, babe."

Malaika took my blood pressure, listened to my heart, and then checked my pulse and temperature. She asked me about my food and water intake, the meds I was on, and we discussed the pain and nausea meds for when the symptoms worsened.

"I, um, saw in your chart you've been prescribed barbiturates, in a high dosage," Malaika spoke slowly, as if unsure how to broach the topic. "Are you planning—"

I cut her off with a flash of my palm, already knowing her question. "I'll be ending my own life."

She glanced at me, then down at the chart. A feeling of dread swept through me that she might be against me, too. I straightened my shoulders, preparing for a fight.

"That's really brave," she replied simply.

"Oh." *Wait...what? Brave? Tell my family.* "Well, thank you."

She went on with business as usual and my entire body relaxed. "Do you have a timeline in mind or an estimated date?" she asked.

I shrugged one shoulder. "Sort of. I think October, after my birthday at the end of September. But it depends on how quickly my symptoms progress. I should be able to have 'til November if the doctors are right."

"So, we're talking two to three months."

I pulled my lips between my teeth, rolling them back out as I considered how truly short a period of time it was. "Yeah."

"Okay, well I'll be here to help you every step of the way. I can't actually be involved in the final step as I'm sure you know, but I'll be there to monitor your heart and vitals, and help your family coordinate aftercare services."

Aftercare? It took me a moment to realize she was talking about my body...about what to do with my remains. They slid through me, emotionless—I liked the separation. *That* wouldn't be me, just be a body. I'd already be gone. My pain would already be over.

Everything would be over.

She continued talking about logistics, palliative care options, and provided me with her contact information for emergencies. She promised to return every morning until symptoms worsened, and then it would be twice daily. She sorted my medications into an easy pill holder and showed me which to take when. By the end of the hour, I felt my entire life had been simplified and the relief was intoxicating. All the unknowns, once so scary, now looked routine.

I may not have the support of my family, but I had someone, and for now, that would be enough.

CHAPTER THIRTY-ONE

Tuesday, August 12, 2014

AFTER MALAIKA LEFT, I ventured into the kitchen for a bowl of oatmeal and actually managed to eat about half before I felt sick. Still, I considered it a success and spent the rest of the morning into the late afternoon writing in my journal.

Actually, it was a word document on my laptop now since after filling a few notebooks, I'd quickly grown tired of the ache in my hand. Thankfully, Kyle transcribed the journals to my computer for me. I could live ten lifetimes and still never deserve such an incredible man.

Opening my laptop, I sat on the back veranda and added paragraph after paragraph to my book. I felt fierce as hell—professional even. I felt like a real writer now, slaving for my craft as I pounded against the keys. It was illuminating...and frightening. I worried I'd never be able to finish the book in time, my memoir cut short like my life.

All I'd been writing about this week was the Death with

Dignity Act—the different people I'd spoken to about it, how I'd researched it, what information was out there about it for different blog articles that I was trying to get posted on the topic—a slight departure from the book, but I figured still a worthy use of my time. I'd laid it out like a pros and cons list, arguing both sides, and then explaining why I'd chosen what I did. If anything, I felt more assured of my decision than ever, yet somehow even more alone.

My dad slid open the back door. "Tessa, you've got a visitor."

Frowning, I glanced back at him. "I'm not expecting anyone?"

He stuck his head inside, and I heard him talking to someone. Poking his head back out, he said, "It's the real estate agent's sister."

I hadn't talked to Carly Wellings since we moved in and the paperwork was finalized. "Um, okay…can she come join me out here?" I was exhausted from a fitful night of tossing and turning in bed thanks to a pounding headache.

A lanky, young blonde who couldn't have been older than twenty-two replaced my dad in the doorway. With a huge smile on her face, she put her hand out when she reached my side. "Hi, you must be Tessa."

I lightly shook her hand. "And you're Carly's sister?"

"I am. My name is Marley." When I gave her a funny look, she chuckled and sat on the patio chair opposite me. "I know—my mom had three kids and named them Charlie, Carly, and Marley. Originality was never her strong suit."

I laughed. "I like it."

"Me, too," she said in a hushed tone, as if conspiratorially. As strange as this surprise visit was, I instantly liked Marley in the same way I'd liked Malaika earlier. Something about both women put me at ease, and I relished having people in my life like that. "I hope it's not weird I came by."

The corners of my lips twitched. "It's a little weird."

"That's what Carly told me." Marley groaned and touched her palm to her cheek, as if to say she was embarrassed. The shine in her eyes and the commanding way in which she held herself told me she wasn't at all. "But I *had* to take the opportunity to come meet with you...and ask you a favor."

My brows lifted, nearing my hairline. "You're here to ask *me* a favor?" I think I liked her even more now. The girl had balls.

"Yes, and I know it makes this even weirder." Marley sat forward, leaning her elbows on her knees as she excitedly launched into her request. "I'm hoping to become a journalist. Well, I am a journalist, but I'm just freelance right now. I'd like to write an article about your journey, shop it to magazines and publications, and hopefully get your story heard."

I opened my mouth to say something, but nothing came out. Closing it again, I furrowed my brows and stared at her through squinty eyes.

"It's a lot to ask, and you don't know me, but when my sister told me about your decision to move here, and why—I couldn't stop thinking about it," she continued. "It's so powerful, and it'll resonate with so many people. Even the people who don't agree, they won't forget your story. It'll spark debates, fire up passions, get the world talking about a real issue we need to address as a society."

I folded my arms across my chest, tilting my head to the side. "What did your sister tell you about me?"

"Not a lot. She's a professional, and doesn't actually know I'm here." I liked how she defended her sister immediately, even if she was sneaking behind her anyway. "She told me about your diagnosis, and how you moved to Vermont from Chicago to go through the legal process of ending your life."

"Well, that's all true."

"Does that mean you'll let me write the article?" Her hazel eyes shone brighter at the prospect.

"I didn't say that." I put one finger up as if in warning. "I'm writing my own story, you know." I gestured toward the laptop computer. "I'm writing a book. A memoir, kind of."

She clasped her hands in front of her. "That's fantastic! I can mention it in the article and drum up more interest about the upcoming release. If I can get the article somewhere big, you'll get more sales from the exposure."

Something between a scoff and a chuckle bubbled up from my throat. "I'm not going to be around to see any sales from this book, Marley."

Marley's eyes went wide. "Oh shit, my fault. Duh, obviously." Her cheeks reddened, but I enjoyed seeing the first glimpse of the vulnerable woman beneath her intense confidence. "Well, what are you going to do with the book, then?"

I pointed toward the house. "My husband will shop it around to publishers, if he wants. Or he may just let my family read it and then put it in a drawer for the rest of time. It's up to them. They're the only people I'm writing it for."

"I really love that idea." Marley clucked her tongue, genuine adoration on her face. "What if they do decide to publish it? Who gets the profits then?"

I lifted one brow. We'd literally *just* met. Since when do strangers talk about finances? Deciding she was harmless, I let myself open up a bit—just a bit though. "Any profits would be split evenly among my family."

"Well, even more so why the article would be a great idea. It could give them publicity for the book, and for their futures. If your husband wants to publish it, I'll help him," Marley said. "I know literary agents and can help get him in touch with one."

I sat back in my chair, squinting my eyes at her. "Can we pause for a minute here? I don't know you. You're young and excited about your future, but I'm not a tool to get you to the next level in your career."

There was an awkward moment where we stared at each other, her expression as shocked as I felt about this meeting. If I was being honest, she was overwhelming me with all this book talk. My book might not be worth publishing, and I sure as hell wasn't going to spend my last few months dealing with rejection letters.

"I'm so sorry." Marley dropped her head, looking down at her lap. "You're right. I really come on too strong—I always have—but this is *not* about my career."

Her eyes found mine and I saw a newfound sincerity. "Carly, Charlie, and me...we didn't grow up with our parents. Our mother has been in jail for the last fifteen years for killing our father."

My mouth fell open, letting out a harsh exhale. "Shit, I'm sorry."

She waved her hand as if to say it was no big deal. "That's not the point of my story."

"Okay?" *Where was she going with this?*

"The point is my grandparents raised us, and they loved each other more than anything. My grandmother got very sick about five years ago—lung cancer. She fought it for a while, but eventually, she was terminal and it was..." Marley swallowed hard and shook her head. "It was really hard. She was in so much pain. She'd reached that point where she'd done everything she had ever wanted, she'd said her goodbyes, her affairs were in order. She was ready."

I bit down on the inside of my cheek as I listened to her story. I understood what she was describing probably more than she did. "I can imagine how hard that must have been."

She sighed, swallowing hard again, the bright and bouncy spirit she'd walked in with gone. "It was hardest for my grandfather. Watching her suffer, waiting for God to take her. She was ready, but her body was still hanging on. So, he..."

A pit stirred in my stomach. "He helped her."

Marley nodded. "He couldn't say no. She was the love of his life, and she begged him."

"Five years ago? Before—"

"Before it was legal," Marley confirmed. "He tried to ask the doctor for help, but they refused. They waited until after my eighteenth birthday, when all three of us kids were away at college. Wrote us all letters, had their affairs in order so we wouldn't have to worry about a thing. They thought of everything, and then they took handfuls of medications."

My eyes widened and I leaned forward. "Your grandfather wasn't sick..."

"I know." The corners of her lips pointed down as her shoulders slumped. "But he couldn't live without her. They'd been married for sixty-two years."

I was quiet for a moment, allowing the story to sink in and burrow into my heart. I didn't agree with what her grandfather had done, but I could understand why he'd done it.

What would have happened if my dad had made that

same choice when my mother had died? How much pain would he have caused Elly and me? I saw glimmers of it crossing Marley's face now, and anger flared in my stomach at her grandfather for leaving them.

My mind flitted to Kyle. There was absolutely no part of me that wanted him to come with me. Even if we'd been together for sixty years, I couldn't imagine ever placing such a burden on him. Maybe I'm young and naïve. Maybe I don't know what love is at all.

I wanted him to have a full and happy life, to have all the things we'd ever dreamt about even if I wasn't there to enjoy it with him.

"The thing is, Tessa—can I call you Tessa?" Marley glanced at me, tears welled in her eyes. She quickly brushed them away and cleared her throat.

I nodded. "Sure."

"After it was over, the autopsy reported that the medications they'd used had been successful, but it was slow. They both suffered in those final moments...*a lot*. If the Death with Dignity Act had been legal in Vermont then, maybe that wouldn't have happened. Maybe my grandfather wouldn't have felt the need to take the journey with her. Maybe my grandmother could have gotten what she wanted without additional suffering."

I sighed, unable to stop frowning. "That's a lot of maybes. Second guessing everything like that will drive you mad."

She licked her lips slowly, consider my words. "It is, and I probably have been driving myself mad over it the last few years, but I can't help myself. I found a cause I believe in, and I'm eager to do whatever I can to help make this law legal in every state. You shouldn't have had to move to make this happen. You shouldn't have to uproot your life with everything else you're already going through. People should have the right to do what they want with their bodies, with their lives. When I heard your story—despite how very little I know—I knew you could help."

I shook my head. "I need to think about this, Marley. Your story is...intense. I'm so sorry you had to go through that. I'm so sorry about your grandparents. But I can't say I agree with what he did. I don't know if that makes me a hypocrite considering what I'm doing, but he was healthy... he had more time he could have spent with you and your siblings."

"He did, and if I'm being honest, I still harbor a lot of anger at his decision," Marley agreed. "But it's another reason why I support the Death with Dignity Act—it wouldn't allow people to commit suicide like he did. It'd help people who are in situations like yours. It allows doctors and nurses to help make sure things go smoothly, pain free, but puts checks and balances into place. The law doesn't allow for rash decisions; it makes everyone jump through hoops instead, which is a good thing considering what's at stake."

I let out a slight grunt, remembering everything I had to do to get the medication. "Believe me, I'm very familiar with the hoops. Took me almost two months before I got my medication."

"So, you have it already?" she asked.

I nodded slowly. "Marley, I'm not saying yes to the article. I need to think about this."

"I understand. I dropped a lot of information on you out of nowhere." She got to her feet and pulled a business card out of her pocket, then handed it to me. "I think what you're doing is brave, and I think you have an opportunity to make a difference in the world if you want to."

"Thank you," I said simply.

Marley headed for the house, and my dad opened the door to let her walk through.

I watched her go, not missing the fact that she hadn't said goodbye, and kind of liking her presumptuousness that this wasn't goodbye.

I faced the lake, the water lapping against the stones as I pulled my feet up under me and wrapped my sweater tighter. Doing this article could mean turning myself into a public spectacle. Definitely not something I wanted, but Marley's insistence that I could make a difference wedged under my skin.

If I were to die today, I wouldn't feel I'd wasted my time on Earth, or hadn't made a difference. I may not have won the Nobel Peace prize or cured cancer—*irony*—but I'd lived a good life, and I had people who loved me and would remember me.

But...I did like to help people. I always had. The idea that maybe I still could, even in my current state, felt exciting. I'd thought those days were behind me, like I was a burden to everyone I loved now. They'd never say that, of course, but I knew they were sacrificing for me.

The realization sat heavily in my stomach. Why I'd felt so empty, so misplaced these last few weeks...everything I'd been doing was for myself. The move, the doctors, the medications. I'd completely turned away from all the things that made me happy, that made me...me.

I'd spent my entire life dedicated to taking care of the people around me. I'd raised Elly when my mother couldn't, comforted my father when he had nothing left, and built a home for Kyle to return to after every deployment that made him feel secure and adored. Taking care of others was my life, and it made me happy.

Marley's promise that I could still make a difference filled me with a familiar feeling of purpose and passion. This article could help others, and my book could help my family. *I could still help.* That's who I was.

That's who I wanted to be when I died.

My resolve hardened and I knew then and there that not only would I do the article, but I was going to finish this book. I was going to make sure it was published.

Cancer be damned—I had a purpose.

CHAPTER THIRTY-TWO

Tuesday, August 12, 2014

"WHAT'S ALL THIS?" Kyle asked, entering the bedroom later that evening.

I glanced at him, taking a second to appreciate his rock-hard muscles pressing against the fabric of his shirt. His biceps looked like they might rip his sleeves completely, and a stirring in my core definitely appreciated the view.

"Hello to you, too," I said, a flirtatious lilt to my words.

His eyes darkened and his jaw set as he stalked over to me. My wandering eyes must have been a dead giveaway to what I was thinking. "Tessa..." he growled, a timbre in his voice that vibrated inside me.

I waved to the pile of books and papers around me. "I'm just doing some research."

"Research for what?" He pushed aside enough to be able to sit on the bed. His fingers trailed down my inner thigh.

"The Death with Dignity Act, not only in Vermont, but

everywhere. Carly's sister was here earlier, she's a journalist—"

His brows furrowed, and he looked confused. "Our real estate agent?"

"Yep, her little sister is Marley—long story—but she wants to write an article about me and what I'm doing. She does freelance, so I'm not sure where it will end up being published, but I think it's a good idea. I think I could make a difference. So many of these laws and cases—" I gestured to the stack of papers around me. "They cause so much suffering, and they take away any freedom we have over our own bodies."

"Tessa," Kyle began, a groan following my name. "This is a sensitive topic. You know that."

Piling up the rest of my papers, I put them on the nightstand. "It's also my life. And I had to upend everything for it. You did, too. We shouldn't have had to do that, and maybe if I talk publicly about it, then we can save someone else the hassle we had to go through."

Kyle's tongue slid across his lower lip and he moved farther on to the bed, resting against the headboard. "Tessa, I don't regret moving here. I don't regret doing anything for you."

My eyes flickered to his. "Wait...you're not mad about what I'm going to do?"

"Mad?" He looked surprised. "I've never been mad at you, babe. I just..." His voice trailed off, like he was still deciding what to say. I took the opportunity to crawl into his lap, draping my legs over his and resting my head against his chest. He wrapped his arms around me and kissed the top of my head. "It just hurts my heart, Tessa. I'm going to lose you, and it hurts that you want to leave me sooner than you have to."

I tilted my head to look at him. His jaw was set, green eyes shining as he stared straight ahead. "Kyle..."

He didn't let me finish. Instead, he dipped his chin and found my lips with his. It was soft and sweet, gentle presses and nips. I slid my hand from his chest to his neck, pulling him closer. Need grew inside me—for him, for our connection. There'd been so much tension, frustration, but it felt different now. The lines were fading, and something new and open had taken its place.

The soft caress of his lips quickly became not enough. His hunger seemed to grow with mine as he pulled me down on the bed, stretching me beneath him. I pressed my hips against his and he growled in my ear before finding my lips again.

He pulled my lower lip between his, sucking on it before moving to my top lip. My tongue slid forward, meeting his, dancing around each other as my nails pressed into his back and one of his hands slid down my side. Slipping inside my pants, he reached between my legs as I anchored my knees to the outside of his hips.

His finger teased me, my back arching off the bed. I groaned into his mouth. He pushed into me and I begged him to keep going. He kissed my jaw, tracing his way to my ear, and whispering how much he loved me. Pleasure built inside me, stiffening my muscles and stealing my breath as his hand picked up the pace.

Stars splintered behind my eyes and I fell over the edge, clinging to him like he was the only thing keeping me grounded, keeping me here. And in this moment, he was.

He whispered in my ear, told me to let go, assured me he had me, he loved me, he'd *always* love me. My heart burst into a million little pieces as my body followed suit.

"Kyle, please, I need you," I begged him when I found

my breath again. I pushed my pants down and wiggled out of them. He quickly did the same and was pressed against me seconds later.

"Tell me if it's too much," he warned, hovering above me and promising me ecstasy with every thrust of his hips.

"You've always been too much," I teased.

He grinned from ear to ear. "You're damn right, I am."

With that, he pushed inside me and filled my heart completely. Our lips pressed together, I wrapped my arms around his neck as we moved together. He was careful, but he wasn't holding back. I needed him, and this was everything we once were and more. I'd spent the last few weeks forgetting who I was, forgetting what made me happy. My singular focus had made me miss time I could have had doing just this. Being with my husband, being in love, being us.

I wasn't going to waste another moment.

My body began to build with anticipation as each press brought me closer and closer to shattering. The strength in Kyle's shoulders and arms as I held onto him sent a thrill through me, our lips fused together as our bodies met again and again.

"Together," he whispered, curving one hand beneath me to lift my hips. "Together, Tessa."

I nodded, as ready as he was. The new angle was everything I needed, my body trembling as the first few waves slid through me. Increasing the pressure, he moved faster and my eyes pressed closed as I tried to find my breath while losing complete control of my body.

Kyle groaned, holding me still against him as I pulsed around him. "Fucking hell, Tessa." His breathing slowed as his grip loosened, leaving me sated and floating beneath him. "You always feel so amazing."

I kissed him softly, telling him everything I was feeling in the way I held his face and touched his lips. He heard me and he replied, returning my affection with more of his own.

He slid to the bed, my back to his chest, wrapping an arm around me. "What can I do to help with the article?" he asked after a few quiet moments cuddling.

I bit my bottom lip to keep from smiling too wide, but I couldn't stop the grin on my face at both his acceptance and his support. "Nothing. I just need you."

"And I need you." He nuzzled his nose against my cheek. "I'll always need you."

I took his hands in mine, wrapping them tighter around me, enjoying the squeezing feeling of being so close to him. "I'll always be around, somehow."

He didn't say anything. I started talking, telling him everything I'd learned in my research, as well as everything Marley had told me. He listened quietly, his thumb gently stroking my forearm.

Kyle kissed my neck again. "I would do that if you asked me, Tessa. If you needed me, I would."

I quickly turned around in his arms to face him, horror in my voice. "I'd *never* want you to kill yourself, Kyle. *Never*. Promise me."

"No, not that. Of course, I'd never do that. I mean..." He looked like he was contemplating it for a moment. "Maybe if I was eighty and we'd been married sixty years."

"Kyle, I'm serious." I shook my head adamantly. "Don't you dare."

"Relax, Tessa." He smiled and kissed me on the tip of my nose. "What I meant was I'd do it for you. If it hadn't been legal and there was no other way, and you asked me to help you...I'd help you. I wouldn't like it, but I'd do it if you were suffering and that's what you wanted."

I stared at him for a minute, both loving he'd do something like that for me and also grateful he didn't have to. Brushing my fingers over his cheek, I cupped his face and kissed him. "You're already helping me. So much."

"It'll never be enough," he whispered against my lips. "You deserve so much more. More than twenty-eight years." His voice trembled, straining. "More than I can give you."

"You gave me all your love." I brushed my hand through his hair and pushed my hips against his so we were completely touching from head to toe. "You've given me everything, Kyle."

He groaned and I felt him press against my hips. "I want to give you more. I want more time. I want...more."

"Take what you want from me." I hooked a knee over his hips and kissed his neck. "I'd give you anything."

He pushed my legs apart, moving over me and cradling my head in his hands. "I've only ever wanted you, Tessa."

"Take me then." I licked my lips, never taking my eyes from his. "I'm yours."

He pushed inside me, his lips hovering above mine. "Tessa, if this is all I get, if a few years with you is all I will have, then I've already lived a better life than I ever could have dreamed of."

Tears pricked my eyes as I pressed my mouth to his. "All my love, Kyle."

"All my love, Tessa."

CHAPTER THIRTY-THREE

WEDNESDAY, *August 13, 2014*

MY EYES BLINKED open slowly from the warm sun beating down on my face. It was higher than most mornings, and when I turned to find the clock announcing it was almost ten, I realized I'd slept in later than usual. Stretching my body, I felt a dull, satiated ache between my legs and grinned, remembering my night with Kyle.

He was still sleeping beside me with Beast curled against him. The sight made me smile—my giant husband spooning a tiny, fluffy white dog.

My heart felt fuller than it had in a long time as I slid out of bed, careful not to disturb either of them. I pulled on a satin robe, cinching it at the waist and stepped into a pair of soft slippers. The more weight I lost, mostly from muscle mass, the quicker my bones began to ache, starting with the soles of my feet.

The kitchen was bathed in sunlight, and I eagerly went to the coffee maker and began brewing a cup for myself.

Staring out the big window over the sink that looked to the lake, I found myself appreciating that I could wake to a sight this beautiful. It felt like a permanent vacation, though our purpose here was anything but.

"Tessy?"

I turned to see my sister standing in the kitchen doorway, my laptop in her hands. "Good morning."

"Morning." She sat down at the breakfast bar, propping open my computer in front of her. "You making coffee?"

I eyed her suspiciously, not wanting to snatch my computer from her, but also wondering why she had it. "Yeah, do you want a cup?"

"Sure, thanks."

Her eyes didn't meet mine, but I didn't push her. Instead, I pulled a second mug out of the cabinet and poured her some.

"Thanks." She held the mug to her nose and took a big sniff. "You always make it better than anyone else."

I pulled out a tall chair next to hers and sat down. We both sipped our coffees for a minute before I finally nodded to the computer. "So, what are you doing on there?"

She blushed and put her mug down. "I read your book. Or what you have so far." She pointed the screen toward me and my manuscript stared back at me.

My brows pinched together. "Jeez, Elly. That's kind of an invasion of privacy without asking me. I mean, I would have shown you if I'd known you wanted to see it."

"I know, and I'm sorry, but you left it open last night and curiosity got the better of me. I stayed up all night reading it." She looked at me sheepishly, her hands folded as if in a prayer. "Please don't be mad."

"I'm not mad, El. Things are just...between us...it's—"

"It's awkward," she finished for me. "I know. And that's

why I read it. You and I have never been like *this*." She gestured between us. "We've never spent this long barely talking, and I hate it."

I nibbled my lower lip. "I do, too."

"I wanted to understand. To *really* understand." She sniffed, the tears welling in her eyes ripping at my heart. "You're everything to me, Tessa. Literally, *everything*. I don't want our last few months to be like this. I don't want you to hate me."

I reached forward, grabbing her shoulders and pulling her toward me. "Hate you? My god, El, that's literally impossible!"

She dropped her head to my shoulder, her arms hugging my waist. I rubbed my hand in circles over her back, cradling her to me. "I love you, baby girl. Always, no matter what. You're my everything, too."

"The book is so great, Tessy." She sniffed again, her words mumbled against my shoulder. "I understand now."

I leaned back, holding her at arm's length as I searched her red-rimmed eyes. "You do?"

She nodded. "Everything about Mom? All those stories about the good times with her, then the not-good when she became sick the first time, then the second. Her death. I didn't know all of those stories."

"You were so young," I reminded her.

"And I missed so much because of that. I missed so much of *her*. If I'd had to watch her suffer...watch her die...I couldn't do it."

I wiped a tear from her cheek with my thumb. She picked up her coffee, taking another sip. I let mine sit, waiting for her to continue.

"I think I was so upset for so long because those pills, this move, this entire plan—it felt like you wanted to leave me sooner than you had to. But, when I read your book, the stories of Mom, all the examples of other people and research...I realized I'd rather miss you sooner than watch you suffer."

"El—"

"No, I'm serious, Tessa." She put her mug down and set her jaw firmly. Her tears were gone, and in their place was resolve. Fierce, tough, determined—this was the sister I knew.

"I don't want to miss this time with you fighting. I don't want to miss a single moment, especially when there are so few left. You're my big sister, but you're also my mother. I just want my mother."

"Oh, Elly, me, too." I hugged her again, somehow even tighter this time. My heart swelled in my chest, simultaneously devastated and elated. I ached for the loss I knew she'd experience soon, but I finally had my sister back.

"I love you, Tessy," she whispered.

"I love you more, El."

CHAPTER THIRTY-FOUR

MONDAY, *August 18, 2014*

"HEY, MALAIKA," I greeted the bubbly, young nurse at the front door. I stepped aside to let her in.

"Good morning, Tessa!" Her tiny frame bounced past me and headed straight for the dining room where we always did morning vitals. "How are you feeling today?"

"Same as the last few days." I shrugged, following her. I sat in the chair at the end of the table as she busied herself setting up.

"So, good and bad, huh?" She slid a stethoscope around her neck, placing the buds in each ear.

I stretched my arm out across the table. "Exactly. I'll be fine for a while, even energetic sometimes. Then suddenly, I'll be drained and dizzy, or get an intense ache and have to sit down."

She held the stethoscope against my arm, carefully monitoring her watch as she listened. We were both silent for a moment, letting her count the beats.

"That sounds low," I said when she announced my blood pressure.

"It is, but not enough to be too concerned." She draped the stethoscope around her neck and then pulled out a small metal clip with a red light inside it, clamping it over my finger until it beeped. She recorded the number and then pulled the small box of daily medications out of her bag. "I'm going to get you some water and you'll take these."

I waited while she walked to the cupboard and took out a glass. She'd been coming every day for a week, and already knew her way around. I was comfortable with her, enjoyed her company even. She came while most of the house was still sleeping, but I enjoyed my private morning chats with her and getting to know about her life. Her baby daddy was out of the picture, but she was working hard to make a life for herself and her unborn child anyway. She wasn't feeling sorry for herself—she was taking charge of her life, and I loved that about her.

"Ooh!" Malaika paused in front of the counter, putting down the jug of water she'd been pouring into a glass. "That was quite a kick!"

"Are you okay?"

She smiled and returned, grabbing my hand. I startled for a second, not expecting her to touch me, but I let her guide my palm to her stomach. She held it firmly against the underside of her swollen belly and I felt the unmistakable movement of a foot slamming against my fingers.

"Whoa!" I exclaimed.

"She's been quiet all morning," Malaika giggled. "I guess we woke her up!"

My smile spread wide as I felt her little girl make her presence known. "I guess we did."

Malaika let go of my hand. "Ready to take your pills now?"

I pulled away reluctantly, missing the brief connection with her baby—with *a* baby. My heart squeezed at the reminder, but I pushed away the thought. I couldn't dwell on things I'd never have. It wasn't fair to myself, and it was something I was working hard to stop doing. "Yeah, I'm ready."

She opened the 'Monday' slot and poured its contents into my waiting palm. I tossed them to the back of my throat and quickly swallowed a few gulps of water, grimacing at the feeling of the giant pills sliding down my throat. I was getting more and more used to it every day, but I hated taking medication—I always had.

I cleared my throat and shook my head. "All done."

"Any fun plans for the week?" She began repacking her bag.

I shook my head. "Nothing in particular. I spend most of my time writing, or being with my family. We take walks around the lake, which I love. Or go to new restaurants."

"Ooh, I love eating out," she exclaimed. "So much better than having to cook for myself."

I grinned in agreement. "It's pretty nice. Gets expensive though."

She waved her hand nonchalantly. "Money isn't something you should worry about at this point, you know?"

I knew what she meant, but sadly, that wasn't how life worked. I wish I could call my bill collectors and say, *hey I'm dying, so you know, freebie?* Particularly my medical bills, which were still coming in at exorbitant rates. The balances stressed me out, and I tried not to think about it.

Thankfully, Kyle had always been over-prepared for the

worst-case scenario so not only did we both have life insurance long before my diagnosis, but it was top of the line. When the terminal diagnosis had become official, a fat check had shown up a few days later that had helped us pay off the medical bills with plenty left over. It was really strange, being able to spend my own life insurance money, but I wasn't about to complain.

"Morning, Malaika." *Speak of the devil.* A shirtless Kyle walked past us in the dining room, stopping briefly to lean down and kiss the top of my head, before heading for the kitchen.

I couldn't stop myself from gawking at his chiseled chest, his muscles expanding and contracting with each step. His pajama pants hung low on his waist, the long muscular lines on his lower abdomen pointing down reminding me of what we'd done the night before.

"Morning, Mr. Falls!" she replied, before turning her twinkling eyes to me and lowering her voice. "Good God, Tessa, you scored with that one."

I blushed, following her gaze to the kitchen and biting my lip at the sight of Kyle's rippled back while he poured a cup of coffee. "He's really wonderful," I agreed.

"And so freaking hot!" she whispered, gently smacking my upper arm.

I laughed loudly, quickly covering my open mouth with my hand.

"What's so funny?" Kyle turned to look at us.

Malaika's eyes went wide and she gave me a conspiratorial grin.

"Oh, nothing," I assured him. "We were just talking about Malaika's baby. She's kicking."

"She is," Malaika quickly agreed, nodding her head and

busying herself with writing notes in my file. "Gonna play soccer, this one."

"Really?" He walked over, interested. "That's so cool."

"Can he feel?" I asked Malaika, not wanting to offer up her stomach without her permission.

She looked at me carefully for a second, as if wanting reassurance she wasn't crossing a line. I didn't mind one bit that she found my husband attractive, because, *hello*, he was freaking gorgeous. But I also knew Kyle only had eyes for me. There had never been a second in our entire relationship I'd ever doubted him and I had no plans to start now.

"Sure," she agreed. "Here, give me your hand."

He held his coffee in one hand, and gave her his other. She positioned it on the right side of her protruding baby bump this time, and his large hand nearly covered half of her.

"Shit!" Kyle suddenly gasped after we'd all been quiet for a moment, waiting for the baby's move. "Oh, I'm sorry. I meant...wow!"

"She's strong, huh?" Malaika's face beamed with pride.

"Definitely," he agreed. "There she goes again!"

Malaika rambled on about the baby and her pregnancy, but I was barely listening. Instead, I watched. The look on Kyle's face made my entire body warm. There was such adoration in his eyes, and I knew in every fiber of my being Kyle was meant to be a father.

I wouldn't be the one to give him that, but I wanted it for him so badly.

The picture of him standing over Malaika, his hand on her belly confirmed my thoughts. Kyle *would* find love again. He would remarry. He would have a family, and children, and love after me. Without me.

A peace settled over me as, for the first time, I realized I was okay with that. I'd gone through the motions before, telling him I wanted him to move on after me, but part of me had never really meant it. Part of me had wanted him mine forever...and to defy death and live another sixty years.

It was time to let go of that part.

CHAPTER THIRTY-FIVE

FRIDAY, August 22, 2014

"YOU WON'T REGRET THIS, Tessa! I'm so excited!" Marley's voice screeched through the phone.

"I'm sure I won't," I laughed, hoping that was true. "I'll see you tonight.

"See you then!" She hung up, not saying goodbye. I was noticing a trend with her.

We'd agreed to meet for dinner to go over the article and let her ask her questions. I'd spent the last ten days thinking about it, even though I knew I was going to do it. I'd wanted to be sure, and make sure my family was comfortable first. In fact, I'd agreed to do it on one condition—my family was left out of it.

If I was going to thrust myself into the limelight, knowingly risking ridicule and anger, then that's one thing, but my family hadn't asked for this. The last thing I ever wanted was for them to have to deal with the consequences of my decision, despite that they'd given me their blessing.

"Where are you going?" my dad asked from behind the newspaper he was reading at the dining room table.

I sat on the chair next to him, my back aching from standing even for a few minutes. "Some local burger joint."

"Need me to come with you? You can't drive yourself."

I shook my head. "No, Kyle is driving me." Ever since my seizure, driving was out of the question. I'd always enjoyed driving—hell, I'd gone through the hassle of getting my Vermont driver's license, which I'd only been able to use for a few days before I'd had my first seizure. "Hey, Dad?"

"Hmm," he barely answered, his attention on the paper.

"Thank you for everything."

He glanced over the paper's edge, gave a small nod of his chin, then turned back to reading. "You got it, sunshine."

I grinned, loving the ease between us, and the simplicity with which my dad approached life. Kyle and I had repaired things last night, both with words and affections. We'd bared our souls and mended everything fractured between us. Elly and I had talked it out, apologized, and reminded each other of what was important. But my dad? He didn't need any of that. He was just...my dad, and there was nothing I could ever do to break our bond.

Beast pushed his nose against my leg, and I glanced under the table to see his tongue wagging as he stared at the porch door. I chuckled. "Looks like Beast needs to go out."

I stood slowly, taking a moment to steady myself as a wave of dizziness rushed me. A shaky breath left me as my vision danced, the table moving left and right and slamming against the ceiling. I clutched the edge in hopes everything would slide back in place, but it went black instead.

"Tessa? You okay?" I heard my dad's voice in my ear and the darkness pulled like the tide being urged back to sea. "Tessa?"

"Yeah." I swallowed hard, blinking as the dining room returned to focus. "Yeah, I'm okay. Just a little dizzy."

"Sit down," he instructed. "I'll take out Beast. Kyle! Come in here—quickly!"

My head pounded at the noise.

Kyle's face rushed into my view, his eyes wide as he looked between my dad and me. "What? What's going on?"

"Nothing. Nothing's going on." I waved my hands as if to accentuate my point. "I was just a little dizzy."

My dad didn't agree. "That looked a lot more than dizzy. Kyle, take her to the couch in case she falls and hits her head. I'm going to let the dog out."

Kyle carefully helped me to my feet. "Babe, let's go watch some television."

"Oh, my goodness, guys, I'm not an invalid. I can walk by myself." I tried to shake off my husband, but he was insistent.

"Babe, it's been a month since your seizure. We're just being cautious. They said it could happen again any time."

I sighed. "I'm well aware of that, but this was different. It was more like the room went out of focus, it was moving when I wasn't, and then everything went black."

I sat on the couch and took the seat next to me, pulling my legs across his lap. "Vision issues is one of the symptoms," he reminded me.

Frustration at my own body poured through me. "It's August. There should be more time."

His lips formed a tight line. "There should be."

CHAPTER THIRTY-SIX

MONDAY, September 1, 2014

"WHAT IN THE EVER-LOVING HELL?" A barrage of pink, red, and white streamed past my eyes. I batted the unknown objects away and Beast jumped around at my feet, trying to save me from the unknown flying objects attack.

When the strange shower finally stopped, I blinked and opened my eyes again. A heap of rose petals in every shade of red, pink, and white was lying in front of my bedroom door. Actually, they trailed all the way down the hallway toward the stairs.

"Beast, stop it!" I admonished when he buried his face in the pile, growling and tossing petals left and right.

The rose-murdering puppy looked at me with feigned innocence, petals sticking out of his mouth every which way. I scooped him up and cleared his mouth, carrying him down the stairs with me.

"Kyle?" I called out when I reached the bottom.

He had to be the one behind this. My sister had gone boating on Lake Champlain with my dad today and I was sure they weren't back yet.

"Out here!" His voice echoed from the yard.

I shuffled onto the porch, my nap barely doing anything to relieve my constant exhaustion. At the very least, the rest had seemed to pause the fifteen mini-hammers pounding on the back of my eye socket.

My jaw fell open as I took in the scene in front of me. The trail of rose petals had stopped at the door, but the porch was decorated with paper pink hearts, pink streamers, red roses in red vases, and tall white candles. In the center was a table covered in a dark red tablecloth with a beautifully decorated centerpiece of roses.

Kyle turned to face me, complete in a three-piece suit that made him look powerful and, impossibly, even more handsome. He held a single long-stemmed rose in his hands. "Happy Valentine's Day, babe."

"What? What is all of this?" I could practically hear my own smile as I put Beast down and walked to my husband. "It's September."

"Nope." His green eyes twinkled mischievously. "It's February fourteenth, and you are my Valentine." He handed me the rose, which I sniffed slowly, holding it in front of my mouth to hide my smile.

"Hmmm," I hummed. "What if I don't want to be your Valentine?"

Wrapping his arms around me, he pulled me against his chest and dipped me sideways, like I weighed nothing—which at this point wasn't that far of a stretch. Then his lips were on mine and he kissed me so intensely, I was floating. My hands cupped his jaw, his lips against mine, kissing him back with everything in me.

When he finally righted me, he flashed me a knowing look. "Would you be my Valentine now?"

"You're very convincing," I conceded without much of a fight.

He laced his fingers with mine, leading me to my chair. "Perfect, because I've made a romantic dinner for my Valentine."

"You *made* it? What do you know how to cook?" I quizzed, never knowing him to cook before. "Or did you order takeout and put it on our plates?"

Kyle laughed. "That counts as making it, Tessa."

"Oh, sure." My words dripped with sarcasm, but he knew I was teasing. The effort he was going through for me had my emotions on overdrive—sarcasm was the safest defense.

"Don't worry. This is certified Kyle Falls cooking, straight from our kitchen." He opened a bottle of red wine and poured me a glass.

I sipped it, relishing the taste of my favorite Malbec. I didn't drink often due to my medications, but I wasn't about to deny myself anything anymore. If I wanted a glass of wine, I'm having the entire damn glass. Maybe the bottle.

"Mmm," I hummed my enjoyment, the blend of flavors passing over my tongue. I'd lost my sense of taste during treatment, but luckily, it had returned, although not as strong.

"I'll be right back with our food," he told me, heading inside.

I took the opportunity to open a card sitting next to my place setting. My name was scrawled on the front in Kyle's famously illegible handwriting that had taken me years to learn. I let my fingers trace his ink lightly, smiling at the thought of him penning my name and wondering how much time he'd have left to do that.

The front of the card had a picture of a small puppy with a surprising resemblance to Beast, and said, *"This isn't just puppy love..."* I opened the card, and the sentence finished saying *"This is forever love"* over a picture of an older dog wearing comically geriatric glasses. It was both funny and loving—everything *us*—and a lump swelled in my throat.

"Ready to be amazed?" Kyle returned with a dish in each hand, both piled high with food. Steam lifted from each, and the smell of meat and potatoes quickly wafted over me.

"I'm already amazed," I choked out, trying to keep the tears at bay while reading Kyle's inscription in the card.

DEAR TESSA,

We may not have another Valentine's Day together, but we'll have tonight. That's all we need. The best years of my life will always be the years I had everything I ever dreamed of—the years I had you.

I love you with everything.

Kyle

"BABE, YOU'RE CRYING." Kyle put the plates down then grabbed a napkin. He knelt next to me—which with his height, brought him to my eye level—and gently wiped my cheeks.

I'd done my best to keep them at bay, but it was a losing battle from the start. "Happy tears, I promise."

"You know what will make you happier?"

I shook my head, putting the card on the table.

"My food." He motioned toward my plate, and for the first time, I really looked at what he'd made. Sliced roast beef topped with gravy sat next to a huge pile of mashed potatoes, a gleaming wedge of butter on top, and a small stack of dark green beans that radiated delectability.

"Kyle, this smells delicious," I raved, my stomach growling. "I can't believe you made all this!"

"And I washed the dishes already," he boasted, taking my hand from across the table. "Plus, I'll do these as soon as we've eaten." He gestured to the plates in front of us.

That made me laugh. *Hard.* Tears were streaking down my face for an entirely new reason. On our first Valentine's Day together, Kyle had cooked dinner for me as well, but had destroyed my kitchen in the process. He used every single piece of cutlery, bowls, plates, and cups I owned, including every pot and pan.

To this day, I don't understand how that's even possible because he only made spaghetti.

I hadn't even thought about the dishes since we'd ended up hopping straight into bed after that dinner. When we woke up the next morning, I realized he'd already gone to work and left the dishes from last night for *me* to clean up. All of them. Piled high in *my* sink. There wasn't even a clean mug left for me to have coffee!

I'd been so mad I almost dumped him then and there.

Instead, I'd left it there and waited for him to get home, then started a huge fight and made him clean it up. I still brought it up here and there, just to bug him.

"It's not *that* funny," he said, though he began laughing with me.

"Oh, it's funny," I choked out between gasps of air. "It's perfect. So perfect." We'd come full circle—he'd grown from that immature young guy, to a responsible, wonderful grown man in our years together.

"I'm doing it right this time, especially since it's..." He spoke quieter this time, his laughter dropping off in a way only possible when it was covering tears. "Our last Valentine's Day."

"It's still September," I reminded him, suddenly nervous and fidgeting.

"I grew up with you." He ignored my tangent and I loved how he never let my nerves pull him out of the moment. He wanted to reminisce, and I wanted to let him—despite how painful I knew it would be. "When I met you, Tessa, I was an immature kid...and kind of a jerk. Everything was about being a U.S. Marine, and no one's feelings or thoughts mattered but my own."

I smiled at the reminder. He hadn't been that bad, but there was a transition period between bachelor to my committed and loving husband.

"I'd never met anyone who cared enough to make me grow up. Not until you. And you didn't even *make* me. You just knew who you were and what you wanted, and you expected the same from those you let into your life."

I squeezed his hand. "You've always been a great man, Kyle."

"Maybe... but I was incomplete. I had zero understanding of how wonderful life could be just by waking up next to the woman you love every morning. And I love you," He paused briefly, a strain in his voice. "And with you, I'm complete."

"Kyle—" I sighed, tears prickling my eyes.

"What am I going to do, Tessa?" His voice was barely above a whisper. "When you're gone? I'll be missing everything that made me complete, that made me happy, that made me... me."

I pushed to my feet and stepped around the table, sitting directly on his lap with my arms around his neck. Our foreheads rested against one another and I kissed the tip of his nose. He cried, and I cried, but we were silent. Tears streamed down our faces, and we didn't bother to wipe them away, but we also didn't heave or sob. No sound could have defined the pain in that moment.

"I don't have the answers," I started, the lump in my throat causing my words to croak out slowly. "But I do know none of the last few years will be erased. You'll still have those memories of me, the things we did together, all that we meant to each other—it'll still be here." I placed my palm over his heart. "You'll still have my family, the things you learned, the man you've become... none of that changes." I swallowed hard as I kept my forehead against his and we both stared down at each other's lips. "And you'll still have me. Maybe not on your lap, but you'll still *feel* me." I traced a small heart on his chest. He covered my hand with one of his and squeezed tightly. "You'll feel me where it matters most."

Tears dropped on our combined hands, and I'm not sure if they were mine or his, but we didn't move and we didn't speak. Everything was already said. We stayed like that, foreheads touching and tears flowing.

He held me, and I held his heart.

We always would.

CHAPTER THIRTY-SEVEN

*T*UESDAY, *September 2, 2014*

"TESSA, HURRY UP!" my sister called from outside my bedroom door.

I finished pulling on my cardigan and moved for the door, feeling slower than usual this morning. I'd woken up so stiff, my joints aching and my head pounding. I was getting used to it, since there never seemed to be a minute anymore when I wasn't in pain. It'd become my new normal, despite its ominous implications.

And it made sense, considering the results of my latest scans. Dr. Morales had done another set of scans to see how far my tumor had progressed. The image of my brain was lit up so bright, there was no mistaking my tumor's presence. Except it wasn't a solid mass on one side of my brain like it had started as. The little feelers that had once looked tiny, extending from the mass into the rest of my brain, were now full on branches. The toxic spindles covered my brain and spine so quickly, so fully, that it was no wonder my head always hurt, or my eyes were starting to see black spots, or the numbness already tingling in my extremities.

"Tessa!" Elly called again.

"Coming!" I finally responded, one last glance in the mirror at my short hair. I fluffed it up with my fingers, hoping to make it look fuller than it was, then I swung open my bedroom door.

"There you are! I've had breakfast waiting!" Elly looked a lot more excited than breakfast warranted, so I cocked my head to the side and gave her a funny look. She waved it off and bounced down the hallway. "Come on! It's a surprise."

My family was standing around the breakfast bar, which was lined with full, steaming dishes of my favorite foods...and everything was green. Green eggs, green biscuits, green tea...it looked downright awful, honestly.

"Um..." I started, not sure what to say when breakfast looked like it'd already been eaten and regurgitated.

My dad laughed. "See? She thinks this is gross too."

"It's not gross," Elly countered. "It's festive." Then she pointed up to a banner I'd missed when I first walked in. "Happy St. Patrick's Day!"

Kyle swung an arm around my shoulder and kissed my temple. "You didn't think we were only celebrating Valentine's Day, did you?"

My eyes widened and I looked between him, my dad, and Elly. "What are you guys talking about?"

"We're doing it all!" Elly clapped her hands excitedly. "All of your favorite holidays!"

"What!" I squeaked out.

Kyle squeezed my shoulders again, but my dad filled in the blanks. "We didn't know, sunshine. We didn't know last year would be our last Christmas, or last March our last St. Patrick's Day. They're not that big a deal in the grand scheme of things, but we're having a redo. All week. We're going to make some memories."

I wiped a tear off my cheek, trying to get the words out to tell them how much this meant to me—how much I love each one of them. Instead, I hugged them.

When I finally let go of Elly, hugging her longer than the others, she ran to grab me a special plate off the counter and presented it to me with such pride in her face. "Since I know you're not a huge fan of eggs right now, I made these for you."

She watched my face for my reaction, but I hesitated. I knew what she was holding; I'd eaten them a million times. They were one of my favorite breakfast foods; soft, round discs topped with a mountain of blueberries and syrup.

I *knew* what these were...somewhere in my brain. But nothing comes out of my mouth. I'd forgotten the words. I'd forgotten...

Elly frowned. "Do you like them?"

I opened my mouth to say something, but a barely audible mix between a squeak and a groan came out instead. "Uh..."

Kyle was immediately in front of me, searching my eyes. "Tessa? Are you okay?"

I nodded my head, but I'm not sure I was actually moving. "I'm okay."

"Are you sure?" my dad asked this time.

"I can't remember what it is," I finally admitted, flushing with embarrassment.

Everyone's eyes followed my finger pointing to the plate of food Elly was holding.

"I know I like it—love it, even—but I can't remember what it is." I heard my own pace picking up, my voice sounding panicky. I felt panicky. *Why can't I remember the word?*

"Pancakes," Elly said softly, looking down at the plate. "I made you pancakes."

I blinked. *Pancakes.* "Oh."

My dad cleared his throat, and Kyle walked to the coffee machine. I could see him pretending to make a cup, but I knew he was trying to hide his face from me.

"I bet they're delicious, Elly," my dad offered, grabbing his own plate and starting to pile it high with green foods. "Very festive."

"I love it, Elly," I added, knowing the stricken look on her face was my fault. "I can't wait to dig in. I love *pancakes.*"

She seemed to jolt slightly at the word, but brought me the plate with a plastered smile. "Thanks. Happy St. Patrick's Day."

Pancakes. What a cruel thing to forget first.

· ભ · ભ · ભ ·

DESPITE MY FAUX PAU EARLIER, the rest of the green-themed breakfast was actually fantastic. The pancakes tasted much better than they looked, and my family moved on to lively, happy chatter around the table. It was fun and silly, and everything I needed to brighten my day.

The afternoon was a no-holds barred April Fool's Day celebration. The first prank caught me completely off guard when Kyle replaced the stevia I use in my coffee with salt.

Not one to be ousted, payback was swift. I covered the toilet seat with clear plastic wrap and waited.

And waited.

The man can really hold his bladder.

Two hours later, when I heard shrieks from the bathroom, I dissolved into laughter on the couch as Kyle came storming out, cursing up a storm.

"Plastic wrap? Really, Tessa? *Really?*" he balked. "Who's going to clean up now?"

My hands tried to cover the smile on my face, but there was no hiding my laughter. I touched my index finger to the tip of my nose as if that would get me off the hook. "Not me!"

He scowled, but the corners of his lips twitched and I knew a smile was near. "There's pee everywhere!"

That made me howl harder, pulling a couch cushion over my face to muffle the sound.

"You're going to pay for this!" he promised as he marched to the bathroom, armed with multipurpose disinfectant and a roll of paper towels. "I'm going to get you."

"Counting on it," I said, teasing.

He returned the favor an hour later when he hid around the corner, jumping out wearing a zombie mask when I walked by. I shrieked and fell on my butt, which immediately made him feel bad and try to help me up. My sister put a fake dead fly in an ice cube in my glass, which my dad had switched out for a dribble cup. I retaliated by cutting two holes strategically placed in the front of her sweater, which she didn't notice until my dad uncomfortably pointed out to her that he could see her brassiere.

By the time dinner rolled around, everyone was laughing, jumpy, and paranoid—and the house was a mess. By far the best April Fool's Day in September I'd ever had.

Exhausted from the day's activities, my head already starting to pound, I stretched out on the couch for a quick nap. Kyle walked by me carrying several packages of hot dogs and hamburgers. My dad was right behind him with a bag of multicolored rockets and sparklers.

I pulled a throw blanket over my legs. "What is that for?"

"Tonight is July Fourth!" Kyle replied.

My dad winked. "Take a nap, sunshine. I'll wake you up when the next holiday is here."

Grinning, my heart warm and full of love, I closed my eyes. "I can't wait."

CHAPTER THIRTY-EIGHT

*T*UESDAY, *September 2, 2014*

"TESSA?" The voice was soft, almost a whisper, but it still roused me from my nap.

"Mmm?"

"Tessa, wake up."

I opened my eyes and stretched out my arms, hit with a sudden wave of dizziness that made me glad I was lying down.

Elly sat on the couch at my feet, sheepishly staring down at a flat envelope in her hands.

"What's up?" I asked, wondering if it was time for our Fourth of July celebrations yet.

"I got you something," she started, holding the envelope out, then quickly pulling it back to her chest. "It's kind of like it's May right now, you know?"

"Um..." I definitely did not know, but I also couldn't remember what pancakes were so I wasn't about to start correcting people.

"I mean, we had March for breakfast, April for lunch, and July tonight at dinner."

"Oh, right." Talk about time passing in a flash. "What about it?"

"Well, it's mid-afternoon, so makes it May...Mother's Day." She looked sheepish again, plucking at the corners of the envelope.

I pushed myself into a seated position, pulling a couch cushion behind me. The dizziness worsened with movement, but dissipated once I was up. I waited for Elly to continue speaking.

"If this is..." she started again, but then swallowed hard. "If this is your last 'May,' your last 'Mother's Day,' then I want to celebrate it."

She handed the card to me, and I took it. Tiny and pink, the front had my name in Elly's handwriting.

"You got me a card?" I asked, turning it over. "For Mother's Day?"

She nodded. "Open it."

I found a simple card inside with a cartoon of two women of similar ages hugging on the front, hearts around them. Flipping it open, I read the inscription, and my heart fell into my stomach and burst through my chest all at the same time.

MOTHER IS A TITLE YOU EARN. You've earned it a hundred times over.

I love you, Tessa. Happy Mother's Day.

"ELLY—" I tried to speak, but my words failed me.

"I know it's not Mom's fault she didn't raise me, and I'll always love her even though I never knew her," Elly started.

I watched her as she spoke, tears brimming her lower lashes. I reached over and intertwined my fingers with hers. She moved closer to me, both of us stretched out side by side on the couch. I cradled her like a child against me, her head on my shoulder.

She sniffed and started again. "But you, Tessa... you're my mother. You took care of me. You raised me. You taught me everything I know—the important things. You taught me it's okay to have high hopes, even if they come crashing down, and how to get up and try again. You taught me how to treat people—with love, kindness, and humor. You taught me how to be happy, even when life isn't. That's what mother's do, Tessa, and that's who you are for me. Happy Mother's Day."

For the very first time since I'd decided to move to Vermont, I wished for a miracle. I wished for life—wished the cancer away. I wasn't grieving for my death, for what I'd miss out on, for what I'd lose... I was grieving for Elly.

And for her sake, I was wishing for a miracle.

Silent prayers were sent up to whatever deity would listen. *She needs me. Please, don't take me when she needs me.* As if in some sort of cosmic answer, a sharp pain shot through my skull and down the base of my neck.

The cancer wasn't going anywhere.

And I cried harder.

"I'm so honored, Elly. I'm so happy I could be that for you." I kissed her temple, not caring that my tears were wetting her hair. "I love you so much. I always will."

"I love you, Tessy."

We stayed curled together on the couch. My tears

continued for how long, I don't even know. Every emotion slammed through me, unrelenting and full of anguish. The beauty in my little sister's words, in her raw emotions, made my heart swell. I'd never once, not even for a second, regretted giving up so much of my childhood to care for her. Getting up early to make her lunch before school, making sure to include tiny love notes—big enough she wouldn't miss it, but small enough her peers wouldn't see it and tease her. Working summers to pay for her to go to pre-med summer camps and classes because she wanted to be a doctor, and then helping put her through college when she'd gotten into one of the most prestigious programs in the country.

She was right—I'd been her mother. I *am* her mother.

I'd spent so much of the last few years wishing to be someone I already was. Mother is a title you earn, and though my womb was empty and my body was failing me... I'd already earned it.

To marry the love of my life. *Check.*

To become a mother. *Check.*

To write a book. Almost.

· ღ · ღ · ღ ·

"HAPPY FOURTH OF JULY!" My dad clinked the top of his beer bottle against Kyle's as we sat around the fire pit they'd built in the yard.

"Can you say that?" Elly questioned. "It's September second. I think Happy Independence Day works better."

"We celebrated *April* Fool's Day today, too," I pointed out.

Elly frowned. "True. Still... 'independence' seems to fit us better. Celebrating freedom, coming to Vermont to pursue your freedom—" She looked at me uncertainly. "The freedom to make your own choices."

A small smile tipped up the corners of my lips. "I like that."

I did feel free. Freer than I'd been since before my diagnosis, maybe longer. Despite the sadness I'd felt earlier in the day over my conversation with Elly, I knew wishing away the cancer wasn't the answer. Knowing I was leaving Elly alone—it was hard and it was painful, but I'd given myself several hours to grieve. I'd cried, and cried some more. I'd let myself feel it, and as the emotion bled out, so did its intensity.

She would be okay. She'd have Kyle and my dad, and even little Beast. She'd have people who would always love her, and who would step in where I was stepping out. She was loved as much as I was, and by people who knew I loved them too.

There was nothing left unsaid. Love said it all.

My family had finally accepted my choice, and I was in control of my life again, despite the sickness that was so far out of my hands. All the angst and stress of the last few months, trying to deny, what was happening... it had melted away.

I was dying, and there was a freedom in that, too.

There was a freedom in accepting this *was* going to happen. Kyle would lose his wife. Elly would lose her sister —and Dad, his daughter. I couldn't fight it. I couldn't stop it, but I could enjoy the time I had left with them.

I hadn't even celebrated the real July Fourth this past year. We'd just moved to Vermont, and I'd been so busy dealing with the process of getting my medication, getting residency established, and everything else that goes into uprooting your life. The last April Fool's Day I'd spent throwing up after my first radiation treatment. The last St. Patrick's Day and Valentine's Day, I'd been planning a family and falling in love with the rest of my life stretching out before me.

It hadn't occurred to me to celebrate the last few holidays because I might not have another chance, which was very unlike me. Who I had become over the last few months... I didn't like that person. For the first time in a while, I felt like the old me again. I was getting a re-do—even if only on holidays.

"Happy Independence Day it is," Kyle agreed, taking another swig of his beer.

I sipped my lemonade and watched Beast sniffing at the bag of fireworks a few feet from us. "How big are those fireworks?"

Kyle grinned mischievously. "Let's just say, it's not completely legal."

My brows raised and Elly scooped Beast into her arms. "Let's put you inside, Beastie Boy."

"Good idea," Kyle agreed. "I'm going to set them up."

"Don't lose a hand—or anything else!" I called out, though I knew he'd be careful.

A few minutes later, there was a row of rockets, poised and pointing over the water.

"Here you go." Kyle handed everyone two sparklers and then lit a match, setting them on fire.

I held the wooden end carefully, keeping the flame away from me as sparks shot out from the tip. It crackled and sizzled and flamed, and I couldn't take my eyes off of it.

Elly ran around the yard with hers, dancing in circles, waving the sparkler to make long ribbons of light through the night sky. "Instead of using ribbons in gymnastics, we should have used these!"

My dad joined her, spelling out her name with his sparkler, and then mine. "Tessa, look! Your name's in lights!"

My smile was as bright as the sparkler he was holding, and I turned to see Kyle watching me. His eyes were dark, his smile barely there, but I recognized the look as his sparkler sailed slowly through the air in front of him, forming a heart. I gestured the same heart back to him with my sparkler, and he gave me a small wink before heading over to light the rockets that would shoot up brilliantly into the sky and flame out over the water.

Half the year was over, in more ways than one, and all I felt was the warmth of the sparklers flames and my family's love.

CHAPTER THIRTY-NINE

WEDNESDAY, *September 3, 2014*

"HOW DO you celebrate Halloween when it's *not* Halloween?" I asked my sister as I flipped through the costumes on the rack in front of me. Luckily, stores put out holiday items insanely early, so though it's only September, there were a ton of costume options at the local department store. "We can't exactly go trick-or-treating."

Elly laughed. "When's the last time *you* went trick-or-treating? I mean, I could probably get away with it, but you're old as hell."

"You're going to be a lot older than I'll ever be," I teased.

Elly's face dropped and she shook her head. "Dude."

I put on my most innocent face. "What?"

"Not a funny joke, you jerk."

I shrugged. "It's a little funny."

"*Anyways,*" Elly emphasized loudly, turning to the rack of costumes. "What about this one for me? Tinkerbell?"

"Nothing slutty." I took it from her and returned it to the rack. "I get to pick your costume."

"Says who?" she balked. "You'd probably pick a nun's outfit."

A wiggled my brows at her. "Do they have one of those, because—yes."

Elly laughed. "Hell, no!"

"Nuns don't curse, El."

"Tinkerbell probably does, but it sounds like this—sheeeeet!" Her voice went up several octaves as she shrieked *shit* in the highest pitch possible.

I dissolved into giggles then pulled another costume off the rack. "What about Cat in the Hat?"

"You just said nothing slutty, but now you want me to dress up as a p—"

"All right!" I interrupted her before she could finish that thought, laughing with my hands in the air. "Pick your own costume! Just nothing with 'sexy' or 'slutty' in the title. You're still my little sister."

"Fine, fine!" Elly flitted off to a rack a few rows over.

The tips of my fingers tingled as I returned to pushing costume after costume aside on the rack. I'd moved over to the horror section, costumes covered in gore and fake blood —which I *loved*. Halloween should be scary, and I'd never understood how it had turned into just another excuse to show boobs and ass.

That's what I was thinking of before I had my second seizure.

Boobs and ass.

The oatmeal I'd had for breakfast churned in my stomach and my tongue felt thick. I tried to ignore it, like the tingling spreading up my arms. The music playing over the store's loudspeakers began screeching like a terrifying carnival ride...the music slowed and sped up, slowed and sped up.

I felt it all so fast, I didn't have time to consider what was happening. I grabbed the rack to steady myself as the room ebbed and flowed around me, black spots clustering in my vision until it faded entirely.

Boobs and ass, and I was gone.

Muffled silence slowly faded into noise—deafening noise. Noise so loud I wanted to cover my ears, but I couldn't move. Pain shot through me, reminding me I was alive, but making me wish differently.

Elly was talking to me. I could hear her—she sounded comforting—but I couldn't make out what she was saying, or where she was.

Minutes went by, or hours? Everything was so slow, and somehow on fast forward. My eyelids parted, and I stared at a bloodied face, mouth split open wide, with an even bloodier skeleton head popping out where its tongue should have been.

WHAT THE HELL?!

"AH!" I shrieked and tried to push away from the monster—which ended up being more of a shimmy, shuffling motion backward since I was still on my side on the floor. "Get it away from me!"

Except my words came out like mush, and the room was spinning. My stomach threatened to empty its contents and I clutched my throat, begging it to stay down.

"It's a mask!" Elly said, her voice sounding garbled. It slowly started to make sense, though she still sounded far away for someone bending over me. She kept repeating herself again and again until finally, I began to understand. "You had a seizure and fell into the rack of costumes. It was just a mask."

"Thank you, baby Jesus." I exhaled loudly, finally finding my words. "I thought I blacked out and woke up in the zombie apocalypse."

Elly rolled her eyes, but she still looked terrified. "This isn't 'The Walking Dead,' Tessa."

"Our loss, really. I'd kick zombie ass." I rolled onto my back and took a deep breath, readying myself to stand. Nothing felt sore or broken—probably thanks to falling on a rack of soft clothes and rubbery masks.

"Only you would be making jokes right now." Elly offered me a hand and helped me to my feet.

I suddenly realized that at least five sales people were surrounding us, looking scared shitless. "Oh, hi. Sorry about the rack."

"Are you okay?" one asked.

"Should we call 911?" another added.

A third had a *manager* tag on. "Are you going to sue?"

"What? No, I'm fine. It's okay," I assured them, giving the manager an odd look. Definitely not the zombie apocalypse. People's biggest fears were still their wallets. "I think I'll take that costume though." I pointed to the one I'd woken up staring at. You know, face your fears and all that.

"Take it," the manager rushed to say. "No charge."

"Really?" Elly looked at him skeptically then scooped it up for me. "Cool."

"Can she have one too?" I asked, pushing my luck. *I'm dying, so why not.*

The manager nodded, wringing his hands. "Anything you want."

Elly grinned and held up the Tinkerbell costume.

• ෆ • ෆ • ෆ •

"YOU HAD A SEIZURE?" Kyle gaped, his eyes wider than his heart.

I dropped to the couch, curling into the corner of the plush cushions and pulling a throw blanket over my legs, still holding my zombie mask in my lap. "It's not that big a deal, Kyle."

He looked around the room, double checking we weren't in ear shot of my dad or sister. "Tessa, it is. This is your second. The doctor said they'll begin to happen more frequently toward...toward the end." He sat next to me and took my hand. "Plus, remember how you're starting to forget things?"

"I'm forgetting things?" I feigned then batted at his chest playfully when a look of horror crossed his face. "Kidding. I was kidding!"

He groaned. "You know, you're a lot less funny than you think you are."

I gasped with all the mock seriousness of a proper diva. "How. Dare. You. Sir."

Kyle smiled, eyeing me with both worry and suspicion. Finally, he kissed the back of my hand and let out a long sigh. "You'd tell me, right? If things got really bad?"

"Of course, but I doubt I'll have to," I replied. "I can't imagine it'd be easy to hide pain, paralysis, vision loss, or seizures."

He took a moment to think about it. "Are you in pain now?"

I nodded.

"Like on a scale of zero to ten, where are you?"

I sighed. "Probably a six. That's kind of my average. A steady drum of pain at all times."

"Does it ever get worse?" He was frowning now, and I hated how upset this conversation was making him, but I wasn't going to hide it from him. I couldn't help what was happening to my body.

"A lot worse. Ten. Maybe twelve. But those are quick flashes, not lasting."

He was chewing on the inside of his cheek now, a tick he only did when really worried. "Tessa..." He snuggled closer to me, wrapping an arm around my shoulders. "I hate that you're going through this."

"I hate that *you're* going through this." The despondent looks on his face, my father's, and my sister's? Those were so much worse than any aches and pains.

I lifted the zombie mask from my lap and pulled it over my head. I made my voice as creepy as possible and slowly enunciated his name. "Kyyyylllllllllle—"

"Shit, that mask." Kyle leaned away from me. "That's creepy as hell, Tessa."

I pulled it off, laughing. "Well, it *is* Halloween!"

"Stay here, I'll be right back." He jumped up and jogged into the kitchen. I watched him go with admiration—his butt, my God. I could bounce a quarter off it, then bite right into it. I decided then and there that unless I was physically unable to, I was going to have as much sex as possible before I died.

I didn't want to travel the world or go on a huge shopping spree or some other fantastical adventure. I just wanted to have sex. With my husband. *A lot.*

"Kyle?" I called out to him. There was no time better than the present to start and the pulsing between my legs was already halfway there.

"Check it out," he said, returning with his hands full. Beast danced around his legs and Kyle tried to step around him. "Six different choices of scary movies—everything from horror and gore to aliens and paranormal—and all your favorite candies in fun size." He tossed bags of mini Twix, Reese's, and Milky Ways onto the coffee table and placed the stack of movies beside it. "And..." He held up a small pumpkin costume clearly meant for dogs. "I didn't forget Beast!"

I burst out laughing and scooped Beast into my arms. "Beast, do you want to be a pumpkin for Halloween?" I cooed into his fluffy face.

He wiggled and made silly growling noises before licking my nose.

Kyle grinned and handed me the costume, which I fitted the dog into with only a small amount of squirming. He jumped out of my arms the moment I got it on, tripped over his own feet, and face planted on the floor.

"Beast!"

Kyle laughed. "He makes a cute pumpkin."

I cooed over my puppy a little bit more as he wobbled around, trying to get used to walking as a pumpkin.

"I know we've done the bar crawls, the Halloween parties, the trick-or-treating kids...I thought maybe it's time to have old married couple fun." Kyle dropped down on the couch next to me. "Scary movies, candy, dogs in costume, and a zombie mask—what do you think?"

I kissed him, soft at first, then a little slower, longer. "I think it sounds like the perfect Halloween."

"Yeah?" His eyes were dark and hooded, and I knew exactly what he was thinking.

I nodded. "But on an unrelated note, how long do we have until the movie starts?"

He glanced toward the clock. "I don't know what your dad and sister are doing but we could start whenever."

"So, we have time to go upstairs?" I wiggled my eyebrows at him.

His green eyes flared, and a low growl rumbled through his chest. "Oh, we have time."

"Yeah?" I said, teasing, but he was already on his feet and scooping me into his arms.

He cradled me against his chest and I wrapped my arms around his neck.

"Wait!" I pointed to the couch. "Bring the zombie mask."

Kyle glanced between me and the mask, his expression not amused with the idea. "All right. I'll power through."

I laughed, grabbing the mask and letting him carry me up the stairs.

CHAPTER FORTY

THURSDAY, *September 4, 2014*

"YOU'VE LITERALLY NEVER COOKED a whole turkey before, Tessa."

I shrugged, clicking to the next website. "How hard can it be?"

Kyle lifted one brow. "I've never heard anyone call it easy before, that's for sure. We were just planning to order it from a store or something like that."

I shook my head quickly. "Nope, I'm making it. I've always wanted to do it before, and this is my chance." I flashed him a confident smile. "You can help me though."

Kyle clicked his heels together, straightened his shoulders, and gave me a true military salute. "Yes, ma'am."

"Ma'am?" I laughed, shaking my head. "How about miss? I'm still young enough to be a miss."

He repeated the salute again. "Sorry, miss. I'll help you burn down the house, miss."

I smacked his chest. "Oh, please."

The corners of Kyle's mouth lifted into a smile, and he winked at me. He didn't get a chance for a snappy retort, however, since my dad walked in carrying a huge cardboard box.

"Guess what I got!" he called over the top.

"If there's a live turkey in there, I'm out," I declared.

My dad put the box on the ground, and Beast immediately ran to it and began trying to chew the edge off of. "The way Beast is attacking the box, maybe!" my dad said seeming to tease, then he waved his hand to say it wasn't. "It's a deep fryer. For the turkey."

"What?" I balked.

"YES!" Kyle fist pumped the air. "Best idea you've ever had, sir."

"Thanks, son." My dad beamed with pride as he started pulling a giant stock pot and other random components out. "Now we need to do this outside, but it'll be so fast. What size turkey do we have?"

"Ten pounds." I eyed the contraption suspiciously, because I'm pretty sure I've heard dozens of stories of deep-frying-turkeys burning houses down. "How long will it take to cook in that?"

"For ten pounds, I think about thirty-five minutes."

My brows lifted. "For a *full* turkey?"

Kyle nodded, confirming my dad's assertion. "That's the beauty of the deep fryer, babe."

I gingerly stepped over to it, going slowly since my body was all aches and pains. "Well...I *have* always wanted to try deep fried turkey, but I get to prep the bird and drop it in."

My dad gave me a thumbs-up. "You got it, sunshine."

He and Kyle began taking everything outside, far

enough from the house to hopefully avoid disasters. I began pulling food out of the fridge for the sides and desserts.

"Ready to start, Tessy?" Elly waltzed into the kitchen, freshly showered after her run. "What are we making?"

I pointed to my computer screen that had a list of dishes and the recipe for each.

She read it out loud. "Mashed potatoes, cranberry sauce, homemade pumpkin pie and apple pie, and green bean casserole. Oh man, we're going to pig out!"

I grinned and handed her a mixing bowl. "That's the goal. Which do you want to do?"

"I'll do potatoes and casserole, you do desserts," she offered.

I nodded in relief, because the potatoes sounded like they were going to take more energy than I had. "Perfect. Oh, and I'm going to prep the bird."

"We should get it in the oven fast. Those take forever to cook."

"Nope." I pointed out the window to where our dad and Kyle were setting up the deep fryer. "Dad bought a deep fryer, so it doesn't take long."

"I thought deep fryers always set people's houses on fire..." She nibbled on the edge of her thumb. "Is this a good idea?"

"Definitely not." I shrugged. "But are you going to stop them?"

That earned me a big grin when she turned away from the window. "Like that's even possible."

We both laughed and returned to our prep work. I fixed the turkey first, getting it washed and seasoned and stuffed full of flavor, ready to be dunked in hot oil. It only took me a few minutes, but I was winded by the end of it and had to sit while prepping the pies.

A couple hours went by and the kitchen smelled so good, my stomach was growling. I hadn't had much of an appetite in months, so I was excited for both the food and another Thanksgiving with my family. Our last Thanksgiving had been lackluster at best. Elly had been at school and hadn't made it home over break. We'd invited Kyle's family, but they'd been finding enlightenment in a yurt in Alaska, or something equally as absurd.

When it was time to deep fry the turkey, Dad helped, both of us fully covered in aprons and long gloves to keep the oil from burning our skin. We lowered the bird into the pot while Elly and Kyle set the table for dinner. Sure enough, a little under forty minutes later, the bird was crispy and perfect.

The weather was beautiful—it was still September, after all— so we set a picnic table outside with a red checkered tablecloth, a gourd filled with small pumpkins as a centerpiece, and neatly folded checkered napkins to match. I felt like a freaking domestic goddess.

I wanted everything to be perfect and memorable, even if I wouldn't be the one remembering it.

"What's left?" Elly looked around the kitchen, having helped me make several trips out to the table already. "Is everything outside?"

"I think just the pies," I replied, pulling open the oven. Beast bounced around my feet, but I pushed him away, worried he'd burn himself.

Elly grabbed pot holders, and we each picked a pie and headed outside. I was only a few steps behind her. My feet felt tingly, and I wondered if I had pushed myself too hard today, spending so much time standing. I was definitely tired, but this was a million pins and needles stabbing my legs. I wobbled and swayed, clutching the pie in my hand, but it was too late.

My left foot disappeared, like it wasn't even attached to me. I looked down and saw it, but I couldn't feel it. The surprising sensation, or lack thereof, tipped me sideways and I stumbled. I tried to catch myself, but with the pie in my hand, it was a losing battle.

In an odd, slow motion slump, my butt hit the concrete patio as I cradled the pie against me—because, damn it, I worked hard on that pie.

I was suddenly sitting on the ground, staring at my feet splayed in front of me. I could see it. I moved my leg, saw my foot move in turn, but that was it. I tried to wiggle my toes—they didn't budge. I shook my leg, but my foot just dangled like it had no other choice.

I can't feel my foot.

"Tessa?!" Panic sounded in Kyle's voice as he rushed to me, Elly and my dad close behind. "Are you okay?"

I nodded slowly, unsure, but not wanting to alarm them.

"Here." My dad took the pie out of my hands and gave it to my sister. "Let us help you up. You okay?"

He and Kyle grabbed me beneath both arms and lifted me into a standing position. They let go and I immediately tipped to the side again and fell into Kyle's chest.

Luckily, he reacted fast and grabbed me, holding me steady against him. "Tessa, what's wrong?"

My bottom lip trembled, and I looked over at the decorated table, devastated I might be about to ruin a moment that meant so much to me. Finally, I pointed at my leg. "My left foot."

"Did you hurt it when you tripped?" my dad asked.

"I can get you some ice," Elly volunteered.

I shook my head. "No, I tripped because of my foot. I can't feel it."

Kyle helped me hobble to my chair. He bent on one knee in front of me and lifted my leg, rubbing up and down my calf. "Can you feel me here?" He touched just below my knee, pushing in slightly.

I nodded.

He moved lower. "Here?"

I nodded again.

He touched my ankle, pushing in lightly and I felt it, but...differently. I could feel a pressure, but couldn't pinpoint where it was coming from. "Sort of. It feels numb but hurts. If that makes any sense."

It was his turn to nod. "How about here?"

I could see he was squeezing my toes. I *saw* it—I couldn't feel it.

A cold wave swept through my body, and I trembled under the knowledge that this was happening. My symptoms were getting worse and there was nothing I could do to stop it.

"Can you feel here?" he asked again, tapping the sole of my foot.

I swallowed hard. "No."

"I'm going to call the doctor." Kyle placed my foot on the ground and headed for the house.

"No!" I called out after him, almost shouting. I hadn't meant to be that loud, but damn it, I'd worked so hard on dinner.

"Tessa, he needs to know about this," he argued.

My dad nodded his head. "I agree with Kyle, sunshine. This is serious."

"It's not," I replied. "We knew numbness would start soon. Paralysis eventually. It'll probably be fine later, and if it's not, there's nothing the doctor can do about that. I just want to have Thanksgiving dinner with my family. We all worked so hard to put this together."

Elly was beside me now, squeezing my shoulder and facing against the men in a sign of solidarity. "It's up to Tessy how she wants to handle this."

Kyle and my dad traded glances, before my dad finally spoke up. "We'll have dinner, but after, we call."

Kyle didn't look like he fully agreed with the plan. "Immediately after, and we follow whatever advice the doctor gives."

That seemed fair. "Okay."

Elly looked between the rest of us. "Well, um, everything is ready, so...dinner is served?"

She seemed hesitant, but I squeezed her arm. "Time to eat!"

Kyle helped me push my chair into the table, and everyone sat down in their respective places. "This smells really good, babe."

I beamed. "It wasn't just me. Elly helped a lot."

"And I put together the turkey fryer!" my dad announced, brandishing a large carving knife. "I'm going to cut this bird up. Legs or breast?"

"Wait!" I put my hand up and shook my head. "Not yet. First, we have to say what we're thankful for."

Elly and Kyle exchanged glances, and I knew they were both thinking the year hadn't boasted a ton of grateful moments. There were a lot of shitty parts to my life, but the people were pretty damn great. They were who I was grateful for.

"I'll start," my dad volunteered. "I'm thankful for my daughters. Beautiful, loving, good. That's all you can ever ask for as a father—to raise children who make you proud of who they are. Not what they do, what they have, or what they accomplished. Just who they are." He lifted his glass, as if in a toast to us. "Tessa, Elly, you two are what I've done right in my life." His voice tensed, and he took a deep breath. "I'm thankful for my baby girls."

I pulled my lips between my teeth and bit down to keep from crying. I'd always felt I'd gotten my optimism from him—always able to find the good. Even in a time like this, he still was thankful for love, for us.

Elly didn't hide her tears, letting several streak down her cheeks as she held our dad's hand. "We love you too, Daddy."

I squeezed his other hand. "So much."

"I love you too, girls." He smiled widely then looked at Kyle. "And I haven't forgotten you, Kyle. I'm thankful you came into my oldest girl's life and have been so good to her. I'm thankful I've gotten to know you as a man, and as my son."

Kyle offered him a smile, tight-lipped and deep, his hand on his chest. "That means a lot, sir."

My dad lifted one brow. "You know you can call me 'Dad'."

Elly's mouth fell open. "He can?"

My dad nodded. "Yeah. I think it's time. He's my son." He turned to Kyle. "You're my son, Kyle. You always will be. Even..." He glanced at me, then my husband. "Even after."

I reached out a hand to Kyle and wrapped my fingers around his, my other hand in my dad's. The two most important men in my life. Here. Supporting each other. Loving each other.

I'm thankful.

"My turn," Elly announced. "Can I go next?"

"Go for it, baby girl," my dad told her.

She smiled at the table—that same innocent, unsure tilt to her grin she'd always had. She was an adult, but when I looked at her, all I saw was the little girl who used to follow me around the playground, hanging on my every word. I saw the child who didn't say her first word until she was five, but who I understood as if she was speaking full sentences. Everyone had called me her translator, and said she'd speak when she was ready.

Our mother had had cancer during the pregnancy, and they said it had affected the baby, but once Elly started talking, she never stopped, and there was never another sign of trouble. My dad had worried, but not me. Never once. Elly communicated with me... somehow. I'm still not sure how I knew what she wanted or was saying, but I did.

To this day, I still just did. I knew her like the inside of my heart, because she was. She was my everything.

I'm thankful.

Elly took a deep breath, then started. "Okay, well, I'm thankful for a lot this year. I'm also not thankful for a lot, too. And it may not be tradition, but I'm going to say both."

Her statement was more of a warning than asking for permission, and no one tried to stop her. "I'm thankful for the little things, like our trip to Niagara Falls. I'm thankful for this move, even if it's temporary. This house is breathtaking, right on the water." She gestured to the lake. "I've always dreamed of seeing water out my bedroom window."

"Me, too," I agreed.

"I'm also thankful I have understanding advisors at school who helped me take this semester off. I'm thankful I only have less than a year of undergrad left. I'm thankful for all you guys have sacrificed to get me through school."

I beamed at her, pride seeping through me. She was

excelling in college, and I'd been pretty guilt ridden at her taking this fall off, but her advisor had assured her it wouldn't put her far behind.

"But also..." Elly sighed, her expression frustrated as she carefully picked what she would say next. "I'm not thankful. I'm not thankful when the real Thanksgiving comes in two months, my sister might not be there to share it with me. I'm not thankful we have to sit idly by and watch a disease we can't see take Tessa from us. I'm not thankful you're dying, Tessa. And that's everything. That's bigger than all the good things. It's the only thing on the list that matters. So, I don't know, but maybe I'm not thankful at all."

I watched her from across the table, feeling the heartbreak in her words as she stared down at her plate. I split open so wide I'm not sure I'd ever be able to close again.

She glanced up at me, and despite everything she'd said, she said even more in that one look. We had an entire conversation with just the tears in our eyes.

And I'm thankful.

My dad and Kyle looked between us, knowing they were missing words they were never meant to hear. "They're doing it again," Kyle whispered to my dad.

My dad grinned. "I'm going to miss that."

Returning my focus to the table, I asked, "Who's next?" Beast barked on the ground by my feet, and I startled. "Jeez, Beast! You're going to give me a heart attack."

"Damn dog," my dad muttered.

I laughed and scooped him in my arms, holding the fluffy white dog in my lap at the table. He tried sniffing his way toward the turkey, but I held him firmly, knowing his agenda.

"It's my turn," Kyle answered my question, draping his arm over the back of my chair and leaning closer to me.

"Although I don't know how I can top those two. That's probably the first thing I'm thankful for—this family. I love my family to pieces, but closeness was never really valued in our home. Everyone did their own thing, and sure, we supported each other, but in our own way. But this family? You guys show up. You show up when it matters, when it's inconvenient, when things aren't fun. And you welcomed me in to that."

"Always welcome, son," my dad echoed.

"Yeah, you're my big brother!" Elly chimed in, smiling at my husband in a way that made my heart explode with warmth. The way my family loved my husband was so beautiful.

I'm thankful.

Kyle nodded his appreciation. "Most of all, I'm thankful for you, Tessa." His eyes were on me now, blazing green with pain and passion and pure honesty. "I'm thankful I found you. I'm thankful you found me. I'm thankful that even if we only have a few years together, at least I had any time at all. If I'd never met you, my life would have been empty and I wouldn't have even known it—but I'd have felt it. I'd have always felt something missing."

Tears were flowing down my cheeks now, because his words were sad, but they were his heart. And I was so damn thankful.

"I love you, Tessa. I'm thankful for you, and every Thanksgiving for the rest of my life—and every day in between—I'll be thankful to have been your husband."

I shoved out of my seat so fast, Beast fell to the ground, casting an annoyed look at me. I barely noticed as I haphazardly threw my arms around Kyle's neck and kissed him hard on the mouth, his arms steadying me as I balanced on one foot. There was nothing sweet or affectionate about my kiss. It was hard and intense and as pain-filled as our hearts were.

My dad had his napkin under his eye, wiping away the evidence of a single tear as he snorted loudly. "Fucking hell, son," was all he managed to say.

Men didn't cry, or at least that's what my dad liked to pretend. I'd heard him behind closed doors shedding tears more than once since my diagnosis, but I hadn't told a soul.

Elly needed a moment to composed herself as well, but then she stood and hugged Kyle. "That was beautiful."

"Tessa, you haven't gone yet," my dad pointed out.

"My turn." I sat straighter in my seat, taking a deep breath. "This year, I'm thankful for chances. The chance to move to a new place, a dream house with a dream view. The chance to go on trips and explore new places I might not have gotten around to before. The chance to spend time with the people I love." I made sure to look at each of them. "I'm thankful for the chance to take control of my cancer, and of my life. I'm thankful for the chance to say goodbye."

Kyle rubbed my shoulder, and Elly sniffed again.

"Happy Thanksgiving, guys," I finally said, shrugging my shoulders in exhaustion at the emotional moments we'd all just shared. "Now, let's stop crying and eat this freaking turkey!"

Laughter burst out all around and my dad picked up the carving knife. "Happily!"

"I want a drumstick," Elly declared, and Beast started barking the moment Dad's knife touched the bird. The dog was claiming his piece, too.

"Happy Thanksgiving, Tessa," Kyle whispered in my ear, kissing me on the cheek before filling up his plate.

I didn't rush to fill mine right away, but instead watched my family laugh and joke and stuff their mouths with food

I'd helped prepare. We were all so raw, and we loved each other so beautifully that I knew my life was already fulfilled. I would have a shorter time than most, but I'd already lived more because of these three people.

I was so damn thankful.

CHAPTER FORTY-ONE

*F*RIDAY, *September 5, 2014*

I LOVE CHRISTMAS. I've *always* loved Christmas. If there's one holiday we could have skipped this week, it would be this because we've never wasted a single one. Last year, we were *the* house to see on our block—covered with lights and nativity scenes and tinsel for days.

My mother started the tradition, always reading me The Night Before Christmas to us on Christmas Eve and letting us open one present each. We roasted marshmallows in the fireplace and made s'mores, staying up way past bedtime in excitement for Christmas morning. After I went to bed, she'd dress up like Mrs. Claus, and Dad like Santa, just in case I'd see them wrapping presents and stuffing my stocking. I did, and I knew it was them, but I loved that they'd tried.

The next morning, I rushed down the stairs, eager to tear through my presents, even though that wasn't allowed until after breakfast. My dad would get such a kick out of slowly stirring the eggs, yawning widely, and purposely dragging his feet while my antsy little body bounced around the kitchen trying to hurry him along.

We made green eggs and ham, or rather scrambled eggs mixed with grape jelly and a side of crispy bacon, every Christmas morning after my favorite Dr. Seuss story that Mom read to me every night. It never tasted nearly as good as the novelty of it, but to this day, it was still a tradition we kept and dying food was a strange addition to most of our holidays now.

Elly never got to experience Mom like that, and so I'd made it my mission to give that to her. Even after Mom died, Dad and I went all out every year. Instead of waiting anxiously in bed for Christmas morning, I was the one downstairs with Dad, helping him wrap gifts and stuff stockings. I got up early and made the off-colored eggs and savory bacon, keeping Mom's tradition alive.

Elly's face when she barreled down the stairs the next morning made every sleepless moment and early morning worth it. I wanted to do that every Christmas for the rest of her life, even if I only had today, and it was only September fifth.

It was a really cruel twist of fate that I couldn't do this one thing for her.

Instead, I was lying in bed, staring at the streak of morning sun cast against the ceiling above me. Tears streamed down my face, or at least I think they were. My body was silent. Numb and tingling as I slowly regained control of my limbs.

Despite the fuzziness in my head, it hadn't taken me too long to figure out what had just happened, that I'd experienced a seizure in my sleep, and was waking from it. My stomach rolled with the room around me as I waited for the dizziness to fade away. My arms and legs were a million tiny pins pricking me, and my body felt swollen, angry...unresponsive. Except my body *was* responding on its own accord, it just wasn't consulting me in the process.

When I smelled a whiff of urine, I began crying harder. Silent tears turned to choking sobs as my body gave me just enough control to allow me this. At twenty-eight years old, I wet the fucking bed.

"Tessa?" Kyle stirred beside me, rousing at the sounds of my sobs.

I quickly shook my head, or at least I thought I did, but I wasn't sure since everything was still spinning. "Kyle, please leave. Please leave the room now!"

I could hear the panic in my voice and it matched Kyle's face when he leaned over me. He needed to leave. He needed to leave *now* and never see me like this. I'd regain feeling in my limbs in moments, I was sure I would. I'd get up on my own and clean myself, and he'd never be the wiser. He couldn't know about this. *He just can't.*

"Babe, what's wrong?" He pulled the covers down off me, and I wanted to stop him. I wanted to hide what I'd done, hide what had happened, but I couldn't lift my arms yet.

"Stop!" I tried again, this time lifting my arm just enough to hold his forearm.

But it was too late.

"Babe? Did you...?" His words petered out as he looked from my soiled pajama pants up to my tear-streaked face. "Oh, Tessa, are you okay?"

I nodded my head slowly, refusing to make eye contact with him. "I'll be fine. Please, just leave."

He was climbing off his side of the bed now, and for a second, I thought he would actually do as I asked. Part of me felt relieved, but another part felt hurt. I wasn't sure how to decipher that mix of emotions.

"Like that's going to happen," he scoffed, a slight tease to his voice. He came around to my side of the bed and pulled the covers completely off. "Come on, I'm going to carry you to the bath."

I stared at him, wide-eyed. The room had definitely slowed, but I was even more aware of my stench now than before. I felt my cheeks flush, my face certainly stained bright red, but his expression didn't hold a single ounce of pity or disgust.

"Can you put your arm around my neck?" he asked, and I nodded I could. "Good, ready?"

He slid his arm under my back and I draped mine around his neck. His other hand slid directly under my soaked bottom without any hesitation.

I prayed for God to take me right then and there.

He didn't.

God has a fucked-up sense of timing.

Kyle sat me on the edge of the tub in the master bathroom—a pretty luxurious Jacuzzi actually. It had been one of the main draws to renting this home, and I'd already bathed in it dozens of times. It eased the aches in my muscles, especially when I added in any of the array of bath salts, aromatherapy oils, and other goodies my sister had gifted me.

Kyle prepared it perfectly—adding the calming scents as he turned on the faucet and stopped the drain up with its plug. He lifted my arms above my head with only some help from me, then lifted my shirt off, tossing it into the dirty clothes basket.

He helped me stand, and I clutched the wall with one hand, and his shoulder with the other, as I tried to stay upright despite my shaking knees. He crouched before me, sliding my damp pajama pants and underwear down my legs, lifting my feet one at a time to step out of them. His arm returned to my back and he walked me to the shower stall next to the tub.

He stepped inside with me, not caring that he was wearing a T-shirt and pajama pants, and turned the water on hot. It beat down against us, and we took a moment to adjust to the temperature, but once we had, Kyle moved quickly. I was able to stand on my own now, despite still feeling weak and slightly dizzy.

Within seconds, his clothes clung to his body and I couldn't help but let my mind wander as I saw his toned muscles beneath the white tee. I tilted my head into the water and he scrubbed shampoo into my hair. He then took a soapy wash cloth to the rest of me, scrubbing me clean.

I stood there, not entirely helpless but not entirely helpful either, as the kind, caring man I'd fallen in love with years ago washed the urine from my legs.

He didn't grimace. He didn't frown. He didn't curl his lips.

I wouldn't have blamed him if he did—I was certainly disgusted with myself—but it didn't seem to cross his mind. And when I was all clean, he turned off the shower and walked me to the now full, soothingly scented tub and helped me inside.

I lay under the warm water enveloping me like a blanket, my muscles aching from the seizure already relaxing.

He peeled off his wet clothes and put them in the basket alongside mine. Wrapping a towel around his waist to cover himself, he picked up the basket and left the bathroom. I heard some noise in the bedroom, and it sounded like he was stripping the sheets off the bed. A few minutes later, I heard the laundry room door down the hallway open and my heart warmed at the gesture.

I looked out the window over the tub, high above the ground, Lake Champlain stretched out before me. A lone tear streaked down my face, nothing else left inside me to cry after my sobs earlier.

I don't know what I did to ever deserve a man like Kyle —so loving, so without judgment. I'd been filled with shame, and in one simple act of love, he'd literally washed it away. Instead of foolish, I felt tender and cared for. It was the sweetest Christmas gift I ever could have asked for.

He returned in a few minutes, dropping his towel and sliding into the tub behind me, his legs on either side of me as I leaned into his chest. His arms engulfed me and I sighed, feeling almost deliriously happy which felt absurd considering what I'd just experienced.

"Merry Christmas," he said in a low rumble against my ear.

I smiled and squeezed his hand, which was currently resting against my breast. I straightened my back ever so slightly, just enough for his hand to fall lower, covering my nipple. "Merry Christmas," I rumbled back with a small shake of my ass against his pelvis.

He growled against my ear and I felt his lips move south, his teeth sinking gently into my neck. "You're making it hard for me to let you just have a relaxing bath, babe."

"That's the point," I teased, wiggling my ass again. "Making it hard."

That got an appreciative chuckle, and I surged with excitement as I felt just that happening against me. His hand cupped my breast harder, his thumb sliding across one nipple as I leaned my head back onto his shoulder and closed my eyes. His other hand slid south, and I felt butter-flies respond in a flurry.

He reached between my legs, finding where I wanted him. His manipulations started slowly, but as my hips thrust against his hand, he sped up and my body responded in kind. The water splashed as the jets pulsed against our skin, while I fell apart against him.

After my body had calmed, he lifted my hips and pressed himself against my core. The warm water swirled around us as we moved in rhythmic waves. His lips traced my shoulder and my hand held tight to his forearms as he hugged me.

We loved, and loved hard, and when we were done, we let the soothing bath drift around us as we quietly held each other. In one simple act, he had reassured me that nothing about what was happening changed how he felt about me.

He still loved me. He still desired me.

In sickness and in health, 'till death do us part.

CHAPTER FORTY-TWO

SATURDAY, *September 6, 2014*

DESPITE ITS ROCKY START, yesterday's Christmas celebrations went well. My nurse, Malaika, had been warned about Thursday's numbness and brought me a cane which I have been using more often than not. The numbness lasts longer each time, rising higher up my leg, as if I can feel it slowly seizing control. Slowly stealing my life.

We followed the traditions we'd always had. Green eggs and ham for Christmas breakfast. Stockings stuffed with chocolate and love notes. I cried as I read each of the letters my family wrote me, just like I had every Christmas for years. We opened presents, and everything was homemade. There had been no rule not to buy anyone anything, but when facing the truth about what was actually important for our last Christmas together, love and memories couldn't be expressed in dollar signs.

I'd given everyone scrapbooks tailor made just for them. Kyle's was filled with mementos of our life together—photos of us, receipts or ticket stubs from our most memorable dates, and other little pieces of who we are to each other. My dad's scrapbook was filled with a lot of childhood pictures, and of him walking me down the aisle, and even a picture of us overlooking Niagara Falls from a month ago. Elly's was about sisterhood. I'd stuffed it full of pictures of us together, doing my best to convey our bond through pictures and sweet captions.

There were letters in the back of everyone's scrapbook, but they were in a hidden pocket. They were meant to be read after everything happened. Morbid, maybe, but I felt the need to leave them with something. A little piece of me to offer some type of solace when it was all said and done. That's what hurt me the most—knowing they will grieve and knowing I won't be there to comfort them.

My dad's gift to me was more of a temporarily loaned item, but unbelievably special. He'd put a small box together which contained the love letters between him and my mother during their courtship and marriage. He'd been deployed so much that their communications were often handwritten. I hadn't even known these existed, and when I read the first one—with Elly eagerly reading over my shoulder—I cried at this new side to my mother I'd never known.

I touched the ink she'd pressed into the paper, reveling in how similar her handwriting was to my own. Her sweet words and the loving exchange between my parents both broke my heart and repaired it all at once. I was honored to be able to see into this part of them, and I'd spent the rest of the day reading through each and every one with my sister.

Elly gifted me with a beautiful canvas she had painted herself. It was a rendition of a photo from our childhood where both of us are looking off into the distance and my hand is on her shoulder. It was beautiful and touching, and I immediately hung it in my bedroom so I'd see it every single day. Well, Kyle hung it, but I supervised.

His gift to me was much more practical, but Kyle had always been a practical man. It was a completed copy of our will and all the documents I'd wanted settled that he'd been putting off. He'd done everything I asked, and the sense of relief I felt knowing he'd have everything he needed was immense.

Beast was not forgotten, of course. That dog got away with at least a dozen new toys, a bone larger than he was, plus a slew of treats he's already dug in to. I spoiled him rotten, it was my last chance.

It was one of the best Christmases we'd ever had.

"Malaika's here!" my dad called from the front hall.

She waltzed in seconds later and scanned the room before looking at me. "How was Christmas?"

"It was amazing. Rocky start, but then..." I sighed happily. "Wonderful."

She had loved the idea of a week of holidays, and every morning this week would ask me what day it was. I loved bragging about my family, so I was more than eager to dish.

Malaika dropped her bag on the dining table and began setting herself up. "Rocky start?"

"Seizure," I said with a slight frown as she positioned a blood pressure cuff on my arm. "I woke up from it."

She seemed surprised. "It happened when you were asleep?"

"A twilight sleep, I think. I vaguely remember some sort of consciousness before, but it definitely woke me up after."

I decided not to tell her about soiling the bed, or what Kyle had sweetly done for me. Frankly, I was still embarrassed.

She continued checking my vitals and I rambled on about the week's activities. She oohed and aahed, and let me have my moment. Malaika took her job seriously, but she also treated me like a friend. Every morning visit felt like having tea with a girlfriend, and that meant a lot to me, especially now.

I'd never taken a job as seriously as that in my life. I'd enjoyed my old job, and I certainly wasn't a slacker, but I'd never been passionate about it. Writing was different—*that* I felt passionate about. But I still wonder if I would feel that way if it was my full-time career over a normal life span, or if it's important to me because of my current situation and what I'd like to leave behind for the world.

It's hard to say what I'd be doing or who I would be if I was planning a life to live, rather than planning for how I was going to die.

Malaika finished the last of her notes before lowering her pregnant self into the chair next to me. "Let's take a look at those legs."

I stretched them out slowly, and she maneuvered them around, asking me about pain and what I was feeling, or not feeling.

"It's not numb right now, but it feels stiff, or, um..." I thought about how to describe the sensation. "It feels like my legs are behind my brain. I plan to get up to walk, but there's a delay between when I think I'm walking to when I'm *actually* walking. I don't know... does that make sense?"

"Sure," she replied. "And why you need the cane."

"I'm using it most of the time. I think I'm just...slower."

She nodded her head. "Without the cane, you're at a serious risk for falling and hurting yourself, which could put you back in the hospital. My understanding is that *that* is the last place you want to be."

My mouth set to a firm line. Definitely a big worry for me. I did not want to do anything that could wind me up back there instead of finishing out my days at home. "Yeah, I'm going to be as careful as I can. I'll use the cane."

She got back to her feet with a big groan and a hand on her belly. "So, yesterday was Christmas, what's today?"

"Um, New Year's Day? Or Eve?" I frowned, wondering why I hadn't heard anything about it. "Actually, it might be over. No more holidays, I think."

"Well, you never know." Malaika smiled innocently, but there was something beneath her words. "What about your birthday? It's soon, isn't it?"

I nodded, the corners of my lips tilted down. "September thirtieth."

"You don't look thrilled?" She draped a hand over her pregnant belly. "Don't want to turn twenty-nine?"

"I don't mind that," I replied. It was thirty I'd always wanted to avoid, not that that was a worry now. "It's three weeks away."

"Okay... I'm not following."

"Three weeks is a long time, and I don't have a lot of that."

She tried to hide it from me, but her face fell and I saw a grief I hadn't expected.

"Am I your...first?" I asked, suddenly curious.

Her brow furrowed. "My first?"

"First patient to..." *Die* felt too harsh, though it's exactly what was going to happen. "To not make it?"

She exhaled slowly. "Technically, no. But other times have been in the hospital, on rotations, things like that. This is my first hospice home care role."

"Oh."

"If you're asking if I'll miss you, or if it will hurt," she started slowly, looking down at fidgeting hands. "I will, and it will."

I stared at her, and for the first time, really saw her. Really saw how young she was. How beautiful she was in a quirky, offbeat way. I saw the way she cradled her belly, like how she would one day cradle her child. I saw strength and honesty and fearlessness and humanity. "Thank you, Malaika. For everything."

"You got it, girl." She was smiling again, turning to put the last of her papers in her bag. She rummaged around in it for a minute. "Oh, I forgot to congratulate you."

"On what?"

She pulled a glossy magazine out of her bag and handed it to me. On the cover was a huge story about a celebrity feud, a reality television star's arrest, and of course, a Kardashian doing... something. I glanced up at her, my confusion obviously apparent on my face because she pointed back down at it. "You haven't seen it? Page fifty-three."

I did, and my picture stared back at me. "What on earth?"

CHICAGO NATIVE CHOOSES TO END LIFE WHEN DIAGNOSED WITH TERMINAL DISEASE, *by Marley Wellings.*

My picture sat under it—the single one I'd let her take. It was me sitting on the patio lounge chair out back, my legs tucked under me, and Beast in my lap. We were both staring out toward the lake, and it looked poignant as hell. I'd laughed when she told me to do that, saying it would have more impact, but now I saw she was right.

"You knew about it, didn't you?" Malaika looked worried now.

I nodded. I did know about it. I had agreed to it. I'd

given her all the information for it. But it felt different seeing it in print, in a magazine thousands of people read.

"Hey." Kyle stepped into the room, giving my nurse a small wave. "How're you doing, Malaika?"

"I'm doing great, Mr. Falls." She beamed. "Thank you."

"I've told you, you can call me Kyle," he said with a smile before kissing me on the top of my head. "What are you reading, babe?"

I hadn't read the article yet, but had scanned it briefly and didn't see any big surprises. I handed it to him. "Marley's article."

"Shit! In this magazine? I thought it was going in a webzine or something."

I shrugged. "She'd warned me she would try to get it in a major publication."

Kyle glanced at the cover of the magazine. "Major might be a bit of a stretch. There *is* a Kardashian on the cover."

Malaika and I both laughed, and my tension dwindled a bit. Kyle always knew how to make things feel simpler, easier, happier.

"Should I call Marley? I haven't heard from her. I should congratulate her, right?" I asked him.

"Babe, you haven't checked your phone in days. I don't even know where it is. She's probably tried calling you a few times." He rummaged in his pocket for his cell phone and handed it to me. "Here, use mine."

Thankfully, he'd saved her number when I'd given it to him a few weeks ago. I clicked on her name and she picked up so quickly, I wasn't sure I'd heard it ring.

"Go for Marley!"

The corners of my mouth tilted up, loving the young energy that surrounded this girl. "Hey Marley, it's Tessa."

"Tessa! Jesus H. Christ, I've been calling you for days—

I've got huge news! Is this a new phone? New number? You're not going to believe what happened!" Marley rambled breathlessly into the phone. "Oh, oh, but tell me first, how are you doing? How are you feeling?"

"I'm doing okay. Mostly the same as before." No reason to burden her with my less-than-functioning feet or random bouts of unconsciousness. "And I think I've guessed at the huge news already."

"You saw the article? Did you like it?" Marley made a high-pitched squeak into the phone.

"I loved it, Marley. You did an amazing job."

I heard her smile and imagined her clutching the phone tighter and dancing around. "I just knew people needed to hear your story, Tessa. It's so amazing, and you will not believe how much my phone has been blowing up since it came out. So many people want to talk to you. Can I come over? I'd love to tell you about it!"

"Maybe tomorrow. I might have plans with my family today, I'm not sure." I noticed the covert look between Kyle and Malaika, and made a mental note to interrogate both of them later.

"Tomorrow works!" Marley replied. "Thanks again for letting me interview you—I truly think this is going to be bigger than either of us knows."

"Sure, Marley," I said, although I had to chalk most of her enthusiasm up to naiveté because tons of stories are run in magazines every week that few people read. "This is Kyle's number, by the way, so if you can't reach me on mine, try here."

"Perfect, I'll see you tomorrow!" She hung up without saying goodbye.

"What did Marley say?" Kyle asked as I handed his phone to him.

"Just that the article is doing really well. She wants to talk more about it."

Kyle nodded. "I just finished reading. It's really good. Not just her writing—which is fantastic—but the story has every component a viral news story needs."

My brows furrowed. "I don't know if I want to go viral."

"I don't think it would be a bad thing," Kyle said. "You could be an advocate for the Death with Dignity Act."

"I agree with Mr. Falls," Malaika spoke up, slinging her bag over her shoulder. "You're an inspiration to me just from meeting you. Imagine being able to do that for people all over the globe."

"If it were up to me, no one would ever have to be in a position to make that decision." I frowned, wondering if I could really be of influence to anyone. A huge part of me wanted to be. I wanted to be an advocate, I wanted to help—but it felt impossible to do since I wouldn't be here much longer. Can I still be inspiring if I'm dead? "Is my legacy only going to be my death?"

"Definitely not," Kyle replied immediately.

Malaika shook her head in agreement with him. "Your legacy is how you lived, Tessa. Dying is only the end of your story, not the entire story."

I stared at her for a second, hoping that was true. Wanting it to be true. Wanting there to be a lot more to me than what someone could read in a magazine about how I died.

CHAPTER FORTY-THREE

SATURDAY, *September 6, 2014*

"THIS WAS A GOOD IDEA." I surveyed my freshly painted toes and fingers. "Do you like this color? Too sparkly?"

Elly glanced at me from the driver's seat. "The perfect amount of sparkly."

I smiled, happy to have spent the last few hours with my sister getting our nails and hair done—not that I had a ton of hair to work with, but a nice scalp massage had really made my day. Elly wasn't usually a girly-girl, so I'd been surprised when she'd suggested we go. After the article's revelation this morning, I was feeling a bit emotional.

Some time to unwind was exactly what I needed.

"Shit," Elly mumbled under her breath as she pulled the car onto our street.

"What?"

"Nothing," she said, suddenly nonchalant.

She was so quick to brush it off, I immediately became

suspicious. Looking around, I noticed an unusually high number of cars parked by our house, and my dad was on the front porch quickly ushering someone inside and slamming the door shut behind them.

"Wait, what's going on?" *Who was visiting?*

"I don't know." Elly cleared her throat, her voice a slightly higher pitch now—a dead giveaway that she was full of it.

"Liar," I accused with a slight chuckle. "Jeez, you're *still* a terrible liar. Tell me what's happening? Is it a surprise? Oh! Oh!" Suddenly it hit me. "Is it a surprise party? For New Year's Eve?"

Elly put the car in park in the driveway and huffed, unbuckling her seatbelt. "It's...not a surprise party totally."

"Okay..." I was lost.

She chewed on the edge of her lip. "It *is* actually New Year's Eve themed, but remember when you said you didn't want people to mourn you after... you know? That you wanted to celebrate your life with everyone you loved?"

I looked down at her all-black outfit—the new one she'd insisted on wearing today. The complete opposite of my entirely white outfit that she'd also picked out for me— white linen pants hung loosely around jutting hips, with a thin white tee under a flowy white sweater open in the front, the sides hanging loosely down the sides of my breasts. She'd even picked out my jewelry, which I so rarely wore but had agreed to today. Not to mention the freshly painted nails and newly styled hair the stylist had fluffed just enough to make my haircut look like a choice rather than a symptom.

It all made sense now.

"Is this—" I took a deep breath to steady my racing

heart. "Is this my...?" The word wouldn't come out, though I wasn't afraid of it.

"It's your funeral, Tessa."

I exhaled fast, blowing the air out of my lungs in one long gust as her words settled in me.

"Dad and Kyle didn't want me to tell you, or to phrase it like that. They wanted it to be a surprise. And it still is a surprise, or it would have been if they'd parked the cars where I told them." Elly sighed then twisted in the driver's seat to face me, her hands resting on my forearm. "I just thought I should tell you before we go in. I don't know, I thought—"

I squeezed her hands. "No, you did the right thing. I'm glad I have this second. I would have needed it. I don't want everyone in there to see me freak out."

"You're freaked out?" She frowned. "Shit, we screwed up."

I clucked my tongue like a mother hen. "Since when did you take up cursing so much?"

A sly smile spread over her face, the mood lightening ever so slightly. "Sorry, *Mom*."

My lips twitched. The truth was I wasn't upset with them at all. I was relieved. I was honored. I was...a little excited? I'd told them long before that the idea of a funeral sucked donkey balls.

Everyone saying nice stuff about you after you can no longer hear it? That's some bull. Let me relish in those compliments. Can't a dying girl get an ego boost?

Plus, I didn't want people reminiscing and sad. I wanted people dancing, celebrating—full of life and love like me. I'd mentioned it a couple of times to my dad and to Kyle, but with the move to Vermont, I'd pretty much assumed it was off the table. I was getting sicker quickly and couldn't make a trip back to Chicago.

Despite this being exactly what I wanted, the initial realization of what this was...yeah, I'd need a second to process that and be a little freaked out. That made me all the more grateful my sister knew me well enough to let me do that in private.

"I'm not freaked out," I finally said after a quiet moment passed between us—at least I wasn't anymore. "Thanks for telling me. I'm glad I knew before walking in there." I glanced down at the cane jutting up from the wheel well and resting against my thigh. "Well, hobble in there."

Elly laughed. "I'm so glad you're not mad. I wasn't a fan of this entire process to begin with, but Kyle insisted it's what you wanted."

"It is," I said, pulling off my seatbelt. "He's right."

Elly gave a happy nod, and then stepped out of the car, coming around to my side. I waited for her, letting her open the door for me. Maneuvering my body to face out, I put the end of the cane down on the asphalt.

"Need a hand?" Elly hovered, looking around for what she could help with.

I shook my head, pulling my partially-useless leg out of the car and taking a deep breath. Exhaling, I pushed myself up onto the cane and my feet.

"I got it," I said, unsure at first until I found my balance and nodded. "Yep, I got this."

"Okay," she said, still looking reluctant.

Moving out of the way, she closed the car door after me. She was back by my side in seconds, acting ready to catch me if I fell—more than a little ridiculous since despite how tiny I was now, my sister had never been much bigger. I'm sure I'd still flatten her like a...what's the word? Just kidding, I knew, *pancake*. Fucking pancakes.

When we reached the front door, I took a second to fluff my hair, adjust my clothes, and scan my outfit. I thought I looked pretty good, especially after a day of glamour, but my body made no secret of my illness. My skin was pale—very pale—and clung to my bones with very little muscle mass left. My clothes were baggy, hiding a lot of it, but the cancer could still be seen in the way my knuckles protruded from my hands, or my cheekbones pushed from my face.

"Do I look okay?" I asked Elly, suddenly nervous to see everyone—and I didn't even know who *everyone* would be.

"You look beautiful," Elly insisted, and there wasn't a hint of high-pitched lying in her tone. "Ethereal, actually."

I smiled. "All right, let's do this."

Elly opened the front door and I stepped inside the dark foyer.

"What happened to the lights?" I asked, purposefully trying to play up the "surprise" act. Elly flipped on the lights, but the room was empty. "Wait, where is everyone?"

She put a finger to her lips, and then pointed toward the back of the house. I could see everyone milling on the porch through the glass door, and by everyone, I mean *everyone*.

Elly slid open the glass doors and I hobbled onto the illuminated porch. It was decorated beautifully—a table and grill to one side with enough food and drinks to feed an army. String lights hung across the yard between the trees, and everyone was adorned with New Year's Eve style glasses with the year on the frames and party hats that said *Happy New Year!*

"Tessa! Surprise!" Kyle stepped forward, both his hands up in greeting. The rest of the party turned their attention to me, greeting me with a big "*Surprise!*"

"What's all this?" I squeaked out, not actually from surprise, but more from the sudden loud noise of an entire crowd screaming at me and Beast running full force into my cane.

Kyle lunged forward to steady me. "You okay?"

"Oh, sure," I laughed. "Nothing like scaring a dying lady to death."

Kyle rolled his eyes. "Morbid, babe."

"So is a funeral for someone still alive," I teased.

"Not a funeral," he replied. "A celebration of life."

"I thought you didn't believe in that kind of thing." I wrapped my arms around him, kissing him softly.

"I don't," he replied, his lips moving from mine to my nose, then to my forehead. "But I love my wife."

I sighed happily. "I love you."

"All my love," he replied, then turned us to face the crowd. Almost everyone was wearing black, or dark shades, but it didn't look morbid. It didn't look sad. It looked like a party—and with the music blaring, it sounded like one too. "Let's get this party started!"

The crowd whooped and for the first time, my eyes started picking out individual people, and that's when my emotions really hit me.

Kyle's parents, Elias and Dixie Falls. His brother, Michael, and his sister, Cat. My dad and sister, of course. Dr. Page and Dr. Morales. Carly and Marley. Friends from Chicago. Classmates. Malaika and her baby bump, a handsome man I didn't recognize with his arm around her shoulder. My old boss. And...Delores.

"Oh, hun," Delores' sweet, familiar voice caressed me. Her chocolatey skin was as smooth and beautiful as I remembered, a toothy grin warming my heart. "I've missed you something fierce."

I threw my arms around her neck, hugging her tightly—no small feat when you have a cane. "Delores! I missed you *so* much!"

She'd been my nurse through the chemo treatments, but she'd been so much more. She'd been my friend when I needed one, a cheerleader when I wasn't, and an advocate when my words dried up. In fact, I'd written extensively about her in my book because of how much she impacted me at the biggest moments of my illness.

She squeezed me tighter, her hand on the back of my head, like a mom cradling her child. I sank into her chest, letting her baby me. I needed it. She knew. When we pulled apart, she gave me a huge grin. "Still got that smooth as hell head, girl."

I laughed, the happiness bursting from me in a loud exhale. "But I've got more hair finally. Like it?" I touched the edges of my mane.

"It looks fantastic," she assured me. I knew she wasn't lying. "How are you doing?"

"I'm..." I shrugged my shoulders, as if there weren't words to fit.

Delores nodded, and I knew I didn't have to explain. "Yeah."

"Yeah," I agreed.

"When's the big day?" She'd never been one to hold her punches. She glanced at my cane and the new pair of reading glasses on the end of my nose. "Soon?"

"Soon."

She hugged me again, and it felt sadder this time. "You do you, Tessy girl. Take care of you."

"I'm trying." That was how we talked. That was all we needed.

"By the way, have you seen my calves?" She pulled up

her pant legs to show very muscular calves on both legs. "Told you that crooked floor apartment would do me good. Like, bam!" She flexed each to her own personal soundtrack and I laughed.

"Just like Serena!" I said, teasing.

Delores clapped her hands over her head. "Yes, girl! I just need me some hand-eye coordination and a tennis racket, and you won't be able to tell the two of us apart!"

"Tessa!" My mother-in-law, Dixie, gave me a big wave from behind Delores. Most people in the party were milling around enjoying food and drinks, but a small line had formed of people waiting to talk to me.

"I'll let you talk to everyone else," Delores said with a sly grin, like she and I had a secret no one else knew about. And we kind of did—the type of secret you couldn't put words to. "I'm gonna find you again 'fore this party is over."

I nodded. "Please do."

"In the meantime, I'm about to stuff my face with your food and beer, hun."

I laughed when she headed straight for the buffet line. My mother-in-law took her place—a vision in a flowing black kimono with chunky wooden jewelry around her neck and arms painted in vibrant neon colors.

"Tessa, darling!" She embraced me, swaying like we were dancing—which made me have to focus on not toppling over. When she pulled away, she kept her hands on my shoulders. "Look at you, you're glowing!"

"I am?"

She nodded emphatically. "You are. How are you feeling? You look like you've lost weight."

I let out a light chuckle, tipping my head to the side —duh, lady. "Yeah, I've lost weight."

"I'm sorry we couldn't come sooner. Elias and I—Elias,

baby?" She turned to look for her husband, who came up and gave me another huge hug. "Elias and I were in Bali."

"You were in Bali?" *Totally normal.*

"It was very *eat, pray, love*, darling. Wasn't it, baby?" She looked to her husband for confirmation.

"Oh, definitely. We re-centered ourselves, found our chi, our inner child yearning to be free. We explored tantric orgasms—though that wasn't part of the course—but I'm telling you, there is nothing more centering than meditating nude inside the person you love."

My eyes widened at the mental image he was painting.

"Jesus H. Christ, Dad! Mom!" Kyle must have heard the last part, circling his arm around my waist. "Can we keep conversations PG, please?"

"Sweetheart, you've got to be more open to living. Sex is a natural part of life—an amazing part." Dixie winked at her husband and Kyle made a gagging noise. "Actually, I wanted to ask you, Tessa—"

I immediately guessed I wouldn't like where this was going.

"Are you two still having sex in your condition?" she finished. "It's so healing, not just for your soul, but your body."

Elias nodded emphatically. "If you guys aren't; you need to be. Every day, all day. I always tell your mother, when I go, I want it to be on top of her."

"Or behind me," Dixie teased.

Yep, I was right. This was the worst.

Kyle grabbed at his chest, his head tilting back. "Lord, take me now."

"This kid. Always with the theatrics." Dixie rubbed her son's shoulder. "Do you want to smoke with me? It'll loosen you up."

"You brought weed?" Kyle asked, not sounding surprised. "How did you get it on the plane?"

"My love center, of course." She shrugged, as if it were obvious.

I still hadn't said anything yet—partially because they were talking a-million-miles-an-hour, and because I was still trying to mentally bleach the image of my in-laws doing naked-yoga-monkey-sex from my brain. I wasn't even remotely ready to process weed from my mother-in-law's vagina yet.

Kyle, however, made a choking noise and grabbed a bottle of beer from a caterer's tray and downed the entire thing in a matter of seconds.

"Ooh, I saw your article, Tessa," Dixie added. "What a blessing. Very powerful, very I-am-woman-hear-me-roar."

"Fuck death," Elias chimed in, in agreement. "*You* have the power."

I put the verbal trauma of their earlier mental images on the back burner for now. "Thanks. I'm honored to reach so many people."

"You're changing lives, Tessa—and in your final hour," Dixie continued, before turning to Kyle. "You've married a real saint, Kyle. Make love to this woman—make love to her feminine power. Bask in it."

Kyle made another throaty, croaking noise, his eyes on the ground.

"Anyways, we're going to go smoke on the dock." Dixie gave me a quick hug. "Get Tessa something to eat, Kyle. She's been eyeing the buffet bar."

I had been, but mostly from a desire to escape, rather than hunger.

"Come join us when you're done eating!" Elias hugged me next. "We've got plenty for everyone."

"Okay, sure. Sounds fun," I replied automatically. "Thanks."

When they walked away, Kyle looked at me sideways. "Are you really going to smoke weed that was in my mother's...*love center*?"

He looked pale, and I couldn't help but laugh.

"I haven't ruled it out," I said, purposely trying to make my face look as innocent as possible. "I like other things that have come out of her."

Kyle made a retching noise. "Oh, oh my God, I'm going to puke. I'm literally going to puke."

"She's right," I laughed. "You really are dramatic."

He gave me the evil eye. "I'm getting another drink. Want one?"

"Definitely."

The line of people who came to see me continued to grow and Elly quickly brought me a chair, since I was officially exhausted after the chat with my in-laws. My old boss cried and told me his new assistant would never live up to me. Our neighbor from Chicago told me she was watching the house for us, and would make sure to keep checking our mail. Several of my friends from high school cried and showed me pictures of their kids, and then I cried, and it was just a cry fest for several minutes as we all faced our mortalities.

My doctors were there, albeit briefly, and told me how strong I was, how impressed they were with my resilience. Dr. Morales even checked my leg and confirmed what I'd already guessed—it wasn't going to get any better. Delores returned and took a picture of her and I together, promising to get it framed and hung in her crooked-floor house.

Everyone said goodbye, but no one actually said *goodbye*. It was under their words, but no one wanted the finality that today truly meant. I wouldn't see the majority of these people again. That was a fact. I wasn't getting better. Things were going downhill fast, and I felt it. I felt the cloudiness, a looming presence, waiting. Waiting to take me, for the last inhale, the last of me.

So, I said the goodbyes instead, even when they averted their eyes and said they'd *see me later* or *'til next time*. I said goodbye. Because it was, and because I had to, and because I wanted each of them to know that it was okay. I'd led a good life, and I was happy, and now I just wanted to say goodbye.

At a few minutes before midnight, Kyle and Elly passed out kazoos and confetti and everyone prepped to ring in the "new year" with me. Kyle handed me a small paper box, and I opened it to find several long-awaited sugar-covered Fried Oreos inside. I cried and stuffed my mouth full of chocolatey fried goodness, offering one to Dr. Page as promised. Dixie rolled enough blunts for everyone, and I tried my first, blowing smoke out onto Lake Champlain.

Then, at midnight, I kissed my husband until both of our faces were covered in powdered sugar. And that's how I rang in the "new year."

Sugar-covered kisses, and my mother-in-law's love center weed.

CHAPTER FORTY-FOUR

SUNDAY, *September 28, 2014*

THE JETS from the Jacuzzi splashed around me, easing the pain from my muscles as I stared out at the lake.

To call the last three weeks a whirlwind would be an understatement, but I barely paid it any attention. Life got busy, and the world became interested in me, but the feeling wasn't mutual. I understood the article about me upset people. I got it. I really did. Death was upsetting. Facing your own mortality was upsetting—and that's what the article about me forced readers to do. But death is a lot like birth—you're afraid at first, and then you're not.

I listened to Malaika's fears about giving birth. A gigantic baby was growing in that tiny woman, and the only way it was coming out looked less than pleasant. Hell, I was scared for her—or rather, I was scared for her lady bits. But closer to her due date, Malaika changed.

She was ready—more than ready—and suddenly the

possibility of hours and hours of painful, lady-bit-destroying labor didn't sound nearly as bad as having that baby kick her ribs all day, or not being able to find a position to sleep in, or the fact that she kept mismatching her shoes because she couldn't see them on her feet.

She wanted to hold her baby, no matter what she had to face beforehand. And wasn't that what death was? A new chapter, or maybe an epilogue...*I'm ready to write my epilogue.*

I had another seizure that morning—I didn't know how many I'd had at this point. I stopped counting two weeks ago. Beast had begun to alert me to them now, which was actually really helpful. When he started barking at me out of the blue, I'd go sit down somewhere my head wouldn't smash against the floor, or a table's edge, or God knew what else. Every once in a while, the barking was just because he was bored and wanted to fuck with me, but nine times out of ten, he sensed (maybe smelled? I don't know how it works.) the seizure coming.

"Tessa?" Kyle's head popped into the bathroom.

I barely glanced up from the bath. "Mmm?"

He leaned against the doorframe, crossing his arms over his chest. "Do you think you'll want dinner? What if I made soup—really light?"

I took a deep breath, assessing my nausea level. I didn't feel like hacking up my guts at the moment, so I nodded. "Yeah, soup sounds good."

"Thank goodness." He smiled and leaned over the tub, kissing my forehead.

I reached out to squeeze his hand. "Why 'thank goodness'?"

He shrugged. "I've been worried. You're barely eating."

"I'm working on my bikini body," I teased.

That made him roll his eyes. "I hope fucking not, babe."

I just grinned, not letting on if I was kidding. I couldn't wear a bikini now even if I wanted to. I didn't have the curves to hold it up, and my skin had already begun to cave in on me as the weight and muscle mass dropped off. There wasn't one particular reason, more like fifteen—food tasted like nothing, it sat in my stomach heavy and unforgiving, nausea was a constant struggle even if I was just having a glass of water, and the list went on and on.

"Are you getting out of the bath soon?" he asked.

"Ish."

"The soup will be ready when you come down."

I gave him an appreciative smile before he retreated. Pulling the plug out of the bottom of the tub with my toes, I then dropped it onto the floor of the bath. The water slowly drained from around me, a loud swirling noise filling my ears for several minutes. I sat still and let the water level lower, my skin breaking out in tiny bumps from the chill of the air.

Once it was finally empty, I pulled myself up and sat on the edge before swinging my legs around to the tile floor. Grabbing at my cane, I hobbled to my robe and wrapped it around my body.

When my hands slid through the thick, plush sleeves, I realized my fingers on one hand were tingling. I stared at them, flexing my hand and trying to wiggle them. They moved—slowly—but all I felt was tingling. I grabbed the door knob, but my hand wouldn't grip it.

I balanced carefully against the bathroom counter and used the hand I'd been holding the cane with to open the door instead. I changed quickly, sitting on the edge of the bed and using one hand to pull on pants and an oversized sweater.

Beast came rushing into the room and rubbed against my legs, but moved out of the way when I stood to head down for dinner, my slowly numbing hand tucked into pocket.

It was almost time. I was almost ready.

CHAPTER FORTY-FIVE

*T*UESDAY, *September 30, 2014*

"HAPPY BIRTHDAY, TESSA," my husband's soft lilt roused me to consciousness, his head burrowed in the crook of my neck.

"Mmm," I sighed, caressing his shoulder with my hand. "Thanks, babe."

"Twenty-nine."

"I'm catching up to you," I teased, despite the circumstances.

He didn't say anything, but I felt him swallow, which made me feel slightly guilty. This was a tough time—there was no way to tiptoe around it. Everything I said was morbid, whether I meant it to be or not.

He kissed my cheek, and I turned my face to his. He smiled, but it didn't reach his eyes, and we kissed for another few minutes. When we pressed our bodies together, a yelp came from under the covers and Beast shoved his nose up between us, making his presence known.

I laughed. "Morning, Beast."

"Damn dog," Kyle groaned. "Come downstairs when you're ready, okay? I'm going to make you breakfast. Malaika should be here soon for your vitals."

"Okay."

"Or call if you need me to carry you down," he added, climbing out of bed and searching the floor for his boxers.

I waited for him to leave before getting up myself. He was right that the stairs were getting to be a little too much of a safety issue for me, but I could still walk around with the help of the cane or scoot down them on my butt.

I sat on the edge of the bed and stared at the full-length mirror across from me. I was *so* small. Not in a skinny or short kind of way—though I was both. My presence, the aura around me that made me...me, it was small and unassuming. Like my body was already beginning to retreat from the world.

I'd gone to visit Dr. Morales on Friday for the results of my latest scans. No one was surprised when the images revealed a body riddled with cancer, but I was surprised at the sheer amount. It seemed like there was more cancer than...well, me.

The doctor upped some of my pain medications, as well as adding in some others to hopefully assist my symptoms— the balance, nausea, aches, etc. It was exhausting.

Pulling on a light tee shirt with a pair of jeans multiple sizes smaller than I'd ever thought I'd fit, I examined myself in the mirror. Clothed, it wasn't as jarring. My hands and face showed how I sick I was, but the clothes hid a lot. My hair was longer and thicker, more lustrous, tickling the bottom of my chin. I slid a hand through it and relished the softness I'd missed.

Cane in hand, I moved into the bathroom and brushed my teeth. Absentmindedly, I opened the drawer to the right of the sink and double checked that the two bottles I needed were still there. Those two little pill bottles were everything. I had taken up routinely glancing in the drawer, kind of like a security blanket.

Still there. Still my choice.

I was in control, despite having just dropped my toothbrush in the sink because my fingers went numb. Cupping my hands as best as I could, I rinsed my mouth and put back my toothbrush. My fingers tingled, but it wasn't any worse than before. I hadn't mentioned it to Kyle, and I probably wouldn't. There was nothing numb about what he was going through.

"Tessa?" Malaika's voice came from my bedroom.

"In here," I called out, seating myself on the padded stool in front of the bathroom counter. I began pulling out compacts, eye shadows, and powders from my makeup bag. I hadn't worn any in months. There had never been a reason why, but there wasn't a reason why not either.

"Hey girl," she said, waddling into the bathroom and dropping her bag on the counter next to me. "What're you doing? I don't think I've ever seen you wear makeup."

I shrugged. "I usually don't. Just felt like it today."

"Oh, cool. I love makeup." She gestured to her face. Being this close, I could see the thick layer of makeup, but she made it look so natural. "Contouring is life. I swear— game changer."

"I tried contouring a few times, followed some online tutorials, but I looked ridiculous," I admitted sheepishly. "I don't think I did it right. You pull it off so much better than me."

"Thanks." Malaika moved her shoulders back and forth, like a fun, little shake. She began pulling a blood pressure cuff up my arm and I tried with my free hand to swirl powder onto my cheeks, but my fingers were still tingling and I kept dropping the brush.

Malaika definitely noticed, but didn't say anything, finishing taking my blood pressure instead. "So, how are you feeling?" she finally asked.

I sighed and held up my hand. "My leg feels barely there, and now my arm is doing the same."

"Your entire arm?" She examined me and massaged my forearm lightly.

I shook my head. "Not the whole arm, but it's getting that way."

"Well, how about I do your makeup today?"

I glanced at her. "Really? Don't you have other patients to see after me?"

"Sure, but it doesn't take too long. I'm a pro, remember?" She gestured to her face again.

I chuckled lightly. "Well, if you don't mind, that would be great."

We spent the next ten minutes with me seated quietly while she colored my face. There's something about someone softly touching and caressing your face that eases your entire body—it was relaxing as hell.

When we were done, I surveyed her work in the mirror and was impressed. Somehow, she'd managed to make me look less pale, a little fuller, and darkened my features that had been fading away. "Wow, Malaika."

"You like?" she asked.

I nodded. "I love it. Thank you!"

She clapped her hands. "Fantastic. I can do it again tomorrow if you want, and every day after that!"

"That would be nice," I told her, then caught myself. "Well, um...for the next two days."

Malaika's expression switched from elated to somber. Her voice was quiet when she finally spoke. "Two days?"

"Two days." I'd already decided. Now I just had to figure out how to tell my family.

CHAPTER FORTY-SIX

TUESDAY, September 30, 2014

"BABE?" I walked out onto the patio holding two plates of colorful, icing covered birthday cake strategically balanced in one hand. "Want a second slice?"

"Sure." Kyle grinned, knowing full well I had wanted the second piece, but hadn't wanted to eat it alone. He jumped up to grab the plates from me, since I was struggling to hold those in one hand and the cane in the other.

We all make sacrifices for cake. Don't judge me.

"You seem pretty energetic today," he noted, as we ate our second dessert.

I was seated on the end of the lounge chair facing him where he sat at the top. "It *is* my birthday. Can't a girl be in a good mood?"

"Did I already tell you 'happy birthday'?" He leaned forward and left an icing-smeared kiss on my cheek.

I grinned. "Like a million times."

We'd already had a big birthday dinner, and everyone

had given me sweet, sentimental gifts, plus this huge cake. I'd actually eaten a large first slice, but it was a few hours later and I wanted more. I was surprised as hell that I could even taste it or stomach it, but I could and it was delicious. So sugary, so perfect.

"Well, happy birthday for the millionth and one time," he said. "It was a good one."

Dinner had ended hours ago, and both my dad and my sister had gone to bed. I'd noticed Kyle sitting out on the patio when I'd gone to get a glass of water from the kitchen. I'd watched him for a minute, wondering if I should interrupt his private moment. He'd looked so sad, so full of grief, and his lips were moving ever so slightly like he was talking to someone. His head was turned toward the sky, and I'd realized he was praying.

My husband was praying. And I knew in my gut, it was for me.

So, I prayed, too—right there in the kitchen. I prayed my thanks that God ever put a man like Kyle in my life. It had never been hard between us—except to be apart. He was as much a part of me, as I was of him. He'd given me a beautiful birthday present—an agent to sell my book. He'd apparently been sending queries out for months with Marley's help, and once the article went viral, they quickly responded. Someone wanted to represent *my* book, and sell it to a publisher.

He'd done his research—this agent was one of the best, a pioneer among women in her field. She'd taken over her agency when her mentor passed away, and she'd even named her daughter in her mentor's honor. Her integrity shown through everyone's adoration of her, and she had always been my number one pick for an agent. The fact that she wanted me—or rather, my book—was an absolute dream come true.

And Kyle had given me that dream.

When I finished my cake, I leaned over and put my plate next to his on the ground. He'd always eaten so much faster than me.

His legs were draped off opposite sides of the chair, so I crawled between them and leaned my back against his chest. His arms circled me and rested in my lap, tangling his fingers with mine. I looked across at the lake, dark and swirling under the night sky with only stars to illuminate the water's movements.

"Tessa?" His voice was so hesitant, I had to look at him to see what was wrong.

Shadows cast over his face that had nothing to do with the darkness of tonight.

"You're ready, aren't you?" There was no inflection at the end of his sentence. He already knew my answer.

I returned my gaze to the lake, settling my head against the front of his shoulder. "I'm ready."

"How long?"

I exhaled slowly. "Two days."

"Two days," he repeated. Kyle held me tighter, the breeze crossing our skin together. "I'm going to miss you, Tessa."

"I know," I whispered, squeezing my eyes shut.

"I don't think I can do this," he said, his voice catching on his last word. He cleared his throat. "I don't know how to say goodbye to you."

I clutched his hand in mine, rubbing my thumb rhythmically over his palm. "Don't say goodbye. Just 'I love you'. That's all we need to say."

"I love you, Tessa. All my love."

"Show me," I said quietly, tilting my face toward his.

His mouth found mine, needy and wanting. It was passionate and sweet, and I rotated completely to face him, scrambling with his help to climb on his lap, chest to chest. His arms wrapped around me, pinning me to him. The kiss was perfect, and beautiful, but I wanted more. If the end was coming, I wanted to spend it in love, and making love.

"Show me," I coaxed him further, my voice a throaty moan against his lips.

He lifted my hips until I was standing next to the lounge chair, balancing myself, even though I didn't need to since he was holding me. My fingers flew to the top of my pants and I shoved them down my legs, along with my panties. Bringing me back to straddle him, I undid his pants and freed him. Our lips locked once again as he pushed inside me.

"I love you, Tessa," he growled in my ear, his hands on my hips, lifting and lowering me on him—hard enough to make my body tingle, but gentle enough not to hurt me. "I love you so fucking much. I'll always love you, Tessa."

"I love you, Kyle," I replied breathlessly. "Always."

A few more strokes and we were both feeling our ascension, clutching each other tightly and whispering again and again and again how much we loved each other. Every bit of strength we'd been holding on to was worn away. The realness and vulnerability of this moment tore at our armors until there was nothing left. Our bodies and hearts were completely overwhelmed, and we shattered.

We shattered, and every pretense fell with us.

The hope I would get better.

The wish things were different.

The pain of being pulled apart.

The lie that we were strong enough.

Kyle buried his face against my shoulder, sobs racking his body as I held him to me. He hugged my waist and I cried with him, stroking his head and whispering to him one more lie. One more hope. One more wish—that it would all be okay. He would be okay, and he would be okay without me. Because he had to be.

I needed him to be.

CHAPTER FORTY-SEVEN

Thursday, October 2, 2014

I STARTED WRITING this book as a way to leave a little piece of myself behind in the world. Instead, I think I'm taking pieces with me. Little lessons and moments that I'll bring into eternity as memories of who I once was, and how much I was loved.

And I'm ready.

The morning sun was beginning to creep across the horizon, the lake shimmering beneath. I'd been awake for hours, sitting on the cushion-covered window seat in my bedroom with Beast curled in my lap. Kyle was still sleeping, his face so peaceful, I couldn't disturb him. I couldn't drag him in to today, knowing what it was.

I was operating on maybe three hours of sleep, but I wasn't tired. I was wide awake, my body humming with nerves, as well as the usual pain. Medications had been upped, therapies had been tried, but the pain not only persisted, it worsened. It was in my brain. Little lies shooting through my nerves, telling me to hurt, telling me to ache.

My fingers rhythmically trailed through Beast's fur, his slumbering body moving slightly with each breath. I could feel his soft fur, but the rest of my caress was mostly guess-work as my fingers didn't respond to my commands. My limbs tingled, numb at times, screaming pain at others. My seizures were daily, sometimes more. And the latest symptom—the one that frightened me the most—my sight.

Things had begun getting blurry in the last few weeks. It wasn't enough to have me walking into walls or anything, but I stubbed my toes, knocked things over, and startled easily when something suddenly came into my vision, even if it had been there all along. I often miscalculated distances, swiping my shoulder against door frames, or drop-ping something on the floor when I'd intended to put it on the table.

Malaika would be here soon, and we'd already arranged for her to stay the day. She'd been staying longer and longer as time went by since I needed her help more. I worried it was too much in her hugely pregnant condition, but she insisted she knew her limits.

Despite the doctors warning of the opposite, I had really thought I'd make it to Christmas. Or at least Thanksgiving.

The corners of my lips tilted south as I leaned my fore-head against the cool, clear windowpane. If I was being honest, I really thought I'd beat this. I went into treatments sure I was invincible. I was the exception. I was *not* the statistic.

My ordinariness is the best part of me, and sometimes, the worst.

The chill from the window sent a shiver down my spine, but I didn't move. I stared out at the golden tinged skyline and watched the sun move slowly, so slowly, into the sky. The streaks of orange and red dipped away, defeated, and calming light blue surrounded the sphere, lifting it higher.

It was my last sunrise, and it was beautiful. I'd watched dozens of sunrises in my life—but, none of those were like this one. None of those were *last*.

Kyle stirred behind me, and I saw him stretching out over the bed and yawning. His hand came down on my side of the bed, landing on the cool sheets. "Babe?"

"Over here."

He lay on his side to face me and patted the bed next to him.

Grinning, I pushed Beast onto the cushion beside me and carefully took the two steps over to the bed, stumbling only slightly. His arms quickly secured me, and he pulled me down against him, spooning me.

"Morning," I whispered.

"Morning, beautiful." He kissed my temple and worked his way down to my neck. "Thank you for last night, by the way. We haven't done that in so long."

We'd stayed up late, just lying next to each other, holding hands, and talking. We'd made love too—sweet, slow, and loving—but it was the talking that truly burrowed its way into my heart. When we'd first started dating, we'd stay up all night telling each other everything on our minds, everything about our pasts, every part of who we were, and are. The closeness I felt at doing that again on our last night, *my* last night, meant the world to me.

"It was really nice," I conceded with a small smile.

He kissed my shoulder, then I turned around to face him. "I'm referring to the talking, by the way."

"I was, too!"

He lifted one brow. "Suuuuure, you were."

I laughed, smacking his chest weakly. "Get your mind out of the gutter."

He didn't reply this time, a small smile permanently fixed to his lips as we stared at each other. After several quiet moments, his fingers trailed down the side of my face from my temple to my chin.

I leaned my cheek into his palm, kissing it gently, surprised it felt so wet until I realized I was crying. His thumb moved across my cheek and wiped the streaks from beneath my eyes.

"I'm glad I can cry with you," he whispered, my face still pressed to his hand. "Laugh with you. Love you. I'm glad for each moment since we met, because I've woken up every morning wondering how the hell I got so damn lucky to be with you. Even if I wanted longer. I'm glad we have *now*."

"You're my fireworks. My heart," I touched my chest, laying my palm flat. "My heart didn't know love until I loved you." He leaned down and kissed me, soft and lingering. "I'm just so sorry. I'm so, so sorry, Kyle."

He shook his head, his brows pulled together. "You have done nothing to be sorry for, Tessa."

I traced a finger down his jawline. "I promised you old age. I promised you a family. Forever."

He squeezed me tighter against him. "We have this. We've had these years, and that's already more than I ever thought possible. Please don't feel sorry—it would break me. You've given me everything I ever could have wanted, Tessa. You're all my love."

My heart squeezed as he repeated the same phrase we've said to each other for years. *All my love.* I'd insisted on it once upon a time. I'd demanded it. I'd also given it.

What I hadn't known was that love was bigger than one person, and fleeting...

I kissed him again, cherishing the softness of his words. "I don't want it anymore."

"Tessa—" he began to interrupt.

"No, please, let me say this." He closed his mouth, his hand trailing down my arm and then resting on my waist. "I don't want *all* your love anymore, just some of it. Save me a tiny piece in the corner of your heart that will never forget me, that's mine forever. Then give the rest to someone else. Someone who deserves you. Someone who can make you a father, and give you the things we dreamed of. You'll always be my forever, Kyle. But I don't want to be yours. Your heart is so wonderful, so loving, so large—promise me, someone else will get to love the heart I love so much." My voice turned pleading. "Promise me, Kyle."

"Tessa," he started, his head already shaking. "I can't even think about that."

"I know, but I'm asking you too." I pulled my lips between my teeth, biting down on them before rolling them back out. "I'm asking you to be open to it...one day."

Kyle dropped his head down onto the bed, burrowing into my neck. I heard him groan, then exhale quickly. "Okay, Tessa. I'll be open to it. I'll try. One day. But not today—no more talk like this today."

I kissed his cheek until he lifted his head and kissed me until we both needed more. Clothes discarded and blankets pushed away, we silently said *thank you*, and *I'll miss you*. We said *I love you* to every part of each other, for the last time.

Souls tangled in grief, I grew old in his arms.

CHAPTER FORTY-EIGHT

Thursday, October 2, 2014

"HEY, YOU'RE AWAKE," Elly greeted me as she entered my bedroom a few hours later and peered into my bathroom. I was seated at the counter toying with my makeup. "Kyle told me it was okay to come up."

"Yep, I took a bath." I lifted an eyeshadow palette. "Want to help?"

"Sure." She leaned on the edge of the counter and toyed with a blush compact. "I can do your makeup."

"And maybe my hair?" I ran my hand through the wet tangles.

"I thought you'd never ask," she said, clapping excitedly. "Hair first."

I chuckled lightly and acquiesced. We both faced the mirror covering one whole wall in the bathroom. She ran her fingers through my wet hair, then grabbed a brush and gave it a few passes. Plugging in my blow-dryer next, she used that and a round brush to give my hair volume and waves I hadn't known was possible.

I admired her work after she finished. "Wow, it actually looks longer."

"It's grown a lot in six months," Elly agreed, fluffing it with her fingers. "But you've always had beautiful hair. I'm jealous."

I laughed at that. Elly was stunning with sharp, dark features and bright eyes that made you feel she truly saw you. "You've nothing to be jealous of, little sis. You're gorgeous."

She did a little curtsy, smiling into the mirror at my reflection. "Well, thank you, big sis. Makeup time!"

I tilted my chin up as she came around to face me, armed with a compact and brush. She smoothed concealer in the dark, sunken circles under my eyes, and evened the splotchy transparent look to my skin with foundation, then dusted it with powder. I watched my reflection, admiring her skill, and how different I looked with only a few products.

A tiny bit of eye shadow, some swipes of mascara, and a gentle gloss to my lips, then Elly smiled and put her hands up. "Voila!" she announced. "Like it?"

"I absolutely love it, Elly. You're so talented." I opened a bottle of lotion and began lathering it into my arms.

Elly watched me, saying nothing for a minute or so. When my eyes met hers, I saw tears glistening on her lower lashes.

"Elly," I sighed, reaching a hand to hers and tangling our fingers.

A loud sob tore from her throat and she slid forward, moving off the edge of the counter and throwing her arms around me. My little sister knelt next to my chair, her head in my lap, her arms around my waist, like a child seeking comfort from her mother.

In a sense, that was exactly what was happening.

Neither one of us said anything. I let her cry against my legs, gently caressing her head and rubbing small circles on her back. I didn't cry, I wasn't even sure I could any more. I'd poured my heart out to Kyle this morning, and cried so much the last few months. But now? I finally felt a strange peace, soothing in an entirely foreign way.

"Tessa, this can't be it," Elly finally managed to get out a sentence.

"Baby girl, it's going to be okay."

"We could have longer, Tessa." She lifted her head enough to look up at me, her red-rimmed eyes pleading. "We could have more time."

"Elly," I sighed. "Whether I do this or not, we don't have more time. I can feel it."

She swallowed hard, and dropped her head back to my lap. Her tears slowed and she hiccupped as I continued to caress her head, my motions clumsy, but well-meaning.

"What do you feel?" Her voice so tiny, my heart squeezed.

I licked my lips and thought of the best way to describe it. "My symptoms are so much worse, and quickly, but it's something deeper. I feel it in my soul...in my heart. It's peace, and...exhaustion. It's a warmth spreading inside me— a force around me I can't keep at bay much longer. It's my time, Elly. It's just my time."

She was quiet again, and I knew she was digesting what I was telling her. "I'm going to miss you, Tessa. More than I even know now."

"I know, baby girl. I know."

"You'll always be my sister, no matter what," Elly

continued. "I'm not going to forget you just because you're gone. I'll tell my kids about their aunt. I'll show them your pictures and tell them how much I love you. I'll make them read your book, and see what a wonderful person their auntie was."

"I'd love that, Elly—and I love you. If I get any say over where I'm going, I'll be watching over you." I smiled at the thought. "I'll be your guardian angel."

"You already have been for years," Elly said softly.

I tilted my head, my heart bursting with love. It suddenly occurred to me that I'd wanted to write this book to pass on something to the world, to leave parts of me behind. But I'd already done that in Elly. She was bits and pieces of me—my legacy.

We were quiet again, taking the time to sit with our feelings.

"It has to be today?" she asked one more time.

"Yeah, baby girl. It has to be today."

She nodded, and I saw acceptance in her expression. "Hey, weird question. If you see Mom, will you tell her I love her?"

My head tipped to the side and I smiled. "Yeah, Elly. I'll tell her."

CHAPTER FORTY-NINE

THURSDAY, *October 2, 2014*

"HEY, SUNSHINE," my dad greeted me when I entered the kitchen, enjoying the smell of the home cooked breakfast that had been wafting up the stairs.

It was still early and Malaika was due to arrive any moment, but I'd been up for hours and had already taken a bath, gotten my makeup and hair done by Elly, and dressed for the day. I'd carefully picked out my outfit—a comfy, form fitting tee shirt under an open sweater I loved pulling tighter around me, like a blanket. My favorite white linen pants and a pair of colorful ballet flats finished my look.

It was strange deciding what I was going to wear to die in.

A shiver ran up my spine and I shook it from my shoulders. The truth was, I *was* nervous. I knew I was doing the right thing, and I knew this was coming whether by my choice or not. I'd accepted that. I had cancer. I was newly twenty-nine years old, and had a tumor in my brain that had spread...everywhere. Conceptually, I had come to terms with it all.

But the moment was literally hours away and I was...scared.

I didn't know what was waiting for me, or what would come after I closed my eyes for the last time. I didn't know if it would hurt, or if I'd be aware of what was happening, or if there was anything after. It was so unknown, a chilling reality. But it was just that—reality.

I leaned against the cane for a moment, then made my way to the kitchen table and sat down, already winded. Inhaling deeply, I felt the air enter my lungs, pushing back out just as fast.

"Hey, Daddy." I was, and always would be, a Daddy's Girl.

He beamed and stood taller. "You look beautiful, sunshine. Radiant, even. Want an omelet?"

Elly's makeup was definitely a key factor in my 'radiance,' but I also did feel surprisingly...better? I had a bit more energy the last few days, and felt a little more alive. Ironic, I know, and it messed with my head a bit. It made me wonder if this didn't have to be the end, if I could get better, and this would all have been a terrible nightmare.

I knew the cancer hadn't changed, and I'd spoken to my doctor who had assured me this was common—albeit cruel. A small burst of energy, a psychological moment where the body has one last hurrah.

"Thanks, and yes, please. I'd love an omelet." My mouth was already salivating despite my lackluster taste buds. "Cheese?"

"Of course, and extra," he declared. "The Barnes family loves cheese."

I laughed, knowing full well of his obsession with

cheese. It must be genetic, since I was just as infatuated. He and I often spent snacks squabbling over perfect cracker-to-cheese ratio. He'd carefully divide the cheese up, enough for each cracker, and God forbid if someone swiped an extra piece of cheese and threw his count off.

Beast barked at the glass door that led out to the patio. I leaned over and slid open the door enough for him to run out. My dad cracked eggs into a bowl while simultaneously turning bacon in a pan on the stove. The bacon must have been what I was smelling upstairs, because my stomach growled at the reminder.

"That smells amazing, Dad," I volunteered, filling the heaviness that blanketed the room.

"Bacon." He grunted like a caveman and pounded one fist to his chest. "Good."

I snorted, laughing as he brought me a fresh cup of coffee. I tipped the mug up to my lips and tasted the delicious, bitter flavor, relishing the way it made my bones shiver with excitement. I swear even my taste buds have been improving the last two days. I'm not sure if that's part of this last hurrah, and it's certainly not back to what it was before I became sick, but it's still amazing to taste anything at all. The boldest flavors tasted the best—the nitrate-filled bacon, the sugar-filled cake, the bitter coffee—I was enjoying every second of it.

"I just got off the phone with the priest Father Jack in Chicago recommended," my dad said, busying himself with flipping the eggs. "He confirmed for three o'clock. Oh, and I spoke to that reporter, Marley? She says she's going to help Kyle with the press side of everything. The article's still popular, and it's mostly positive responses now. The charity you made that video with, the one you're donating part of the book proceeds to? They're working on the legal side, lobbying for the act with your case study and all that."

I nodded my head. "Thanks, Dad. I really appreciate it."

Not only was my book being bid on by several publishers, but my new agent had guaranteed a portion of its profits would be going to a non-profit charity working to raise awareness of the Death with Dignity Act, as well as lobbying for it federally. I'd filmed a small YouTube video for them, detailing my story and what I thought about the Act, and hundreds of thousands of people had viewed it. I was proud, glad that maybe all I've gone through could make a difference for other people.

But in the grand scheme of things, it was a very minor part of my life. I didn't want to be a media sensation. I didn't want to do interviews. I didn't want to be famous. With so little time left, none of that mattered and I had only promised my time to family and loved ones. I did the video, the article, and I finished the book. That's all the world would get from me, and I had to hope it was enough.

"Malaika should be here any minute. She has the papers we need to sign, and she'll call the funeral home to come pick up..." He swallowed hard, and cleared his throat. "To come pick up the body. They'll do whatever is needed to ship..." He cleared his throat again. "To Chicago. The cemetery has already been notified and the family plot prepared."

He ticked off everything like he was reciting a list of groceries we needed. I appreciated his efficiency because these things needed to happen, and I needed to know someone was taking care of it. Kyle was the last person I wanted to have to deal with this, and Elly was way too fragile. My father was loving—so, so loving—but he was also practical, objective, and non-emotional most of the time. I could trust him to get these things done without falling apart.

I took another sip of my coffee. "Will I be near Mom?"

"Not directly next to her. You're on the other side of my plot, and there's a few feet of space between. You've been there, do you remember?"

I nodded. I remembered.

I'd visited my mother's grave many times, and I knew our family plot well. Some distant relatives were there, my grandparents, and my mother. There was a space beside her for my father, and several other spaces set aside for me, Elly, and our future generations.

I'd already told Kyle the spot next to me would always be open to him if he wanted it, but if he remarried and wanted to be buried with his second wife, I wouldn't hold any hard feelings. I'd already be around my family, and I'd be okay. The rest was just dirt and ashes.

I don't know exactly what happens after death, or where you go, but I don't think you sit around chained to a box under six feet of dirt. I think you're around the people you love, watching out for them, guiding them, and making sure they feel loved.

I'd never seen a ghost, but I believed they existed in some form. I'd *felt* my mother dozens of times over the years. I'd just known somehow that she was nearby, and felt a love and warmth from her presence. I want to be that same comfort for the people I'm leaving behind.

"Is that spot okay?" My dad glanced at me then flipped an omelet onto a plate and stacked bacon next to it.

"It's perfect," I said, because honestly, it was.

He'd taken care of everything, and I felt the weight of responsibility lifted from my shoulders. He'd always been my rock, ever since I was a little girl. He'd been my protector, my provider, and the one I sought out for advice when life got hard.

He was everything to two little girls who had no one else.

My eyes welled up at the memories and I wondered if there was any way to properly express how grateful I was.

"You okay, sunshine?" He positioned the plate of delicious smelling food in front of me, and sat in the chair caddy corner from me.

I nodded my head, then shook it no, then nodded yes again. I didn't know if I was okay, all I knew was I loved the big, gruff man in front of me. "Thank you, Daddy."

"You're welcome, but you should taste it before you thank me," he teased, pointing to the plate of food.

"No, not about the food." I grabbed his hand, holding it in mine on the table top. "Thank you for getting the little things taken care of so none of us have to worry. Thanks for...being my Dad."

"Don't mention it, Tessa." He squeezed my hand. "It's no big deal. I like to stay busy, you know?"

I smiled at him, not at all surprised he'd deflected my compliment. "I love you, Daddy."

He looked down at our hands, his throat bobbing as he swallowed. "I love you, too, Sunshine on a Cloudy Day," he repeated the famous lyric that had created the nickname he'd called me all my life. "I just, uh..." He exhaled sharply and looked up at me. "I'm going to miss you, baby girl."

"I'm sorry, Dad." No parent should have to bury a child, and here he was preparing to do just that. "I'm so, so sorry."

I could see the glimmer of tears in the corner of his eyes, but he blinked them away quickly. "There's nothing for you to be sorry about, Tessa. I'm the one who is sorry," he replied, shaking his head emphatically, his brows furrowed. "I wish there was something I could do. I wish I could fix this."

"Dad..." I began to say.

"No, Tessa." He shook his head one more time, exhaling loudly. "I wish it could be me."

I didn't say anything, the lump in my throat making it impossible to speak. He stood and grabbed a napkin off the counter, handing it to me so I could clean the tears from my face. I blew my nose into it, not caring how gross I sounded.

When I was done, my dad leaned down and wrapped his thick arms around me. I hugged him back, my tears soaking his shoulder. "I love you, Daddy."

"I'm going to miss you, little girl," he said again. "I'm going to miss your shine."

Scraping glass suddenly pierced the room and we both startled, twitching at the jarring sound we felt down to our bones. An onslaught of barking quickly followed as Beast scratched at on the glass pane door to come in.

"That damn dog," my dad cursed under his breath before letting him in.

"He's a beast," I laughed, wiping at my tears.

The moment the door opened a crack, the dog ran straight at me, slamming into my legs and then twisting this way and that, his tail wagging a million miles an hour. I tried to pick him up, but he was like a floppy fish on land and wouldn't hold still. "Beast, calm down!"

"He's going to miss you, too," my dad said.

My heart felt heavy when I finally held Beast and kissed his wet nose, then snuck him a piece of my bacon. I wondered how he'd handle this afternoon, and if he'd know what was happening. I knew he could already sense something inside me—the way he'd scratched at my head before I was diagnosed, or the way he barked to warn me about oncoming seizures now.

I was going to leave him, and he wouldn't understand why. He'd just know I'd promised to love him forever, and then I'd left.

I squeezed him closer against my chest and gave him a second, then a third, slice of bacon, and buried my face in his fur one more time.

CHAPTER FIFTY

*T*HURSDAY, *October 2, 2014*

WHEN I WAS BORN, the room was crowded with people. Nurses and doctors carefully watched over my mother, but my dad was also there with both of my grand-mothers. They welcomed me into this world with so much love and affection, because that's really all anyone needs when starting the journey of life—people to love you and support you.

That's all I needed when my journey was over, too.

"Tell me one more time," I repeated to Malaika. I sat on the edge of my bed and looked up at her. "I know, I know it, but I want to go through it one more time."

She nodded, not bothered by my question in the least. "This bottle has the pill you'll take first. It'll make you fall asleep and you'll drink some water to make sure it gets down and stays down, since we can't have you throwing them up." She held up a small pill bottle then placed it down on the nightstand, and lifted up a second bottle.

"Then once we're sure you've swallowed the first, you'll open these pills—they're capsules, actually—and pour the contents in the remaining water, and drink it all. Every last drop. This one will stop your heart." She placed the second bottle back down next to the freshly poured glass of water. "I can't help you take either of these, but you don't need my help. And, of course, legally I have to advise you...in no way do you *have* to do this. You have everyone's support either way, but there *is* the option of waiting for nature to take its course."

"I know," I replied. "Malaika, thank you. You've been so helpful already."

There was no one else in my bedroom at the moment, except for Beast who was sleeping on the bed next to me. Everyone was waiting downstairs for us to tell them we were ready. I'd chosen to be here in my bedroom at the end, looking out on Lake Champlain with everyone I loved around me.

It was simple and peaceful and all I needed.

"No need to thank me." She squeezed my hand affectionately. "It's my job. Though, even if it wasn't, I'd still do this for you." She stood up straighter, one hand on her pregnant belly, the other on her lower back for support. "I'm going to miss you, Tessa."

I gently rubbed the front of her belly. "I'm going to miss you, too. Give this baby kisses for me, okay?"

She smiled. "I promise."

I inhaled slowly, filling my lungs as much as I could. I pushed the air out just as fast in one long exhale. "All right, well...I guess it's time."

"You're sure?" Malaika looked at me pensively. "There's no rush. No pressure at all, you know that, right?"

I nodded. "I'm ready. I've been ready for a while now."

Her lips formed a tight line, and she tipped her chin down. "I'll call everyone in."

Malaika stepped out of the room. I pushed back on the bed, leaning against the headboard. Still not comfortable, I played with the pillows until I finally found an angle I liked.

Beast moved next to my hip and curled up in a ball. I kissed him and told him how much I loved him. He squirmed and wagged his tail, but stayed in his spot by my hip. He sensed something, I knew he did. Anyone who's ever owned a dog can tell when they know too much.

"Hey, babe," Kyle greeted me, a clearly forced smile on his face when he entered our bedroom first. He looked around the room, shuffling his weight from one foot to the other. "Where, um, would you like me to be?"

"Here." I patted my side. "Definitely here next to me."

He kicked his shoes off into the corner of the room and grabbed the throw blanket stretched across the bottom of our bed. "Want this?"

"Ooh, yes, perfect." It seriously was the softest blanket in existence, and I'd been obsessed with it since we moved here.

Kyle handed it to me and then climbed onto the bed. I fluffed the blanket over both of our legs, and Beast moved to my other hip, this time on top of the covers. Kyle leaned against the headboard and pushed in as close to me as possible, so he was partially behind one of my shoulders. I leaned my head back against his shoulder and he kissed my temple.

"I love you, Tessa," he started, a hoarseness to his voice made him sound almost raspy. "I love you so much."

I pulled one of his hands to circle around me, holding me, and intertwined my fingers with his. Lifting our hands, I kissed his knuckles. "I love you, Kyle. More than anything. Always. Every last drop of love."

"Always," he responded, his lips pressing to mine. I appreciated how he respected my wishes and hadn't responded with *all my love* like we'd normally say.

My heart ached with how badly I wanted to stay with him, how badly I wanted to live out forever with him. I loved this man more than I'd ever know how to describe, and being in his arms at this moment was right. It was just...right.

"I love you," I whispered, kissing him again and again, and wishing this wasn't goodbye.

"I love you," he whispered, his voice catching and his lips pushing hard against mine. "Always know that. Wherever you are, and whatever life has in store for me, I'll always love you, Tessa."

Our words became more frantic, because I just *needed* him to know. There was a fundamental urgency in me that knew there was nothing more important right now than making sure he knew how I felt before I died. Nothing I'd ever earned, accomplished, or done in my life crossed my mind.

Love, kisses, closeness...those are the meaning of life. End of story.

My dad cleared his throat from the doorway, trying to signal that we weren't alone. I felt my cheeks warm slightly, but Kyle didn't look the least bit embarrassed.

"Come in, come in." I waved the group of people inside the room. I guessed they'd let Kyle have a few minutes first, which touched me.

My dad entered first, seating himself on the end of the bed by my feet. He dropped one hand on my shin and rubbed gently. "How're you feeling, sunshine on a cloudy day?"

"I'm good, Daddy. I really am," I assured him, and it

was true. I was nervous, definitely, but mostly, I was full of a calm peace that felt like the soft blanket over my legs. "I'm ready."

My sister entered the room next. Her face was blotchy and red, tear-stained cheeks under puffy eyes. She hugged me tightly before laying on the bed against my side. Thank goodness, we had a king's size bed, because there were officially four people and a dog on it, yet we were comfortable. Physically, at least.

Elly placed her head on my chest and wrapped an arm around my waist. The rest of her body curled against me in the fetal position, and I heard her sniffling as I rubbed her head gently. There was no numbness in any part of me anymore; I felt everything in my final minutes.

"I love you, Tessy." Elly's words were muffled against my shirt. "I'm going to miss you so much."

I kissed the top of her head. "I love you, too, Elly."

My dad cleared his throat again, less to interrupt us this time and more to hold back his tears. I smiled sadly at him, and he just nodded. A silent acknowledgement we both understood.

"The, uh, priest and nurse are both here. They're giving us a couple minutes before they come in," my dad finally said.

I looked around at the group of people I loved. Exhaling slowly, I squeezed Kyle's hand in one of mine and tangled my other hand in Beast's fur. Elly cuddled closer on one side and Kyle sat on my other, his arms around me. My dad squeezed my toes and gave me a smile that didn't meet his eyes.

"Well, guys..." I felt the need to say...something. Waves of memories and emotions hit me, pieces of my life, moments I'd cherished—there was so much to say, and I didn't have the words. "I can only imagine how hard this is going to be...after. A little over six months ago, I thought I'd have forever. We were going to have a family." I squeezed Kyle's hand. "And then the diagnosis came, and the three of you were so strong. Elly, you came to support me and still managed to do well in school. Kyle, your job has so many demands, but you didn't miss a single moment with me. Dad, you were a rock for all of us, not just for me."

Elly let out a small sob.

"I thought I'd beat the cancer—I swear to God, I did. I knew my chances, and I knew about Mom, but I thought I'd be the exception. I thought by now we'd be looking back on this as a bad dream, that I was strong enough to get through it."

I paused and sniffed lightly, not wanting to fall apart right now.

"But I discovered I *am* strong. I am stronger than cancer, even when cancer wins. And it's because of all of you. It's because of the love I experienced, and the memories I'll take with me. Even if I didn't beat this...I won so much."

The room was quiet, and I looked at each person carefully. I purposely spent a few seconds just staring in their eyes, trading a memory. Telling them with a small smile and a pointed look that I loved them so much.

I needed them to know. I *needed* them to remember me.

"If I can ask any favor," I started again.

"Anything, sunshine," my dad quickly responded.

"Babe, of course," Kyle said simultaneously.

I smiled at their attentiveness. "Stay a family. Don't let me be the glue that kept you three together, and once I'm gone, so is this." I let go of Kyle's hand and motioned between everybody. "If Kyle remarries, love his new wife and future kids. They're our family. All the big moments, be there for each other. Be a family—for me. Can you promise me that?"

Elly sat up, reached across me, and grabbed Kyle's hand. "You're my brother, Kyle. No matter what. I love you."

"I promise, too," my dad said, dropping a hand on Kyle's shoulder. "This is my son. If you ever fall in love again, and I hope you do, that'll be my daughter. My grand-kids, too."

"I'd really love that," Kyle replied, his eyes welling with tears again. "I'd love that so much."

Elly turned back to me. "We promise, Tessy."

"We do," my dad agreed.

"Me too," Kyle chimed in. "You two will always be my family."

I smiled wide as everyone moved in and group-hugged. We kissed and exchanged I-love-youes. I asked them to take care of Beast and to explain to him what was going to happen and where I was, to talk to him so he didn't feel lonely, to give him kisses on his little nose like I would always do. They cried and agreed and I felt a little better about leaving them all. That feeling of family, of an unbreakable bond, surrounded us, and my heart swelled and thumped against my rib cage.

"You guys ready for us?" Malaika peeked her head in the bedroom door, then smiled widely. "Group hug time, huh?"

"We're ready." I settled back against Kyle's chest and my dad returned to his seat at my feet. Elly resumed her place by my side, her head on my chest. Beast licked my hand and stayed by my hip, and I kissed his little nose one last time.

I looked around at my family, the loves of my life, and a

single tear spilled down my cheek into my smile. "I'm ready."

A tall, thin man followed Malaika into the room, a leather-bound Bible in his hand. He wore head-to-toe black, except for a thick white collar around his neck.

"Tessa, this is Father Michael," my dad said, gesturing the man forward.

"Good to meet you in person, Tessa." The middle-aged priest came to the edge of the bed then shook my hand.

He and I had spoken on the phone days ago after I'd gotten his name from Father Jack in Chicago. Father Michael had driven over an hour to give me Last Rites, which I appreciated since I hadn't been able to find other priests so open to my situation.

"You, too, Father." I smiled as we shook hands. "So, how does it work? Prayer and oil?"

He pulled a small vial from his pocket and held it up. "Prayer, then I'll say the Sacrament of the Anointing of the Sick, and place this oil on your forehead."

"Doesn't sound too hard." I inhaled deeply, feeling hopeful. "Should we do it now?"

"Since this is to cleanse you of your sins, to be safe, we're going to wait until after you've ingested the medication. We'll have a small window of time, but enough," Father Michael said, a comforting smile on his face that reminded me a lot of Father Jack.

I thought back to what Father Jack had told me. *He loves me. That will not change.* I knew in my heart, and had to hope I wasn't kidding myself. This was the right choice for me. There was a peace and comfort in the depths of my soul when I thought about it. But I also knew that whatever God thought, the bottom line was as simple as what Father Jack had told me.

Whatever I decide, whatever I do, He loves me. That will not change.

I looked at everyone around me. My dad gently rubbing my legs. Elly's face tilted to me, her arm flung around my waist. Beast between us, his chin resting on thigh and his little eyes on mine. Kyle, holding me, his lips pressed to my temple. Malaika stood off to the side, her eyes full and sad, and her arms resting on her stomach as if hugging her child. The priest, poised and stoic, stood next to her, the Bible in one hand, and blessed oil in the other.

I took everything in, as if it could be a memory I'd hold on to forever. And maybe it was. Wherever I was going, whatever would happen to me...this moment would be the sum of my life. This would be my legacy. These people, these hearts, this spirit... this is who I was when I lived.

"I'm ready." I picked up the first bottle.

No one moved as I unscrewed the lid, and dropped its contents into my hand. I placed the empty container on the nightstand and grabbed the glass of water. Placing the pill on the back of my tongue, I held the glass of cool liquid to my lips and swigged down a few gulps.

The pill slid down my throat easily.

Nothing happened—not that I'd expected it to—and I reached over to grab the second bottle. I took a couple more sips of water, double-checking the first pill would stay down, before opening the second bottle and dropping the capsules in my hand.

I balanced the glass of water between my thighs and cracked open each capsule, dumping its contents inside. Swirling the glass, I watched it dissolve and mix.

I glanced around one more time at everyone I loved, then I lifted the glass to my lips, surprised at the tears stinging my eyes.

I swallowed the first gulp, grimacing at the bitterness of the taste. Rushing, I chugged the rest—every last drop. My stomach churned, and my mouth felt prickly and chalky. I dropped the glass down on the nightstand with a slight clang.

"That tasted like ass."

Everyone burst out laughing around me, even the priest.

I quickly covered my mouth. "Sorry, Father."

Malaika handed me a small chocolate bar. "Here, I got you this for the taste."

My mouth fell open, and I took it from her with a big smile. "Malaika, you are everything good."

I unwrapped the square of chocolate and placed it on my tongue, rolling it around my mouth and letting it melt. The bitter taste of the medication was gone in seconds.

Father Michael moved forward and took my hand, his head bowed. He began to pray and I closed my eyes with him. He prayed for my salvation, for my soul, and for my sins. My heart swelled when he prayed for my family, that they would be healed from the pain my death would cause.

Finally, he let go of my hand, and I looked up at him as he spilled several drops of oil from the bottle onto his finger. He wiped it on my forehead in the shape of a cross. "Through this holy anointing, may the Lord in his love and mercy, help you with the grace of the Holy Spirit. May the Lord who frees you from sin, save you, and raise you up."

"Amen," my dad said, squeezing my foot.

"Amen," Kyle repeated, kissing my temple.

"Amen," Elly said, hugging my waist tighter.

"Amen," I said, my eyelids feeling heavy.

Father Michael stepped away, and I thanked him and Malaika once more.

"I'm so glad I met you," Malaika said, her voice thick

and heavy with emotion.

I smiled and put a hand over my heart. "You, too, Malaika. Thank you."

I looked down at my dad, his shoulders were slack, but his jaw set in a tight line, as if in pain. So, I said the only thing I knew to say...the only thing that mattered anymore. "I love you, Daddy."

"I love you, sunshine on a cloudy day." He blew me a kiss. "Rest now, there's nothing more you need to do. You've done it all, and I'm so proud of you. We're here now. You can go."

His calming words filled my tired soul, and I squeezed Kyle's hand in mine, my other hand stroking Beast one last time before moving up and squeezing Elly's shoulder.

Everything was done. Everyone was here. The papers were signed, the plans were scheduled, and all the things I'd ever wanted to accomplish in life were completed.

Twenty-nine years I'd walked this planet, and it was summed up in this moment. To the people here with me in the very end.

To marry the love of my life.

My head felt heavier as I kissed my husband. "I love you, Kyle."

"I love you, Tessa. Always."

Check.

I ran my hand slowly through my baby sister's hair. "I love you, Elly."

To become a mother.

"I love you, Tessy," she replied, tears streaming down her cheeks.

Check.

To write a book.

Check.

EPILOGUE

CHICAGO, IL - October 2, 2014 - Tessa Falls, maiden name Tessa Barnes, of Chicago, Illinois passed away on October 2, 2014 in her lakeside cottage in Burlington, Vermont. Her father, her sister, and her husband surrounded her in her final hours. She was the third person in the state of Vermont to end her own life with the newly passed Vermont Patient Choice and Control at the End of Life Act. Her husband Staff Sergeant Kyle Falls, her father Master Sergeant Glenn Barnes, her sister Elly Barnes, and her dog, The Beast, survive her. She will be returned to her hometown of Chicago, IL for internment in the family plot, and a small, private funeral will be held on October 5th, 2014 for close friends and family.

MY WIFE, Tessa Falls, died on a Thursday at 3:47 p.m. after six months battling cancer. She was in our bed in our rented home in Vermont, her head on my shoulder as I lay next to her with my arms around her. I caressed her head gently, running my fingers through her hair and whispering to her how much I loved her.

Our dog lay against her hip, and when she passed, he whimpered quietly.

Her father sat at the end of the bed, and he sang softly to her until she was gone. His melodic voice slipped from love to sorrow, and the grizzly man I'd come to know as stoic and rarely emotional, bowed over his daughter's legs and cried against her knees.

Her sister, Elly, lay her head on Tessa's chest. She told me she was listening to her heart, because she couldn't stand to miss the final beat. She said someone needed to hear it and remember it had happened. And when it did, she cried too, refusing to move from her sister's body as much as I refused to let go, too.

The first drug kicked in after only a few minutes, not long after she received her Last Rites from Father Michael and telling us each she loved us one more time. She fell asleep then, and to be honest, I don't think I've ever seen her face look more peaceful. I felt the slump in her frame as consciousness left her, but none of us moved, no one let go.

The nurse checked her vitals, but her heart was still beating.

The second drug took effect about forty minutes later. I watched my wife's chest rise and fall with each breath slower and farther apart. Elly tapped her finger against Tessa's hand every time she heard a heartbeat. The time between taps lengthened, until each one seemed it would be the last. Our bodies would tense and we'd look at each other and wonder if this was it... if she was gone. Then her chest would rise once more and Elly would tap her finger.

Until there wasn't one more.

The nurse, now a close friend named Malaika, stepped

forward and checked again. Her eyes closed as she concentrated. When they re-opened, her sorrow was evident and she shook her head slowly.

My Tessa was gone. Our Tessa.

And still none of us moved, no one let go.

Elly cried, hugging her sister's body harder, calling her name over and over, her voice so full of grief, it broke all of our hearts. Her father no longer tried to be stoic or strong, but instead openly sobbed for his daughter. Tears streaked my cheeks, but I didn't make a sound. I held my wife's body against my chest and closed my eyes tight, praying things could have been different.

That we could have been forever.

They let us cry for as long as we needed, until each of us was too exhausted to shed one more tear. Her father left first, kissing her cheek and whispering his love one last time, before leaving with Father Michael, who was praying over him. Elly left next, her voice hoarse, and her eyes swollen and red. She kissed her sister's cheek, told her she loved her, and left with Malaika who would go call the funeral home.

After they had both left and I was alone, I laid Tessa's body out flat against the bed and folded her hands across her chest. I kissed her on the lips, my forehead on hers, and said goodbye to my wife, to the love of my life, to my soulmate.

I tried to pick up Beast from where he lay against her hip and take him away, but he growled at me, and I understood how he felt. So, I left to go find my family. Beast stayed with the love of his life, curled against her side, until her body was eventually removed. He refused to eat for days after, and hasn't been the same dog since, but sometimes I see glimmers of the old Beast, and the ferocity he was once famous for. I miss that Beast.

And I miss Tessa.

I flew home the next day with her body. Her father and sister drove back after packing what little belongings we'd brought with us in a trailer and hitching it to the car. Her obituary was published in the local paper and in Chicago, and the national news picked up her story yet again. I fielded phone calls and emails, only replying to some. Catholic officials asked me to reveal who had performed Last Rites, but I wouldn't say. Media outlets called her death a tragedy, and I agreed. People vilified her choice, and I ignored them.

There was no wake or huge funeral, we'd already done that at her New Year's Eve party. It was only a small group of people who loved her and stood around her grave trading happy memories as her ashes were lowered into the ground. We covered her with dirt, and hugged one another, and then everybody went back to their lives as normal.

Except me.

I returned to an empty house in Chicago, and stared at the bed we'd slept in so many times together. In that moment, I realized for the first time, I was a widower.

I slept on the couch with Beast instead.

A week later, I received a beautiful card in the mail. Malaika had gone into labor the following day, and birthed a beautiful baby girl, who now had the middle name 'Tessa.' I cried and called her, thanking her for carrying on Tessa's memory in such a beautiful way. She told me Tessa was a special woman, and should always be remembered, and I agreed.

Marley came to Chicago for the funeral and ended up never leaving. She said she fell in love with the city, and she landed a job in media at the same nonprofit that Tessa's book is partnering with. She still did freelance writing on the side, and I read all of her work. There was no doubt with her talent, she was going places.

Tessa's book sold quickly to a publisher who worked with me to keep Tessa's vision. They asked me to be the face of the launch, doing the interviews and spreading awareness of Tessa's message, and I reluctantly agreed. I wasn't one for being on camera, but I knew what this book meant to Tessa, and her words were beautiful—the world *needed* to read it.

There are no blatant messages or call to arms in this book. It is just Tessa's story about the way she loved and what's important in life.

That's who she was, and that will be her legacy. Everyone who reads this will be her legacy.

Around the time this book was released a little under year after her death, there were twenty-five states, including Washington, DC, considering Death with Dignity. California eventually joined in passing it, but as of this writing, no other state has. Despite that, her book quickly became a bestseller, and I ensured the profits were split between the charity she'd chosen and her sister's schooling.

Beast and I moved closer to my job, to a small apartment in the center of Chicago where everywhere I turned didn't remind me of her. I was honorably discharged from the Marines the following year, and took a six-month sabbatical to decide what I wanted to do with my life.

Beast went to live with Elly during that time as I, for reasons I still don't fully understand, agreed to travel with my family all over the world seeking 'spiritual enlightenment,' as my mother called it. I don't know if I ever found that, but I did find some peace and a renewed energy that grief had long since drained from me.

Elly continued to live in New York City and graduated

college, only to start medical school a semester later thanks to the book sales paying her tuition. She had planned to be a doctor of physical therapy once upon a time, but is going the oncology route instead.

Tessa's father still lives just north of Chicago, and has actually met a woman his age that he calls his special friend. She's lovely and a little strange, and I know Tessa would have approved.

Both Elly and he are still very close to me.

We talk on the phone every week, spend holidays together, and have dinner together as often as we can. On the one-year anniversary of Tessa's death, we went to her grave and sat there for hours, just telling stories about her.

Beast sat by her headstone and wouldn't let any of us hold him until it was time to go. He just kept staring past my shoulder, something he does frequently now, and I wondered if he saw her...if she had kept her promise and is watching over us.

I like to believe she is.

She would have been thirty years old a few days ago—an age she said she never wanted to be. I still miss her like it was yesterday.

I know I promised her I'd be open to moving on one day, and I think I will be eventually, but today, I'm still Tessa's husband.

And I still love my wife.

Always.

ACKNOWLEDGMENTS

This book broke me. I spent so long fighting it off, begging it to stay silent, but it refused. Tessa's story needed to be told, and I needed to tell it. When I finally typed Tessa's last words, I cried...hard. I sobbed against my computer so much, I was sure I'd short-circuited it.

And then the fog lifted, and the intense feeling of need to get these words through my fingertips was gone. I'd done Tessa justice. I'd told her story.

And now the rest is up to you.

I want to thank Nicole Resciniti, who brought life into the world the same week I took Tessa's to the page. My agent and friend, she believed in this book before anyone else even knew about it, and she cried over it before anyone else ever could. She has always been one of my biggest support-ers, and I can't possibly say thank you enough.

Thank you to everyone who had read my books, shared with friends, and helped spread my work with other read-ers. It's because of support like that I can continue to live my dream, and that means more to me than I'll ever be able to express.

Thank you for opening your mind to a difficult topic, whether you agree with Tessa's decision or not. Thank you for giving her a chance and for talking about it. That's all I ask—whether you hate it or love it—talk about it.

Talk about the women like Tessa who never had her choice.

ABOUT THE AUTHOR

Sarah Robinson is the Top 10 Barnes & Noble and Amazon Bestselling Author of multiple series and standalone novels in the romance genre, including the *Exposed* series, *The Photographer Trilogy*, *Kavanagh Legends* series, the *Forbidden Rockers* series, and *Not a Hero: A Marine Romance*. She has recently penned her first women's fiction title, *Every Last Drop,* and is branching into a whole new genre.

A native of Washington, D.C., Robinson has both her bachelor's and master's degrees in forensic and clinical psychology and works as a counselor. She owns a small zoo of furry pets and is actively involved in volunteering in her community.

Follow the Author on Social Media

booksbysarahrobinson.net
subscribepage.com/sarahrobinsonnewsletter
facebook.com/booksbysarahrobinson
twitter.com/booksby_sarah
goodreads.com/booksbysarahrobinson
instagram.com/booksbysarahrobinson
Snapchat: @booksbysarahrob

ALSO BY SARAH ROBINSON

Standalone Women's Fiction Novels

Every Last Drop

The Photographer Trilogy

(*Romantic Suspense*)

Tainted Bodies

Tainted Pictures

Untainted

The Photographer Trilogy Boxset

Forbidden Rockers Series

(*Rockstar Romances*)

Her Forbidden Rockstar

Rocker Christmas: A Logan & Caroline Holiday Novella

Logan's Story: A Prequel Novella

Logan Clay: A Box Set

Kavanagh Legends Series

(*MMA Fighter Standalone Romances*)

Breaking a Legend

Saving a Legend

Becoming a Legend

Chasing a Legend

Kavanagh Christmas

Exposed Series

(*Hollywood Standalone Romances*)

Nudes

Bare

Sheer

Exposed: A Box Set

100 Proof Series

(*Contemporary Country Romances*)

Wylde Fire

Wylde Spirits (Coming 2020)

Wylde Hearts (Coming 2020)

Standalone Romance Novels

Not a Hero: A Bad Boy Marine Romance

Misadventures in the Cage (Coming 2020)